"Layla returns to London tonight."

At the mention of her name, Sin's heart stilled within his breast. His childhood friend. The one woman who could take his breath, his reason, simply by laying eyes upon her.

Stuffing his shaking hands into his trouser pockets, Sin forced himself to keep an even tone. "So then I am to begin watching over her?"

God, but he did not want to. It would be agony, staying so close to her and never being allowed to show his true feelings.

"Are you ready?" her father asked, though his expression told Sin he fully expected an affirmative answer.

So Sin told him the only truth left to him. "I will not fail her."

Praise for the Darkest London Series

Soulbound

"A tight plot and fascinating characters make Callihan's sixth Darkest London historical paranormal her best to date. It's easy to get delightfully lost in Callihan's story; her masterly prose immediately pulls the reader into the deeply detailed universe she's created. Callihan ably lays the groundwork for the next installment, which readers will hungrily await."

—*Publishers Weekly* (starred review)

"Top Pick! 4½ Stars! Another unique, gripping read. Just when you think you know what's coming next, she throws a curveball, leaving readers enraptured with the story."

—*RT Book Reviews*

Evernight

"[A] perfectly paced, tremendously sexy romance set against a beautifully wrought backdrop."

—*Washington Post*

"Top Pick! 4½ Stars! Callihan never disappoints or fails to surprise as she spins her tales of Darkest London. With extraordinary storytelling skills, mesmerizing characters, and plots that twist and turn readers around and around, she delivers a remarkable non-stop read that sucks you in and doesn't let go. Here is a book you will think about, talk about, and dream about for a long time."

—*RT Book Reviews*

Shadowdance

"Top pick! From page one, Kristen Callihan had me. She weaved a tale so powerful, so compelling, that I had no choice but to follow it through to the end... It's a rare talent, being able to do that, but Callihan has it."

—NightOwlReviews.com

"Grade: A. The Darkest London series is one that everyone should be reading... It is hard to put it into one category, but if I was forced, [that] category would be pure excellence. If you aren't reading these books you should be!"

—FictionVixen.com

Winterblaze

"Top Pick! 4½ stars! Not only a gripping novel, but also one that elevates the genre with its depth of emotion, passion, and mesmerizing storytelling... Once begun, it's impossible to put down *Winterblaze*."

—*RT Book Reviews*

"Dark, dangerous, and totally enthralling, this latest edition in Callihan's Darkest London series treats fans to a heart-tugging, satisfying romance, fills in a few series blanks with well-handled flashbacks, and nicely sets the stage for stories that are sure to come."

—*Library Journal*

Moonglow

"Action-packed... This richly textured tale of 19th-century London interweaves intricately imagined and historically accurate scenes with red-hot sensual interludes. Like the first, a deeply compelling and imaginative story."

—*Publishers Weekly* (starred review)

"Simply fantastic... beautifully written... A Perfect 10 is rare for a debut author, probably more rare for the second novel, but *Moonglow* more than deserves the accolade."

—RomRevToday.com

Firelight

"*Beauty and the Beast* meets *Phantom of the Opera* in this gripping, intoxicating story... An exceptional debut and the first of what promises to be a compelling series."

—*Library Journal* (starred review)

"4½ stars! Top pick! Seal of Excellence! Like moths to a flame, readers will be drawn to the flickering *Firelight* and get entangled in the first of the Darkest London series... Callihan crafts a taut tale filled with sexual tension. This is one of the finest debuts of the season."

—*RT Book Reviews*

Forevermore

Also by Kristen Callihan

Firelight

Ember (short story)

Moonglow

Winterblaze

Entwined (short story)

Shadowdance

Evernight

Soulbound

FOREVERMORE

Kristen Callihan

FOREVER

NEW YORK BOSTON

Forever
Hachette Book Group
1290 Avenue of the Americas
New York, NY 10104
hachettebookgroup.com
twitter.com/foreverromance

First edition: June 2016

Forever is an imprint of Grand Central Publishing.
The Forever name and logo are trademarks of Hachette Book Group, Inc.

ISBN 978-1-4555-8169-6 (ebook edition)
ISBN 978-1-4555-8170-2 (mass market edition)

10 9 8 7 6 5 4 3 2 1

OPM

To Rachel, Claire, Jen, and Susan, my first beta readers and the ones who encouraged me to keep writing Firelight, *the book that started it all.*

To Kristin, Alex, Lauren, and Amy, the ones who took a chance on me and championed this series.

To my family, always.

To the readers, whose love made one book grow to seven.

Acknowledgments

It wasn't easy saying good-bye to the Darkest London world. I've lived in it for so long, the characters feel like family. But I'm extremely happy with where I've left them. They are happy and secure in their lives.

When I wrote *Firelight*, I never expected I'd go on to write a seven-book series. For that, I have you readers to thank.

While my agent was trying to sell the Darkest London series to a publisher, my husband told me not to worry, that I'd find the perfect editor. He was right. Alex Logan has been my partner every step of the way. Her knowledge and advice has made me a stronger writer. These books would not be what they are without her. For that, I will be forever grateful. I could not have asked for better.

I would also like to thank the staff at Grand Central/Forever. They are not only hard working and dedicated, but I consider many of them my friends. Darkest London would not have been the success it was without them.

And lastly, I'd like to thank my agent, Kristin Nelson. She is astute, tenacious, and has looked after me for the entire ride.

FOREVERMORE

Prologue

Boston 1868

Boston was not like London. The streets, though properly paved and lined with stately buildings, felt wider. In truth, everything about America felt bigger in some essential way. Even here, on this side street where taverns and quaint shops lined the block, could not compare to the cramped and sinister darkness of London.

No, Boston was too picturesque, with snow falling like lazy feathers to cover the ground in pristine white. Merry lanterns glowed at every doorway and lit a trail that was easy to follow. Pedestrians did not huddle down in their coats, avoiding eye contact, but gave a distinct nod, as if to say, Welcome to our fair city. Indeed, they all smiled. It was ridiculous. Never, in all her years, had Lena seen so many sets of teeth.

She outright scowled at the simpering woman in a bright pink bonnet and felt a flutter of pleasure when the woman gasped and hurried along. But the pleasure was short-lived. A gust of icy wind rushed down the lane, forcing her to hold the little bundle in her arms closer. Which in turn had her icy heart clenching just a bit tighter too.

It was fortunate, then, that she'd reached the Howling Wolf Tavern. With grim determination, she pushed open the door. Warm air, heavy with the scents of roasted meat, pipe smoke, and the ever-present sweetness of human blood, assaulted her lungs. Ignoring her hunger, Lena strode towards the back of the room. She needn't search for her quarry; she'd felt him before she had even entered the building. His scent was part of her now, a poison in her blood. She would always be able to track him, even if she didn't want to.

And though she'd been expecting to find him, the moment Lena set eyes on Augustus, his stern profile limned golden in the lantern light, a punch of feeling tore through her. She simply could not look upon him and not want him.

He did not acknowledge her presence until she slid into the worn wooden bench opposite him, though she knew perfectly well he'd felt her approach too. They'd always known when the other was near.

With careful precision, Augustus pushed his tankard of peaty ale aside and rested his forearms upon the table.

"Lena." His pleasant, calm voice was a roll of sensation down her back. "Lovely as ever."

She did not miss his fleeting glance at the basket and the subsequent tightening of the skin around his mouth and eyes. Curiosity there, but not fear or anger.

"As I recall, when last we met, you compared me to a black widow spider." Lena unwound the red silk scarf covering her hair and tossed it down on the seat next to the little basket she'd been carrying.

Augustus's smile was thin, but his dark eyes shone with

affection she did not deserve. "Well, as they say here, if the shoe fits, wear it."

"Touché," she said with a nod. For, really, she *did* possess the ability to turn into spiders—not one, but dozens—so he was correct.

"What brings you here?" he asked.

So solid, was Augustus. The calm in the eye of the storm. Not even her reappearance after thirty years of separation had him rattled. Was it wrong of her that she wanted to unnerve him? Likely so.

"Would you believe I missed you?" she offered lightly.

"Yes." His gaze stayed steady on her. "I missed you too."

Well. She was not expecting that. It deflated her, damn him. "Let us not play games. You could find me anytime you wanted, Augustus."

"It is not the finding that proves troublesome, my dear. It is the welcome I shall receive once found."

"Fair enough." Lena settled back onto the bench, trying to convey ease. "I have to go away for a time. Perhaps to Nowhere." Nowhere being another plane of existence where demons such as her could escape. Augustus, along with all manner of supernatural beings, could travel there as well. Though there were realms, such as what supernaturals commonly called There, that pure of heart Augustus could enter, and she, with her tainted soul, could not. A fact that never failed to irk her.

As expected, his dark eyes flashed silver upon mention of Nowhere. "Why?"

"I have a few things to take care of." She had some hunting to do, and her prey was currently skulking in the darkest corner of Nowhere. But Augustus needn't know that.

He frowned at her caginess. "No one simply chooses to go to Nowhere."

"I'd prefer it to here. Tell me, are you happy living amongst these simple colonials?"

He didn't bother to answer, merely gave her another one of his eloquent looks. Which only made her want to needle him.

"What pet are you following now, Augustus?"

He always had a few souls he guarded over, guiding them this way and that way, like some overzealous hand of God. They were little pawns in his ultimate chess game. And yet, she knew he loved every one of his "children."

Augustus did not bother to deny it. "A girl named Eliza May. She's an Evernight—the Boston branch."

Odd coincidence, though, as she was intimately tied with the Evernights, an old and powerful family of Elementals who lived in Ireland. She'd recently placed St. John, a young babe who was in need of hiding, in their care. The irony almost made her laugh.

"And who is Miss May destined for?"

"Never you mind," Augustus said with sad predictability. "Now, answer my question. Why are you really going to Nowhere? Do not tell me you have a sudden urge to holiday there."

She lifted her shoulders in a shrug. "Believe what you will. I shall confide in you this: it is safer for me to go." This was true.

"Explain, Lena, and use long sentences for once."

A brief smile touched her lips. "If I stay, I shall be hunted down by the father of this." With a flourish, she lifted the basket and pulled back the woolen blanket draped over it. Deep in a nest of red silk lay a tiny babe. The few wisps of hair she had were a rich brown, and her plump, little cheeks flushed pink with life as she slept, oblivious to the chatter around her.

All color drained from Augustus's skin, leaving little streaks of silver at the edges of his hairline. He managed to get himself under control quickly, but his mouth remained agape. "Please do not tell me you've stolen a baby. Anything but that."

"Stolen? Ridiculous. What would I do with a baby?"

His stern look spoke volumes.

Though Lena had been waiting for this moment, relishing it with a sort of sick glee, she suddenly faltered, her cold heart thumping hard against her ribs. "It is mine," she got out.

Absolute silence. Around them, the tavern's patrons laughed and talked, drank and ate foul-smelling ale and food. But here, at their little corner table, the air stirred with rage. Against her palms the pitted wood table began to vibrate as if it soon might shatter.

"Temper, my love," she murmured.

And his eyes went full-on silver. "Whose is it?"

The question was a whip against her skin.

"I'll not tell you."

"Lena. Please."

It hurt her, she realized, to see the pain in his eyes. They'd known each other for nearly a hundred years, neither of them aging. And though she'd had many lovers, none of them meant a thing to her. He was the only man she loved. The only man she hated. Had he done similar and conceived a child with another, her rage would have known no bounds.

Softening her tone, she leaned in. "Augustus, I did not plan this. Indeed it is a shock. Sanguis do not procreate without intent. Believe me, having a child was not part of my plans."

"And yet you have one," he whispered with a harsh breath.

"Yes. And the father, he cannot know. It would be dangerous for her."

At this, Augustus's gaze went back to the babe. His expression shifted to one of longing and regret. Lena could not stop from reaching out to him, touching his warm skin with the tips of her gloved fingers. "Please believe this of me."

"I do," he said, still looking at the babe, ignoring her touch. But then, as if waking from a dream, he stirred, and a frightful expression tightened his familiar features. Again the air began to hum. "You cannot take the child with you to Nowhere."

"No." It hurt to utter the word.

His fine lips curled back on a snarl. "Why are you here?"

He knew. She could see it in his eyes. In his rage.

"She will be safe with you."

"No."

"She needs a good influence. A protector."

"No." It was nearly a shout. Flushed and breathing hard, he glared at Lena. "Do not dare ask this of me. To bring me your child by another and..." He broke off, grinding his teeth.

"Look at her," Lena pressed. "Really look. Use your gift and tell me that she isn't destined for you to protect. If she is not, then I shall leave and never bother you again."

It was cruel, using his gift against him. Only she knew what he could do, how he saw the future paths of all but his one, true love. That it was her fate he could not see was a stab in the heart and the only thing that kept her going.

He did as bided. And promptly cursed. "I will never forgive you for doing this to me."

"I may never forgive myself. But it must be done."

She could not, would not, look at the babe. Already her chest was too tight, her eyes burning. "You are the best thing that could happen to this child."

He snorted and looked away.

"You must promise me this," she said over the lump in her throat. "She cannot know who she is. Never let her return to England."

His dark eyes pinned her. "You beg of me to watch over this child, then you must trust me to raise her as I see fit."

"And what do you see?" Lena could not help but ask it.

"England. Judgment. St. John." A shudder went through him. "She is the key to St. John's future."

"Margaret's boy?" Lena thought it over, and it made sense in a way. He was just a baby now, but the child had the blood of greatness in his veins, the son of a powerful Elemental and a demi-god of chaos. One day his power would be fearsome. What then would her child be? Lena longed to see her babe come into her own.

"Well then," she said slowly. "Keep her away from England until you sense that it is safe for her to return."

He gave a grunt of agreement, his gaze returning to the babe.

A strangled breath left Lena as she prepared to leave. *Do not look at the child.*

Quick as a flash, Augustus caught her cold hand, squeezing it tight. "Stay. Stay with me. I will protect you. On my life."

A watery smile pulled at her lips. "You and I both know that is impossible." She was the one person Augustus could never save. It was their curse. Doomed to love and never be together.

"Lena." It was an agonized plea.

Gently, she broke free of his grip. "I came to you. Only you."

His chin jerked in a nod. "Only you would I do this for."

She needed to go. Moving was akin to tearing off strips

of her flesh. But she did, standing slowly and feeling every bit of her two hundred and twenty-seven years. The babe had not stirred but her soft, steady little breaths seemed to fill the silence. As if prompted, Augustus lifted the basket and brought it close to him, careful not to wake the child.

His expression was one of reverence and wonder. Lena knew he was already in love. That hurt too, selfish creature that she was.

"She is a half-breed," he said.

"Yes." She fought the horrid tears that wanted so badly to bloom in her eyes.

Thankfully, Augustus was too busy peering at the child to notice her disquiet. "You refuse to reveal the father, fine. It saves me the trouble of having to hunt him down and kill him. But I demand to know her origins."

"Nothing you can't handle."

When he shot her a glare, she snorted. "Come now, Augustus. You are a Watcher, the creator of Judgment angels. You mean to tell me you fear this child might harm you?"

His lips pursed. "I fear what she might do to others without the proper training."

Fair enough. Theirs was a world of strange and powerful beings. Some capable of complete mayhem. But to reveal the child's origins would be to reveal the father. So Lena merely gave him a bland look. "It will be clear when she fully matures."

"How helpful."

Yes, wasn't it? Being annoyed at Augustus helped, however. Another deep breath and she could back away.

He glanced up at her, and instead of anger, she saw endless sorrow and reluctant understanding. "Tell me her name."

Lena hadn't dared to name the girl. Why? When she'd

never have a chance to know her? Lena almost confessed as much when her mouth opened, and she blurted out a name.

"Layla. Layla Starling." *Her little night bird.*

Ireland
Ten years later

Layla knew that Augustus was not her father. He'd always been very clear on that account. And yet he had always been very clear that he loved her as much as any father could love a child. Therefore she did not truly mourn the loss of parents she'd never known. Indeed, she had a fine life. Fine home. Lovely dresses. And her favorite doll Annabelle.

There were times when Augustus had to go away. But it was never for very long. And when he returned, he'd seek her out first thing, set her on his knee, and ask after her day. Layla loved her guardian very much. And there was Mrs. Gibbons to look after her when Augustus was away. So, no, she never experienced loneliness or fear.

How odd, then, that she knew the boy in the tree was both lonely and afraid.

"Why are you up there?" she asked, peering up at his dangling legs, all covered in soot. "Are you hiding?"

His strange, pale green eyes seemed to glow in his equally soot-covered face. "Hiding? Hardly."

"In trouble, then?"

"Nosey boots," he muttered in that thick Irish accent of his. "Don't you ever climb trees?"

"Yes. But not when I'm crying. Unless I want to hide, that is."

His scowl was fierce. "I am not crying."

The silvery tracks through the soot told a different tale.

Layla caught hold of a lower branch and easily climbed up the tree. She smiled as the boy scrambled farther up as if he didn't want her near. Perching on a nice, sturdy branch, she looked him over. "Were you helping to put out the fire last night?"

The barn on the Evernight property had burnt down, and the flames had been so great that the very night sky seemed to glow orange. That was, until Mrs. Gibbons had shooed Layla away from the window and ordered her to bed.

"Why would I be doing that? I'm just a boy." He looked off, his nose wrinkled in a scowl.

It was then that Layla saw the book resting on a thick branch. He made a reach for it as she picked it up, but she was faster. "*Tom Sawyer.* Oh, I liked that one."

As he huffed, she glanced at the front page. "Says property of Saint John Evernight. Is that you?"

He glared down at her. "First off, it's not Saint John. It's pronounced *Sin-jin.*"

"Why on earth would you pronounce Saint John as *Sin-jin*? It does not make sense. My name is spelled L-a-y-l-a, and you pronounce it *Lay-lah*. Just as it ought to be."

He snorted. "Lass, if you had a look at how the Irish spell most of their names, it would do your little head in."

Layla had no response for that. Ireland was a strange and wonderful place to her. So fresh and green. At least out here in the country. Augustus had only just moved them here to a large manor house, surrounded by a carpet of emerald that stretched all the way to the sea. Since St. John, or Sinjin, was an Evernight, that meant he lived on the adjoining property.

"I think they ought to call you Saint. Wouldn't that be lovely?"

He appeared rather ill at the prospect. "Who in the bleeding hell would want to be called a saint?"

Bleeding hell were bad words, she knew, but she liked the way they rolled off his tongue and the fierce way he glared made her smile. Perhaps because, at the very least, this boy paid her attention. She hadn't any friends her own age since she'd arrived from Boston.

"I don't know," she said with a shrug. "I just thought... well, if you did something wrong, you'd be the last person anyone would suspect if your name was Saint." She lowered her voice in her best grown-up impersonation. " 'Who stole the last currant tart?' 'Well, I do not know, but surely it could not be Saint. A boy called Saint would never stoop so low.' "

St. John snorted. "They call me Sin, not Saint."

"Oh," Layla said in a small voice. "Well, then you are in a bad way. A boy named Sin is bound to get into trouble."

He rolled his eyes at her jest. But she did not miss the way he seemed to hug himself and turn his face from hers, or the way his chest hitched with a sharp breath.

"Did you get hurt in the fire? Is that why you were crying?"

"For the last time," he spat out, "I was not crying."

When she simply waited for an explanation, he gave an expansive sigh, the sort Cook did when Layla asked for her meat to be served rare. Layla never felt badly about that, though. She loved bloody meat. It tasted sweet to her. Why Cook couldn't understand this, she'd never know.

"I..." Sin bit the corner of his bottom lip and then blurted out, "I started the fire. It was an accident."

"Oh." Layla pulled one leg close to her chest, leaving the other to dangle. "Were they very cross with you?"

"They don't know."

They were silent for a moment, listening to the birds chirp.

"Once, when I was six," Layla said, "I took it to mind to have a bath. I turned on the taps myself. Only I had to get my doll Annabelle ready, and then I'd forgotten I'd promised her a tea party, and well... Mrs. Gibbons came charging in, shouting about a leaking ceiling."

Oh, the memory still burned.

Sin snorted. "You flooded the bath?"

"Yes."

He laughed and laughed. A very nice sound. And she told him so.

Unfortunately, it made him stop. But he didn't ask her to leave. Instead they sat for a long while, until her legs grew cramped. "I have to get down. Will you come and play with me at the pond instead, Saint John?"

"Call me Sin. It's what my friends do." And then he jumped right out of the tree as though the height was nothing to him. Well, Layla could do that too.

"I'd rather call you Saint," she said, once safely on the ground.

His pale green eyes crinkled at the corners. "Why?"

"Someone ought to think the best of you. I shall apply myself to the task."

He looked annoyed but she did not miss the way his mouth fought a smile. "You are a strange little bird, Layla. Are we going to the pond or what?"

"Lead the way, Saint."

And he did. For five wonderful years, he led her on adventures, became her dearest friend. And then Augustus ruined it all. He took her away from Sin and Ireland, and she'd never see either again.

Chapter One

London 1890

St. John Evernight ran full-out, his bare feet hitting the cold, slick cobbles with nary a sound. He did not need footwear, for his skin would never tear, and clunky boots affected his speed and balance. Both of which he needed during a chase.

His prey was just ahead, moving at inhuman speed and agility through the dark alleyway. Too far to catch or get a proper look at. Irritated, Sin put forth the effort and increased his pace, pushing himself to his limits.

Christ but this *thing* was fast. For Sin had no clue as to its nature; its scent was a strange mix that he'd never before encountered, though it appeared human in shape, which really meant nothing in his world of shape shifters and demons.

The moonless night reduced everything to dark shapes, echoing sounds, rank smells. This was London, after all, a city of foul, coal-leaden fog and evil lurking in shadowy corners.

Breath burning in his lungs, he dashed around a corner, following the slim figure ahead, a dark cloak fluttering behind it like a flag.

Closer, closer.

Sin stretched his arm out, his silver fingers appearing like glass in the darkness. Almost...

His prey leapt, straight up.

"Shit."

Slate and dirt rained down, clacking and clattering as the thing took to the rooftops.

Well then.

Sin leapt too, landing lightly on his feet and taking off even as part of the roof began to cave under his weight. Scrambling up the steep slope, he reached the spine of the roof and dashed along the narrow space.

His quarry was getting away. Not bloody likely. He'd seen what it had done, gorging itself on a helpless human before Sin had appeared. He'd taken one look at the cloaked figure huddled over the body, blood thick and redolent on the ground, and attacked. Sin would not give this creature another opportunity to kill again.

Unfortunately, whatever it was he chased was *slightly* quicker than he was. It chafed.

"Sod it." He halted, sliding a few feet on the slick surface before stopping. The creature kept going, but Sin had had enough. Tearing off his clothes, he watched his prey leap from rooftop to rooftop, its moves akin to a lycan's but slightly *off*. Hell, everything was off about this thing.

Nude, Sin took a breath and let his wings free. They unfurled behind him like sails snapping in a full wind. And then he took to the sky, his crystal clear skin now invisible to those below.

Gods, he'd never grow accustomed to that first burst of

power and motion of flight. No matter how hellish his life got, flying was bloody glorious.

Up he went, his gaze intent on the creature, who was headed for the Thames, near Parliament Bridge. It was slowing, unaware that Sin was still stalking.

With a hard grin, Sin angled his body, his wings slicing through the air, sending a ripple of pure pleasure along his spine. He dove, the wind whistling in his ears.

The tiny form moving along the rooftops grew larger, larger. Sin was almost on top of him when, out of the corner of his eye, he saw another form racing from the opposite direction towards them both. A massive, hairy werewolf.

Collision was imminent, but Sin did not slow or hesitate. His arms wrapped around his prey, noting its slim form, the scent reminiscent of lycan, mixed with blood and something oddly floral. Then the world exploded in a riot of fur, flesh, and snarls as the werewolf hit them both.

They all rolled in a tumble of limbs, wings, and teeth, dropping over the edge of the roof and landing upon the Victoria Embankment with a massive crash. Pavers cracked; Sin's wing did too. He registered the sharp pain with a grunt, lights popping behind his eyes.

He did not let go of his prey. And yet his arms were empty and dozens of tiny black birds flapped around his face, with frantic wings obscuring his sight. They took to the sky, leaving him with an enormous, brassed-off werewolf crushing his chest.

Sin watched the birds take flight and then roared his outrage, letting loose a bolt of lightning—his greatest weapon, and one he still had yet to get under full control.

The *were* yelped, its big body writhing and launching into the air from the force. It tumbled several feet before righting and leaping to its feet.

When it stood, it was no longer a wolf but a man, as naked as Sin, and glaring bloody murder his way.

"Impudent pup," growled Ian Ranulf, Lycan King and Sin's brother-in-law. "You nearly burnt my cods off."

Sin vanished his wings with a thought and willed the color of his flesh from that of clear crystal to the human tone he'd been born with before standing and dusting off his sore arse. "And you cost me my prey. What the bloody hell were you thinking, Ian?"

Ian's mouth opened as if to retort then slammed shut as he scowled. With a sharp breath, he tilted his head and glanced at the sky, his expression thoughtful. "You know, dear brother, I really cannot say."

Dressed in borrowed clothes, which consisted of a fine lawn shirt, wool coat, and heavy kilt, Sin sat back in his chair by the fire and took a bracing sip of brandy. The liquor burned smooth and luscious down his throat, yet it did little to soothe him.

He had not entered this study in years, and he felt every single one of them acutely. While he'd never called this place home, he'd been welcome here once. And he'd been cast out of here once too.

After a small but irritating debate, Sin had agreed to follow Ian back to his home. They clearly had much to discuss and standing stark naked in the middle of London was hardly an intelligent course of action. And Sin couldn't bring Ian back to his place. No one could ever know where Sin lived. So to Ian's they went. Sin could not leave here soon enough.

"She's visiting Miranda and Archer at their country estate." Ian's casual comment broke their silence.

Sin straightened in his seat and glanced at his brother-in-law, who lounged in the chair across from him. Firelight gleamed in Ian's blue eyes, giving him a faintly demonic appearance, but his elegant sprawl and watchful manner spoke of pure lycan.

They spoke of Daisy, Ian's wife and Sin's sister. Sin had three sisters: Daisy, Miranda, and Poppy. All three of them had cut Sin out of their lives. For good reason.

An ugly sludge of regret and shame pushed through his gut. He tapped it down by force of will and faced Ian without wincing. "Are you going to tell her?" *Does she ever speak of me? Do any of them?* He couldn't ask.

"I do not keep things from my wife." A lazy smile drifted across his lips. "However, I shall refrain from speaking of it until she is in a . . . receptive mood."

Sin's mouth twisted at the thought of how Ian would get his wife in such a mood. "Careful, Ranulf, she's still my sister. I'd rather think of her as pure and untouched, if it's all the same to you."

Ian grinned outright. "Warms the cockles of my heart to see you ruffled over Daisy's honor, even now." His open expression shuttered. "What was it that you chased tonight?"

Sin set his glass aside on the small table between them. "I don't know. Which is rare." Since becoming Judgment, he'd studied all manner of beasties. It was his duty to find those who practiced evil and deliver their souls for final judgment. "Its scent was like nothing I've encountered. I was hoping you could shed some light on it."

After all, Ian, as a lycan—a man capable of turning into a wolf—had the far superior sense of smell. Oddly though, Ian fidgeted in his seat, plucking at the bit of lace at his cuffs.

Sin narrowed his gaze as a thought occurred. "You were chasing the thing as well, were you not? Or was that hit meant for me?"

Ian gave him an irritated look, his body tight and almost

hunched. Sin had learned early on in his life to read people, and he knew the wily bastard was hiding something.

"I caught the creature's scent from my terrace," Ian said suddenly. "Went out to have a fag—Daisy doesn't like smoke in the house." His expression said it all: he loved Daisy's grousing about cigarettes and the like. "At any rate, the scent washed over me before I had a chance to strike my match. It intrigued me enough to follow it."

Sin leaned forward, the worn leather creaking under him. "You caught the scent nearly a mile out and through all the..." He waved towards the window. "Foul smells of London?"

Ian lifted an auburn brow. "You doubt my word?"

Sin huffed out a laugh. "Hardly. More like, you have my extreme sympathies for possessing such a highly acute sense of smell."

Ian grimaced. "I shall not lie; there are times when it is truly a curse. Ordinarily, I ignore the majority of them. But there was something about this scent." He glanced at Sin, the corners of his mouth turning down. "It was female, a stranger, and apparently lycan. Hardly something I could ignore."

As king of the lycans, Ian would expect to know every lycan that resided in London. But even more troubling was the fact that a female lycan hadn't been born in centuries.

Sin hadn't been thinking about the sex of the creature he'd chased. But now he could recall that, when he'd grabbed hold of his prey, he'd felt the softness of breasts against his palms.

Sin tapped the side of his bent knee. "I thought lycan as well; however the scent was slightly off."

"Because she isn't."

"Are you certain?"

Ian stopped just short of rolling his eyes, which Sin deserved for yet again questioning his sense of smell. "Her scent is close to lycan yet not. It's akin to…" Ian's brow wrinkled. "The difference between a white wine and a red. Or perhaps an apple to a pear."

"So if she isn't lycan, what could she be?"

Ian appeared deflated. "I haven't a clue. It's nothing I've personally encountered before."

While Sin was still in his twenties, Ian was over a century old.

"Why did you tackle me?" Sin had to ask. From the angle of attack and the timing, Sin knew Ian had aimed for him, not the unknown creature.

Ian had the good grace to wince. He looked off into the fire, his shoulders hunching. "I don't know."

"You don't know?" Sin repeated, dubious and more than curious now.

"No." Ian's expression turned mulish, then he caught Sin's gaze and sighed. "Bloody hell. I have no earthly idea. I felt compelled to track the scent. Then I saw you swooping down and…" He lifted his hands as if to convey his utter confusion. "Instinct told me to protect."

"And yet you still do not believe that she is a lycan." Sin softened his tone. "If she were lycan, it would be your duty to protect one of your own."

"No one knows that better than I," Ian said with a snort. For a moment, his aqua eyes appeared completely lupine. "But getting that close, it struck me that she is not lycan. Even more? There is a scent pattern to her that my inner wolf regards as an enemy. Honestly, St. John, I am confounded. I'll have to think on it."

Sin sighed. "Well, whatever she is, she half-devoured a man tonight."

"Christ." Ian ran a hand through his hair. "Do you require assistance?"

Despite his resolve to blot out his personal life, a lump of gratitude filled Sin's throat. He'd betrayed everyone he ever cared for, including this man. And yet Ian still offered help.

"I shall let you know." Because Sin could not bring himself to fully close that door. It was hard enough to stand now, force himself to leave. It did him no good to linger, for he would merely crave what he could not have: family, acceptance.

"One thing," he found himself saying. "Am I dreaming, or did our mysterious creature turn herself into a flock of birds?"

Ian blanched, but he did not appear to be shocked. Sin would have bet his best hat Ian had not wanted him to mention that little fact. "She did," Ian said slowly.

"And aside from the obvious," Sin said, "this disturbs you, why?"

Ian seemed to search for his words. "It is a rare power. One not often seen."

"Perhaps we were chasing a shifter."

"That was no shifter."

"Odd you say so, since she did shift."

"Shifters change into other shapes, animals, not multiple birds."

"Ian." Sin braced a hand on the back of the chair. "Spit it out, man. Why are you bothered by this?"

Those lupine eyes glowed with irritation. "I know of only one being capable of doing such a thing, though I've only seen her shift to spiders. Her name is Lena." A hint of fang dropped from behind Ian's lips. "She is responsible for capturing and torturing Jack Talent."

Jack Talent was Ian's foster son. Once he had been Sin's good friend. Until Sin had disappointed everyone with his betrayal.

"And yet you did not recognize this creature as Lena," he said to Ian.

"She might be disguising her scent. If it is Lena," Ian went on in a silky tone, "I will destroy her."

Sin did not point out that Ian had had the creature nearly in his grasp and protected her instead. Truth was, now that Sin had begun the hunt, he would not stop until he'd won. It was his nature, and his duty. "Not," Sin said, holding Ian's gaze, "if I catch her first."

It was always the same. She came back to herself in stages. First her hearing. The ragged raps of her breath through her lips, the muted thud of her heart within her breast. Then feeling. This was often different, for she never ended up in the same place.

At this moment, something cold, hard, and a bit gritty pressed against her cheek, her side, the swell of her hip. She was lying on something—the floor, if she had to guess. With a careful breath, she opened her eyes. Dusty, dark floorboards greeted her sight, and just beyond, the deep reds of a fine Turkish carpet.

It was vaguely familiar. Another breath and it rushed back to her. A stateroom. She was on a luxury liner, on a deck that served the upper echelon, though given the dirt that had accumulated on the floor, it was more show than substance. She was traveling, nearly at her destination. The ocean ought to be a safe haven. But she knew now it wasn't.

Rising slowly, she winced at the various aches and pains shooting through her body. And then glanced down. Sweet butter, she was nude. And cold. She rubbed her arms and stood on wobbly limbs.

She stumbled towards the bathing room, thankful that, despite the unswept dust on her bedroom floor, the chamber had a lovely, deep tub with taps that delivered piping hot water.

Watching the water fill the tub, she sat on the edge of it and shivered. It was strange how she could remember that waking this way was not an uncommon occurrence, and yet she could barely string together a proper thought beyond the need to get warm and clean. She could not even remember her name, which ought to cause her fear, but it did not.

Soon. Soon it will all come back to you. She knew she'd heard that refrain numerous times before.

So she relaxed, sank into the filled tub, and let her body soak up the water's warmth—her head lolling to the side, her eyes closed in quiet bliss. It was not until she'd reached for the little cake of soap, scrubbed her body and face, and rinsed clean that she noted the water's now pink tinge.

Blood. Her face and neck had been covered in blood. Only now did she recognize the faint metallic taste on her tongue and in the back of her throat. As if she'd been drinking it down. Hot, thick, wet. A fine shiver ran through her. So very delicious. And that was enough to have her scrambling from the tub, her shin banging on the edge as she fell out of it and onto the hard tiles.

She barely made it to the privy before being sick. Blood. So much blood.

Exhausted, she slumped back, her shaking hand to her mouth. Always waking up with blood on her skin. What was she?

Memories surged forth. She was Layla. Layla Starling. The world saw her as an innocent heiress and a talented singer. But she knew the truth. She was a monster.

Chapter Two

One might think being an immortal was a blessing—never grow old, never grow sick, never die. At one time in St. John Evernight's life, he'd considered it a blessing too. He would be around long after the simple humans who surrounded him were nothing but dust. They could stare all they liked at his "strange" hair and frosty green eyes. They could gossip and speculate about him until they lost their voices. It didn't matter. He was untouchable, and they were but fragile sacks of blood and bone.

How naïve he'd been. Because living forever merely meant a lack of escape from the desolation of regret and loneliness. He knew now that he could walk down Jermyn Street endlessly, see the sands of time shift and rearrange before him, and never be a part of life.

"Brooding, Mr. Evernight?"

Sin almost jumped at the sudden sound of Augustus's voice by his side. Damn, the blasted man loved to startle him. He gave Augustus a passing glance. Dressed in conservative brown tweed and a bowler hat, the angel appeared every inch the English gentleman, save for his dark coloring that marked him to be from Southern climes.

"It's really quite the trick, popping up like a soap bubble whenever you choose, Augustus. You must teach me how one day."

The man's mouth twitched. "With your luck, you'd pop up in the middle of a parliamentary session."

Yes, Sin had abominable luck. Or perhaps it was more a matter of making abominable choices.

"You're brooding again," Augustus remarked.

"I'm not brooding. This is simply my face."

Augustus snorted but remained silent as they walked along, past Trafalgar Square and down Whitehall.

"Care to tell me why you called me here?" Sin asked when they came upon the grounds of Westminster. For the past year, Sin had been in Rome, soaking in the warmer temperatures, drinking espresso in cafés along the Piazza della Rotonda, under the shade of the ancient Pantheon. He'd eaten simple but delicious food, and listened to the rapid fire of Italian, and felt... well, not peace, but a measure of contentment.

Until Augustus had sent for him last month with a message to "sit tight" until Augustus could meet with him. Returning to England sat like a stone in his gut. But he would obey. Augustus was his mentor, and the man who'd given him salvation. The price was a lifetime of servitude. To be fair, his role was for justice, not evil, which was a nice change of pace.

A massive dray rattled past, kicking up dust and sending a fug of stale manure into the air. They hurried past the cloud and headed for Westminster Abbey. Sin hadn't planned on visiting today, but here they were all the same. He wondered if Augustus somehow had led him to their usual meeting place or if Sin had merely headed that way because of the man's sudden arrival.

He'd like to think the latter. It did not sit well with him having another control his actions. Not since a certain evil fae had kept Sin as a blood slave for years. Even now, the memory made his stomach turn.

Not a soul acknowledged them as they walked through the abbey and into the cloisters. Here, a rare bit of sunlight peeked through the constant cloud cover and cast lacy shadows along the walkway. The sound of their boot heels clacked out a steady rhythm as they strolled along.

"Layla returns to London tonight."

At the mention of her name, Sin's heart stilled within his breast. He'd tried his best to ward off all finer feelings, to remain numb, detached from life. And yet he could not, for the life of him, remain immune to Layla Starling. His childhood friend. The one woman who could take his breath, his reason, simply by laying eyes upon her.

Stuffing his shaking hands into his trouser pockets, Sin forced himself to keep an even tone. "So then I am to begin watching over her?"

God, but he did not want to. It would be agony, staying so close to her and never being allowed to show his true feelings. And yet a thrum of anticipation went through him at the mere prospect of seeing Layla once more.

"Are you ready?" Augustus asked, though his expression told Sin he fully expected an affirmative answer.

So Sin told him the only truth left to him. "I will not fail her."

Chapter Three

Layla Starling had not been in London for over a year. She'd been touring the continent—Paris, Vienna, Prague, Austria, Venice. After a while, the cities began to blur, and no matter how luxuriously appointed the hotel rooms were, they did not feel like a home.

She longed for a permanent home. But she'd never really had one. Augustus, her guardian, had always kept them moving, never settling in one place for too long. It had changed something in her, made her into a restless vagabond. So, really, she couldn't quite fathom *why* she longed to remain in one place now. Perhaps it was loneliness.

She felt it keenly now that she was an adult. Augustus's company, while always a comfort, was not enough anymore. She hadn't any friends, only employees. Ones that looked after her newfound career as a singer.

For her entire life, Layla possessed a love for singing. It was her joy, the soaring power of freedom and love and sorrow all rolled into one. She sang and she was alive, wholly and completely. Even better, she sang, and people stopped to listen. It seemed only natural to take to the stage. A dream made reality.

Only reality was not a dream. She felt drained. Her throat hurt constantly, and her body battered. Layla had sent her manager and her assistant on holiday, cancelled all further performances, and took the first steamer back to London where Augustus lived. Now she wanted nothing more than to find her room in Augustus's newest town home and sleep for two weeks solid.

And as the fine carriage turned into the circular drive, rocking slightly as it took the corner, she nearly wept with relief. Home. At least for now.

A footman dressed in crisp black awaited, opening the door as soon as the coach halted. Gathering her skirts, Layla stepped down. She ignored the strange, sweet scent of the man, unnerved that she knew it was the rich blood running through his body. Since hitting womanhood, Layla had smelled the blood of others and found it...tantalizing. The older she became, the stronger her sense of smell.

The stronger *she* became. As it was, she had to watch herself or she'd snap the stem of any wineglass she held. Yet another reason to take a holiday. Her gloved hands began to shake as the faint smudges of a memory began to sharpen in her mind.

No. She would not think of the waking up on the stateroom floor, or of Venice. Of The Incidents. Her fingers curled into a tight fist. But they still felt cold and slick, as if old blood lingered on her skin.

Frowning, she alighted the stairs. She needed to talk to Augustus. He would make sense of this. He always seemed to know just the right thing to say.

A butler waited for her at the front door, letting her in with a nod. "Miss Starling, I am Pole, at your service."

Another oddity about Augustus's household; he never

employed the same people for very long. It did not matter how well they did their duties; he simply liked new faces.

"Hello, Pole. Is the master in?"

"He and the gentleman are waiting for you in the drawing room, Miss."

In a breath, Layla deflated. She had little patience to entertain or make nice with a visitor. But she knew without doubt that Augustus was aware of her arrival. To slink off now would be unforgivably rude.

Squaring her shoulders, Layla followed Pole.

She spotted Augustus first, standing by the mantel, his lean frame silhouetted by the fire crackling in the hearth. His coal black hair glinted in the flickering light of the gas sconces flanking either side of the fireplace. His skin was smooth and golden.

He never aged. This was simply fact. Layla recalled the day he'd sat her on his knee in her nursery and told her that he, unlike other men, would never have a gray hair upon his head, and his skin would never wrinkle or sag.

"It is simply my nature, child," he'd told her then. *"As much a part of me as are the freckles upon your little nose."*

Because she'd been a girl of merely five, she'd accepted his story. It was only when she'd grown older and understood more of the order of things that she'd begun to realize there was nothing natural about it at all. It did not, however, alter her affection for the man she thought of as her father. But she feared. Deep in her heart she worried that, while Augustus remained unchanged, she would grow old and eventually die. Who would look after him then? And why did he not age? She'd always been too afraid that she'd upset him if she asked.

Now, she simply gave him a happy smile. "Augustus, it is so good to see you again."

Layla moved to cross the room and embrace her guardian when she caught sight of another man, standing just to the left of Augustus. He'd been clinging to the shadows as if not wanting to be seen. But it was too late; her attention lit upon him and she promptly froze, the blood draining from her cheeks then rushing back with a force that made her skin prickle.

She had not laid eyes upon that face since she was fifteen years old, when this man had been no more than a youth himself. And perhaps she ought not recognize him at all. But there was no forgetting those eyes, green sea glass, surrounded by long, ink-black lashes. Or that strange, unearthly hair that had caused the boy such trouble—shiny black with red tips, as if his very hair was aflame.

He used to shear that hair right off his head, hating the sight of it. Only to despair when it grew back thick and full in a fortnight.

And here he was, standing in her parlor, his pale green gaze so potent it made her knees weak and her breath short.

Happiness fluttered in her heart. "Saint?"

Until then, his expression had been stoic, a frozen mask she knew he often wore among strangers. That had hurt. But at the sound of his nickname, the firm curve of his lower lip kicked up at one corner, and his eyes grew warm, the pale green darkening.

"Hello, little bird." His voice was much deeper now, carrying a resonance that spoke of power. "I wondered if you would remember me."

"Remember you?" A small laugh left her, as her heart did that fluttering thing again. "Not a day goes by that I don't think of you in some small way."

At that, he blinked with the slightest jerk of his head, a look of extreme discomfort flitting across his features. Layla winced, cursing her loose lips. But the moment was gone, and he was looking upon her as if she was some exotic bird suddenly let out of its cage.

So she did the only thing she could. Uttering a little sound of apology mixed with self-deprecation, she hurried forward and embraced him, just as she would any other dear friend.

A mistake realized in hindsight, as the smoky, amber scent of him surrounded her, and his intense warmth buffeted her skin. He held himself stiff as new starch, his chin grazing the top of her head as he peered down at her. Lord but he was unmistakably a man now, tall and strong. His shoulders were like oak beneath her palms.

"Hello, Sin," she murmured, flushing a little as she drew away. "I'm so happy so see you."

The gentle brush of his fingertips at her elbow sent awareness skittering down her spine. Or maybe she imagined it, for he remained as reserved as ever, and both of his hands hung at his sides, as if he'd never moved at all.

Unable to look him in the eye, she quickly turned to Augustus, who wore an irksome smile as if she'd amused him greatly. She gave him the slightest reproving look, one well-hidden from a silent Sin, before giving her guardian a kiss on his smooth cheek. "Are you going to welcome me home, old man?"

He huffed out a laugh. "I deserved that," he said at her ear. "Welcome home, dear girl."

Fortunately, the arrival of tea gave Layla a moment to settle. After she'd served them all a cup, she sat back with a sigh of relief. Regardless of whether Sin was here or not, it was good to be with Augustus once more.

"Please do not take this as rude, Sin," she said, "but we haven't seen each other for years. What brings you here now?"

It was Augustus who spoke, however. "St. John and I have become well acquainted since you've been gone. I've asked him to stay here with us while he is in London."

Sin made a slight sound in his chest, then leaned forward in his seat, resting his forearms upon his bent knees. "I am here to watch over you."

"What? Why?" Her gaze darted from him to Augustus, who was glaring at Sin.

Sin returned the look with a placid one. "I'll not lie to her. And Layla needs to know. Duplicity will only make my task more difficult."

With one last frown at Sin, Augustus turned back to her. "I did not want to cause you undue concern. However, St. John speaks the truth. He is to be your guard."

When Layla had performed on stage, Augustus had employed men to protect her. Some admirers could be aggressive. And while that was all well and good then, she could only gape at Augustus, hurt pressing into her ribs. He knew that was all moot now.

"Are you deliberately trying to be cruel?" she asked him.

"No," Augustus said quietly as Sin frowned on, his gaze darting between them.

"Then why throw this at my head? Because it feels very much like a sick joke."

Sin tried to speak. "Perhaps we had better—"

"No," she snapped, getting to her feet. "I'm going to assume you had no part in this, so let me inform you, St. John. I can no longer sing." A sob struggled to break free. She would not let it. "My voice is gone. Destroyed, and I cannot bring it back."

She had not gotten past the complete devastation she'd felt when, a few weeks ago, Layla had opened her mouth to sing and ugly, discordant tones tumbled out instead.

Sin blinked up at her. "You cannot sing?"

"Is that not what I just stated? At first I thought I'd come down with the ague or some such thing, only I felt fine in all other regards. My voice was simply...broken." She shot her quiet guardian a hateful glare. "Something Augustus knows."

Sin's expression turned sorrowful, and she stiffened. "I am finished with all that. So you can see why I will not be needing your...services."

For a moment, she thought she caught a flash of humor in his eyes but he did not smile, only turned his attention to Augustus. "Care to explain to the class, old man?"

Layla had embraced him. Sin could still feel the imprint of her body against his chest. Her fragrance, like that of summer cherries, lingered on his coat. It had taken all his restraint to keep still and back away from her. Because, in truth, her touch and nearness had been like nails dragging over his skin.

Ever since his enslavement by the evil fae queen Mab, he abhorred the touch of others. It did not matter who touched him; he reacted the same, as if he'd sooner flay his skin off rather than endure another moment of contact.

And yet, he'd *wanted* to touch Layla. As it was, he could not keep his eyes off her. He drank in the sight of Layla like a man does a mirage in the desert. She could not be real. Not be here in front of him. Sin fought the urge to reach out and run his fingers along the smooth crest of her rosy cheek just to make certain.

But he had a task to do and it did not involve flights of fancy. And his mentor was finally willing to talk, which felt like a minor miracle in and of itself. So he tucked his hands in his pockets and leaned against the arm of the couch.

"I'm quite comfortable now," he told Augustus. "I do believe Layla is as well." He glanced at her and she sat back in her chair, tucking her heels under her skirts as if to settle in. Sin wanted to smile but turned back to Augustus. "Shall we continue?"

Augustus snorted softly through his nose. "Cheeky, the both of you." He sat as well, resting his hands upon the arms of his chair. "There is a saying: pull the thorn out quickly. I suppose it applies here." He looked at Layla. "My dearest girl, I am not what I seem."

"What you seem?" she asked with a little laugh, and Sin was struck by the husky quality of the sound. She was a contralto, her beautiful voice smooth and low. And nervous now.

"Human," Augustus answered. "Though perhaps you might have suspected this already."

A furrow grew between Layla's winged brows. "I don't..."

"Come now, my dear," he said. "I haven't aged a day. You know as well as I that isn't normal."

She flushed prettily. "I thought you said that was just how you are."

Augustus smiled. "Yes, and I lied. And I think you know it."

At that, Layla frowned. "All right, it's true, I knew something was not quite right. But I did not want to hurt your feelings by questioning you. And now what am I to believe? That you were having a laugh on me? This entire time? Of course I'd trust your word. I was a child. And you were my family."

"I was an ass to do that. But I had no other way to protect you at the time. You are no longer a child, though, and now you need the truth."

She looked off and the light of day hit the line of her neck, her profile, setting her skin aglow. It was a lovely honey-cream color, a sharp contrast to her glossy mahogany hair and eyes. Again Sin felt the urge to touch her, to trace the delicate curve of her jaw up to the plump earlobe just visible beneath her updo. He'd been in her shoes before and knew the shock and discomfort she was surely feeling. But Augustus was right. It was best to get the truth out and over with.

"Tell her what you are," Sin ordered.

His mentor lifted a brow but did not argue. His voice was calm and easy when he spoke again to Layla. "I am a Judgment angel."

Layla was silent for a moment then broke out in an inelegant and distinctly loud snort. "Oh, do tell me more. An angel." She laughed again. "Of all the things—"

Her mouth stood agape as Augustus calmly called forth his wings, unfurling them with a sort of majesty that Sin had yet to accomplish. He had to admit, however, that it was an awe-inspiring sight.

Augustus's wings spanned at least seven feet in either direction. Pure, pale silver, they were feathered, unlike Sin's, and reflected the light as if one were looking into a mirror.

Layla's mouth moved several times before words came out. "I... That is... you..."

"Am an angel," Augustus finished.

Layla's slim hand rose to her head. "I might faint."

"You'll do no such thing," Augustus ordered mildly. "Come, child. You knew. Deep down, you knew."

"I did not know this," she snapped. "I thought... well, I don't really know what I thought. True, I wondered why you did not age. But an angel?" She shook her head. "Why are you even here? Don't you have a harp you should be playing on a cloud somewhere?"

A chuckle left Sin's lips before he could contain it. Layla shot him a glance. "You knew?"

Sin straightened. "Of course I knew. Why do you think I'm here?"

Her brown eyes grew wide. "Oh, please do not tell me you're an angel too."

"All right," he said easily. "I won't."

Augustus cleared his throat, drawing their attention. "Harps are for Putti, Layla. Angels are warriors. And I am not the sort you've learned about in your lessons."

"I gather," she muttered.

"I am the creator of Judgment. 'Angel' is actually a new term," Augustus explained with a wave of his hand. "We actually go back to Egyptian myth. Where hell was called Duat, and the queen of Judgment was named Maat. I, like my brethren, am an eater of souls. I hunt down other immortals and supernatural beings who have done wrong and take their souls for final Judgment."

"Other supernatural beings?" Layla's lips parted in expectation. "Such as?"

"Demons, Lycans—which human fairy tales often call werewolves—Elementals, capable of controlling the elements—fire, ice, earth, electricity."

Layla frowned, her body tensing, and Sin wondered if she was thinking of him. He'd never quite been able to control his powers as a lad. But he'd never full-out shown them to her either.

"Ghosts in the Machine or GIM, who have clockwork hearts and the ability to leave their body in spirit."

Layla's mouth opened in a gape.

"There are many beings," Augustus went on. "We shall teach you all about them."

At this, Layla did look at Sin. "What are you, then? I know you are something."

"It's my hair that gives me away, isn't it?" he teased, his heart suddenly beating too hard. He didn't like exposure.

Layla glanced at his head. "Well, it isn't exactly normal, no. But I've always found it quite lovely."

He would not smile. His hair was not at all normal. Black as pitch, except for the tips, which always, always turned a vibrant scarlet red. It did not matter how many times he cut his hair; the tips would turn back to red within hours. Sin had taken to pomading the lot of it back, resulting in his hair having a sort of red-black tint. Not ideal but it hid its strangeness well enough.

"Thank you," he said tightly. "As to what I am. I was born an elemental."

"The barn you burned," Layla said, her gaze turning inward as if remembering when they'd first met.

"An unfortunate flare of temper," he admitted.

"St. John is unique in that he has control of all the elements," Augustus said. "Most only have power over one."

Yes, jolly great, that. All it really meant was Sin had to learn to control himself at all times or risk crumpling buildings or striking some poor innocent with a bolt of lightning.

Augustus was still talking, however. "But what St. John is now is something a bit more." His smile was proud, which surprised Sin. "St. John is now Judgment as well. The most powerful after myself, for he brings with him the elements."

Layla's gaze was curious and a little afraid. "Show me."

"I'm not a parlor trick," he muttered. But she had to believe.

So he drew in a breath and let himself change. Fully, not the half measure Augustus had done. And Layla let out a strangled sound as his skin color shifted from ivory to the palest mercury. As with Augustus's wings, Sin's flesh also appeared to be mirror-like, the heart of fine crystal. He looked like a man made of out of moving, living crystal.

Another breath and his wings came forth, called to life with a thought. They snapped out, shaped like his mentor's, but without feathers. Augustus had explained that only a true angel-born would have feathers. Judgment created by other means would have smooth wings.

"Oh, my," Layla said, standing as if in a trance. Her trembling fingers rose up to touch him, and Sin flinched. It was a reaction to contact, nothing against her, but she saw and quickly lowered her hand. "Sorry," she said. "But you are... utterly beautiful."

"Augustus too," Sin murmured, trying to deflect.

His mentor inclined his head and transformed as well. "It is but one of our forms. Designed, actually, to make us invisible. Mostly in the sky."

Layla took a breath. "So you..." She laughed a little. "I don't know how to think anymore. Why are you telling me this now?"

"Because I am fading," Augustus said calmly.

Sin sat up straight as Layla balked, her color rising. "What?"

They both spoke as one.

"My time here is growing limited," Augustus continued as if speaking of going on a day trip. "At some point, I will be pulled back into the realm where only angel-born and their mates can enter. I changed St. John into Judgment so that he might watch over you when I am gone. But more than that, I need to know that you are protected for all time."

"Oh, Augustus," Layla sighed. "You've given me your fortune. I'd rather have you around. But it's there and I will use it wisely. I don't need anything more."

"You need someone to protect you. A husband."

Everything within Sin stilled, his heart slowing down to a painful thumping. *No. No. No. She could not go to another.* On the heels of his internal protest was another: *He could not watch this. Not her.*

Augustus glanced between an appalled Layla and a frozen Sin. "I had hoped St. John would be that man for you."

"No!" Sin was shouting and on his feet before he knew it.

The denial rang over the room, and he cursed inwardly as he glanced at Layla, who was ducking her head and flushed pink.

"You needn't be so vehement," she murmured in the awkward silence. "I have no intention of marrying. And certainly not..." Her breath hitched just slightly. "Not to someone who does not want me."

Sin winced, his heart squeezing. He could not look at her. "It isn't a matter... I am Judgment. We are akin to... warrior monks."

Augustus's piercing gaze made a mockery of that statement, and the clouds of disappointment Sin saw just beyond that reprimand furthered his regret. But, hells bells, what was the man thinking? Sin wasn't for Layla. He carried such ugliness. He couldn't even bloody touch a woman without wanting to retch. He would not shackle Layla in that way.

"As I was saying," Augustus went on dryly, "I had a hope but I knew it was not entirely optimistic."

Sin crossed his arms in front of himself, and Layla swallowed a snort.

"Well, then," she said thickly. "Seeing as that is off the table, shall we continue and clear the notion of a husband entirely?"

Augustus shook his head. "St. John not coming up to snuff does not negate the need to see you safely settled."

Sin had more than a few choice words for Augustus just then, but Layla huffed loudly.

"So you keep saying," she snapped. "But I cannot see why. This is the modern age, Augustus. A woman of means is perfectly capable of living a happy life without a protector."

Sin cleared his throat. "Why don't you explain to us why you feel Layla must be guarded?"

His mentor sighed. "Judgment all have special gifts. Mine

is foresight. And what I see for you, Layla…" His expression grew tight and pinched. "What I've always seen is you, just as you appear at this age, being hunted by Damnation."

Everything in Sin went cold and hard. He loomed over Augustus, the room heating and humming with a crackle that was unnatural. "And you tell me this now?"

Layla's eyes shot to him. "What is damnation?"

Sin ran a hand through his hair as he began to pace. "They are our dark counterpoint. We take a soul, send it to Judgment, where it will be either sent to a version of hell or a version of immortal afterlife. Damnation takes a soul and keeps it."

"Keeps it?" Her eyes were round and fearful.

"Absorbs it as his or her own," Sin explained. "And gains any powers that person might have."

"Right." Layla stood. "Precisely. Demons and werewolves and soul-sucking fiends." Her hands were clasped, knuckles white. "Simply another normal day in London." With an off-kilter laugh, she wrung her hands again. "If you'll excuse me, I need some air."

Layla did not wait but promptly quit the room as if the hounds of hell were after her.

Sin cut Augustus a look. "Marriage? Truly? You couldn't have given just a wee bit of warning about what you wanted out of me here?" He didn't wait for an answer but strode off to follow Layla. He'd leave her be, but having her out of sight now was no longer an option.

Chapter Four

It was the 1890s now, Layla thought as she strode along the pavement, ignoring the bustle of coaches, drays, and omnibuses rattling past. A modern age where a modern woman could walk on her own, without a companion hovering at her shoulder.

Her skirts kicked up as she lengthened her stride. A modern age where women were not married off to appease lying, *immortal angel* guardians. Guardians who thoughtlessly humiliated their charges. She cringed, her cheeks heating at the memory of Sin's vehement refusal to so much as think about her as a wife. She'd been as shocked as he, but she'd been able to hold her tongue. It wasn't as if she expected marriage from him. Good grief, the idea was ridiculous, considering they hadn't seen each other since they were youths.

But you always thought he'd be the one to ask for your hand, did you not? You'd kept all other suitors at bay because you've been waiting for him to return, haven't you?

Layla told her conscience to shut up.

"You're muttering to yourself," a male voice said at her side. "Keep on and you'll be carted off to Bedlam."

Her pace halted, and she glared. Augustus strolled along, derby atop his head, walking stick in hand—the perfect English gentleman. *Ha. What rot.* "Just imagine," she drawled, "what they would do if I told them what you said to me today."

His mouth curled, but there was little humor in the gesture. "I've heard they're experimenting with electric shock treatments these days."

Layla shuddered. "Don't jest. It's horrid. And I very well might end up there." She felt decidedly unhinged as it was.

It was his turn to break stride. "No, you won't. You will lead a full and happy life."

Together they slowed. Her brisk pace had taken them to the corner of Hyde Park, and the sun was still out, shining brightly for once upon the path.

"Augustus, are you truly..." A lump formed in her throat, and she couldn't finish.

His black gaze grew soft. "Yes, darling girl, I'm not long for here." When she made a little sob, he rested his hand on her arm. "Don't cry for me."

"How can you say that when you tell me you are dying?" Truly, she was going to start a crying jag right here on the street in a moment, and she did not even have a proper kerchief.

As if he'd heard her internal struggle, Augustus pulled the yellow silk handkerchief from his suit breast pocket and handed it to her. She dabbed at her watering eyes.

"It isn't death as you think of it," he said quietly. "I simply move on to another plane of existence."

"One in which I cannot go," she said. "Which is just as bad."

"So you pity yourself," he said with a little laugh.

"Of course," she snapped without heat. "Why do we cry over death if not for our loss? You believe I will not mourn you every day? Miss you? Silly old man."

He chuckled then and leaned in to kiss her brow. "Sassy girl. You always were." He stepped back and offered her his elbow. When she took it, he began to stroll along the path.

"Are you quite certain you are dying, or fading, as you call it?" she asked. "Perhaps you're being overly dramatic and paranoid."

"My dear girl, I am an angel of Judgment. *The* Angel of Judgment. I don't do dramatic."

She snorted. And he ignored it.

"I broke a law. Long ago. I saved a being I was charged to hunt down. And in doing so, I was punished. First, stripped of my ability to act as Judgment, only to guide other Judgment angels. Second, I was allowed smaller and smaller windows of time in which I could live here in this world." He glanced up at the blue sky. "I feel it, child, in my heart and soul. I'm soon to be called back and won't be allowed to return."

"How very unfair. You should be rewarded for your kindness in sparing another, not punished."

He glanced at her. "Even if the being I hunted was evil? Had done many a foul deed?"

"You say you are 'the' angel of Judgment. Does that not mean you are able to see into the heart and soul of another and deem whether it is worthy?"

"It does," he said carefully, still looking at her.

"Then your decision to spare this being ought not be questioned."

His lips curled again, this time with amusement. "So you say, child."

Layla grumbled in annoyance over his unjust fate. They were quiet until they reached the Serpentine. "I'm still cross with you. How could you throw Sin at my head in that manner? It was badly done."

One of his dark brows rose. "Reprimanding me, are you?" He shook his head. "I was not in jest, Layla dear. You need guarding. Were Sin your husband, it would solve that problem."

"Oh, neatly, indeed." She glared off at the lake. "He was horrified. And, in turn, I was mortified."

"I do apologize for the way I handled the situation," Augustus murmured. "But not for the idea."

"Why Sin?" she asked, the sting of rejection still sharp in her belly.

Augustus halted and turned to face her. His expression was kind but unyielding. "Because you love the boy."

Layla flushed hotly, her mouth opening to give him a good piece of her mind. But he talked over her.

"You do. You always have. Lie to me if you must, but I've seen the truth since you were a girl."

"You took me away from him," she blurted out, close to crying once again. "You kept us apart."

His jaw tightened. "It had to be done then. For your safety."

"My safety. Always my safety." She flapped her arm as if she could strike down the very notion. "Never mind my feelings."

"Not when it means your life, no."

She huffed then, wanting to stamp her foot.

"I see you did not deny what I said," Augustus pointed out.

Layla hugged herself close. "What does it matter how I feel? He does not want me."

It hurt to say and brought a fresh wave of hot humiliation over her skin.

"He does not know what he wants at the moment," Augustus said quietly. "Sin has had a rough go of it, these past years. He needs to find his way again." He held up a hand when Layla moved to ask why. "I'll not divulge what is his story to tell. But know that what St. John says and how he truly feels are not in complete accord at the moment."

Layla blinked down at the rough gravel path. "Then we are at an impasse."

He was silent until she was forced to look up. As always, his dark eyes seemed to see straight to her soul. Layla supposed he probably did, and wasn't that an uncomfortable notion. His voice was deeper than usual when he spoke. "What would you do, Layla Starling, to find your happiness? To secure his?"

When he looked at her in that manner, his voice compelling and strong, she was unable to hold her tongue. "Anything."

He nodded. "Even swallow your pride?"

She'd never thrown her pride down before. Never had to. But she found herself saying, "Yes."

"Then heed me, child, and have faith that all will turn out right."

A part of her did not want to. That cowardly self preferred to crawl into her bed and hide for a good, long while. But Augustus stood before her, steady and sure, a world of love for her in his eyes. He would not harm her. And so she would trust him. "Very well," she said. "What shall I do?"

As soon as Sin saw Augustus headed for Layla, who had been stomping towards Hyde Park in a fury, he backed off. Augustus had much to say to Layla, at any rate, and Sin did not.

Wrenching his tie loose, he made his way towards Covent Garden, where the broad streets narrowed to twisted lanes and crowded houses. The sun had a few hours left in the sky but there was a shimmer of wrongness in the air—more so than usual. He'd never noticed these markers before becoming Judgment. Now he could see glittering, dark trails and vapors of ill intent running through the city, the sight of them like black diamonds in the moonlight, beautiful in their own, strange way.

That he found evil and corruption attractive was unnerving. However, Augustus had once told him that to be Judgment was to appreciate that the world was made up of both good and evil. That one must accept that there must be balance. Sin had countered by asking why they bothered eradicating great evil then, only to be patiently told that their task was to even the playing field. In other words, wipe out great evil and leave the smaller, petty crimes to play out for themselves.

At the moment, he was in the mood to fight. Energy crackled over his skin and dug into his bones. It took all his concentration not to let it free, lest buildings topple or some poor sod be suddenly burnt to a crisp or frozen solid.

Gods, but he wanted to let out a blast of power though. One good hit, perhaps at the monstrosity that was the Tower Bridge. Londoners would likely thank him. Sin ground his teeth. All this preparation, all these dire warnings that Layla needed protecting, and what did it come down to? Augustus wanted to see her married off. And he had Sin in mind for the task.

"Fuck's sake," he muttered under his breath. Of all the stupid ideas…

His fist flew out and he punched the side of a building as he passed. Brick crumpled, leaving a large hole. A coffee monger yelped at the noise, his eyes wide, but Sin kept walking.

Then there was the treat of Damnation to contend with.

This he could manage, though the thought of Damnation coming after Layla left him cold with fear and white hot with rage. Sin had never encountered a damnation demon. But he'd been thoroughly schooled on them.

Fully turned, they possessed blood-red skin and batlike wings. Sin's own sire, Apep, was a sort of grandfather of all Damnation, which meant Sin's blood was as tainted as it was saved. He might have one day been turned into Damnation, only Apep was trapped in hell and the only being capable of doing the deed. As it was, the appearance of a Damnation demon was so rare, the only being who had seen one in living memory was Augustus.

What worried Sin was that one had no way of knowing what powers a Damnation would possess. He'd have to go in blind when he fought one. Ordinarily that was fine, but Layla's safety was not something he was willing to risk.

Layla, Layla, Layla. It always came back to her. Thank god she'd rejected the idea of marrying as much as he had. He would gladly guard her, but watch her give herself to another? Sin couldn't stomach that.

The further into the older warrens of the city he went, the darker it became, the streets so narrow and crowded they blotted out even the strongest of rare London sunlight. Around him the poor went about their business, none of them even bothering to look his way. They never did. It was but a matter of thinking himself invisible to humans and he all but became so. They simply did not notice him.

Sin found himself moving through Covent Garden and heading towards Whitechapel. A shudder worked over his shoulders. That place. A few years back, a deranged demon had done his best to terrorize London with his games, preying on women and ripping them apart in the most gruesome of ways. The press had dubbed him Jack the Ripper.

Augustus, Sin, and the Society for the Suppression of Supernaturals, casually referred to as the SOS, knew him as an evil destruction demon with a taste for human organs. His had been the second soul Sin had sent to hell.

The idea that there might be new and violent evil lurking in the already traumatized district did not sit well. The horrid place suffered the lowest sort of poverty and needed no further inducement to misery.

Sin's nostrils pinched as he moved from Whitechapel High Road into the tight maze of lanes just off it. Here was humanity at its most desperate. Filled to bursting with poor Jewish and Irish immigrants, there simply wasn't enough room or hope. Filth and sewage ran free in the streets, dead animals lay in gutters, barefoot and ragged children ambled about. Beggars and thieves mixed with honest workers who tried to make their way in this ugly world.

He passed a gaggle of prostitutes, the very type who had been terrorized by the Ripper, their health so poor they were old before their time.

Had they noticed him, he'd have been approached ten times over already, his pockets picked clean by light-fingered babes, while older, more capable fiends would try to gut him.

Humans may not be an issue for Sin but Whitechapel was home to a great many nonhuman fiends as well, demons and strange beings who fed off misery and rage. They hid themselves well, but they were here. And they were watching him.

Yes, something dark and powerful lurked here.

Sin wove his way past idling humans, going deeper into the warren. Ragged linens hung on lines, brushing the top of his head as he walked along. He could hear the cries of children, the discordant yowl of a cat, and the distant clamor of the traffic on the high street. But here, however, all was still and cold.

He did not bother to quiet his steps. Whatever he was tracking had clearly tried to entice him here. It radiated its power in the way a human would ring a bell. A trap, perhaps. But Sin wasn't easy to take down. He had a feeling this unknown being understood as much.

The wind changed, and with it came the unmistakable scent of blood. Deeply metallic and tempered with the fug of offal, the blood scent was clearly that of a gutted human. His steps quickened and then halted.

The body was spread over the alleyway. A bit here, a bit there. Nothing recognizable as the human form. He swallowed convulsively. Such carnage. He'd seen the like before, but not to this level. Blood dripped from the rough clapboard walls and ran along hard-packed dirt.

He was not an expert on death. But the kill appeared to be a few hours old. Already the rats and bugs were at it, lazy flies circling, the blood black and congealing.

The sound of footsteps had him stilling. Sin looked around then leapt up to a roof overhang tucked into a nook. Perching lightly, he watched as a tall, hulking form appeared out of the gloom.

Fists clenched at his sides, the man was scowling, his nostrils flaring as he took in the scene. Sin watched him for a moment, then cleared his throat—not wanting to startle the man, for Sin knew him, and his strengths, well.

Jack Talent started then glared up at him. "Piss and shit, Sin, what the hell are you doing up there?"

Talent was SOS, tasked with hunting down rouge supernatural beings and strange anomalies. At one point, he had also been Sin's friend. Not so much now, since Talent was Ian's adopted son, which also made him Daisy's brother-in-law. Talent had kept his distance once Daisy had stopped speaking to Sin.

Sin jumped down easily. “Watching you. Honestly, that was badly done, Talent. I could have had you without a fight.”

Talent’s brow rose. “Oh, it would have been a fight.” He glanced at the mess of body parts as his nose wrinkled. “What’s all this, then?”

Sin knew what he was asking and was grateful that Jack hadn’t immediately thought it was Sin’s doing. “I’m not certain,” Sin said, surveying the scene again. “I followed a trail of darkness here.”

Jack gave him a look but nodded. “I did too. Felt it in my gut.”

Jack was the son of a fallen angel, and thus, like Sin, had immense power running through his veins. Jack could sprout wings, which had the same characteristics of Damnation, blood red and batlike. But Jack was honest and hunted down evil. The only true difference between their jobs was that Jack simply killed offenders. Sin took their souls as well.

Jack set his hands low on his hips. “Ian sent me out, truth be told. Said he smelled something off in the air. But he was headed to the theater with Daisy and didn’t want to leave her.”

Sin snorted. “Had you do his dirty work, eh?”

Jack almost smiled. “He’s a king, after all. I’m but a servant of justice.” His expression grew serious. “Ian wondered if I’d see you here.”

“I met Ian a few nights ago,” he said to Jack. “Both of us chasing an unknown being who I came upon gorging on a dead human. The scent was much like a lycan’s but off in certain ways.” Sin tried to breathe in the scents around them and catalogue the different notes but it was impossible, and all he got for his efforts was a rolling stomach. His lip curled. “I smell nothing but death and rot.”

Jack let out a short laugh. “Me as well. But I sense something dark. Something…” Jack rolled his massive shoulders. “Like us.”

"Yes," Sin said. "I think it might be Damnation."

Jack's green eyes narrowed. "I've heard of those bastards but never seen them."

"That is where you are wrong," Sin said, turning away from the carnage. "Amaros, the fallen you destroyed, was Damnation. Or so says Augustus. Had Amaros been at full power, that is." But the fallen had been cursed and was both weak and mad.

Jack cursed sharply. "Are you telling me that whatever did this..." He gestured towards the ground. "Could be more powerful than that sick fuck?"

"That is exactly what I'm saying." And Augustus had seen it coming after Layla. Sin had the sudden need to get back to her and to stay at her side come hell or high water.

Jack ran a hand through his brown hair. "Right. I'll alert the SOS."

"Don't bother. Augustus is the one who warned me, which means the SOS already knows."

"Well, I bloody didn't," Jack snapped.

"Because Augustus wants me to take it down."

Jack gave him a long, measured look. "Regardless, you are not alone. I don't care when or where: you call for me and I will come to your aid."

Sin blinked a few times. But he did not answer. All his life, he'd wanted family and acceptance. He'd had a taste of it but it had been bittersweet, tempered as it was by Mab's ugly influence. Now he was accustomed to being on his own, often talking to no one for weeks at a time.

Jack gave his shoulder a hearty slap and then he walked off, leaving Sin alone in that foul alley. He stood for a moment, his spine cold and his shoulder blades itching.

"Did you ever wonder," said a silky voice in his head, *"if you picked the wrong side?"*

Sin closed his eyes as a shudder worked through him. It felt like lust, dark and thick and dirty. Not the clean, sweet need he experienced while looking at Layla. It was the familiar ugly sort he'd felt servicing the bitch Mab.

Sweat broke out over his skin. He wanted to turn heel and run but he let the lust ride through him.

"Imagine," said the voice, *"if you were in control? If it were you giving the orders?"*

Unbidden came the image of Layla, naked and bound, her peachy arse in the air, waiting for him to strike it. He could see her flesh wobble as his hand smacked.

Sin did turn then, striding out of the alley with inhuman speed, his cock at full mast and painful, his heart thrumming fast and insistent. And he swore he heard laughter follow.

Chapter Five

Layla was very quiet as she climbed the stairs to the top floor of the house. Not because she was trying to hide. Skulking around seemed ridiculous, as if she was doing wrong. She crept because it was part of an old game, one that she found she wanted very badly to resume.

In truth, she wanted her old friend back, the one she could talk to about anything. And he'd tell her anything as well. She missed those interactions with a keen intensity that made her ache all over.

Her heart pounded in giddy anticipation as she reached the topmost landing. Muscles quivering with the effort to hold still when she really wanted to pounce, Layla laid her hand upon the doorknob in front of her.

Only to have it ripped from her grip as the door flew open and a hand reached out to grab her. She gave a little cry of surprise as she all but tumbled into Sin's arms.

He adjusted his grip, holding her steady by the upper arms, but setting her away from him so that her body did not come into contact with his. "What," he asked, "are you doing?"

Layla couldn't repress her grin. "What does it appear to be? I'm sneaking into your room, you noodle."

His expression remained unaffected save for the very slight lift of one dark brow. "Why?"

Layla broke free of his impersonal grip. "Oh, for Pete's sake. You are frighteningly obtuse these days." Strolling away from him, she looked around. "We always snuck into each other's rooms."

He watched her with narrowed eyes. "We were children then."

"Captain Obvious rides again," Layla murmured. She ignored his response in favor of inspecting the room. Layla had not been up here before and was surprised to find not a warren of small rooms, as was the case in most top floors, but a wide open space that ran nearly the length of the house.

Plain, wooden columns broke up the expanse and obviously held up the roof. The floors were clean but worn and unwaxed. For all its openness, it was downright Spartan in its furnishings.

A brass bed that had been Layla's as a girl—before she'd discarded it in favor of a pretty, white-enamel, cast-iron bed—faced the set of French doors that made up the wall overlooking the mews. There was a little, old writing desk and chair, and a gaudy black and gold Louis XIV dresser that had once sat in the second floor hall. Nothing more. Not even a rug to warm one's feet.

"Why do you choose to stay up here?" she asked, walking over to the far side of the room that was completely devoid of furniture. The open space reminded her of a dance floor.

Sin stayed by his spot close to the door, as if he'd like nothing more than to boot her from the room, or perhaps run from it himself. "I value privacy."

Layla ignored the heavily implied reprimand in his tone.

"You should at least make yourself more comfortable. A rug and a few pillows would help immensely."

She reached one set of French doors and looked out, only to discover a narrow balcony. She hadn't been aware the house had one, as it was hidden by the roofline. "This, however, is quite nice. I've always wanted a balcony."

"I remember. Now, are you done with this little impromptu room inspection?" Sin asked, bland as ever.

Layla's lips twitched—part in annoyance, part because he amused her. "Be warned, Saint. The nastier you are, the more I want to needle you."

At this, he glared. Their gazes clashed and did battle, and though she refused to show it, the action sent a little thrill through her veins. Staring at Sin was no hardship, after all—he was ridiculously handsome, beautiful in a way a master sculptor would create. But it was the strength of his gaze, all that glaring, green fire, and obstinacy, that hit her solar plexus and weakened her knees.

She wondered if Sin was similarly affected. It was difficult to tell, for his stony expression never altered. How horrid to think of him being unmoved, but she began to notice little things, such as the way his taut chest lifted and fell a bit more quickly, the way his fine nostrils flared just slightly and his irises widened.

Those small signs sent heat throughout her body and quickened her own breath. She drew in more of his scent, which was now stronger, headier. Her gums began to ache—something that had been happening more and more when she was roused. Layla feared she might growl—an utter humiliation which would have her fleeing the room.

But before she could do just that, Sin broke their war by slicing his gaze away from hers. His shoulders lifted in a shrug. "All right then," he said lightly. "I've been an inhospitable arse. Apologies."

Layla gaped at him, not believing his words for a moment.

Sin didn't notice. He strolled over to his bed and then plopped down upon it, as if a man without care. Leaning against the headboard, he folded his hands behind his head and gave her a genial look. "I don't have any tea, but feel free to make yourself comfortable. Perhaps we can tell each other stories. Or you can plait the ends of my hair, as you once attempted one night long ago."

The words were right, but the delivery cut through the air like a scythe.

Layla's canines itched. She had the violent urge to remove her slipper and hurl it at his head. But the anger was only second to the blue feeling of hurt.

"You never used to mock me," she whispered through the pain.

Sin sighed, all the starch flowing out of him like a paper dropped in hot water. "Layla," he said softly. "I'm here to guard you, not be your old friend who climbed trees and left fake snakes in your bed."

More's the pity. She swallowed down a wave of utter disappointment then drew herself up. "As I am in no need of guarding at the moment, I believe I shall turn in. Good night."

She walked across the room with a few long strides, but paused at the door. Nerves fluttered in her belly but she made herself say the words. "I have decided to appease Augustus in his request to see me married."

Sin lurched up, his black brow knitted and his eyes flashing silver. "What?"

"You heard me." Her fingers curled over the door lintel. "Augustus is going to arrange for balls, parties, and the like. And I'm going to search for a husband."

More silver spread through his irises. "You do not have

to do this. I shall guard you regardless of whether he is here or not."

"That is big of you. However, I want to do this. For him. For me."

"Layla—"

"Protests?" she snapped then, glaring at him. "Forgive me, but you have no say in this."

Sin shot off the bed in such a quick and graceful movement she wondered how she had not seen his supernaturalness before this. "That may be," he said. "But do not expect me to hold my tongue when you make foolish decisions."

"Fair enough. But don't *you* go expecting me to listen." She drew herself up. "Were you my husband, I might feel differently, but since you were quite clear on rejecting that role, I'm afraid you have little recourse in these matters."

Oh, but his glare was a fearsome thing when he put his mind to it. "Very well, Layla. Ruin your life. Don't expect sympathy from me when it all goes to hell."

Sin waited until he heard Layla's bedroom door shut on the floor below then let out a hard breath. God's teeth, the woman was going to drive him over the edge. Never had he wanted more than to give in and just . . . play.

When they were younger, she'd use those nimble fingers of hers to tickle him until he teared up, and he'd retaliate by pinching her knees. How on earth he'd figured out she had ticklish knees was lost to time. It seemed as though he'd always just known Layla and what made her tick. Although his idea of play was far less innocent now.

He could picture it—tossing Layla on his bed, her mahogany locks spreading out like a silken web on his pillow, her bright eyes smiling at him. He'd start on her knees straight away, burrowing under her skirts where it would be warm and fragrant.

"Bloody hell," he muttered, a fine sweat breaking out over his skin. Sin stalked to the window and opened it. The London air was far from fresh but it was cold, and that was enough for now.

Drawing it into his lungs, he tried to calm his heated blood. Yes, Layla made him crave, but tonight, he'd hurt her. And hurt himself too. Leaning his forehead against the windowpane, Sin stared at the skyline, now hazy under a burgeoning moon.

Augustus wanted to marry her off, see her safe and settled. And she had agreed to the nonsense. Who was Sin to argue? He wanted the same thing. Only…It did not matter what he wanted. He was Judgment. It grounded him and gave his life purpose. There was no place for domesticity in that life. Which was a good thing, considering that he was not fit to be with anyone.

He told himself this. But, on a deeper level, he knew that he hadn't any protection against his heart when it came to Layla. Nor any way to keep her at arm's length, save for being cold and cruel. It disgusted him to treat her so callously. But Layla would persist otherwise. She was rather like a puppy that way—all boisterous energy and eternally optimistic.

Sin feared he'd destroy that light before all this was over.

Archer

Throughout his long life, Archer had known pain—both physical and mental. He'd grown accustomed to tolerating both, though between the two, he'd take physical pain over mental anguish any day.

Not that he'd had much experience with mental pain in the past years. For he'd been happy. So much so that there were mornings when he'd wake and fear it was all a dream. Then his lovely wife would make a sound as she slept, perhaps move a little beside him, and the bliss of peace would wash over him once more.

Yes, he'd been happy. For he was in love. Deeply. Eternally. Miranda was his heart and soul, and the idea of ever leaving her was more than he could bear to imagine. So he never did. Even when the realities of life became difficult to ignore.

As he descended the steps of his carriage, Archer knew what he appeared to be—a man in his thirties, tall and well formed, his thick black hair touched with strands of silver. In truth, he'd been born over a hundred years ago. Once cursed but now fully human and vulnerable to all human frailties.

Despite his advanced age, he'd never felt it. Until now. Gripping the handle of his walking stick and leaning on it as much as he could without actually toppling over, he stared up at the household he'd come to visit.

The town home was in the middle-class neighborhood of Notting Hill. Narrow and of newer construction, it had nevertheless already accumulated a dark patina of London grime.

Slowly he took the steps, his chest heavy, his breath short. By the time he reached the door, painted a hopeful emerald green, he was sweating. His hand shook as he pulled out a kerchief and pressed it to his brow. Tucking the cloth away, he knocked upon the door.

Silence answered.

Lights flickered behind the front parlor windows, so he knew someone was in residence.

Fighting a smile, he knocked again, more forcefully. "I

shall not leave until you face me, young Evernight," he said in a voice just a shade louder than normal. "Better to answer the door and get it over with."

After a beat, the door swung open, and a stone-faced St. John stared at him. It was a tad unnerving how greatly Sin resembled Miranda. They shared the same eye color, the same facial features, although Sin's were undeniably masculine whereas Miranda's were delicate and utterly feminine. And while Miranda had hair of red-gold, Sin's was an odd, inhuman shade of deep black fading into bright scarlet. Even so, the similarities were enough to warm Archer's heart towards the boy.

"Hello, Sin." He fought the urge to lean against the doorway. He needed to sit, and soon.

"Archer. You look..." Sin's black brows rose. "Well, not to put too great a point on it, you look like—"

"Hell," Archer finished for him. "Yes, I know." He'd lost weight. Shadows haunted the skin beneath his eyes.

Sin's mouth quirked. "I was going to say like death warmed over, but that will do."

Archer hated to think how close Sin's estimation really was. "As amusing as it is to stand here and let you analyze my appearance, I wonder if you plan to let me in at any time soon."

Sin snapped to attention. "Right. Pardon." He shot Archer another curious glance as he stepped aside. "Do come in, brother Archer."

Archer snorted at Sin's overly formal tone but gratefully followed the young man into the parlor. It was clearly a bachelor's room, bereft of excessive ornamentation. A fire crackled in the hearth and an old but large armchair covered in gold velvet was pushed close to it. A pile of newspapers lay in a heap by the chair, as if Sin had dropped them to attend to the door.

Running a haphazard hand through his hair, Sin looked around and then grabbed another chair that sat by the window. This chair was smaller and covered in brown leather, but no less battered. Sin set it by the fire then gathered up his newspaper.

"I don't receive visitors," he mumbled, moving to bring a little table between the two chairs.

"It appears you've hardly set up house," Archer observed.

"Because I haven't been here for a year. I was in Rome, and as of tonight, I'll be living with Augustus for a time." Sin dusted off the velvet chair then gestured towards it. "Have a seat."

Archer took the leather chair instead. The velvet was obviously Sin's preferred chair, and he was not here to put the boy out any more than necessary. He thought he heard Sin mutter "stubborn" under his breath but the young man was already turning to a little sideboard.

"I've brandy, port, and gin," Sin said, nodding to the crystal decanters. "What shall it be?"

None of those things would agree with his stomach so Archer waved it away. "If it's all right with you, I'd rather smoke my pipe." He did not smoke often, but lately, it soothed him when nothing else could.

"Of course." Sin helped himself to a glass of brandy then sat as Archer pulled out his pipe and prepared it. Sin watched the motions with a narrowed gaze. "Out of curiosity, how did you find me here?"

"Poppy alerted Miranda and Daisy that you were back in town, and where you dwelled." Archer winced at his words, but there was no getting around that particular elephant in the room. Sin was on the outs with his sisters, and there wasn't a damn thing Archer could do to persuade his oft-stubborn wife to forgive her brother. "As for the rest, I paid a boy to keep an eye out on the house and find me when you arrived."

Sin's smile was tight but amusement lit his eyes. "Augustus always warned me, never ignore the children. They're often the eyes and ears of the underground."

"To be sure."

Sin's smile faded. "Why are you here, Archer?"

Taking a draw on his pipe, Archer sat back and let the smoke out slowly. It perfumed the air and made his aching back relax just a bit. "Just as direct as your sister."

Sin flinched, his gaze sliding away. Archer did not like the way Miranda had cut Sin out of her life. He knew her reasons, but family was family, and Sin deserved a chance.

"Is she well?" Sin asked quietly.

Archer's heart warmed further. "She is."

Sin nodded, his gaze on the fire.

Archer let his pipe rest on the arm of the chair. "Why haven't you explained yourself to your sisters? I'm certain, whatever it is, they shall understand."

Sin's shoulders tensed. Eyes flashing green fire glared Archer's way. "I appreciate you coming here in an obvious attempt to arrange peace between me and my family, but there are things I will not discuss."

"Bedding the Fae Queen being one of them."

Sin's skin took on a deep shade of pink before going a sickly white. He swallowed hard before drawing a deep breath. The next instant, Sin was a different man—hard and cold, his body appearing almost larger somehow.

Archer's pulse missed a beat. He could have sworn he saw a flash of silver in Sin's eyes, but the younger man blinked and all he saw was jade green.

"Speak of that again and I shall remove you from my home, Lord Archer."

A formidable opponent. Sin Evernight had officially grown into full manhood.

Archer nodded. "I understand I've overstepped. However, it must be said. I would see your relationship with Miranda and your other sisters restored."

"Why does it mean so much to you?" Sin's tone was hard and quick. "My character is not that of a gentleman's. I'll make no excuses for what I have done. Is it not better for all concerned if things simply remain as they are?"

Archer took another draw on his pipe. "Would you consider it a favor to me to try?"

Sin made a noise of dry amusement. "You'll forgive me, Archer, but why should I? We haven't spoken for over a year."

Despite Sin's stone-cold demeanor, Archer could hear the faint accusation and hurt that laced his tone. And felt rather ashamed.

He faced his brother-in-law and did not withhold the truth. "I am dying."

Sin's head cocked as if Archer had slapped him. "What?" he asked in a thin voice.

"Miranda believes I have simply been ill. Stomach ailment." Archer had not yet found the strength to tell her the truth. But he must. "However, I am a physician. I know the signs. It is cancer, and it is advanced."

Sin stared at him, his throat working. "How long?"

"It is hard to determine. A few months, perhaps less."

"Jesus."

"She'll need you," Archer said in a rough voice. "No matter what you might believe, Miranda loves you. And I'll need you to be there for her."

Sin wiped a hand over his face. "Archer... She'll want to know why I did what I did. I have no answer."

"I have never believed you went willingly to ... that creature," Archer finished, avoiding her name out of respect for Sin.

Sin snorted but would not meet his eyes. "I was not forced."

There was a world of evasion in that statement. Archer studied Sin, who was tense and sullen once more. "I know well there are things of which a man cannot speak. Mistakes that take him down dark roads he cannot escape."

If anything, Sin grew more uncomfortable. "Then do not ask of me what I cannot give."

Silence fell between them, drawing attention to the crackle of the fire and the clip-clop-rattle-clank of a carriage passing on the street. Then Sin sighed. "I will go to Miranda, try to offer my support. Whether she agrees to accept me is up to her."

"That is all I ask."

Sin looked at him for a long moment, and Archer had the same unnerving sensation of catching a fleeting glimpse of silver in the man's irises. But he was imagining things. There was no silver, only sorrow and a bit of thoughtfulness, as if Sin were thinking things over.

"Will you do me a favor in return?" Sin asked.

"Of course."

"Tell me when you grow worse. I want to know before ..." He swallowed hard. "I should be obliged if you kept me informed of your progress, Archer."

Seemed a fairly maudlin request, and Archer was surprised at the level of caring Sin displayed. But he nodded. "That I can do."

Chapter Six

"Quite the spectacle, is it not?" Layla murmured at Sin's side. Her voice was smooth as honey and warm cream. Not at all what he'd remembered, and every time she spoke when he wasn't prepared for it, that lovely, silken voice slid right over the length of his cock.

He swore he could feel her along every inch. Sin pushed his fists deeper into his trouser pockets. "It is at that," he agreed as they strolled along the narrow walk of the greenhouse. Greenery hung dense and thick around them, the air so humid it felt alive.

Much to Sin's underlying disgruntlement, Augustus had organized a party for Layla's return. And, in a display of shocking showmanship, the man had chosen to throw it at the Temperate House at Kew Gardens.

Sunlight filtered through the massive iron and glass structure and touched on Layla's glossy, dark hair. "So then," she said. "Augustus has dubbed you an excellent judge of character—"

Sin snorted so loudly that several heads turned. It could

not be helped. "I am a terrible judge of character," he murmured.

"Bollocks," Layla said smartly. "Augustus does not lie."

Sin was tempted to snort again. "He is an expert at twisting truth and evading outright lies." He flicked a palm frond out of their way. "As are we all in this strange little world."

Layla paused, and her pink lips turned down at the corners. "Such a cynic you've become."

She had no idea.

Layla shrugged as if she heard him. "Regardless, do tell me. Have I any promising prospects in this lot?"

Sourness coated Sin's tongue. This lot. He'd like to kick all of them out on their arses.

What had surprised Sin was that the majority of guests were Other in some way. Sanguis, lycans, undetermined but odd—there was a sampling of London's supernatural community. Most, he assumed, were SOS, but not all. Some were merely outliers who lived simple lives among an unknowing human society.

Most noticeably absent, however, were his sisters, all of whom would usually attend this sort of monster's ball. That they were likely avoiding Sin stung.

"You do realize," he said to Layla in a casual tone, "that almost all of them can hear you perfectly well?"

"Really?" She did not sound scandalized but intrigued.

"Mmm. Advanced senses are the most common trait among supernatural beings."

As if to punctuate his statement, a group of sanguis demons dressed in dapper gray morning suits turned away, purposely giving their backs to them as if to demonstrate their ignorance of Layla and Sin's conversation. Sin glared their way.

"To answer your question," he said in the same, almost

bored tone, "twenty percent of these...*prospects* appear to be mainly attracted to your money, while the other eighty clearly want the chance to bed you."

A lycan in pinstripes took an over-long sip of his champagne punch, never glancing in their direction.

"Which is why," Sin went on clearly, "if any of them so much as puts a pinkie on you without your express permission, I shall snap it off and stuff it down his throat."

Layla burst out laughing, a husky yet lilting sound that had more heads turning, this time in rapt interest. "Saint John, protector of virtue and destroyer of pinkies across the kingdom."

Sin grunted, about to retort, when a man stepped into their path.

"A true gentleman," the man drawled, "would always seek permission first." He smiled down at an openmouthed Layla. "Something I shall endeavor to do."

Sin didn't know who the bloody hell this sod was, but he did not like him. He was not human, that much was clear, but what he was remained a mystery.

They were of an even height, though the man in question was thinner, giving an appearance of being taller. His hair was so light it gleamed nearly white in the sunbeam shining down upon him. Crystal blue eyes stared at Layla.

Oh, he'd make a fine dandy for the ladies to fawn over. Sin ground his back teeth. "And you are?"

The man didn't look away from Layla. "Eron St. Clair."

"Another Sin name?" Layla glanced from Sin to the smarmy bastard before them. She appeared amused. Sin was not.

"Yes," said the bastard, "but only in the best possible ways."

"A clever one, he is," Sin offered dryly to Layla.

The man looked at him now. "I'm sorry, was that your line?"

"Not even a little."

St. Clair tilted his head as if in confusion. Sin knew the arse wasn't confused in the least. Especially when the man's pale blue eyes gleamed with smugness. "One would expect a former consort of Mab would know all about sin."

The air left Sin's lungs as hot prickles broke out over his face. He knew better than to assume his time with Mab wasn't common knowledge. He'd been forced to attend too many parties and sordid orgies of the rich and bored on her arm for people not to know. It did not matter. His shame was now hanging in front of Layla.

And that fucker St. Clair knew it.

For a hot moment, Sin saw himself reaching over, tearing out the man's spine, and wrapping it around his throat like a bow. He could do that. But he'd taken a vow: do no harm to innocents. No one was truly innocent, but unless he caught the man doing foul deeds, he could not touch him.

Something St. Clair seemed to know as well. "I did not mean to shock..."—*Oh, yes you bloody well did*—"However, one hears tales..."

He let his words trail off suggestively.

Sin could feel Layla at his side, feel her curious gaze on him. He couldn't look, couldn't move, really. As if from a great distance, he heard her voice.

"I do love a good tale, Mr. St. Clair. However, I much rather tell them than hear them. Is that a fault, do you think?"

St. Clair's voice was equally muffled by the buzzing in Sin's ears. "I find that utterly charming, Miss Starling."

"Do you? Shall I tell you about the time my guardian took me to Rome and I got lost in the Colosseum?"

There was a light touch on his hand. Bemused, Sin

glanced down and was caught in Layla's soft gaze. "I'll meet you by the punch in a quarter hour?"

She was leaving him. To go stroll with the bastard. And there was not a damned thing he could do about it. This was his job. His duty. Dully, Sin nodded, not daring to look at St. Clair or it would be all over; the man's blood would be decorating the glass panes in a heartbeat.

Another soft touch and she moved away, once again chattering about Rome. Sin watched her pleated skirts of dusky blue swaying with each step. In his head, he sang a Gilbert and Sullivan tune to drown out the sound of Layla conversing with the twat. But he followed along at a discreet distance. For he would watch her until it was no longer his privilege.

With every word and step she took, Layla felt a sense of misery and rage. She was walking away from Sin, which she knew upset him, and she was doing it while giving the impression that she'd chosen this arse over her friend.

But what was she to do? Whoever this Mab woman was, her mere name had made Sin recoil with a physical shudder. Oh, it was small, his reaction, nothing more than a tightening of his flesh and a twitch of his fingers. But, for Sin, it might as well have been an outright shout.

Layla hadn't known what to do other than draw this bastard St. Clair away from him. She might have simply given the man the cut direct but then it would have implied that he'd unnerved Sin, and that wouldn't do. Better to get him away from her friend. Surely Sin understood that?

"And so there I was," she prattled on, "lost in the maze of little passageways of the ground floor."

"Where they kept the lions and other exotic animals who attacked the gladiators," St. Clair provided helpfully.

"Yes, there." She glanced at him. "Am I boring you?"

His smile was sly. "Not at all, Miss Starling. Tell me, did you know that some of those small rooms you described were actually lift shafts? They would set the animals on a platform, and slaves would turn a crank to raise them up to the Colosseum floor. Quite the spectacle, really."

"You sound as though you were there," she teased. Layla could flirt if need be. Flirting was nothing more than playing a part. It was soulless, really.

St. Clair leaned in, his strangely pale blue eyes twinkling. "Perhaps I was."

She could not tell if he teased, so she shrugged. "Perhaps you were indeed. I keep forgetting how much my world has changed with a single revelation. I have to remind myself that not all is as it seems."

"It never was, Miss Starling." His attention stayed on her face. "You are quite lovely. I should like to call on you later. Would that be agreeable?"

Layla's steps slowed, and she realized that, a ways behind her, another set of footsteps slowed as well. Sin following. She did not know if she wanted to laugh or cry. Perhaps a little of both. But now she was in a quandary. She did not want to encourage a man who would so callously toss another man's past indiscretions in his face. And yet the entire point of walking with him now was to lead him away while not letting on that he'd gotten to Sin.

She glanced up at St. Clair. Something in the way his lips canted to the side as he so patiently waited for her response made her believe that he knew this all quite well.

"I am receiving callers between the hours of three and four. You may call on me at that time, if you like." There. She'd given him a time not reserved for friends, and made it clear he was but one of many. She might have said no but this man intrigued her. What did he know of Sin?

His tight smile grew. "So very formal, Miss Starling. You know, we Others are far more relaxed in our *intercourse*."

Cheeky.

"As you say," she replied smoothly. "However, as I am fairly new to your world, I expect it shall take me some time to grow accustomed to your ways."

St. Clair stopped. Before she knew what he was about, he'd taken her hand and brushed his lips over her gloved knuckles. "Never change, Miss Starling. You are a breath of fresh air."

She could have sworn she heard Sin snort.

St. Clair bowed his head and then turned on his heels to walk off.

She waited for Sin to saunter up. His hands were stuffed into his pockets as usual, his expression bored. "Fifteen minutes of my life wasted."

"And to think," she added lightly, "you'll get to relive the fun all over again tomorrow."

He glared down at her then. "What game do you play, Layla? You cannot possibly find that sod attractive."

"No?" Layla gazed off in the direction St. Clair had exited. She wanted to needle Sin. Just a little. Wanted him to show anything other than cool acceptance of Augustus's ridiculous quest to see Layla married off. "I'd think it is safe to say most would find him extremely so."

"Only on the surface," he said, still cool, still annoying.

"Why? Because he was rude to you? I do recall two men in that conversation, both equally matched in ill manners."

Sin's features smoothed out like glass. "Then I suppose you've a liaison tomorrow." He nodded towards the clusters of party goers who were idling around. "Are you finished here?"

Irritation surged up her throat. "No. If you'll excuse me, I've been ignoring my guests."

Layla left Sin and spent the next hour flirting with every man who approached her. And why not? As St. Clair said, the rules were different here. And Sin certainly wasn't attempting to stop her. But he did follow. Always. And it only fueled her irritation more.

Chapter Seven

This time, when Layla stole into Sin's room, he did not stop her. She wondered if he were truly sleeping, for he lay upon his bed, tucked under the covers, his head a dark blot on his white pillow. He'd warned her about creeping up on him unexpectedly, and while she'd teased him at the time, she did not want to catch him unaware.

Slowly she padded across the room towards his bed, and he turned his head. His eyes appeared to glow in the darkness as he tracked her movements. But he said nothing, nor did he move. So Layla did not stop. She crawled under the covers and laid her head on the spare pillow, facing him.

For a long moment he simply stared back, his gaze darting over her face as if to suss out what her motives were. When he spoke, his voice was warm and intimate in a way that had Layla's toes curling.

"This is going to become a habit, isn't it?" he said.

If she had her way? Yes. Layla snuggled further into the bedding that smelled of Sin, like the first bite of winter frost mixed with the warmth of a newly started log fire.

He'd been quiet and withdrawn all evening, keeping to himself. She hated to think that their squabble at the garden party had put a rift between them. But as he wasn't escorting her to the door at the moment, she would remain as close to him as she could get.

"The wind is howling," she pointed out. As if to punctuate the statement, a gust hit the windows with rattling force, moaning and wailing. Layla shuddered.

Sin's lush lips pursed on a bitten back smile. "Ah. So it is."

Layla had always hated the sound of a mournful wind. Made her think of death hunting down poor lonely souls in the dark. When she was little, she'd confessed this to Sin, and he'd told her that, whenever the wind howled, he would think of her and she was to think of him too. That way, they would be connected by their thoughts and would never really be alone.

Oddly, it had worked. She'd always felt connected to him on nights such as this.

Keeping her eyes upon him, she spoke in a hushed tone. "I used to dream of you."

The sharp lines of Sin's beautiful face did not move, but his eyes were alive, shining and wide with wonder.

"I used to dream that you were with me," she went on in a whisper. "Doing mundane things, riding in a carriage, having tea. Once you helped choose a hat. But you were there. So many nights."

He swallowed hard. "I dreamed of you too. Every night. It was the best part of my day, going to sleep."

Such a softly spoken confession, yet it had a weight, warm and wonderful, that wrapped around her heart. Her hand lay between them, and her fingers stretched wide, wanting to touch him, not wanting to break the rare spell that was Sin opening up to her.

"Do you suppose," she said, "that we dreamed of each other at the same moment? And perhaps we were together in that dream world?"

His hand slid out from under his pillow, slowly. He stopped just shy of touching her. "Perhaps we were."

"I missed you so, Saint."

His breath made an audible hitch. "I missed you too, little bird."

She lay perfectly still, afraid to move or breathe.

His gaze bore into hers, and meeting his stare was quite like facing the sun. He blinded her with his perfect beauty. But he was also so perfectly familiar to her, the face she most wanted to see for what seemed like her entire life. Right now, that wonderful face was tight with buried pain.

"Why did you not write?" he asked in a ghost of a voice.

A pang of regret hit her full force. "Augustus would not allow it." She licked her dry lips. "In the beginning, I tried to sneak out a few letters. He always caught me. No matter what I did, he seemed to know exactly what I was up to."

A hint of a wry smile lifted his lips. "He reads minds, you realize."

Shock froze her. "No," she breathed. "Does he truly?"

Sin gave a bare nod, amusement lighting his expression.

Heat colored her cheeks. "Oh, how horrid." There were quite a few thoughts she most certainly did not want her guardian to know. "How horrid of *him* not to tell me."

Sin made a sympathetic sound. "To be clear, Augustus has a certain code of honor. He has never, to my knowledge, crept into my thoughts without permission. I do not believe he'd invade yours for any reason but to keep you out of trouble."

"That's hardly comforting." She chewed on her bottom lip, remembering every interaction with Augustus in a new light. "Hmm... When he forbade me, he did expressly say that, in this, he would know immediately if I tried to defy him. At first I thought it a jest. But then..." She shrugged. "Well, he clearly came out on top of that argument."

Sin's chuckle was low and brief. Then his smile faded and he merely watched her as the wind outside groaned. The way he studied her, as if he were trying to memorize every line of her face. No, that wasn't quite it. He was reacquainting himself, learning the new lines she'd gained with maturity and comparing them to the youthful face she'd once had. Layla knew this because she did the same with him.

"Did it hurt," she asked, suddenly, "becoming Judgment?"

His brows furrowed a bit. "Remember the time you ate those sour apples?"

"Lord. And Mrs. Gibbons made me drink that syrup to purge my stomach." The mere memory had her innards quaking.

He flashed a quick, bright grin. "Yes. A bit like that, I suspect. Only worse."

"Well, then you have my sympathy," she muttered darkly.

He snickered. And she found herself grinning back. Their hands moved an inch closer.

"How does it feel to fly?" she asked, without thought.

Remarkably, he answered just as quickly. "Bloody brilliant. It's like nothing else. Thrilling and yet oddly peaceful."

"It's so strange to realize you have wings that you can call forth with a thought," she said.

He gave her a tilted smile. "You want to see them again, don't you?"

"Yes." She certainly wasn't going to deny that.

On a breath, Sin's flesh turned the color of quicksilver, so very clear and clean that he appeared to be made of cut crystal, yet not transparent in the least. As she stared at him, it seemed the air crackled and then the sheets rustled. Something touched her arm, and Layla glanced to see a silvery wing—an honest-to-god wing—slide beneath her.

It was warm and smooth, and the wing kept moving until it wrapped itself around her. Sin's other wing snapped out and then settled down on top of them, and so they were cocooned in the shelter of those enormous wings.

Layla stared in wonder. The wings were shaped like an angel's and yet they did not possess feathers. They were a sleek, glossy, pale silver color.

Once, when she'd vacationed in Brighton, a whale had been beached. The poor thing had lay dying and Layla, devastated, had walked close to it, placing her hand upon its flesh, knowing her touch would not help but wanting to give comfort.

Sin's wing felt a bit like that whale's flesh but so very warm, almost hot. Layla smoothed her fingers over the edge of the wing resting on her shoulder, and Sin's lids lowered, his gaze narrowing to silver slits.

"What does it feel like?" she whispered, stroking him.

His chest lifted on a breath, and the wings moved with him. "Odd. They are a power, not part of my body in the same way my limbs are. It feels... as if I were to touch your hair."

Carefully, he reached out and caught hold of one of her brown locks spilling over her pillow. His fingers slid along the smooth length, and a delicate shiver spread from her scalp down her back.

Layla ran her hand along the leading edge of his wing and saw Sin repress a shiver as well. Silently, Layla caressed his wing, and Sin played with the ends of her hair. Neither of them spoke. The warm weight of his wings seeped into her flesh, and she grew sleepy, her eyes fluttering closed.

She drifted off and dreamed of Sin, kissing her brow, telling her he'd never leave her side again. And in some foggy corner of her mind, she wondered if he dreamed of her too.

Sin could watch Layla endlessly and never tire. His life, it seemed, was destined to be surrounded by beautiful women. He'd seen beauty in so many forms—the women beautiful, each and every one of them. Thus he knew beauty could hold a golden heart, or hide a befouled soul. The surface of a person meant nothing in the larger scheme of things. He knew this as much as he knew his own face had been touched by a benevolent hand when he was created.

Thus it wasn't Layla's beauty that attracted him—though lord knew she was gorgeous; she was a Titian, sweetly erotic, with her pink bud of a mouth, wide eyes, and tumble of dark hair—it was her soul. He could see it clearly, shining through every part of her, a beacon to his battered and ravaged heart. He'd always seen it, even before Augustus had given him the power of Judgment.

To Sin, Layla was perfection. His best dream of heaven. Laying with her made him ache—not just his cock, but his heart, his tarnished soul. Every woman in his life had either left him or used him. But Layla had returned.

She slept now, utterly at peace by his side, caught in a beam of blue-white moonlight that slanted over the bed. The creamy oval of her face was smoother in sleep, her lips parted just a little, the dark sweep of her brows like wings over the fans of her thick lashes. He watched the soft swell of her bosom rise and fall with each breath. He shouldn't be looking at her breasts, but he couldn't seem to stop.

They were plump and high, the size of ripe apples. Perfect to fill up his palms. He fisted his hands, trying to ignore the way they suddenly became sensitized, as if demanding the right to find out if his estimation was correct.

Layla sighed in her sleep, her breasts rising with the action, and the stiff buds of her nipples poked against the thin linen of her nightgown. Hell's teeth, he both cursed and blessed his superior eyesight right now, for that scrap of fabric was no match against it. He could see the exact shape and stiffness of those detectible tips, their color dusky in the pale light. And his mouth watered. So much so that he had to press his tongue against the roof of it to ease the rampant want that bade him to lean forward, to draw one of them into his mouth and suck.

The thought crested in his mind then crashed down with a violent start. He wanted not only to suck her nipples. He wanted to roll on top of her, spread her smooth thighs, and fuck her. Sin hadn't wanted to do anything basely sexual for years. The only experiences he'd had were foul, tainted, and filled with loathing.

Sin gaped at Layla, his breath agitated and hard. He wanted. He wanted so badly his body tightened with need and heat. His fingers dug into the bedding, holding on.

As if she sensed it, Layla gave another sigh, more breathy. No; it was a moan, a fucking moan.

Sweat broke out over his skin as he began to shake, his fingers tearing into the down feather bed. He could not move, nor blink. His entire being was fixed on her.

Layla's lips parted, her breath growing light and quick, perspiration glistening over her smooth skin. Beneath her gown, her nipples were hard little points that he ached to pinch. And as if he'd done just that, she arched her back, her brow furrowing as another whimper of sound left her.

Christ.

He had to leave, leave now and get far away. Only her scent was filling the air, invading his space—all honey sweet and tinged with a lick of salty tang.

Sin's teeth ground together, his heart threatening to beat out of his chest.

Layla's nostrils flared on an indrawn breath, and a fine shudder went through her. Did she smell his desire? Did he have a scent?

Sin inhaled and nearly groaned. He could smell himself, deeper and musky, mixing with her sweeter scent, as though they'd already come together. At his side, Layla panted, her hips now moving. She seemed to glow in the moonlight.

"Layla," it was a plea out of his lips before he could stop himself.

Her eyes snapped open, the irises a thin band of brown before going wide as her focus sharpened on him. For a moment, they almost appeared to gleam gold.

He took a breath, ready to say something—what he did not know. Plead for her to let him have her? Beg off and get the hell out of there? He did not have a chance.

A low growl escaped her, and before he could blink, she was on him, her slim body slamming into his with the speed of a bullet. It knocked the breath from him. Sin's back met the mattress as she straddled him.

"Layla—"

Her mouth found his neck. He sucked in a breath, but then he felt them. Fangs. Razor sharp. They punctured his skin and sank in deep.

Shock and rage hit him all at once. She was drinking him down. Never. Never again would another take his blood. Not like that foul bitch had. Sin roared. His arms pushed between them. Another shout and he flung her back.

The room seemed to explode into chaos, dozens of fluttering birds suddenly swirling around him, their tiny wings slapping his skin. Their distressed cries culminated in a cacophony of sound that had him shouting again in irritation. And then there was silence. The birds gone.

Sitting upright in bed, his chest worked like a bellows, hot blood trickling down his neck. Then his mind cleared enough to truly think.

Layla. He'd thrown her clear off the bed. "Layla!" He leapt to his feet, his heart in his throat. Terror rang like bells in his ears.

She lay facedown, sprawled upon the floor, her bare body pale, her limbs akimbo against the dark wood. Shreds of her nightgown and feathers fluttered like snow to the floor.

"Fuck." His knees bashed into the boards. "Little bird." He was afraid to touch her. But he had to. With a shaking hand, he gently lifted a thick lock of her hair, just as the door to the room burst open and Augustus hurtled in.

Helplessly, Sin looked to Augustus. "She..."

"Is fine," the man finished, kneeling at her other side.

Layla appeared to be sleeping once again, her expression peaceful, almost happy, her breath even and deep.

"I flung her. She might have..." Sin swallowed, feeling sick.

"She tried to feed from you."

Sin followed Augustus's line of sight and touched the wet blood now cool upon his healing neck. "I didn't mean to throw her. I... She... Christ, what a cock up."

"Understandable. I suspect she'll have learned her lesson. Let me get her to bed." Augustus went to the bed and pulled the sheet from it. Draping it over Layla's nakedness, he then moved to lift her.

Sin grabbed his shoulder. "No. I'll do it." He did not give his mentor time to argue but pulled Layla into his arms and stood, cradling her against him. With a sigh, she snuggled closer, her body warm and pliant. Sin gave in to the urge to rest his cheek against her brow. Just for a moment. "Forgive me, little bird."

He was supposed to protect her. Do no harm. Especially not to Layla. But, god—she licked her lower lip, lapping up the crimson gloss of his blood. His stomach lurched, the rage he kept a tight grip upon threatening to break free.

Mab hadn't been a blood drinker out of necessity. But when she took him, she loved to bite and tear his flesh with her small fae fangs and lap at his blood. He'd hated every second of it. Hated the bitch clear to his soul. *May she rot in hell.*

To see Layla do the same, to want his blood . . . He felt sick and cold. And frightened. Not for himself. But for what he might do if she tried it again.

Even so, he held her close and tenderly as he made his way out of the room. But at the last moment he stopped and glanced at Augustus. "I'll put her to bed, then you and I shall be having a talk, old man."

The leader of Judgment blinked once, then nodded. "I suppose we shall."

Chapter Eight

Sin stalked into Augustus's room. The door was open, which made it clear he was welcome. "What the hell is she?" he demanded without preamble.

Augustus sat back in his reading chair, setting his book upon his crossed thigh. "Now, now, St. John; you know perfectly well that she is Layla."

"Do not be cheeky with me, old man." Sin closed the door behind him and crossed his arms over his chest. "What has happened to Layla?"

"She is maturing into her true nature." Augustus gestured to the empty chair.

Sin ignored it and paced instead. Gods, but he hated Augustus's vague answers. The damn angel never gave a solid one. No, he always made Sin work for it. "What, pray tell," he ground out through his teeth, "is she becoming?"

His mentor's shoulders fell a touch, and he glanced away. "I do not know." His usually dark eyes went Judgment silver. "That is the truth."

Sin's mouth snapped shut. He took another turn around the room before speaking again. "You must have some clue."

Augustus rested his chin on the tips of his fingers as he watched Sin's progress around the room. "A blood drinker, obviously."

Sin snorted. He had the puncture marks on his neck to prove that assessment.

"Something related to the Elementals but not quite," Augustus continued thoughtfully.

Sin turned on his heel, frowning down at the carpet. "I nearly caught her before. Ian was there. He too saw her change to birds." Sin glanced at Augustus, who regarded him with an overly bland expression. "Ian told me the only being he'd seen before with the power to break up into multiple, smaller beings was a demon named Lena."

The way Augustus's face went even smoother, his eyes devoid of all emotion, told Sin more than any expression would.

"You know this female," Sin said.

"Yes."

"Is this Lena pure Sanguis? Or is she something different?" Sanguis were the most infamous of blood drinkers. "Will Thorne is a Sanguis. I knew him well, and while he drank blood he never changed into insects or birds."

Augustus rubbed the crest of his forehead. "Do sit down, St. John. You're making me dizzy, prowling about."

Because he wanted answers, Sin did as bidden. "All right. I'm still. Continue."

Augustus pointedly stared at Sin's bobbing knee.

"Fucking..." Sin took a breath and willed his body to quiet down.

A smile twitched on Augustus's lips before fading. "What I say stays in this room."

Sin glanced towards the doors. "Not to put too fine a point on it, but are you certain Layla does not possess superior hearing?"

The angel snorted. "And yet you came in here demanding to know about her biological makeup without a qualm?"

"I must know if I am to fully protect her, but I am not trying to hide it from Layla. I'd share what I learn with her."

At this, Augustus's gaze went hard. "Not this. Not yet."

"It is her right to know."

"I know." Augustus leaned his head back on the chair. "But not until certain things are resolved. She might be in danger."

Sin's fingers dug into the arms of the chair with enough force that the wood threatened to splinter. "So you keep saying. Enlighten me as to why, or I walk and take her with me."

He'd protect her with his life, regardless of whether Augustus helped him, but he was bloody tired of dancing around the angel's hints.

Augustus's mouth pinched. "As to your last question, she does indeed have superior hearing. When she was a girl, I'd have to watch everything I said."

"I remember that as well," Sin whispered, the memory hitting him like the dawn. "She'd always seem to know everything that had occurred in my house, even though she wasn't there. It irritated the hell out of me." Sin laughed shortly. "I couldn't understand how she knew."

Augustus allowed himself a smile but it was strained. "I can imagine. However, I doubt Layla realized that her hearing was anything exceptional. A child assumes their senses are the same as everyone else's."

Sin glanced at the door again. "So then, she can hear us now?" Despite his former claim of not hiding anything from Layla, he felt a pang of guilt and shame in openly discussing her as she listened on.

"No," Augustus said. "First, she is sleeping soundly. I can hear that quite well." He paused, giving Sin another pointed look as a wry smile crossed his lips. "Second, I'm able to mute sound when I please. Both abilities are gifts all Judgment possess if so inclined to use them."

Sin cursed and sighed. He'd forgotten that. Having been Judgment for only a little over a year, he had much to learn and powers to develop.

There were times when different senses seemed to burst to life—sudden occurrences that had him reeling. Such as the time he'd heard a train rushing into a station, only to realize that it was twenty miles away. Or when he'd found himself retching in an alleyway when all of London's lovely stenches came to potent life in a tidal wave of utter rot.

For all intents, Sin was a fledgling Judgment. He had the added protection of his Elemental powers, but he was hardly the force Augustus was.

It irked but he had to address the obvious. "Perhaps it is better that you watch over Layla. I . . . I would not put her into jeopardy due to my inexperience."

At this, Augustus full-out smiled. "Ah, my boy, but this is the quality that makes you a perfect guardian for Layla. You would die before you let her come to harm."

"I just flung her across a room," Sin said wryly.

Augustus waved this away. "Comparable to a light shove for an immortal."

Sin had the urge to give *him* a light shove. But he held back. "You too would die to protect her," Sin pointed out instead.

"But I do not watch her every move as you do." Augustus's expression warmed. "I do not love her the same way you do."

Sin flinched, a scowl pulling at his face. "Do not put

some romantic spin on this. You know as well as I that I've vowed to remain chaste." A vow he had happily accepted. His experience with bed sport had been ugly, forced, and, until tonight, had left him ill at the mere thought of doing those things again. He'd been looking forward to a life of chastity.

Which made the sudden base and intense lust he'd just experienced over Layla even more confusing. How could he crave her? Want to touch her when he could scarcely accept touch himself?

Augustus watched him, his eyes kind and a little sad. "Your vow was to remain chaste until there was love in your heart. Should you find the one you want above all others, you are free to take her."

Sin resisted the urge to tug at his collar. "As interesting as this all is, you have neatly dodged the one question I came to see answered. What is Layla? Why does she seem to possess the same abilities of this Sanguis Lena?"

"Well, I did try," Augustus murmured with some humor before growing solemn. "Have I your word that you will not reveal to Layla who she is until the time is right?"

Sin's back teeth met but he wanted the truth. If he had to hide things from Layla to protect her, he would do it and have no regrets. "By my soul."

Augustus gave a nod at Sin's use of Judgment's most ardent vow. "Lena is Layla's mother."

Sin sat up, his spine growing stiff. "The woman who kidnapped Jack Talent and is a current enemy of Ian Ranulf?"

"Yes," Augustus said slowly.

"Layla, my Layla, is a spawn of evil too?" Sin said it without thought, only the horrible feeling that he did not want her to know.

But Augustus snapped forward, his eyes flaring bright silver. "Lena is not evil." He leaned back, some of the starch ebbing out of him. "She is . . . complicated."

She sounded like a right bitch, but Sin kept this to himself. He glared down at his bare feet upon the fine rug. "I came across Layla gorging on a human, Augustus."

A wave of despair flooded him as he let himself fully realize what he'd discovered this night.

"Tell me what you saw," his mentor said calmly.

"A murdered human, the body destroyed. Layla leaning over it, drinking its cold blood." He shuddered then faced Augustus. "I have sent demons to final Judgment for less."

"You witnessed her drinking this cold blood?"

Sin closed his eyes, replaying the scene in his head. "Did I see her throat work on a swallow? No. I saw a cloaked figure, face deep in gore."

"Then you do not know for certain that she drank the blood or even killed the human. If Layla is attracted to the scent of blood, she might well have been drawn to the scene. Given her fascination, she might have also tried to taste the blood."

Sin groaned, leaning his head back on the chair. "You realize how you sound? You are making excuses for her."

"I am laying out perfectly logical scenarios. Or would you rather condemn Layla before you have all the facts?"

"Do not try it, old man. I'll not fall for that bait. I need facts, not your scenarios." Sin lifted his head. "You're trying to protect Layla against herself, not an outside source."

Augustus's jaw clenched for a second before releasing. "In part. However, it is not who her mother is that concerns me, but what she is."

"Explain."

Augustus sighed, appearing old just then. "Lena is not sanguis. She is Damnation."

A cold wind seemed to flow through Sin. "Tell me you jest."

"Never about this." Augustus lifted his hand as if to rub his forehead but let it drop at the last moment.

"You said you saw Layla being hunted by Damnation. Do you mean her mother?"

"No," Augustus said sharply before taking a deep breath. "Lena would never harm her child."

"So sure, are you?" Sin snorted. "Forgive me if I remain dubious."

Augustus gave him a quelling look. "What you do not understand," he said as though Sin had never spoken, "is that when a child of Damnation reaches maturity, all of her brethren know instinctively. They would seek the newest member out, wanting her to join them."

"And tonight, we saw proof of Layla reaching maturity," Sin said as his innards rolled sickly.

"Yes." Augustus frowned. "Layla's future has always been a bit murky to me. I do not know why. Perhaps it is because she is Lena's child, and..." He waved a hand, his cheeks flushing, "Lena's future has never been clear to me either. I must discover who Layla's father is."

Augustus closed his eyes, a long, slow blink. Despair lingered in his gaze when he finally looked at Sin. "He may well be the Damnation I see hunting Layla down in my visions. Or not. I fear...Lena was adamant that Layla's father not find her. Which is why I shall have to find Lena. We need answers." With that, he stood and leaned an arm against the mantle, staring down into the flames.

Sin peered at the man before him. He'd never once blushed in their entire relationship. Why now? Sin fancied Augustus had feelings for Lena, but he certainly wasn't going to point that out now. "There is more you fear in regards to Layla, isn't there?"

Augustus's expression went blank. "A child born of Damnation and another species would be seen as an abomination. One that needed to be destroyed."

Sin uttered a ripe curse. "Over my dead body."

"It just might come to that," Augustus said baldly.

Sin gave a mirthless laugh. "Your faith in my skills is heartening, truly."

"You have not gone up against Damnation. They are nearly impossible to kill. However..." Augustus put his hand up to forestall Sin's protests. "The issue here is that they are all but extinct. A millennium ago, I destroyed Cain, the original Damnation. But should one of his brethren exist and be out in this world, he would try to make contact with Layla."

"Christ."

"What concerns me most isn't that a Damnation contacted Layla..."

"No? It concerns the hell out of me."

A smile pulled at Augustus's lips, but his expression remained stoic. "No. It is the possibility of a male Damnation finding her. Understand, he would likely be one of the last living of his kind." Augustus blanched. "He would be desperate to create more Damnation."

"And just how would he do that?" Sin asked through clenched teeth, for an ugly idea was taking root in his mind.

Augustus appeared just as pained. "Damnation were either created by Cain or they were bred by later generations. Because Cain is no longer here, he cannot create more Damnation. Thus any remaining Damnation would need one of his own to breed pure-blooded and strong Damnation demons. He would need to mate with Layla."

Sin's wings snapped outward. "The bloody hell he will." Sparks shot off the tips of his wings, little fissures of electricity running amok over his body.

"Which is why I want Layla mated soon. If she were to get with child from another, Damnation would consider her womb tainted." A mirthless smile spread over Augustus's lips. "They are rather odd in that way."

Sin hunched forward, pressing the heels of his hands into his eyes. "This is why you wanted me to offer for her, wasn't it?" Gods, he couldn't do it. Be no more than a stud service. Again.

Even for Layla? No. She ought to have better. She lives in the light. I am darkness.

Augustus was watching him. He could feel that cool, logical gaze like a spike between his shoulder blades. "St. John, if you cannot set yourself free of this self-hate, then you must let Layla go."

Sin's heart squeezed tight. It hurt. Too much. "I know," he whispered thickly.

Augustus nodded once, sorrow lining his features. "My time here grows to a close. You must rely on your instincts. Even if they defy the logical choice or my instructions." Black eyes bore into him. "Do you understand? In every situation. Do not ignore your heart. It is the very best part of you."

Sin did not agree, but his mentor had saved him in more ways than one. And he would not let him down. "I promise, I shall do my best."

The sky was turning pale gray when Augustus woke her. Layla rubbed her eyes and sat up, only to quickly grab her sheet when she felt it slide over her naked skin. Shocked, she gazed around. Hadn't she fallen asleep in Sin's bed? Why was she nude? Her heart began to pound.

Augustus's expression was kind as he handed her a thick cotton nightgown. He promptly turned his back so she could slide it on. "What do you remember?" he asked her.

Layla pulled the gown down her legs then covered up

once more. She was ice cold and shaking. "Falling asleep." Her cheeks heated. "I... ah... I snuck into Sin's room. It was windy, and I was lonely. We didn't—"

"Layla," Augustus cut in, turning then. A smile crinkled his eyes. "You are a woman grown. It is not my place to question what you do with men."

"Only try to marry me off to one, then?" She was only half teasing.

His sidelong glance told her he knew that very well. "You turned, Layla." When she ducked her head, he continued in a soft voice: "How long has this been going on?"

She cleared her throat. "A little under a year. I cannot be sure, though." With a deep breath, she looked up at him. "I don't remember what I do. I wake up nude, sometimes there is blood..." A choked sob left her. "I taste blood on my tongue, and it is delicious."

Her guardian sat and drew her into his embrace. Layla rested her head on his shoulder and tried not to cry. Theirs had always been a close relationship, but Augustus had been formal with her, never one to hug her tight as he did now. But she relished it.

Her fingers curled into his lapels. "I'm frightened."

"I know," he said.

"Why do I end up nude? Do you suppose..." She could not finish. The thought was too horrible.

He gave her shoulder a squeeze. "No, child," he said as if he'd read her thoughts, which, given what Sin had told her, he just might have. "It is because, when you are cornered, you shift into a flock of birds."

She choked out a horrified laugh and drew away. "You're serious? Birds?"

His expression was solemn. "Starlings, actually." A small smile pulled at his mouth. "Quite ironic, given your name, no?"

She had to laugh again. "Quite." She wiped her bleary eyes. "I'm not human. Why didn't you tell me?"

"I wanted to keep you from the ugliness of our life for as long as possible. Most immortals don't discover their 'otherness' until they reach maturity and develop their powers."

"And mine? Changing to birds? What of the blood?" Layla gripped him again. "What have I been doing?"

"I do not know." He peered at her. "I believe you like to drink it."

She gagged. "God. Am I a killer, then?"

"Some blood drinkers are. And some are not. I do not believe you to be a killer, my dear."

"But you do know what I am." She eased farther away from him. "Augustus, you told me my parents died in a coach accident. That wasn't true, was it?"

"No." He frowned down at his hands, neatly folded upon his lap. "Your mother's name is Lena."

"She is alive?" Excitement warred with hurt. If she was alive, why had she never claimed Layla? Why had she left her? And could Layla find her?

Augustus's dark gaze bore into her, as if he could see her roiling emotions, as if he too felt them. "No one knows where she is. The last time I saw her was when she brought you to me. She begged me for help." Tentatively, he reached out and cupped Layla's cold hand. "She was in some sort of trouble, not that she would tell me what. But she was headed for Nowhere."

"Nowhere?"

"Another plane of existence which humans often think of as hell."

She jolted. "How horrible."

"Agreed." He gave her hand a squeeze, then let go. "But Lena has the ability to come and go from that dark place. Many of the more powerful supernaturals do."

"Was she... Is she evil, then?"

"Not evil. But those of us with great powers always walk the line between good and evil, for it is quite easy to fall into greed." He held her gaze. "Remember that. Fate is nothing more than the repercussions of the choices we make."

Layla sighed. "So my mother is gone. And my father? What of him?"

"I do not know who he is. Lena wouldn't tell me."

Frustration and sadness seemed to swirl around him. And she found herself reaching out to comfort him. Augustus gave her a weak attempt at a smile. "I'm leaving now to search for her. And answers. When I am gone, watch over St. John."

"I thought he was here to watch over me."

"You're here for each other, dear girl. Do not forget that."

Chapter Nine

Layla was still sitting in bed, the morning light peeking through the curtains, when Sin knocked on her door. So great was her anticipation in seeing him, she thought nothing of leaping out of bed and running to the door to let him in.

He opened his mouth to speak but seemed to take notice of her attire and the words died in his mouth. His serious green eyes tracked down her length, not a slow or very rushed tour. No, simply thorough and intense.

Caught in the snare of his gaze, she couldn't find it in her to move, but stood stock still, one hand on the door, the other limp at her side. She was not wearing anything provocative, simply a fine linen nightgown that covered her from neck to toes. But she was bare beneath it, and having his gaze on her made her suddenly feel every place the fabric touched her skin—from its caress of her backside, the way it skimmed her knees, to the soft weight of it over her breasts.

Her nipples peaked, growing tight and hot. And his breath seemed to hitch in response.

His eyes met hers, and for a moment his were wide open,

hiding nothing. Heat, want, longing, lust, fear. Then he blinked, and it was gone. All he left for her to see was cool indifference.

"I have brought you these."

Only then did she notice he held a pile of dark clothing. He thrust it forward, forcing her to gather the pieces before they dropped to the floor.

"What are these for?" She glanced down at her gift. It appeared to be two garments made of black linen.

"Practice." Sin kept his attention on the clothing. "You need to know how to defend yourself should someone attack when I am not near."

Layla's hands pressed into the cool fabric. "Forgive me, dear friend, but did I not nearly tear your head off last night?" She hated that knowledge and the vague, blood-tinged memories that spoke of violence and rage. But they could not nullify simple facts—she was a killer.

Sin gave her a measured look. "Oh, you are quite capable when you are turned and nearly mindless."

Layla winced.

"However," he went on, "the likelihood of you being attacked in that state is far less than when you are in your current state." His expression told her exactly what he thought of her current state: she was helpless.

Unfortunately, he wasn't wrong. Layla hadn't a clue how to defend herself should the worst occur. Well, aside from giving a good scream and aiming a knee at a man's cods. Something told her neither of those things would be very effective in Sin's world.

"All right," she said, holding the clothes to her chest, where her heart kicked up in a nervous rhythm.

Sin peered at her for a moment. "It will be all right, little bird. You are more than what you seem. We simply must teach you to draw your powers out."

His sudden, quiet kindness touched her heart and she found herself leaning towards him. But his brusque manner returned. "Get changed and meet me in my room in a quarter hour."

With that, he turned and strode down the hall.

Sighing, Layla closed her door and inspected the garments. The first was a set of loosely tailored pants with a tie to keep them in place. They were quite like her knickers, only longer; the thought had her flushing. The top was a long-sleeved, military-style tunic—though the linen was fine and light.

"Good lord," she muttered as she lifted the last offering. Sin, the devil, had even given her short stays. With wide shoulder straps, lightly padded cups, and ending just beneath the bosom, the stays were merely to hold her breasts in place, giving her the freedom to move and take deep breaths.

Layla rather loved them and instantly wanted more. But the thought that Sin had picked the stays out, that he had put his hands on them, selected the proper size, felt too intimate, as if he were still in the room with her.

He remained foremost in her thoughts when she slipped the stays over her bare breasts—for the outfit left no room for a chemise. Her fingers trembled as she pulled the ties close and secured it with a bow.

Standing in front of the mirror, dressed only in the flowing pants and the plain, functional stays, Layla took stock. The fighting outfit was mannish, the stays holding her breasts flat and secure. And yet she felt more erotically charged than when she wore one of her pretty corsets and lacy knickers. For all its functionality, the outfit was quite naughty. One rip of her tunic, a good tug of her laces, and she'd be utterly bare.

And she was going to spar with Sin, who could pull apart

this fabric as easily as a normal man could tear fine tissue paper.

In the mirror, her cheeks went red. But then Layla laughed. Whatever wicked thoughts Layla entertained, her old friend certainly wouldn't act upon them. Yes, he sometimes looked at her as a man does a woman, but he just as clearly did not want to. Sin was not remotely interested in dallying with her. No, all *he* wanted to do at the moment was teach her how to punch. Wonderful.

Layla found Sin waiting by the far mirrored wall, where the area was devoid of all furniture. When she had been here before, the floors had been bare. Now thick cotton mats covered the space.

Sin stood in the center of the mats, his lean body at ease, his hands set low on his hips as he watched her join him. Like her, he wore a set of black linen trousers and matching tunic. His feet were bare so Layla toed off her slippers before stepping onto the mat.

Sin looked her over once more, then frowned.

"What is it?" she asked, glancing down at her body. "Have I got something wrong?"

Slowly he padded over to her, moving to her side. "Your hair."

"My hair?" She blinked back at him, confused. She'd braided it nice and neat.

Sin didn't answer. Instead, he slipped behind her. His warmth radiated along her back, not touching, but so very close that his proximity held all her awareness. She was about to turn her head to question him when he gently picked up the long rope of her plaited hair and began to feed it down her collar. Her hair tickled the skin of her back as it went, and she shivered lightly.

Sin's soft breath brushed over the edge of her ear, his voice low and intimate. "Do not give anyone such an easy target to grab hold of. Either wear your hair up or tuck it in like this."

Blood rushing in her ears, Layla only nodded. His hand lay heavy and warm upon her shoulder. She had the mad urge to simply lean back against his chest, perhaps rest her head upon his shoulder and ask him to put his lips to the exposed length of her neck where she was most sensitive.

She did none of those things and he stepped away, leaving her cold and alone. He put a good five feet of space between them before he faced her once more.

"Now then," Sin began. "What you must understand is that this will not be conducted as would an ordinary sparring match."

"How fortunate that I do not know what an ordinary sparring match entails," Layla murmured, unable to help herself.

Sin's dark brow quirked, but he pressed his lips together hard and fast for a moment before going on, his tone now dry. "Whereas one would normally execute certain moves, feints, and parries, we are going to act on instinct. Do whatever feels correct."

"So, then, if my instincts are to windmill my arms about in a frantic manner, that is all right?" Layla grinned wide.

Sin stared.

"Fine," she grumped. "Throw a wet blanket on my fun."

"This is not fun, Layla." Sin was in full professor mode now, all dour and pompous. "You are here to learn."

"Learning ought to be fun," Layla groused. When she was met with yet another unyielding stare, she rolled her shoulders to loosen up. Blasted Sin. She was nervous, and he did nothing to help alleviate that.

Layla moved her weight to the balls of her feet, having

absolutely no clue what she was doing. "All right, then. I'm ready."

He looked rather dubious as he strolled forward, his bare feet light and nimble on the mat. It gave the illusion that he barely touched the ground. In truth, the man moved with such lithe grace, he seemed more sleek lone wolf than six feet of beautiful man.

Ordinarily, Layla would let herself enjoy the spectacle of Sin prowling about, wearing nothing more than loose linen shirt and trousers. Now, however, she felt stalked, those green eyes of his holding a gleam of anticipation.

"Off the mat is out of bounds and signifies a loss," he told her casually.

"So," she drew out, her heart pounding loudly in her chest, "what do I do?"

His mouth quirked. "Let's start by staying on your feet."

"Staying on my f—" She landed on her back with an "*ooof!*"—her breath fleeing her lungs. Stunned, she blinked up at the ceiling until Sin's face came into view. He bent over her, a lock of his hair dangling down from his forehead. "Too slow."

Layla found her voice. "St. John! How could you?" She hadn't even seen him move, damn his eyes.

His brow furrowed. "What did you think we were doing here? Having tea?"

Bastard. Layla stood, dusting off her bruised rump. "Fine friend you are."

He cocked his head. "Again. Come at me."

So she did, a little more aggressive now. And he clipped her chin with an almost lazy cuff of his open hand and then swept her feet again.

Again she plopped onto the mat. "You bloody, despicable..."

His face hovered. "Again, Layla."

"That hurt!" Horrifying, but she wanted to cry. She'd never been hit before. That Sin did so hurt more than the actual physical pain.

His expression did not alter from its normal state. "Yes, I know. It will hurt worse when someone attacks you. You must learn how to ignore the shock of being hit."

Refusing to move—for, good gravy, her body throbbed in protest—she glared up at him. "You propose we practice by you breaking my back?"

The man managed to convey an eye roll with a simple lifting of his brows. "You're an immortal. A couple of hard hits will not gravely injure your person. Nor will the discomfort last very long."

He was correct in that. Already the pain in her jaw and ribs were gone. Gritting her teeth, she got to her feet, pausing to straighten her clothes and take a calming breath.

Sin sneered. "Christ, Layla, stop dithering like an old ninny. You are clearly quite powerful when you want to be. It took all I had to chase you down that first night. Now move your arse and hit me."

She swung before all the words left his mouth. And caught air. Snarling, she advanced on him, swinging and kicking in pure rage. And the smarmy cur dipped and spun, easily evading her.

Again he batted her on the side of her head. Another blow to her middle. One swift kick on her arse. None of them very hard. No, he was toying with her.

She saw red. Again she lashed out. Again she missed. And he began to laugh, a pleased chuckle.

His heels reached the edge of the mat. Layla grinned with evil glee and kicked. He leapt high and began to descend, his fist out and aiming for her. Instinct had Layla dropping, rolling her body beneath his and kicking up into him.

Her heel caught him directly on the cods. Sin grunted, his body falling awkwardly and with a great thud on the mat. Groaning, he pulled his knees up.

Unrepentant, Layla jumped up and stomped down, intent on hitting his chest. But he rolled, evading. Even down and in pain the dratted man wouldn't let her get in a good shot. The need to crush him was a sharp, throbbing want in her blood. He no longer looked like Sin, but like prey.

His face was red, a sheen of sweet covering him as he chuckled and hopped to his feet—less graceful than before, but still competent. Still faster. "Good, never stop an attack solely because you hit your target. Always—*oof!*"

Her fist found his chin. Layla tossed a smile his way, her blood hot and racing. "You were saying?"

Sin glared. "All right. You made your point—" He dove away from her elbow. "Christ. I get it. Now, let's take a break and—"

Layla had no intention of stopping. He wanted her anger. Now he had it.

She jumped straight at him and somehow managed to wrap herself around him. His sharp inhale spoke of surprise. Layla bared her fangs with a deep-seated need to sink them in his strong, delicious-smelling neck.

Sin grunted then cupped her bottom. With infuriating ease, he flipped her and pinned her to the ground by her wrists, his ankles hooking over her kicking legs. "Would you stop," he huffed, "trying to kill me?"

Layla glared up into his amused face. "It is not funny."

The corners of his eyes crinkled a bit more. "It is a little."

With a growl, she jerked against his wrists and thrashed her hips to get loose. His hold was not painful but as effective as iron cuffs.

"Layla," he warned, his humor still high but now touched

with a note of strain, "you do not want to continue doing that."

"Oh, no?" She thrashed again, her knee smashing into his thigh. It gave her great satisfaction to hear him grunt. The bastard was too strong to truly hurt, but at the very least, he could feel her ire.

Silver flashed in Sin's eyes, like sunlight rippling over a still lake, before they went bright, jade green. It caught her attention enough to give her pause. Then he simply dropped onto her, his chest against hers, his hips wedged between her parted thighs.

And then she understood. He was hard as iron and grinding that stiff pike *there.* Everything within her stilled—her body, her heart, her breath. This was Sin. Hard for her.

They were both lightly panting now. His nose was a mere inch from hers, and he stared back, unrepentant, if not a wee bit put out. "I see I've made my point," he murmured dryly, not taking his eyes from hers.

She could feel him there, pulsing like a heartbeat. And it felt utterly…wonderful. Her breasts crushed against his chest as she drew in a deep breath. "Do you think," she said, letting that shaking breath out, "this will get me to concede defeat?"

His lush mouth tilted wryly, even as he seemed to settle more comfortably into place. "No…" His hips rocked an infinitesimal degree. It had the effect of a full-out thrust. He watched her shiver, and his lids lowered a touch. "I must say, however," he went on, "I do appreciate this position far more."

She might have melted into a hot puddle of want right there, were it not for that damned wry amusement still lurking in his eyes. He was laughing at her, even as he slowly drove her mad with his hard, lean body. Layla stiffened, forcing herself to ignore everything but his smug face.

"Oh, do get off."

Sin paused, his brows raising. "But we're so comfortable." As if he could not help himself, he moved again, just that small exploratory rock of his hips.

And Layla growled again, a low warning rumble deep in her breast. "Now, Saint. I do not like this."

Instantly she was free. So fast and completely that her lungs expanded with a gasp. Sin stood a foot away, his fisted hands in his pockets, that hateful blank expression back upon his handsome face. "My apologies, Layla. It shall not happen again."

Layla got to her feet, her ribs protesting a twinge. But her heart hurt more. He appeared so wounded, as if her words had sliced into his gut. "Sin..."

He turned and straightened his shoulders. "Shall we continue or are you done for the day?" He looked at her, patient and waiting for her answer, as if nothing had occurred.

Layla took a breath, wanting to scream, wanting to demand he give her his secrets. "Let us continue."

She'd be damned if he forced her to quit. And so they sparred once more, hard, fast, but never playful, never with joy. Sin was once again that solemn stranger, keeping her out.

Chapter Ten

The rules of the supernatural world were not the same as those of human society. When one could easily level a townhouse with a pulse of power, safeguards must be put in place. Therefore, one must always stand down. If one found oneself becoming annoyed, it was imperative to walk away.

On the other hand, when one couldn't be killed short of a beheading, one tended to be more…lax about rules of comportment. Supernaturals usually skipped stuffy formalities such as seeking an introduction and, instead, acted on instinct.

All of which meant that Sin was in a hell disguised as a ball. For he could not step in between the numerous males who flocked around Layla, nor could he throw out the tosser who hovered too close to her elbow. If Layla did not want their attention, all she had to do was say so. Instead she fairly beamed with happiness.

Well good. Wonderful. Bloody great.

He turned away from the spectacle. And ran straight into a woman. Stepping back before he made full contact, Sin was already muttering his pardon when he caught sight of the female. Red, curling hair, and dark brown eyes tilted at the corners. His stomach lurched, a cold sweat breaking out on his back. The woman looked like *her,* the evil, foul witch who'd ruled him for so long. Instinct had him wanting to shrink back or lash out.

It was not *her*; it was just an ordinary female. He was safe. *She* was gone. Dead. He'd annihilated her with his own power, seen her body break apart, and had sent her spirit to Judgment.

Apparently oblivious of Sin's unease, the female sauntered closer, her green gown all but painted on her curves. Sweet hell, she even wore green. Bile rose in Sin's throat. He might well retch before he could escape.

"I've been watching you," the woman said with a lyrical voice. She had the scent of fae. Not exactly like the evil bitch's, but one of her kind. "I know you."

He was certain she did. Most London court fae knew that Sin had been the bitch's blood slave. Humiliation pressed in, but Sin kept his expression neutral by sheer force. "You do not, in fact, know me, madam. You might recognize my face, but only my friends know me."

Her smile was coy. "Very well. I know of you. Is that better? I'd like to know you, however." She moved to touch him.

Sin struck out, grabbing hold of her hand and lowering it. A steady but firm action that could not be avoided. Like hell would he let a fae female lay her hands on him again.

The woman pouted. "I only wanted a dance. Perhaps take a tour of one of the alcoves." Her pink, overlong tongue flicked out to lick her upper lip. "I've heard you're quite the lover."

Rage fell in a red haze over his vision.

"I'm afraid," Layla said, suddenly at his side, "my friend here is otherwise occupied."

Her fingers just touched the edge of his elbow. His first instinct was to throw it off, but this was Layla. So he let her guide him away from the foul fae woman, who huffed in irritation as they left her behind.

Neither of them spoke as they walked towards the terrace. But Layla made a point to drop her hand from his arm. He felt the loss like a cold spot upon his skin. Even so, as soon as he was out of doors, Sin took a deep breath, attempting to purge the sick feeling from his flesh.

She was dead. Annihilated.

"Sin?" Layla's voice brought him back. Her eyes, now wide with worry, peered up at him. "Tell me what happened."

Sin could only stare back at her, a certain horror coiling through his insides at the mere idea of explaining any part of his life concerning the fae bitch.

But Layla was Layla and she would never be dissuaded by silence. "She claimed to know you, and it was clear you were repulsed by the notion." Layla gave him a sad little smile. "Do not worry, I doubt anyone besides me noticed. I know your tells well. They do not."

Another breath and Sin glanced into the inky night. "I did not know the woman."

"She reminded you of someone?" When his gaze snapped to hers, she grimaced. "The way you're looking at me now, as though I'd strung your union suit up a flag pole. Can we not speak honestly anymore?"

He cleared his throat. "I do not wear union suits."

Her smile was sly. "Yet another bit of information I shall store away for later."

Hell. He actually flushed. From a little flirting. But it felt... good. Pure and sweet. So far from the tainted ugliness he'd experienced in the hands of his first sexual experiences that Sin wanted to soak in it, like a cool bath on a hot, sticky day.

And he found himself drawing closer to Layla, setting his hand upon the balustrade where hers rested. "I fear you have me at a disadvantage. You now know what I do *not* wear beneath my trousers, and yet I haven't the same information in regards to you."

Her smile grew, her gaze going dark. "Well, for one, I do not wear union suits."

A laugh huffed out of him, soft but surprising. He hadn't laughed in a long time. His hand moved closer to hers. "No?" he murmured. "How disappointing."

Though he could picture it, all too clearly, Layla's rounded curves filling out a pair of men's long underwear. In his mind, he turned her to her stomach and slowly unbuttoned the little panel that covered her pert bottom. When exposed, he'd run his hand over that smooth, plump flesh, slip between her rounded cheeks.

He took a ragged breath, and she watched him. Her hand slid nearer. The touch of her pinky against his was a match strike along his cock. The ground beneath the house rumbled a bit, the air turning balmy around them.

She didn't appear to notice, but gazed up at him with parted lips. Another tiny stroke of her finger to his. "Are you really disappointed that I don't wear union suits?" she whispered.

The ground rumbled again. Enough to send a tremor up his legs. Sin tried to tamp down his power even as he kept his gaze on Layla. "No," he whispered back. "In truth, I'd prefer to picture you in noth—"

"There you are," a male voice interrupted. Sin's back teeth met with a click.

St. Claire strolled across the terrace, his focus on Layla. "Miss Starling, I do believe you promised me a waltz."

The beginning notes of the waltz drifted out from the open ballroom doors.

Layla glanced between Sin and the rat bastard St. Claire. "Oh yes, I did."

St. Claire stopped beside her, his hand going to her elbow. Sin wanted to tear his fingers off one by one. St. Claire's expression was doting, this side of possessive. "Shall we?" He glanced at Sin. "I'll take it from here, Evernight."

Take it from here. As if Layla were a parcel to be fobbed off. Frustrated rage punched through Sin's chest. But Layla had agreed to dance with the bastard. And she was letting him lead her away. From him.

Her wide, brown eyes glanced back, an expression in them that replaced his rage with guilt. Condemnation, disappointment, and a dare. *Do something if you do not like this*, she seemed to say with that one look.

Nothing had been promised between them. They were merely childhood friends reunited once more. And yet, Layla, with one quiet look, had slashed through that falsehood and exposed the truth: she was his for the taking. If only he dared.

In the golden light of the ballroom, St. Claire took Layla into his arms. He held her close enough to stake a claim, close enough that Layla had to arch her back into his embrace, the tips of her pert breasts nearly grazing his chest.

Sin's hands curled into fists as the air around him grew sweltering hot. Condensation beaded on the French door glass.

Layla smiled up at something St. Claire said. Another twirl and St. Claire was facing Sin's direction. The bastard glanced his way, and a flash of smug humor lit his eyes. His hand slipped down Layla's waist just a fraction. Enough that another surge of rage coursed through Sin's body.

And still he did not move. Sin tore his gaze away and

looked out over the dark garden. The waltz played on, mocking him. The urge to turn back and watch Layla dance with St. Claire had his neck locking up. Laughter drifted through the air. It wasn't hers but it might as well have been.

Here he was again, on the outside while others within enjoyed their lives.

Life is what you make of it, a voice whispered in his head. *You are the one choosing to be out here.*

Out here he could breathe. In there, people knew what he'd been: a slave, a plaything for a bored fiend. He'd been a whore. Betrayer of family. Who was he to take away Layla's opportunities to find someone respectable?

Only she hadn't looked at St. Claire the way she'd looked at Sin. In his mind's eye, he saw her again, pleading, daring.

Something within him snapped. He'd been fortune's fool for long enough.

Honestly, attempting to make a man jealous was bloody tiring work. Layla reflected on this as she danced with St. Claire, tittering like some inane bit of fluff over every word he uttered. The man ought to be rolling his eyes, but he appeared to be quite pleased with himself.

As for the man she wanted to notice? He was still on the terrace, presumably without care that she was dancing with another man.

Well just bloody perfect.

"I would love to hear you sing, Miss Starling," St. Claire said, drawing her attention back to him.

He really was a handsome devil, with his golden hair and well-shaped features. Not in the breathless way of Sin's male beauty, but no less attractive. She held back a sigh. Not appealing to her, however.

"I have retired," she said, giving him her standard polite smile.

His brow drew in a frown. "Retire? You are so very young. At the top of your profession."

Insensitive boor. Did he not realize that she would only retire with good cause? The polite thing would be to drop the subject or not to have brought it up at all.

Her smile grew tight. "There are those who believe it is best to leave the stage while on top." They made a turn, and she went on. "Do you know, Mr. St. Claire, it was always my great regret never to have attended a performance by Miss Jenny Lind."

"The Swedish Nightingale," St. Claire murmured, his eyes flashing with humor. "Yes, she was wonderful but very controlled in her expression. It is said that you, Songbird, are much more passionate in your delivery."

So much for deflecting the conversation. Layla made a noise that one could either interpret as, *this is so* or *please do shut up*. Hopefully he'd do the latter. Her gaze drifted over the crowded ballroom and came to an abrupt halt as she spied Sin striding into the room.

Everything else fell away. She was a lost cause where Sin was concerned, for there was no one else who inspired her regard the way he did. Good Lord but he was magnificent, tall and strong, his angular features fierce, his jade-colored eyes shining bright beneath the black slashes of his brows. Inky strands of hair fell over his forehead, making her believe he must have run his fingers through them in agitation.

When he was a boy, he'd been not shy but quiet, keeping to himself. He was still self-contained but now power radiated from him with such force it affected the very air around him. She fancied he would laugh if she pointed out the way he commanded a room. He merely had to enter it and people turned to watch him, stepping out of his path when he walked past.

They did so now, not that he appeared to notice. His gaze was still focused directly on her. And she flushed hot, her skin prickling. She wanted him to catch her, haul her close, and…

He cut in front of St. Claire, knocking them apart, and wrapped his warm hand around her wrist. A gentle tug and she was stumbling after him as he headed off the dance floor.

Behind them St. Claire called out, protesting.

"Sod off," Sin said over his shoulder, not bothering to look at St. Claire or even at her.

Layla's heart pounded as they entered the hall. Sin guided her to the front door, leaving the house as a footman opened the door for them.

"Sin," she said as they rushed down the stairs, "I'll trip on my skirts if you do not slow down."

He stopped entirely. Still holding her wrist, he turned to face her, and they ended up nearly toe to toe. "Right then," he snapped. "Did you want to dance with that ponce?"

Layla didn't know what a ponce was, but she gathered it wasn't pleasant. "No," she said truthfully.

Sin's nostrils flared on an indrawn breath. "Then why did you?"

"Because he asked and you would not protest."

He gave her wrist a squeeze before letting it go. "It is not my place to protest."

"Oh, but it is yours to drag me off the dance floor like some…some…ruddy barbarian?"

He made a noise of exasperation. "You gave me that look." He pointed an accusatory finger. "That bloody 'why don't you do something, Sin?' look."

She had, hadn't she? Layla bit back a smile, trying valiantly to keep a straight face. But he noticed, and his green eyes narrowed. "Right there, I see that, Layla. You're enjoying yourself, aren't you?"

"Well, I wouldn't say I am enjoying myself, precisely. You are, however, amusing at times."

A blast of heated air brushed over them as his jaw bunched. "So help me..." He took a breath. "You keep pushing me, Layla, and eventually I will push back."

She took a step closer, her satin skirts swirling around his legs, the tips of her breasts nearly touching his chest. "So push."

Sin's body jerked, his head dipping down as if he just might silence her with his lips. But then he froze. His gaze strayed to her mouth, and it seemed he swayed closer, his lids lowering just a fraction more.

Her breath came on in quick, deep pants. *Please. Please.* Heat bloomed wide, washing over her skin, plucking at her nipples. They grew stiff beneath the tight clasp of her bodice.

As if he saw her physical reaction, a visible shudder went through him and he closed his eyes, swallowing hard. "Layla," he rasped, almost weakly. "When I became Judgment, I took a vow."

"A vow," she all but croaked.

He opened his eyes, his gaze flat and pale green. "To remain faithful to my duty. To make it my one and only mistress."

"You mean..." She could not finish the sentence without sobbing. Or stomping her foot. Or something equally horrid.

His voice was low, placid. "I told you Judgment were akin to monk warriors."

That he could stand there, telling her he would never be anything more than her guardian, that he would choose his duty over her...It was noble, honorable. It ought to have made her proud. Instead a thick, sticky emotion came over, thwarted rage and frustration.

She stamped her foot then. "Then why drag me out here, St. John? Why this display of jealous temper?"

His brows rose. "Jealous—"

"Yes, jealous," she snapped. "You appear to appreciate forthright talk. Well, that goes both ways. You were jealous. Admit it."

He glanced away, his jaw bunching again, making it appear sharper. "Leave off, Layla. This is useless."

"Oh, bollocks to that! Admit it, you . . . ponce!"

A shocked laugh escaped him, his cheeks dimpling, the corners of his eyes crinkling in a way that was irritatingly boyish. "Ponce, eh?"

"Yes." She stomped her foot.

He leaned in, tilting his head. "Do you know what that even means?"

"A cad?"

His smile grew. "Try again."

"Boor?"

He began to chuckle, low and rolling. "No."

"Oh, who the bloody hell cares!" She tossed up her hands in defeat. "All I need to know is that it isn't nice. And neither are you . . ."

She stopped talking when he dipped his head until his lips brushed the shell of her ear. His deep voice worked over her like a delicious shiver. "A ponce, little bird, is a man who manages prostitutes."

Layla reared back. "Well, then why would you call St. Claire one?"

He burst out laughing, his entire frame shaking with it. "Because it isn't nice and neither is he."

She wanted to wring Sin's neck but she could not help it;

she laughed too, hard enough that her corset pinched. "You awful man," she said between gasps. "Awful, horrid..."

He reached out and hauled her close, wrapping her in his arms. It shocked her into silence, and he hugged her sweetly, his lips pressing against the top of her head. "I'm sorry, Layla," he murmured into her hair. "I acted the ass. Because I was jealous."

A little lurch went through her heart. As if he felt it, Sin gently rubbed her back, his broad hand warm.

"You don't have to be," she said into his hard chest.

His heart thudded against her cheek. "Yes, I do. He is free to court you. I am not."

Layla closed her eyes as if she could blot his words from existence. "Saint..."

The muscles along his arms bunched as he gathered her closer. "Layla, might we just stand here for a moment without arguing? Just..." He took a breath, and it seemed he burrowed his nose farther into her hair. "Just stand here and be?"

What could she say to that? Her heart was breaking a little more every day. His stubbornness was thicker than the walls of Jericho.

Yes, but eventually even those walls toppled, said a little hopeful voice within her.

She thought of what Augustus had told her before he'd left. *"For too long, St. John has only known to hate himself. It will take a will just as stubborn as his to break him of that notion."*

Slowly, she let her arms relax and wrap around Sin's trim waist, and he stiffened a little before taking a breath and easing once more. Layla let herself rest against him. "We can just be," she told him. "For now, Sin. But eventually, life will go on. Whether you want it to or not."

She'd wanted to impart on him that they were no longer simply friends. Not given the depth of feeling she had for him.

But Sin, the damnable man, simply nodded. "When the time comes that you've found a man you want to dance with," he said quietly, "I will not stand in your way."

And her heart broke all over again.

Chapter Eleven

Augustus

He had not been to Vienna in over a century. Though beautiful and rich with tradition, the city held painful memories, ones that he'd never forget or even try to. But to return to the scene of those long-dead moments in time made his losses all the more real.

Walking along its enchanting streets, taking in the scents of confectionaries behind shop windows, catching the lilting strains of a violin in the cool breeze, tugged on his heart and forced him to remember a time when he'd been his most happy—and his most sorrowful. Yes, the pretty little city on the Danube that called to mind a fairy tale, the place that had inspired human genius such as Strauss and Beethoven, made his heart ache.

He strolled past St. Stephen's Cathedral and moved farther into the twisting streets that made up the old city. Over a millennium ago, when he'd posed as a Roman soldier, there had been a camp near this city. So long ago, when the native people were little more than savages, superstitious and fearful. And so very fierce.

When Augustus had returned the second time, it was the seventeen nineties, and Vienna had turned into a city of culture and refinement. Amadeus Mozart's music was causing a stir. Augustus remembered the first time he'd heard the young composer's work. He'd wept, his heart swelling and his throat closing tight. The music had captured his soul and spoke to the melancholy sweetness of life.

That too, however, was long ago. Now, in the eighteen nineties, the city was still beautiful but a place he'd rather not be. His steps were slow and weighted with more memories as he entered the Griechenbeisl, one of Vienna's oldest and most beloved inns and dining establishments.

It had been two centuries since he'd dined here, yet it had not changed. The dark wood paneling and pale stucco vaulted ceiling remained. He requested a table in the Music Room and was soon tucking into a plate of *schnitzel,* golden and light and delicious.

Augustus drank his ale and ate his meal as musicians played and patrons chatted. And all the while, he ignored the empty seat before him. Night after night, he'd dined here. Every day for two weeks. They knew him by name now, Herr Augustus. And night after night, he made the same request, for them to fill one of their old steins with fine Russian vodka. He would not drink it, no. The vodka sat on the table before the empty seat.

No one ever claimed the drink. It was to be expected. The wait staff clearly found it odd—though they never mentioned it to him. They had no notion that Augustus could pluck those thoughts straight from their minds. They did not realize that he wanted them to talk, wanted the gossip that a foreigner haunted their dining room, ordering this specific drink and not touching it.

Every night, Augustus held out hope that his proffered drink would finally be accepted.

Not tonight, it seemed. He finished his fine meal and left. Alone once more on the winding streets, he reflected that he might never succeed.

Sadness and regret pressed in on his chest, so heavy and encompassing that he nearly missed the whisper of sound behind him. The attack was nearly upon him before he spun with inhuman speed and lashed out, grabbing his predator about the waist and hauling her close.

They met with a small thud and a gasp of sound. Augustus held fast to his catch, knowing that she'd try to break free. But she did not. She merely glared up at him, her eyes shining liquid black in the streetlights.

"A fine way to greet an old friend," Lena murmured.

He held her more securely, moving one hand up between her shoulder blades and the other to the small of her back. An embrace he'd longed to indulge in for centuries. She tensed in his arms, but did nothing more.

"Forgive me," he said, "for confusing your attempt to obtain my attention with an outright attack. He glanced down at the gold dagger pressed between them, caught in her grip. "Is that a peace offering then, dearest?"

With a noise of annoyance, she shook free of him, and the carnelian, beaded enamel hair sticks she favored clattered. He remembered that sound. It had his cock thickening, for he'd often heard that very sound when she pulled those sticks free to unravel all that lush, inky hair. When she'd smile at him as if he were a delicious meal and then tempt him, make him yearn to take her to bed. He'd always resisted. A decision he did not quite regret, but he mourned the loss of opportunity all the same.

"Why is it that you haunt my city?" she asked in exasperation as she pocketed the dagger.

Her city. Augustus considered it *theirs*. But he was the only being in existence who knew she favored this place. Lena was very adept at hiding. Even knowing she might be in Vienna, he had to resort to drawing her out, as opposed to hunting her down.

He gave her a curious look. "Need I a reason other than wanting your company?"

The pale circle of her face gave nothing away. "We stopped seeking each other's company two centuries ago."

That would be the night he'd asked her to give him her heart. To be his for all time. And she'd destroyed his hope and sealed his fate by telling him no.

"Not quite true," he said. "You sought me out not very long ago. Or have you forgotten Layla already?" A cheap shot, he knew, but he could not seem to help himself when it came to Lena.

As expected, her nostrils flared and her eyes narrowed. "Do not dare try that on me." Her ire dimmed, and an odd, expectant look came over her. "Is she well? Is she... strong? Happy?"

Most mothers would ask after their daughter's looks, their deportment. Lena was a fighter and knew that what was most important in their world had little to do with appearance or manners.

Even so, her question caught him off guard. "You mean to tell me you haven't checked up on her once?" True, he'd likely have felt Lena's presence but he'd still expected her to keep an eye on her daughter.

Lena ducked her head, and the gaslight struck the pale curve of her cheek. "Once. But it was easier to know nothing."

Her quiet confession softened his old heart. He cleared his throat. "She has grown to a headstrong, forthright, capable young woman."

Lena nodded but did not meet his eyes. Augustus moved a step closer.

"As to her strength, that is why I am here."

Lena's gaze snapped to his. "What has happened?"

"She is coming into her immortal maturity. There have been human slaughters, and Layla has been drawn to them."

Lena's expression went smooth and blank. "Sanguis at the cusp of fully turning are generally drawn to blood."

"True," he said. "But then we both know we are not dealing with a pure Sanguis."

It had been a convenient cover for Lena to pretend she was something that she was not. And Augustus had played along. Mainly because she'd behaved and he was a fool when it came to her. But now he was done playing games.

Lena sniffed and began walking. "It's rude to mention a lady's origins, Augustus."

He followed, his mouth tight. "Good thing I'm not speaking to a lady."

"Hurtful words." She did not appear offended.

Together, they walked past human pedestrians who spilled from taverns and restaurants. As always in this city, music filled the air.

"Lena, I have protected your identity, kept the supernatural world from knowing what you truly are. Layla needs guidance." He squeezed the back of his neck. "It would take but one act to turn her down a bad road."

She snorted. "You mean for her to become as me."

"Yes." He grabbed her elbow and tugged her to a halt. Her nostrils flared but Augustus did not heed. "Is that what you want for her? To become Damnation? To crave the blood and destruction of others?"

And there was the truth of their ugly past. Lena was Damnation. And Augustus was Judgment. He'd been sent out to destroy her and had ended up in a cat-and-mouse game with the beautiful young fiend, so that he'd found himself enjoying life once more. He'd found himself falling in love with the enemy.

Lena blinked up at him, her expression blank—as it always was when she became most distressed. "No," she said finally. "It is a lonely and dark life."

"Then help me. Is she full Damnation? Who is her father?" Even now, the question was bitter on his tongue.

"I told you years ago, she is only a half-breed," Lena said calmly. "And capable of good. Give her the push and she will be extraordinary."

"That is not enough, Lena." He tried to let her arm go but his fingers would not obey. "Who is her sire?"

She stepped closer to him, bringing her slight breasts against his chest. Everything in him went tight. Her slim arm wrapped around his neck. "Tell me," she murmured, her breath gliding over his parted lips. "Do you ask for Layla or for yourself? Is this not a simple case of jealousy?"

"God's teeth," he ground out. "Do you not know me at all? To think I would put personal feelings before Layla's safety—"

The blasted woman put her finger to his lips. "Oh, I know you care. And I do know you, which is why you cannot hide your petty jealousy." Her red lips curled. "Really, Augustus, as if I'd have anyone else but you."

But she wouldn't have him. That was the point.

The thought ran heavy through his heart, distracting him from her hands upon his cheeks. He blinked down at her, a warning blaring in his mind a moment too late. Lena gave his head a sharp twist, breaking his neck in an instant. Her dark, lovely eyes were the last thing he saw before everything went black.

Resentful as he was towards Augustus and the position he'd backed him into, Sin wholeheartedly appreciated one feature of his changed nature: wings.

He bloody loved having wings. Nothing on this earth quite compared to the rush and freedom of flight. Even in those first days of his training, when Augustus had warned that most newly turned Judgment became air sick, Sin had never faltered in his love. Nor had he ever felt ill when flying. More like exhilarated, joyous. The world looked different from a few thousand feet up.

He flew now, catching wind currents that shot him upward, swirled him this way and that. The cold, wet air did not bother him in the least. It was a kiss against his skin. Up here, over the black layer of clouds that covered London, everything was clear, the night sky so deep black it appeared a cloth of the finest velvet, strewn with a million glittering diamond stars.

For a long time he simply drifted, his wings spread wide, his body relaxed. Then he tucked his wings in and dove. Down. Down. Wind howled in his ears, cold prickles of water stinging his cheeks. His insides lifted against his spine, protesting the rapid fall. Sin tightened his body further and kept his head down.

Like a bullet, he punched through the thick cloud layer, black and dense and laden with the stench of coal. Sin held his breath. Another few seconds and he was shooting out of the clouds.

All of London lay before him. A vast, intricate network of streets and lanes, glittering with lanterns and lit windows.

Gray snakes of smoke coiled from countless chimneys, and people bustled to and fro. Sin took it all in on a glance, then snapped his wings wide.

The instant drag pulled at his muscles and yanked his body back, slowing him considerably. His wings protested in pain, but it was a delicious sort of pain, one borne of pushing his physical endurance.

Holding himself steady, he floated a ways then angled towards his landing spot. Using his wings now, he flew towards the great dome of St. Paul's, now silver-gray in the night. The mere sight of the cathedral soothed him, made him feel at home. For better or worse, London was his home, and St. Paul's dominated the city's skyline.

With light feet, he landed on the balustrade of the Golden Gallery, the little balcony that circled the uppermost portion of the dome. And then nearly lost his footing as a feminine voice spoke.

"About time," said Layla, leaning casually against the wall. "You're quite the showman, Sin."

Glaring, Sin willed his wings gone and jumped onto the balcony. "Sneaking up on me is dangerous, Layla. I might have ripped your head off."

Her pretty eyes rolled. "First, I cannot sneak up on you when I've been standing here all along. Second, you might try to rip my head off, but that does not mean you would succeed."

Sin snorted. "I wouldn't try, because I have fast enough reflexes to stop myself before making that strike."

"Hmm…I seem to have missed the demonstration of those reflexes tonight."

Bloody annoying woman. Though he was more annoyed at himself for failing to notice her in the first place. "How did you know I would be here?" he could not help but ask.

Layla pushed off from the wall. She was wearing a man's

suit, her hair neatly plaited in a rope down her back. When she came abreast of him, she stopped and looked up at the sky. "You shot from the clouds like a comet." Amusement lit her eyes. "Did you know your wings glow with white fire when you dive?"

"Hell." He ran a hand through his now wet hair and scowled. "I did not."

"I suspect Londoners would rationalize the sight as a rather large shooting star. But for beings such as us, you give them a perfect beacon to follow."

Good god, it was akin to listening to Augustus's lectures, only worse because this was Layla, the woman he was supposed to protect.

"That does not explain how you arrived here before I landed."

A small smile played over her rosy lips. "When you were a boy, you used to climb a tree or go to the rooftop of Evernight Hall whenever you were upset." The thick fan of her lashes swept down, hiding her eyes to him. "Always the highest spot. I figured you would do the same now."

He'd been alone in his thoughts for so long now that it was a strange sensation to realize someone knew him to the core.

Layla turned a fraction, lifting her face up to him. "What troubles you, Saint?"

The old nickname had him wanting both to smile and press his hand against his aching heart. He did neither. "It is nothing, little bird."

"Ah. And now you lie to me." Slowly she shook her head. "Rather disappointing, that."

What he wouldn't give to tell her everything, to kneel down at her feet and beg her to hold him just for a little while. Or perhaps forever.

The angry possessive side of him wanted to rail at her for

having the temerity to even ask. How could she not know why he'd needed to fly? Did she honestly think he enjoyed watching her dance and flirt with dozens of men? When he could not be one of them?

God, he wanted to shout his ire, tell her that she belonged to him and he to her.

But he could do none of those things. So Sin moved away from temptation, running his hand along the cold granite balustrade to keep his mind grounded in the here and now.

"I tend to disappoint a great many people, Layla. Do not expect me to fall into some sentimental heart-to-heart confession. I am no longer that boy."

He could feel her gaze like an icy weight upon his shoulders. It took everything in him to turn and face her, keeping his expression bland. Even so, the sight of her large brown eyes, now wide with something that looked very much like pity, was a kick in the gut.

When she spoke, her melodic voice was low but strong. "I have not thought of you as that boy for some time, St. John. Nor am I that girl. More is the pity that you do not realize we are both very much adults."

A pained look spasmed over her fine features and then she broke apart before his eyes. One minute whole—the next moment, a fluttery flock of birds rose into the night sky.

Sin watched them go then bent down to pick up Layla's discarded clothing. Bringing the linen shirt to his nose, he closed his eyes and inhaled. Green Irish grass and the salty tang of the sea—Layla. Home. Need. Lust.

Oh, he was quite aware that they were no longer children.

Chapter Twelve

It was amusing to Layla that Sin apparently thought he was being sly in his attempt to slip out of the house unnoticed at the stroke of midnight, for he was as quiet as a British regiment marching down Whitehall. Which was decidedly odd, considering he appeared to be creeping along the front walk, sticking to the shadows, as if trying to blend into them.

Layla watched him go from her hidden spot beneath the front porticos. He hadn't heard *her* follow, so perhaps he had some sort of hearing impediment. This did not bode well if he was to be her guard. Which was why she decided to keep watch over him.

Dressing in a young lad's costume was nothing new. When she had been at the height of her fame, singing concerts every night to packed halls, the only way Layla could enjoy a bit of anonymity was to go out as a lad. Thankfully her curves were slight and her jawline more curved than narrow. No one noticed her at all.

She used that trick now as she followed Sin down the lane. Unfortunately, he was also quite quick, his stride having the grace of a predator and the speed of a racehorse. Layla silently cursed as she struggled to keep up but still remain hidden.

But her quarry did not seem to notice her at all. His stride remained intent and focused. He cut a slim figure through the foggy night, his tall form a mere blot on the horizon.

They were coming up on the Wellington Arch when he vanished. Layla halted, blinking at the mists eddying around the iron fencing that enclosed Wellington Park. How could he simply disappear? She hadn't even seen him make a move to hide; he'd been walking along and then... nothing.

Thus she nearly leapt out of her skin, a scream tearing from her breast, when he grabbed hold of her from behind and hauled her against his hard chest. His big, gloved hand rested over her mouth, muffling her voice as he leaned in close, his lips at her ear. "You didn't really think I was unaware of your presence, now did you, little bird?"

Though it was buried deep beneath a dark tone, there was amusement in his voice—a little huff as if he was fighting not to laugh. And she relaxed against him—for really, what was the use in fighting?

His hand slipped away and he turned her, setting her far enough away that they no longer touched but close enough that he could grab her in an instant. "Need I ask why you're following me?" The corners of his eyes crinkled just a bit.

She could not help smiling back a little. "You were skulking about in the night. I wanted to know why."

"Skulk." His fine nostrils narrowed with a sniff. "I do not skulk."

"Fine. You were innocently going out for a midnight stroll and I wanted to join you to take in the fresh air." She waved her hand about, and the thickening brown fog that surrounded them swirled with the movement.

Sin's lips compressed. "Curiosity killed the cat, Layla."

Cat? The back of her neck bristled. "I am no cat."

His beautifully carved lips softened and curled just a little at the corners. "No," he said softly. "But you can be skinned just the same."

She supposed that was true. Yet, oddly, she felt completely safe knowing he was near. She always had. "Where were you going, then?" The dark night and the cool fog made her feel compelled to keep her voice low. "Are you… Are you having an assignation?"

The very idea that Sin might be meeting a lover was repellent to her but not out of the realm of possibility. He was stunningly handsome. The most extraordinary man she'd ever seen, really.

Apparently he was not aware of his qualities, for he huffed out a laugh as though she'd said something absurd. "There is no lover, Layla. There never will be."

"Never?" she repeated, suddenly downcast at the idea of Sin going without love.

His strong jaw bunched as he looked her in the eye. "Never."

He sounded utterly certain. And utterly haunted. And that hurt her.

"But… Well…" Layla struggled to find an argument. She really didn't understand why she wanted to argue. She certainly didn't want him going off with some other woman. And yet… "But surely at some point—"

Sin took a step closer, enough that the warmth emanating from his body touched her skin. "Do you want me to seek a lover, Layla?" He frowned, tilting his head a little as he regarded her. "Do you fancy yourself some sort of Austen heroine, set on seeing everyone settled before finding yourself a man?"

He remembered her love of Jane Austen then.

"But, Saint," she countered in a soft voice, "if I were Emma in this scenario, certainly you'd be Knightly." She leaned in a touch, because he smelled divine and was irresistible to her, even when he tensed up as he did now. Her smile grew. "Surely you cannot have forgotten how they end up?"

He stared down at her for a long moment, a myriad of emotions flitting over his face. It was a subtle show but she knew him well enough to see them. Annoyance, horror, shock, longing, and finally wry amusement.

The longing interested her greatly. But he snorted and then sighed, his chin dropping down so that the long, crimson-tipped strands of his raven hair fell over his brow. "Layla," he groaned, "what am I to do with you?"

Keep me. Be mine. Make me yours.

She said none of those things but merely tucked a lock of his hair back behind his ear, careful not to touch his skin. She did not know what had happened to her old friend, but his once deep affinity for touch had dissolved like acid to paper. With a quiet plea, she answered him. "Tell me where you're going?"

On a breath he leaned in, coming just shy of resting his forehead to hers. But she felt it. She felt it everywhere, as if his body had melded to hers. And her eyes fluttered, wanting to close. But she needed to keep her eyes on him, for fear he might leave her again.

Hands fisted at his sides, he simply stood, swaying a bit, perhaps fighting the same urge to hold her close.

Please, she thought. *Please.*

But then he inhaled and drew himself away, his spine stiff once more. "Come along, then. You've made me late as it is."

Despite the loss of his warmth, she could not help but grin wide. "You're truly taking me with you."

Sin gave her a sidelong glance. "Would you truly stay put if I took you home?"

"No."

"Then you have your answer."

Sin had finally fallen off his nut. That was the only explanation for why he'd decided to take Layla with him. He ought to take her home. Go another night. And yet, having her walk beside him, her gait happy and light, as if they were out for a stroll in the park at midday instead of creeping about at midnight, made him feel lighter too.

No matter how dark his mood, no matter how hard he tried to harden himself against her, Layla broke through. It was as if the ghost of his boyish self recognized her as his safe harbor, his little friend who'd always made him laugh, and would not let older, dour Sin turn her away.

Lightly touching her elbow, he guided her up to the Wellington Arch.

At some point in time, all leaders apparently felt the need to grace their cities with victory arches, commemorating their military's great feats. Rome had the Arch of Constantine, Paris had the L'Arc de Triomphe, Munich had its Victory Gate, and London had the Wellington Arch.

What the human world did not know was that every arch hid an entrance that went down to a hidden underground. Depending on the city, that entrance either led friend or foe. And while Sin knew the Wellington was "friendly," he was not certain of his reception.

By the time he'd walked beneath the vaulted arch, his skin was clammy and his heart pounded a hard, uncomfortable rhythm. Layla stayed quiet as they stopped before a door on the side of the arch's base.

"We're going to the gift shop?" Layla asked in a dubious tone.

"Not quite." Sin pulled a skeleton key from his pocket—a golden key that, aside from opening nearly all locks—was actually shaped like a skull at the top. A bit of whimsy that he supposed its creator had found ironic. A pang went through him as he realized that his cousin Holly might very well be that creator. Her absence in his life cut deep.

Pushing maudlin thoughts away, Sin inserted the key into the lock. The door opened with a faint click. "Take hold of my coat."

"Why?" Layla whispered, even as her small hand grasped the edge of his suit coat.

He thought the reason fairly obvious but answered anyway. "It is dark in here and I cannot risk using a light."

"Oh." She said nothing more but followed close behind as he led them into the gift shop.

With only the ambient light coming in through the glass at the front door, the space was as dark as a tomb. Sin's sight shifted from a normal human's to Judgment's superior abilities and the world went from pitch black to cool blues and grays.

To her credit, Layla kept pace without hesitation or stumbling as he wove past shelves housing picture books and wire racks displaying post cards with pictures of Queen Victoria, Buckingham Palace, Hyde Park, and the like.

Crossing the room, he made his way to the lift in the far back corner. Ordinarily he would have taken the stairs down to a hidden door. But tonight was no ordinary visit. Damn, but he hated the gnawing pit in his stomach that seemed to grow wider with each step he took.

Layla's soft breaths sounded loud in the silence as they stopped and he inserted the skeleton key once more. A faint hum filled the air, then soft vibrations tickled the soles of his feet. Pale white light shot through the edges of the inner lift doors as the cab within glided to a stop.

Sin pulled the wrought-iron gate doors open and then slid the inner doors open. The small cab, illuminated by an ornate electric lamp at its ceiling, lay empty and waiting. "After you." He held out an arm, directing Layla to enter.

She shot him a look but walked forward. Sin followed, closing the gates and the door.

"Why not take the stairs?" Layla asked. "After all, the lift is rather loud. We risk attention this way."

"True. Unfortunately, this is the only way." To demonstrate, Sin pulled off his gloves, tucking them into his pocket, and then grasped the brass operator handle that would drive the cab up or down. Squeezing it tight, he let his power go, sending both little zings of electricity and heat into it. The lift hummed again. Then he moved the level indicator to the letter "G."

With a slight jerk, the lift began to rise.

"I don't understand," Layla said, glancing from him to his hand upon the lever.

"There are certain safeguards in place come nightfall. Tonight, the lift is set to rise only by my power."

"And the stairs?" She appeared fascinated.

"Rigged to prevent anyone using them at the moment."

"Curious," she muttered.

Sin found himself flashing a quick smile. "To be sure."

They grinned at each other, and the action was disorienting to Sin, making the muscles in his face ache. When had he last willingly smiled just for the fun of it?

The lift came to a halt at the top floor. He moved the lever to "hold" and then opened the doors. They were on top of the arch, at the viewing gallery floor, and the cold night air touched Sin's cheeks.

Layla's hand rested once more on the tail of his coat, and he paused, wondering if she had trouble adjusting her vision from the lit elevator cab to the dark terrace. But she glanced at him, her perfect brow lifting in question, and he realized she'd merely wanted to hold on to him.

Flushed, he led them towards the middle of the arch.

A slim figure moved from around the corner, and Sin's chest grew tight. He halted, waiting as the figure came closer. Layla gave a little jerk of surprise, likely shocked that he was, in fact, meeting a woman.

The woman came to a halt before them. She was tall enough that she barely had to tilt her head to meet Sin's gaze. As always, he was struck by the steel in hers. She was the only one who still spoke to Sin, and that was more out of necessity than actual need.

Augustus had told her Sin was working for him. Poppy Lane, his eldest sister and leader of the SOS, had demanded to know why, but Augustus would not relent, only informed her that she *would* be sociable to Sin. It was awkward and painful, if Sin were truthful with himself, but he would not hide from her or any of his sisters.

Poppy had always been a cold one, but now she was downright icy for most of their meetings.

"St. John. You look... well." She appeared a bit amazed by this observation.

Sin inclined his head. "As do you, sister."

A small gasp escaped Layla, and she moved forward. "You're Sin's sister?"

Poppy's pale, sharp face turned her way. "One of three. And you are?"

"Layla Starling," Sin said for her. "My old friend."

Poppy's red brows lifted high. "The neighbor girl and heiress."

Well, he wouldn't have put it *exactly* in those words.

"Yes," Layla said. "Pleased to meet you. I did not know Sin had sisters."

Poppy peered at Layla, a frown on her face, then it cleared and she almost smiled. "I know you, though. Layla Starling. You are the famous soprano." The look of pleasure grew, turning Poppy's stern features almost soft. "My husband and I saw you perform in Rome last year. You were marvelous."

Layla ducked her head. "Why, thank you. That is most kind of you to say."

"Merely honest." Poppy glanced back at Sin. "Though I do wonder why my brother brought you along. Forgive me for saying, but we have a private matter to discuss."

Sin held Poppy's gaze and was about to reply, but Layla beat him to it.

"Oh, I followed him and wouldn't give up until he relented."

Poppy's lips compressed, and Sin knew she wanted to laugh. Surprised amusement was in her eyes.

Sin glared. "That scenario," he drawled, darkly. "Or, perhaps, the fact that Layla is the reason I asked for this meeting."

"What?" Layla said a bit shrilly.

But Poppy went still, her gaze slashing from Sin to Layla and back again. Oh, but she was a quick one, clearly putting it all together. Sin gave her another long look. "I need answers, dear sister."

He had sisters. Three of them. How had she not known this? Layla felt an odd sense of loss. Truth was, she did not know St. John Evernight the man very much at all. As a youth he had been cagey and yet oddly sweet, watching out for her wherever they went. But she'd known him. Known everything that happened in their day-to-day lives.

He was still cagey and oddly sweet, but now he was a man of secrets and hidden pain. And as he exchanged a look with his sister, one full of silent understanding, jealousy stabbed through Layla's heart. He had an entire history that did not include her.

Poppy, a tall, pale woman with flame-red hair that glowed a dull copper in the night, gestured towards a stone bench by the gallery wall, where one could sit and look out over Hyde Park. All was quiet now; a few bobbies strolled in the distance as they took the night watch.

"I believe we have much to discuss," Poppy said.

Layla hadn't a clue what they were going on about, but Sin had said it had to do with her. That irked too. She'd thought he'd wanted her presence for the simple fact that he enjoyed her company. She ought to have known better. The dratted man did nothing without a plan.

Layla sat and Poppy joined her, but Sin remained standing, thrusting his hands into his pockets. "Tell me about Lena."

Poppy clearly detested Lena, for the woman's long nose wrinkled as though smelling something foul. What would she think of Layla if she knew her to be Lena's child?

"She was my second in command. Though, honestly, it ought to have been the other way around, for Lena had been a part of the SOS before I'd been born. Before my mother had too." Poppy leaned back against the wall, crossing one long leg over the other in a way that was almost a mannish slouch. Layla approved.

Poppy glanced at Layla. "In my family, membership in the SOS followed a matriarchal line. I, as my mother before me, entered into service. Lena trained me."

Sin's expression was as bland as ever. "And she was a compatriot of Father?"

"I suppose," Poppy said. "They were certainly the eldest members. And they always seemed to know what the other was doing. But I never saw them together. Ever. Which is decidedly odd." She gave a brief, wry smile. "Then again, most things in our world are odd."

"She was your friend. What went wrong?" Sin asked.

Poppy's gaze went utterly cold. So cold that Layla shivered. And then she realized that it had actually become colder. A lacy dusting of frost edged out from where Poppy sat, until Sin gave her a pointed look. At once, the cold died down, but it still lingered.

"She hid you from us," Poppy said crisply.

"Me?" Sin edged closer. "When Miranda found me, she said I'd been a surprise. That you all believed me to be dead at childbirth. But she never told me who kept it from her. Only that it was a misunderstanding. "

"It was Lena. Just before our mother died, she made Lena promise not to reveal your hiding place to any of us. She feared you'd be found by our father." Poppy glanced at Layla before looking back at Sin. Poppy's lips stayed shut.

Sin waved a hand. "No secrets between us now, Poppy."

His sister snorted. "Fine one to talk," she muttered.

Sin went stiff but Poppy continued. "As you know, our father was a powerful primus demon. A primus is one of the original and oldest demon kind," she explained to Layla. "Our father believed that Sin could be talked over to evil and become a powerful ally."

Sin's fine lips curved down a touch. "Why did he believe that?" His voice was soft and raw.

"Because he was drunk on his own delusions." Her hard expression eased. "He thought the same of me as well, St. John. And I destroyed him for his efforts."

Sin blinked slowly, then a small smile pulled at his mouth. "Good."

Brother and sister stared at each other in perfect understanding. Then, in a blink, Poppy resumed her cool manner. "Lena disappeared then. I have not seen nor heard from her since."

Sin nodded almost absently. "Did Lena ever take a lover that you know of?"

A strangled, embarrassed snort left Poppy. "That wasn't something I'd want to know."

"But did you?"

Poppy shrugged. "She's a sanguis demon, Sin. I assume you understand that sanguis crave and feed off sex as well as blood."

"I know what Sanguis demons are, Poppy." Sin kept his gaze decidedly away from Layla.

This was news to Layla, however, and she wondered if she'd suddenly want to tup every male she encountered. The thought turned her stomach. She glanced at Sin, standing tall and elegant in the night. Now, with Sin, she could see the appeal.

Poppy's cool voice broke through her heated thoughts. "Well, then you'll understand that she had many, many lovers."

He sighed and turned away to pace. "As I feared."

"Why do you ask?" Poppy called out.

Sin stopped and turned. But his gaze went to Layla. An awful sort of sinking feeling came over her at his hesitation. It grew worse when he drew near and hunkered down beside her. He spoke to both of them but kept his attention on Layla. "Augustus claims that Lena is your mother."

Layla let out a breath. "I know."

Sin cocked his head as if she'd pinched him. "You know this?"

"Augustus told me before he left."

"Bloody hell." Sin ran a hand through his hair, upsetting

the black locks. "Thing is, love. I believe the bit he did not want you to know is that Lena isn't sanguis. She might drink blood, but she is Damnation."

"Bollocks," Poppy said with a sharp breath.

Layla, however, went utterly cold. "I am part Damnation? Augustus's enemy?"

"No, little bird." Sin knelt close. "He loves you. Never doubt that. He told me not to tell you until I felt it was time for you to know." Sin squeezed her hand. "That time must be now, for I cannot keep this from you any longer. In truth, it hurts my heart to keep anything from you."

Poppy gave him a ghost of a smile. "Come now, little brother, you know as well as I Augustus can be a cagey fiend. I cannot pretend to understand his reasoning here. If I had to guess, however, I'd say that he asked you to wait because he wanted you and Layla to get to this point of trust in each other before you told her."

"A test, was it?" Sin's lip curled. "I've had about enough of those, thank you."

Poppy snorted. "I've dealt with the man since I was a girl. I empathize, believe me."

Layla stood then. "So then, my mother was a woman of loose morals and multiple bed partners. I could be anyone's." She gave a weak laugh. "At least it explains my lust for blood."

"You crave it?" Poppy asked.

And Layla winced. "At times. Other times, the mere smell and sight of it makes me ill."

"Perhaps your sire's ilk detested blood."

"Putting my very nature in opposition of itself?" Layla offered with a frown. "How horrible."

"Nothing about you is horrible, little bird," Sin said at her side. He glanced at Poppy, who stared at him with quiet bemusement, as if his words shocked her. Sin's high-cut cheeks flushed, but his tone remained neutral. "Augustus told me he was going to track down Lena. Where could he have gone?"

Poppy's red brows knitted. "I cannot imagine. Lena has been missing since we found you, St. John. Not a trace of her remains in London. To look for her abroad would be next to impossible. He must have some idea of where to search if he had any hope of finding her."

"And when he found her?" Layla was compelled to ask. "How would she receive him?"

Both Sin and Poppy appeared troubled. Poppy spoke first. "Many do not know this, but Lena and Augustus created the SOS together. There is good in her; I know it. She was my closest confidant until we quarreled. But Lena, when cornered, is volatile, and no one can ever predict how she will react."

Chapter Thirteen

Lena

There had once been a time in her life when Lena fed off violence and blood the way humans sat down to a thirty-six-course meal. Such lovely decadence. Enough to bloat her belly and leave her lethargic, replete with satisfaction. And yet, when the happy glow faded, she was left empty and ashamed. What a horrid thing to realize that she was defective, unable to think and act as a proper Damnation.

Augustus had done that to her. He took one look at her, seeing deep into her soul, and deemed her *worthy*. Worse still, he'd fallen in love with her. What was she to do, then?

In the beginning, she had not wanted his love and had lashed out in an attempt to keep him at bay. But the stubborn man kept coming back for more, chasing her to the ends of the earth. And she found herself yielding to him. She fell in love. With a Judgment angel, of all things. Hideous.

What she did not realize then was that, once she'd let love

into her heart, she wanted more. She began to crave connection, friendships, to be part of something whole and good. And once she found that, she did everything in her power to protect it. She'd changed, no longer true Damnation but hiding out as a simple sanguis demon. Well, not *simple*. She was the most powerful of her supposed kind.

And then it had all gone to hell because of one selfish act. Two, actually, for the first had been falling for an angel. It was wrong to love someone so pure. Her soul would forever taint his.

Lena sighed, looking out over the dancers in the Viennese dance hall. Truly, there was nothing like it in the world. The enormous room glittered, as if one had walked into the heart of a diamond. Mirrored walls, the panels gilded by ormolu; rows of crystal chandeliers dripping from the ceilings; flickering sconces—all of it designed to illuminate the patrons in the best light possible.

Oh, the patrons.

When she'd first come to this dance hall, the women's bodices had been formed into flat V shapes, laced so tightly, bosoms plumped high. Skirts had been so wide one had needed to angle to the side to get through doors. But the men had been the true peacocks—with golden heels, silken hose, and vibrant, often outrageously colored frock coats and knickers.

Now they wore boring, staid black suits, leaving the women to have all the fun with color. Dresses were still tight on the bodice, which now plunged as low as one dared, but the skirts were narrow, structured bells. Colors were jewel-toned but somber and muted.

An arrow of longing shot through her. She wanted to go back to those days. Back to when a handsome, black-haired angel of Judgment and mercy stalked her through the crowds. He'd asked her to dance. And, fool she, had accepted.

Lena had not enjoyed breaking his neck the other night. It had been badly done but necessary. Still, it hurt to see him crumple to the ground, his sightless eyes staring up at her as if in accusation.

The orchestra began to play an old favorite, the Blue Danube waltz. Tears threatened. She did not want to think of waltzes. Why had she come here?

Turning quickly, she bumped into a body. Only to look up and suck in a breath.

"Augustus."

His beautiful dark eyes peered down at her. There was a hint of humor in his eyes, tempered with a larger amount of annoyance. She had, after all, broken his neck. Likely it had pained him for a few hours after he'd revived.

"Thanks to you," he said by way of greeting, "street punks stole my billfold."

She gave him a look and he took her hand, all but dragging her onto the dance floor.

Just like that, they were waltzing once more. For a long moment, they simply enjoyed the music, spinning circles around less graceful human dancers. And it was perfect. He guided her around as though he were born to do just that, to lead her wherever he pleased.

And then he had to ruin it all by speaking. "Come back with me, Lena, and face them. We'll do it together."

Blood rushed out of her heart and down towards her toes. For a moment, she could only gape at him, and then her blood surged back through her, filling her with hot rage.

"Face them? As though I were some recalcitrant child in need of reprimanding?" She sneered. "And to be brought in by you, of all beings? Oh, that is quite ironic, is it not, Augustus?"

He stared at her, his onyx eyes unblinking. "Tell me why you think so."

He did not sound curious in the least. No, he wanted to hear what he already knew.

Lena tossed her head, the beads clicking with a familiar sound. It did little to soothe her now. "You've fooled them all, haven't you?" she said. "Made them believe you are their benevolent leader, when really..." Her chest tightened, the horrifying urge to sob rising up from within.

"When what, Lena?" he murmured, encouraging her to go on, as he danced them around the room.

"Who was it that, a millennia ago, placed the Sword of Maat in a cave, knowing that it was the one weapon able to destroy a Judgment angel, knowing that one day Miranda Archer would use it to save Benjamin Archer by plunging it into their enemy's breast?"

"It was I," Augustus said.

"Benjamin Archer, whose love and care for his wife would help her reunite with her sisters, Poppy and Daisy. Poppy, the leader of the SOS, who'd been losing heart until that moment."

"So it happened," he agreed.

"Who was it that stepped between Aodh and Mab on that long-ago day in the glen," she shouted, unable to hold it in any longer. "Who turned Aodh into Adam, the king of the GIM? The man able to create clockwork hearts, the very sort of heart that would whir in Mary Chase's breast, the girl who would one day save Jack Talent? Who did that?"

"It was I," he answered, conducting a turn.

"Who was it sweeping out of the sky to save a wounded Winston Lane, Poppy's husband, from certain death? Lane, who with that one act would suddenly be beholden to Apep? Lane, who would force my hand into revealing to Poppy that St. John Evernight lived?"

"Go on," he said.

"Lane who, with Jack Talent's help, would finally outwit Apep and see him sent permanently to Judgment."

"It was I who saved Lane," Augustus said.

"And when Apep was sent back to hell, did it not open up a crack that let out the fallen Amaros? The fiend who captured inventor Holly Evernight and sanguis demon Will Thorne?"

"It did."

"And in creating Adam and the golden clockwork hearts, did it not give inventor Holly Evernight the means to create her own heart to place inside Will Thorne?"

"Yes."

"Will Thorne who was thus transformed into a being capable of destroying the entire head of the Nex, the very organization that we've been striving to silence for centuries."

"He did at that."

"And in using Adam's magic without his consent, did it then make Will Thorne the one being capable of freeing Adam's soul mate Eliza May from Adam's hold, thus forcing Adam to become Mab's plaything?"

"That did occur," he agreed, his expression blank.

Lena seethed, her breasts pressing against her bodice with each deep breath she took. "And when Mab finally had Adam, she became obsessed with keeping him, blind to any danger. Thus giving her desperate blood slave, St. John Evernight, the opening he needed to destroy her."

"She was quite distracted," Augustus said.

"Oh, yes," Lena said. "All that was required to get rid of your long-time enemy Mab was for St. John to become Judgment. And what do you think he would say should he discover that it was you who put the idea into his housekeeper's mind to tell him of the fae? You who willingly set him up to be a blood slave to give him the proper motivation to become a killer."

"I suspect he shall be cross with me," Augustus answered.

"You manipulated them all. You used your dark talent to see into the future, and you pushed each and every one of them towards your own end game."

Augustus's careful expression shattered, and his grip upon her waist tightened, his dark eyes blazing silver. "Yes. I saw the possible outcomes and helped them achieve the best ones."

"For you or for them?"

"Are they not happy?" he snapped. "Have they not found their soul mates?"

"Do not pretend you did it for love," Lena snarled. "You had them do your dirty work. Get rid of Mab, destroy the Nex, keep the SOS alive."

"Are you saying these deeds were for naught?" He tilted his head as if confused. "That they did not need to be accomplished?"

"Of course they did," Lena retorted hotly. "But that is not your end game. What is it, then, Augustus?"

His fine jawline bunched. "Balance. St. John needed to become Judgment, not simply one of many, but its leader."

"You are their leader."

His gaze shot to her, and she froze under the onslaught of anger she saw reflected there. Anger and despair. "I am fading, Lena. As you well know."

The words punched into her. Each one a brutal hit. She missed a step. Then another.

Augustus corrected their course, navigating the floor as though he hadn't just destroyed her. "Fading. I have but days to set my affairs, such as they are, in order. And then I am no more for this world, or any world that you can reach."

The unspoken truth hung between them. He'd lost his chance at forever leading Judgment when he let her go. He'd been ordered to collect her soul. And he had refused. Under their laws, the only acceptable reason he could have for sparing her soul was if she was his true soul mate. But Lena had rejected him.

She swallowed hard. "And what of Layla?" It hurt to utter her name. "You left her under St. John's care. Why?"

He huffed out a breath, clearly not expecting the question. Likely he'd expected her to say something of their own predicament. But she could not do so and keep her composure. Not yet, anyway.

"Because I know what she is, Lena." Such accusation in his voice.

Her heart gave a great thump. "Oh? And what is she?"

"Damnation and Judgment in one." His dark eyes blazed. "You joined with a Judgment angel. Who? And why?" He punched his chest as if he could not contain his rage any other way. "Why would you do that to me?"

Lena laughed then. It was that or cry. "Oh, Augustus, you old fool. Always seeing so clearly except where your own affairs are concerned." Her laughter cut off abruptly. "Have you not figured it out? In all these years?"

His brows drew together. "Do not toy with me, Lena."

"You don't like how it feels? To be toyed with by another? Imagine that."

His nostrils flared in warning. Lena shrugged as if it were nothing. "You have always loved Layla as your own. Did you not wonder why?"

"Oh-ho, no," Augustus uttered with a humorless laugh. "Do not even jest about this. Not even for a moment. You and I have never lain together." His eyes glowed bright silver. "Never."

"Because even though you wanted me, you would not lie with me until I agreed to be yours in heart and soul," Lena said with disgust. "Holding your virtue over me like some great prize."

"It is all I have left of me to give," he ground out, finally snapping. They stopped at the edge of the dance floor. And he stared down at her. "And it isn't enough, for you won't take it."

"I wanted it," she snapped back. "Wanted it, wanted you, so badly that I'd do anything to get it."

The air seemed to suck out of the room. Around them "Blue Danube" bubbled and bounced, the notes so light and happy, it brought smiles to faces. Not theirs. They were in a bubble of misery.

"What did you do?" he whispered before his voice grew in strength. "What did you do, Lena?"

"Apep." The name was bitter on her tongue. "You know him well, demi god of chaos and lies. A being capable of granting any wish for a price."

All the color drained out of Augustus's face. He simply stared at her as if suddenly seeing a stranger.

Lena forged on, knowing she was destroying all hope for them. "In return for telling him that Margaret had a male child, I asked for a wish of my own. You." Hells bells, of all the foolish things she'd done, that had been the greatest.

"You..." Augustus's voice cracked. "You asked for me. How so?"

She glared at him. "You know very well. One night together. One night of your total complicity. And you would not remember."

His throat convulsed as if he'd be ill. "Are you saying..."

"We fucked, my virtuous friend. All night long—"

Her words cut short as he suddenly raised his hand as if

to strike her. But he did not. He made a tight fist and let his hand fall. Growling, he caught her arm and walked them into an alcove, half hidden by a massive potted palm.

"You did that to me?" he whispered thinly. "To us? Cheapened what we could have had?"

"You cheapened us when you made what should have been a natural step into some bloody prize." Lena almost believed her words, but regret lay heavy upon her heart. Because he was right too.

He shook his head, his features pinched with hurt. "I would have given you everything if you had only given me your heart. Your love. Instead you took from me. And… Layla? You took that from me too, did you not? She is my child, and I never knew."

"I gave her to you," Lena cried. "You saw her grow. You have her love and affection."

"Do not try to disguise this as an act of benevolence. You know there is a world of difference in the truth and your twisted little version of it."

"Which proves we are more alike than not."

He glared, and the air around him began to crackle. "Apep killed Margaret because of you."

"I know." It was one of her greatest regrets. "Which is why I did what I could to keep St. John's location hidden. Until you mucked that bit up. See? Alike."

When he did not speak, she went on. "Go back to Layla. Watch over her. She does not need me."

"I am weak now. Unable to do more than guide. She needs all the help she can get," he retorted hotly, then sighed. "Lena…I see Damnation. Coming for her. Claiming her soul."

Ice lashed around her heart and squeezed. "All the more reason to keep me far away."

"You are no longer true Damnation." His dark eyes

searched hers. "She will die, Lena. And this Damnation, whoever he is, shall break open a permanent crack between Here and Nowhere. Hell, Lena, will be open to us all."

Everything inside her screamed in protest at the idea of returning. How could she face the child she had left behind?

Augustus stood before her, his gaze burning.

"I..." Her throat constricted. "I...I cannot."

Augustus's irate shout rang in her ears as she fled.

Sin did not join Layla for luncheon. He wondered if she would be cross with him for leaving her to eat alone. He probably should have kept her company, but his appetite was not cooperating, so he'd gone to the library instead, leafing through weighty tomes about Damnation demons Poppy had delivered from the SOS libraries. It made for dry reading, and he currently had a kink in his neck.

So when Layla appeared in the doorway, he wasn't about to complain. He did, however, raise a brow at her attire. Dressed in a brown wool sack suit, her glossy hair braided and tucked beneath her collar as he'd taught her, a newsboy cap tilted over her brow, she appeared a young boy just then. If a young boy had luscious curves, that was.

"Tell me," she said from her slouch at the door. "What is it that you believe I am?"

Adorable? Irresistible?

He set down a book on ancient immortals and crossed one leg over the other. "I'm afraid you're going to have to elaborate a bit more, little bird."

She walked farther into the room, her hands shoved deep into her pockets as though she were emulating him. Definitely adorable. Her slim shoulders lifted in a shrug. "I'm not human. What am I then?"

"Ah. Let's take what we know for certain into account.

You are part Damnation. You crave blood." Her nose wrinkled at that. "You develop fangs. You are supremely fast and agile when need be. And you have the ability to transform yourself into a flock of birds." Sin found himself smiling. "Which is rather brilliant, if you ask me."

She flushed pink. "Thank you."

"Damnation enjoy blood and grow fangs. But as for your father? Perhaps he is the type to grow fangs as well. A shifter or lycan could do that, but they generally hate blood drinking."

Her nose wrinkled again as she paced. "Well, that doesn't narrow it down very much."

"I'm afraid not."

Layla nodded as she nibbled on her lush bottom lip. Then her brown eyes met his. "Regardless of what I am, you do have some idea as to what I can endure." Her eyes narrowed. "Hard hits, for example."

He refused to cringe. Sin hated striking Layla. Every single time he'd lashed out during their sparring, his mind had cried out in protest. But he'd ignored that, for he knew she needed to learn. He merely gave her a level look now. And she smiled, her cheeks plumping. Her easy manner and good humor were a constant revelation to him. She was unlike anyone he'd ever met.

"Could I survive knife wounds?"

"Yes. You'll heal quickly, though I don't advise getting one. It still hurts like the devil." Though he said it lightly, the idea of Layla being knifed had his innards rolling.

Again she nodded. "I am stronger than the average human, yes?"

"Stronger, faster, more agile. Yes."

"And aging? Augustus does not. Will I?" Her eyes went wide. "Will you?"

He sighed, wanting to rub his aching neck. "I will not. As

for you? It depends. Elementals do. And some others. But I suspect you will not."

She expelled a breathy sigh. "Good."

"Good?" He gave a humorless laugh. "Why on earth would you not want to age? For I'll tell you truthfully, Layla. Those who are forced to see the world age and die around them often go mad. I, for one, do not look forward to that."

Slowly she shook her head, her expression soft. "Nor I. But I would hate to think of aging while you remained the same, Saint."

Hell, but she could slay him so easily. His battered heart squeezed at her simple words, and his throat threatened to close tight. "Layla..." His voice drifted off. He really did not know what to say at any rate.

Perhaps she understood, because she straightened her spine and faced him. "Right then. Well, thank you for explaining." With that, she turned and headed out of the room.

Sin stood. "Where are you going?" He took a step or two, ready to follow. "And why on earth are you dressed in that manner?" He'd been meaning to ask but the woman had a way of distracting him.

She stopped by the front door and accepted a big, mannish overcoat from Pole. "Out," she said to Sin as she slipped the coat on. A big, cheeky grin spread over her face. "Dressed as a man, obviously."

"Care to elaborate where 'out' entails?" he snapped, accepting his coat from Pole before doing a double-take. The butler had had the coat in hand, brushed and ready to go. Sin wrenched it on as Layla left the house.

She set off down the walk. "To wander the city. Get some fresh... well, not fresh air, but some air."

"Why not take the coach?" Sin did not like Layla so exposed.

She gave him a sidelong glance. "St. John Evernight, you've just told me that I am an immortal woman, stronger than the average male. Do you really believe I'd hide myself away in a carriage anymore? When I can walk free as I please, without fear of being assaulted?" She shook her head as if he were daft. "You cannot understand the freedom I've just been given."

"Keep your voice down," he said as they wove past a pair of slow-strolling women. "And I do understand. At one point, I too went from believing myself mortal to understanding there was a new world waiting for me."

"No," she said. "You only think you understand."

"You're reading my mind now, are you?" he said with a small laugh.

"You are a man, Sin. Which means, even at your weakest, you've never experienced the worries that women must face." She took wide, swinging strides and grinned down at her legs, encased in loosely cut trousers. "Even your clothing is not the constricting torture chamber that is a woman's gown."

"All right, then, Miss Newly Emancipated. Where shall we go?"

Unfortunately, as Sin suspected, she led them to one of the worst parts of London.

"You're actively trying to drive me mad, aren't you?" he grumbled as she insisted on heading for the London docks.

"Hardly." Layla leaned close, her voice low but pleased. "We have to go somewhere rough. How else are we going to be attacked?"

Sin stopped short, grabbing hold of Layla's elbow in the process. She swung around to face him. "Now see here. Pretending to be a young lad out for a walk is one thing. Actively looking for trouble is another." She moved to protest, and he hauled her closer. "You do not have to worry about most humans, little bird. But there are monsters out here more than willing to take a bite. It is nothing to treat lightly."

Her wide, brown eyes searched his face. "I know that, Saint. It is the monsters I intend to fight."

His blood ran cold. "Jesus, Layla. I could put you over my knee for the very thought."

She laughed then, a seductive, drolly amused sound. "Oh, dear Saint, I should like to see you try."

"There will be no trying involved, Layla."

Her lips twitched and, God help him, he wanted her to needle him just a bit further. He liked the idea of spanking her round arse until it was pink. And that caused his blood to run cold. Mab had loved to tie her men up, inflict pain until they pled. Had she turned him so vile?

He blinked and straightened enough to put a reasonable distance between him and Layla. Not that she noticed. She frowned up at him, a little furrow working over her brow.

"Saint, sparring with you is well and good, but it isn't real. When I sang for my instructor, it was not the same as standing on a stage in front of others." She let out an exasperated breath. "One might well freeze under the strain. Applicable experience is necessary."

Sin's ire deflated. She was right, of course. Augustus had trained him in the field.

"All right," he said. "We'll wander around. But you listen to me. If we encounter something you cannot take on, we leave. No arguments."

Her eyes flashed with excitement. "And you expect them to simply let us leave?"

Sin gave her a look. "No. I expect to knock them senseless, and then we leave."

Chapter Fourteen

Layla had expected Sin to follow her out of the house. She'd counted on it, in truth. To the point where she'd asked Pole to have Sin's coat ready as well as hers. What she had not expected, however, was his capitulation when it came to seeking out a fight.

Oh, he'd fussed but she suspected that had far more to do with his enjoyment of verbal sparring with her rather than any true objection. So then, they were going to hunt for monsters.

Layla could not think of them as anything else. It was simply too fantastical for her to wrap her head around, this whole notion of demons, werewolves, and beings capable of changing shapes. How extraordinary that she too was one of these strange fiends. She wished she remembered the change. She wanted to look at herself in a mirror and see what she became.

"Do you miss singing?" Sin asked at her side. They were walking through a crowded section of The Strand, headed towards Covent Garden. It was nearing five in the evening and many a clerk were already at the pubs. Men spilled out onto the streets, mugs of ale in hand.

"Yes," she said simply. A thud of pain hit her chest. "Deeply."

Frowning, he glanced at her. "I'm sorry, little bird."

She could not speak so she gave a tight nod.

"What happened?"

Layla cleared her throat. "Augustus tells me it is because I reached my immortal maturity. All I can tell you is that one day, I opened my mouth and instead of hearing sweet, clear notes, ugly garbled sounds came out."

She shuddered, burrowing deeper into her overcoat. "I didn't know what to think. Perhaps I had picked up a throat chill. Which would make better sense if I'd felt ill. I was fine, however, save for my voice."

Sin's arm brushed against hers. Though they both wore suits and heavy coats to ward off the frosty air, she felt the touch along her entire side. And when his gloved pinky found her gloved pinky and he hooked his over hers, her body went warm.

They walked for a time, linked by that small contact. And then Sin spoke again. "Do you miss the stage?"

"No," she said without hesitation. When he raised a brow, she shook her head. "Honestly, I do not. When I first took to the stage, it was…How can I explain? It was exhilarating, exciting. All those people watching me, rapt and adoring. I had them in the palm of my hand, just by singing them a song."

Oh, she did miss that bit. She missed the way her body would flush with heat, her nipples tightening along with her sex—the way her heart beat strong and the sense of pure power that flowed over her when she sang. But she could not explain that to Sin, not without blushing, hot and red.

"But it was exhausting," she said truthfully. "And the

pressure to perform taxed my nerves. For there were always those who loved nothing more than to pick me apart."

Sin's pinkie twitched as if he wanted to fist his hands. "Critics, you mean."

"They are a part of the world." Layla took a breath. "At any rate, I was ready for a long rest. But to never sing again? For my personal enjoyment? That does hurt."

Sin threaded all of his fingers through hers, clasping her hand in a firm but gentle grip. "Little bird."

That was all he said, but it was enough. She held onto him. "Do you ever sing, Saint?"

His lips curled, just a bit. "Sing? No, I cannot say I've ever tried it."

"You should try. I would love to hear you sing."

Those green eyes of his crinkled at the corners. "And what would you like to hear me sing?"

"Oh, anything," she said with a sigh. "As long as it was for me."

"Who else would I sing for, if not you?"

Layla smiled at that.

The streets grew close. The light was dim, the foul smell of rotting food and waste thicker now, the clothing others wore thinner and ragged. Women lounged around doorways and street corners, while men idled in groups, laughing and eyeing people who walked by.

An emaciated dog skittered past, chasing what appeared to be a rat.

"No one is looking our way," Layla murmured. She'd expected to be noticed. Hers and Sin's clothes were too fine, their good health too apparent. People here were sallow of skin and thin to the point of being gaunt.

"We are cloaked," he said. "Humans will not notice us unless I let them."

"Can I do that?"

His lips curved up at one corner. "Sorry, love, that's a Judgment power."

"Drat."

His low chuckle cut short as the wind changed and a terrible odor drifted past.

"What is that?" she asked, pinching her nostrils closed. It was thick, foul, with a sickly-cloying tinge that had her nerves twitching.

The square hinge of Sin's jaw bunched. "Death." He eased her behind him as he stared down the dark maw of an alleyway. "Stay close."

Layla followed him deeper into the alley, and the narrow walls seemed to close in on them. The sounds of the streets dampened, the air growing colder, fouler. The passage veered to the left and then opened up at a crossway behind a set of dilapidated buildings. There, in the middle, a woman's body lay sprawled upon the dirt.

The body was clothed in a tatty dress the color of mud. Her neck was torn open, and thick, glistening blood painted the front of the woman's bodice. A lake of blood spread out beneath the body, little eddies of it running along the crevices in the dirt.

Layla knew she ought to be disgusted. And part of her was—her skin going clammy, her insides lurching. But the moment her gaze strayed to the blood, her gums began to ache, her heart pounded hard and insistent.

Sin moved like mist, his long body silent and graceful as it seemed to glide along. She tried to focus on him. But the blood kept calling her attention. Beneath the foul scent of death, it tickled her nostrils, enticing her. Gods, why did it smell so marvelous? Like bitter hot chocolate one moment, then new pennies the next—both delicious and then not.

Something sharp touched her bottom lip, a point on each

side of it. Shocked, she tentatively let her tongue move to one of the protuberances and discovered a long fang. She had fangs. Her breath hitched, which caused more of the blood scent to invade her senses.

Before her, Sin was crouching over the body, his features tight with concentration. Inky strands of his hair fell over his brow and the tips shone the color of new blood. The strong line of his neck peeked out from the velvet lining of his collar. Layla did not know why the sight fascinated her so, but she could not look away from that exposed flesh.

His skin was already winter pale. Skin the color of fresh cream, smooth and tight. If she peered hard, she could just see the blue river of his vein. Which was odd. She'd never noticed his veins before. But there they were, flowing with fresh blood. Her gums throbbed, her throat suddenly so very dry.

"...Appears to be a demon kill," Sin was saying. "They like to steal blood and use it to take on the victim's identity. The blood helps them take the victim's shape, you see..."

Blood. That would make this sharp hunger abate. But not that old, cold blood upon the ground. No, Sin's blood would be better. Warm and luscious.

"...What I do not understand is why this poor woman. Usually they go for wealthy or powerful victims."

He craned his head, studying the body, and even more of his neck came into view. Strong flesh, taut skin. A shudder ran through her, and she bit back a groan.

Sin's head whipped round and he pinned her with a narrowed gaze of brilliant green. "Layla," he said in a low voice.

She shook her head, unable to speak. Saliva filled her mouth, her tongue pushing up against her teeth. It would be so easy to knock him down, press her body against his lean strength, and that smooth skin would break like the finest sugar crust under her fangs, letting hot blood flow over her tongue.

In a fluid move, Sin stood. "Layla, tap it down." His voice was hard now. "Look at my eyes, Layla."

His eyes? Yes, they were lovely, but not as lovely as his flesh. He smelled divine. She licked her swollen lips and his gaze snapped there. For a long moment he stared at her mouth, and she felt it as if he'd stroked her sensitized lips.

One taste. Her body flushed with heat. One little sip.

"Layla!" Sin's sharp tone made her flinch, and she glanced up at his eyes. Silver-green now, he glared at her. "Do not look away from my eyes."

Slowly he advanced on her, never looking away. A strange noise rose up from her throat. A growl.

"You will look at my eyes and hear my voice," Sin said in a deep tone.

She could not ignore him when he spoke that way. He moved closer. His scent surrounded her, smoky-spice like Christmas pudding. She swayed, her vision blurring.

And then he was before her, his hands clasping her arms hard enough to capture her attention. His commanding voice flowed over her. "Look at me."

She did, suddenly frightened and cold. "Sin . . . I want . . ." She licked her dry lips. "I need."

"Yes, I know," he said, soothing but firm. Green eyes peered down at her, his black brows drawing together. "I know, little bird. But you must come back to me now. Focus on my voice."

His voice was lovely too, beautifully modulated and clear. A tenor if he sang. His hands caressed the sides of her arms, and she felt she could breathe. She leaned into his hold, letting him brace her. His caresses did not stop—up and down, up and down.

Suddenly her head was clear. "Saint, what happened just then?"

"Blood lust," he said, frowning again. He gave her arms a squeeze then his hands left her.

"Blood lust." A tentative flick of her tongue told her the fangs were now gone. "Yes, I wanted..." A shudder went through her, and she felt ill. "God, Sin, I wanted your blood."

His expression grew wry. "So I noticed." He touched her cheek, a fleeting stroke. "It's all right, little bird. I don't hold it against you."

She wanted to smile, but the sound of laughter, ugly and thin, filled the air. Layla stiffened and looked round. "Did you hear that?"

"Hear what?" Sin glanced about. "What did you hear?"

Layla hugged herself close. "I thought...no, I heard laughter." She did not like his worried expression. "You didn't hear it, did you?"

"No," he said slowly. "But that does not mean I don't believe you did."

Again came the laughter, and again Sin did not react. Tiny feet of icy cold seemed to dance up her spine, and she leaned closer to Sin. "Take me home. I do not feel up for fighting anymore today."

"Of course," Sin began, but stopped when six men appeared at the mouth of the alleyway.

Ugly-looking thugs, they spread out, blocking the exit. Layla might have thought them street roughs but their eyes were all yellow.

"Raptor demons," Sin said at her ear. "Looks like we'll have our fight after all."

But then the leader did something truly odd: he bowed. "Mistress, we have come to ye."

* * *

Mistress? Sin had to have heard wrong. But there they were, six raptor demons bowing and edging closer to Layla as if she were the queen herself.

She frowned at him and then at the demons. "I'm sorry, but I believe you have me confused with someone else. I don't know you."

The leader, a large and lumpy brute who was wearing his human form rather shabbily, for it kept flicking in and out over his true shape, stepped forward. "Aye, but we know you. Our lady. Our leader. Did ye like our offering?" He gestured to the body on the ground. "Nice an' fresh, it is."

"You..." Layla blanched. "Did this for me? Why?"

The demon tilted his head, his thick brow furrowing. "Does my lady prefer male bodies? We could gladly—"

"No," Layla nearly shouted, her skin white with horror. "Not necessary. I should merely like to understand why you left this for me. Who do you think I am?"

"You are Layla Starling, daughter of Lena, our lady. Thus you are our lady as well."

They all bowed again.

"Our lady Lena preferred blood to all other foods. As do you, yes?" The big lug looked so hopeful that Sin wanted to laugh. But he was too unnerved.

As was Layla, who pressed her hand to her cheek. "That is very...kind of you. However, I'd rather...acquire my own..." She swallowed hard. "Food."

"But my lady, it is our pleasure and duty."

Layla stood up straight, the wings of her brows lifting. "Have you been leaving bodies before now?"

"Of course."

Another one chimed in. "You liked them well enough. Drank all their blood right up."

"I'm going to be ill," she murmured. Then in a louder voice, "You must stop. I cannot abide by murder."

At this, all six demons reared back, their expressions displaying varying levels of disgust and shock.

"No murder?" said their leader. "What would ye have us do, then, if not murder?"

"Look," Layla said, "I do not know what sort of arrangement you had with my mother. But I am not her."

"No," said one, his lip curling over a lowering fang. "You are not."

"Nor are you fit for my lord king?" said another.

"And who is this lord king?" Sin asked.

Apparently they'd either forgotten he was there or never really paid him heed to begin with, for all six demons' gazes snapped to him. The air of goodwill grew decidedly chilly.

"You? You've the glow of angels on ye."

Glow? He glowed? Sin glanced down despite himself. Layla gave him a glance too. Her lip twitched. "Well, I don't see it."

"Rudding, angelic being, with our mistress."

"Not ours if that's the company she keeps."

"Aye, she's a right disappointment. Unworthy."

"Whoring with angels."

"Enough," Sin snapped. "Go now before I show you how very angelic I can be."

The leader sneered. "As if we'd be afraid of a bloomin' angel."

Sin grinned. "I'm afraid I'm not an angel." Not the being they considered an angel, at any rate. "Though I do have wings." He let them snap out and turned full Judgment.

One of the demons backed up. "What the hellfire is that?"

"Looks like an angel to me. It's got wings."

Raptor demons weren't the smartest lot.

He looked down at Layla. "Do you want to practice fighting or shall I simply dispatch them?"

The demons had shed their human skins, growing larger, their skin turning shades of earthen green or blood red.

Layla edged closer to him. "You mean to take them all on?"

"This is nothing, but if you'd like to fight them, I'll wait a bit before getting rid of them."

Truthfully, he did not want them getting anywhere near Layla, but she had asked for applicable experience. He would not deny her that. But Layla shook her head. "They brought me gifts. I cannot raise a hand to them."

"True. And now they mean to hurt you."

"Take a taste of her too," said the leader, clearly listening in. "Royal blood and flesh in me mouth, on me bob and tackle. How sweet."

Sin glared. Enough was enough. They weren't touching Layla. Not now. Not ever.

The leader jumped, intent on toppling Sin. He met with Sin's fist instead, his body flying back with a crash. The others attacked. Sin let the ice within him go. Frozen demons fell to the ground. Sin might have been inclined to let them go, had they not made it clear they'd intended to hurt Layla. The mere thought of her being defiled by their hands had whips of lightning arching from Sin's hands, snapping into them.

The demons vaporized, leaving behind only trails of smoke and scattered bits of black ice.

Layla gaped up at him. "Good lord, is that what you do as Judgment?"

Sin rolled his tight shoulders while returning to his natural-born form. "No, that was what I do as Sin Evernight. As Judgment, I would suck out their souls and send them to hell."

Her brown eyes were round and glossy in the pale oval of her face. "Why did you not do that this time?"

Because it felt too good to simply kill, didn't it? You relished the moment their bodies blew to bits, didn't you?

Sin frowned. "Did you hear that?" For the voice had most definitely not come from inside his head.

Layla's pretty mouth pinched. "I heard the laughing again. What did you hear?"

Tell her, St. John. Tell her how good it feels to kill. To fuck. To cause pain. Take her with you into the hells. Do what you were born to do.

Sin took a deep breath. "Nothing." He grabbed hold of her elbow. "Let us go."

Layla heard laughter; he heard mocking. Something was out there. Something powerful enough to send thoughts into one's head. It wasn't Augustus, but Sin had a bad notion that it was something equally ancient and strong.

You would be correct, young Evernight. Run, run, run, as fast as you can.

Chapter Fifteen

Augustus

He'd failed. The disappointment was so crushing that it took effort to walk back to his hotel. For some time now, he'd known Lena would never be his. Nor would he force the issue; love was worthless if it was not freely given. But he had not thought she would turn her back on her child in need.

Anger swirled in his chest, making it hard to breathe. He rarely became enraged; it was not advisable. But the emotion would not be denied and it seeped from his body, infecting the very air around him.

As he passed them, humans began to stir as if agitated. Their movements became jerky, quick, as they glanced about as if to seek the source of their disquiet. One man looking over his shoulder bumped into another man. Immediately they began to fight, shoving and shouting. It rippled outward from them; more humans fighting, little groups of squabbles.

For a sharp moment he wanted to enter the fray, hit and slash, slice that soft human flesh into bits. He could taste their blood on his tongue, feel their bones crunching under his fists just as surely as if he'd actually done the deed. A shiver went through him. This was why he did not lose control. The angel in him, that inhuman warrior who knew only battle and retribution, craved the fight.

Augustus picked up his pace, knowing that as soon as he was out of range, their anger would ebb. Even so, the shrill sounds of a policeman's whistle cut through the air, the cries of annoyed humans growing louder.

When he neared St. Stephen's Cathedral, the streets thinned of all pedestrian traffic. He did not think much of it until a wave of unnatural heat, like that of a baker's oven doors being thrown open, flowed over his shoulders. The rotten scent of brimstone followed in its wake. Damnation. He turned, half expecting to see Lena yet knowing it would not be her.

Some fifty feet away, a male figure lounged against the doorway of a now-empty tavern, his silhouette limned in gold by the gaslight flickering overhead. The male gave him a slow, easy smile, his fangs glinting white in the dim. "Quite the disturbance you caused just now, Judgment."

Augustus kept his back to the cathedral. "I'm beginning to wonder if it was all my doing."

The Damnation pushed off from the wall and sauntered forward. "I'm afraid so. Though their rage made such a lovely song, I could not help but follow it."

When he was ten feet from Augustus he stopped. His skin was a deep, blood red, his hair like pitch. They were evenly matched in height, but Augustus knew that, when at full power, the Damnation could grow to top twelve feet.

"And you thought you'd drop in for a chat, did you?"

Augustus said mildly. Inwardly, however, he took stock of his powers and found them sadly lacking. If this Damnation was pure blood or bred, he'd be in for trouble. Augustus did not know this particular one on sight; so few of them existed on this plane anymore.

The Damnation gave a brief smile. "You know why I'm here."

Augustus suspected he did. Thing was, he didn't particularly want to die today. Unfortunately, the Damnation chose that moment to unfurl his wings. They snapped open, revealing wings that were not batlike but angelic in shape. Wings like St. John's, only so deeply red they appeared almost black.

This was not a half-breed but one made by the source of all Damnation. Perhaps Augustus would die today after all. "What are you called?" He would know that much about his attacker.

The Damnation smiled again. "Such manners." He gave a little bow, and his wings rose high as little flames began to dance down their length. "My maker calls me Enoch."

Son of Cain. So few knew that Damnation had started with Cain—not an angel but a son of the first fallen. Child of the devil. In Egyptian times, he'd been known as Anubis. So many names, but all led back to one constant.

As if reading his thoughts, the male named Enoch spoke again. "You may call me Death."

Augustus laughed then, slowly gathering up anger. "And you may call me Judgment, servant of Maat and Thoth. And death, my dear fellow, is just the beginning of another journey."

Enoch launched at him with a snarl. Augustus leapt high and quick, flipping over the male and landing on the other side. Just as Enoch turned, Augustus kicked high, catching the Damnation on the chin. His head snapped back with a loud crack. Augustus kicked again, low and sweeping his opponent's legs. But Enoch was quicker, jumping at the last moment.

His volleying hits smashed into Augustus with the force of a cannon. Flames shot from Enoch's fists, incinerating Augustus's clothes. He turned full Judgment, his wings snapping out, his flesh going hard and clear.

They fought with equal fervor. One good kick to the gut sent Enoch crashing into the side of the cathedral. The ground shook, the bells gently rang.

"That is all you have?" Enoch asked with a laugh. "Kicks and hits?"

A rolling wave of white-hot flame rushed over Augustus. And another. Taking his breath, singeing his lungs. He snapped his wings in front of him like a shield then used the one true power he had left.

What is it that you fear, Enoch?

The Damnation flinched as Augustus's voice filled his head.

"Is that your power?" Enoch asked with a sneer. "Silly parlor tricks? Oh, very sad."

Oh, but I see you. I see your fear. Cain found you a failure, did he?

Enoch shouted and threw another blast of fire at Augustus. "You know nothing."

I know you cannot return to his side. You've been cast out. Doomed to wander just as the Cain of myth was doomed. You hate this world, and yet you cannot leave it.

"Cease!" Enoch flew forward, his body colliding into Augustus's.

They fell to the cobbles, the stones flying upward upon impact. Enoch's fist smashed into Augustus's face, breaking his cheekbone.

You will fail. Always. It is written in your soul.

Enoch lashed out again, but Augustus rolled, evading the hit.

Damnation. Never loved. Never accepted. Cold and lonely.

Enoch screamed, his eyes flashing yellow. He shook with rage and the terror Augustus thrust into his mind. But it was not enough. Augustus knew he was merely buying time. He was not strong enough anymore. He had to run from this.

But it was too late. Enoch caught hold of his wing. With a roar, the Damnation ripped it from Augustus's body.

Unlike St. John's wings, Augustus's were part of his flesh, and the loss sent shards of jagged agony along his spine. The wing landed with a wet thud on the ground. Augustus rolled, throwing up an arm to deflect the next blow, but Enoch's clawed hand knocked it aside and punched into his chest.

"No!" The scream seemed to ring from his very soul. But it was not his voice Augustus heard.

A blur of shadows descended upon his failing sight. Enoch was thrust away, his body battered from side to side as hits rained down upon him.

Augustus blinked, clearing his vision. It was Lena, her eyes flashing red, her body growing taller and taller with wings the color of obsidian stretched out behind her. Wings the shape of a bat's with razor sharp claws at the tips and joints. Those claws sliced into Enoch's middle like a scythe through wheat.

Enoch stumbled back, grabbed hold of his spilling guts with one hand. He hissed, his fangs descending. Swiping with a speed too fast to track, the Damnation knocked into Lena.

Augustus lurched up, shouting out as Lena's crimson blood sprayed wide, her wings falling to the ground.

But she did not fall. Even as she bled she attacked, obsidian blades conjured in hand, whirling in the dim light. Enoch fled, gone into ether and leaving them alone on the street.

Augustus

For a moment Lena stood tall, her slim form a slice of blackness against the streetlights. Then she sagged and turned back to Augustus. From across the way her gaze met his, and his chest, gaping and flowing silver blood, constricted. She mouthed his name, her expression shattered.

And then she was at his side, her arms pulling him close against her breast.

"Lena," he whispered, his shaking hand touching her cheek. "Love, your wings."

She touched her forehead to his. "Yours too." She pressed a palm over his wound, and he hissed. Warmth flooded the area.

"Do not drain yourself to heal me," he snapped, though his voice was weak.

"Shut up," she answered softly. The streets were abandoned, their emptying caused by Enoch's powers, but they would soon fill with humans once more. They'd certainly notice a nude man and a woman covered in blood. Lena helped Augustus stand. Together, they walked the short distance to the inn where he'd let a room, Lena using her powers to cloak them from sight.

"You knew I was here," he observed mildly. "For how long?"

She made a scoffing noise. "I knew the moment you stepped foot in Vienna."

Once in his room, she helped him into bed. That she utterly ignored his undressed state was rather insulting but, as he was in no condition to do anything, he supposed it was for the best.

To his surprise, she stripped down to her chemise and knickers and followed him under the covers, holding him against her side.

They sagged into each other, and he felt the strangest sensation. Light, soft brushes against his temple. His breath caught, and his eyes closed as she gently kissed him.

"Augustus." Her voice was broken. "Why won't you heal?"

Silver blood oozed over her fingers where they pushed against his chest.

"As I said, I am fading."

She stilled. When she spoke again, it was snappish and demanding. "Do not be ridiculous. You don't fade from this life because of a wound. You heal. Heal yourself this instant and stop playing games with me."

He could not help but smile. "Not from this. Or perhaps so." His weak attempt at levity was met with a scowl. And he suppressed a sigh. "It is the curse. My time here is at an end, Lena."

He thought her still before. Now she was stone. They sat in utter silence.

Her sob broke it. "Do not make me choose, Augustus." A shudder went through her. "Do not make me do it."

He closed his eyes, utterly weary. "I am not asking anymore, Lena. I am done."

He felt her jerk, heard her swallow. Guilt crept over his heart but he ignored it. He would no longer beg. He'd go and be at peace. But he needed to fix things with Layla first. He needed to set eyes on her one last time.

Lena's voice flowed over him, sad and thin. "My soul would taint yours."

It was his turn to flinch, and his eyes flew open. Her expression was forlorn but stubborn—as usual. But the dark sorrow in her eyes was new. For a long moment, he stared at her.

"Is that what you think?" he said finally. "It that truly why you've resisted all these years? For fear that you will taint me?"

Her pert chin lifted a touch. "I do not *think* it. I *know* it. We join souls, and mine will corrupt yours."

Augustus lurched to a sitting position, his body swaying with effort, but he half-turned so that he might face her. "Woman, were I not so weakened, I might have a true fit about now. How can you be so utterly stupid, so incredibly blind—"

"Do not throw names at my head! I state only the truth—"

He grabbed her by the nape and hauled her close, his mouth crashing into hers. Damn it all, he was done. Her lips were plump and perfect. She resisted for a breath but then yielded, her kiss as angry as his, biting, seeking, her tongue thrusting into his mouth as if she was the one starved for a taste.

His fingers threaded through her silken hair as he kissed her back, letting himself take what he'd always wanted to be offered. And there were only the sounds of them enjoying each other's mouths until, with a snarl, he broke away, not letting her go, but pulling back enough to meet her slightly dazed gaze. "Who am I?" he demanded.

She frowned, licked her wet lips—which made his cock pulse—then frowned again. "Augustus."

"No." He gave her nape a small squeeze. "Who *am* I?"

Her dark gaze bore into his. "You are Judgment."

"And my word is law." Another squeeze, a little shake. "And how did I judge you?"

"I... You deemed me worthy to live." Her cheeks flushed red at that.

"I deemed you *mine*." He ground his teeth to keep from shouting. "I deemed you my other half. So tell me, Lena mine, if you can accept that I am Judgment, why can you not accept that my word is law?"

She pulled back, her gaze cutting away.

"No," he said, "do not evade. Answer the question."

"How..." Her teeth met with a click before she looked at him again, her dark eyes flashing. "How can you love me?"

"I don't know," he answered truthfully, almost laughing when she appeared hurt by his reply. "But I do. Love just is."

Gods but she was stubborn. Her chin lifted again, her sweet mouth set in a straight line.

"The question is," he said, "do you love me? If you do, then get off your arse and claim me. For once I go, so does your chance."

Chapter Sixteen

Another ball, another bloody night of watching Layla dance with other men, laugh and chat with them. And all night her gaze would collide with his, the elegant sweep of her brow lifting upward slightly as if to say, *Well, when shall you throw your hat in?*

She was not taunting Sin; no. Layla was simply showing him that life would go on with or without him. Which stung just as painfully.

He could choose her, choose to live among light and happiness. But he would not take what was offered without her knowing all of him. And there was the rub. To do that, he would have to tell her of his past, of the things he had done.

Call it pride, self-preservation, it did not matter; Sin thought about opening his mouth and letting the truth pour out, and he promptly felt ill. He remembered his sister Miranda's look of utter disgust when she'd found out he'd been with Mab. It gutted him then; it gutted him now.

To see even a shadow of that in Layla's eyes would be a wound from which he would not recover. Better to watch her from afar and do some good in the world than lose all and fall to bitterness.

Still, it chafed. And when it was time to go, as Sin escorted her down the wide stairs of some fussy lord's townhome it was all he could do not to pull her aside and claim her mouth. He wanted to imprint himself on her skin, surround her with his scent so that any Other within a hundred miles would know she was his.

Like a damn dog, he thought with a shake of his head. He would not do that to Layla. St. John Evernight's name was as good as mud.

"Had you a good time?" he asked her politely—or as damn well near it as he could manage—as they made their way along the side of the drive.

"Well enough." She kept her eyes to the pavement, the line of her shoulders hunched beneath her silver silk cape. "I am tired now."

The ball had been a crush and carriages were lined three deep on the drive, not one of them making headway. Drivers sat casually on their seats, smoking pipes and cigarettes, knowing full well they weren't going anywhere for some time.

Sin had asked his driver to wait on the road to avoid the traffic snarls. The night was clear and cold, the moon drifting in and out of sight behind the lacy clouds. It was coming on three in the morning. Behind them came the light sounds of the ball, still going on. But here on the street, where the lamps were flickering and shadows lurked where their light could not touch, it felt too quiet.

Sin moved his hand to the small of Layla's back. She stiffened, going straight, her eyes clear and focused now. "What is it?"

He loved the way her mind worked, as if she was his

partner, not his charge. He pressed his hand a little more securely to her back, feeling her warmth and the neat curve of her spine through the layers of clothing. "I do not know. Something is off."

She nodded, her fine features tight with concentration. "And that scent… I cannot quite place it."

"Scent?" He drew in a deep breath. There, just a hint. Brimstone. Sin tensed. "Shit."

"What?"

Sin did not have time to answer. In a blink, a figure stood in the middle of the street.

"St. Claire?" Layla said. He hadn't been at the ball, something Sin had been grateful for at the time.

"Hello, my dear. Did you miss me?"

Layla's nose wrinkled. But Sin spoke first. "You smell of hellfire, St. Claire."

"Mmm… So I do." St. Claire shrugged. "I grew weary of cloaking it."

That wasn't all he'd been cloaking. Sin could feel the power coming off him in waves that rippled through the air and punched into his chest. St. Claire was not some low-level demon or bored Elemental.

Brimstone marked him as a being of Nowhere. A Primus—or one of the original supernaturals, born of the fears of human thought and not diluted with centuries of human interbreeding. At least, that was what Sin hoped St. Claire was. However, he feared it was not.

"Is this a social call, then?" Sin asked lightly. He would not be able to use fire on a being who smelled of brimstone. They loved heat. Ice, earth, lightning. Those would have to be his tools, for he knew full well St. Claire had no intention of letting Sin walk away.

As if he heard Sin's thoughts, St. Claire gave him a lazy

smile. "I rather thought I'd take Layla home with me. Get better acquainted."

Sin laughed. "And here I thought Primus were without humor."

"I am no Primus, boy." St. Claire transformed before their eyes, growing in height, his skin darkening to blood red, his hair fading to black. Powerful wings rose behind him.

"Damnation," Sin said, his blood pumping with the need to kill. *And so it begins.*

Yellow-gold eyes flashed. "Sired by the Original."

Bollocks. Sin did not want to fight this thing with Layla here. It would be messy and brutal, his chances of survival about even with St. Claire's. But he'd long ago discovered that what he wanted and what he got were two different things. St. Claire had no intention of letting them walk away. And Sin had no intention of cowering.

"Jolly good for you, mate," Sin said as if unaffected. "That still won't help you tonight."

St. Claire's grin was wide and crooked. "So self-assured for a young one." He shook his head, tutting under his breath. "Before we start, I thought you might want this." He tossed something through the air, and it landed with a sick thud at Sin's feet. St. Claire shrugged. "I have no use for it, at any rate."

A strangled cry left Layla, and her grip tightened on Sin's sleeve. He stared down at the dull-silvery shape on the ground as his body began to tremble: Augustus's wing. The stump raged—a knob of bone, like a broken joint, poking from its end.

The ground rumbled as ice raced along the pavers and over his skin.

"Layla," he said, not taking his eyes from St. Claire. "I need you to step back."

"Not a bloody chance," she growled.

He almost smiled at the belligerence in her tone, but he was too angry. "Yes, love, but I need a bit of room."

"Oh," she whispered. And when he felt her drift off, he let forth a blast of ice.

St. Claire jumped high, straight into the lightning bolt Sin released. The bastard's body thrashed about in midair before falling down. He landed in a tumble then leapt to his feet, his wings smoking, his white-blond hair blazing.

"Not bad, St. John. My turn now."

He came at Sin like a storm. His speed was blinding, too fast for Sin to keep up. Razor sharp claws slashed through him again and again. Sin's hot blood splattered over St. Claire's grinning face.

From a distance, he heard Layla shouting. Sin could only fight back, try to get a hit in, try to freeze the air around them to slow St. Claire down. And then St. Claire let loose another power, a high-pitched sound so strong that Sin's head felt as if it would break apart.

He stumbled back and got a kick to the ribs. Crashing to the ground, he rolled away just before St. Claire's foot smashed down.

Bollocks to this. Sin sent a punch of power just beneath St. Claire's feet. The ground opened up, and the Damnation toppled into the deep cavern. Sin closed it tight; then, using his waning power, froze it solid.

It was a struggle to get to his feet. But he only had moments. And he was going to use them to fight another day. Layla ran to his side.

"Saint. Oh God, I thought he'd kill you." Soft hands fluttered over his flayed skin. "Sin. What did he do to you?"

He caught her up in his arms. "Hold tight, love."

She did, pressing herself close, her arms going around his

neck. Sin took a breath and launched himself upward, praying that he'd have the strength to carry them both.

Layla knew she ought to be afraid. She kept telling herself this as Sin opened his massive silver wings and launched up into the sky. She ought to be terrified seeing the ground grow farther away, the houses appear smaller, the fissure caused by Sin's fight with St. Claire nothing more than a small crack on the street. But she was not scared. She was exhilarated.

Wind whistled in her ears; her innards felt buoyant and her head oddly heavy. She laid it on his shoulder and heard the gentle *whoosh* of his wings. Blood, deep red yet glittering with flecks of silver, soaked his shirt and crusted on his skin. He'd had so many deep gashes that she'd wanted to scream. But they were already healed up now, leaving behind nothing but smooth skin. Even so, she could not help but flick out her tongue and catch a line of rapidly drying blood. It tasted like butterscotch and bitter chocolate.

Sin stiffened at the touch. "Quit that, Layla. You'll make us fall."

Cringing, she burrowed her nose just under his chin. "Sorry."

"Lick me all you want later." His tone was only half jesting, but his grip was secure, and she was not afraid of falling. The air was cold and somewhere along the way she'd lost her cloak. But Sin was warm, almost too warm. Below her, the Thames shimmered like a black snake, winding through the glittering grid of the streetlamps and house lights of the city.

Just in front of them, St. Paul's familiar dome loomed. Layla glanced back from where they'd risen and saw a small, black blot rise up into the sky.

"I think he's following," she said, wanting to somehow crawl further into Sin.

He did not look back but held her tighter. "Steady now, we're going down."

She gave a little squeal when he dove, her stomach rising up into her chest. The ground rushed to greet them. At the last moment, Sin pulled up and landed on light feet just before St. Paul's. Not pausing, he rushed to the doors. They flew open with one well-placed kick.

Sin pushed inside then kicked the massive door shut again. Then he set her down. "Come," he said, taking hold of her hand.

The church was dark and cold, the sound of their footsteps echoing in the cavernous space.

Layla had been here many times, but not when it was closed. It felt wrong, somehow, to be invading this space now, as if the faces in the stained glass windows frowned down at them.

Outside she heard the unmistakable sound of thunder. It was loud enough to rattle her bones and echoed through the cathedral.

"Hurry," Sin said, not glancing back. "He's here."

Sin led them to the back of the church and down the stairs to the crypts below. Down the old stone steps they raced, Sin holding her hand so tightly and going so fast that she feared she'd lose her limb. But she clung to him like a lifeline. Fear skittered up her spine, and she'd rather not be trailing behind. Something Sin seemed to realize as well, for he glanced back, his expression grim.

"I'd carry you if I could." There was no room for that. Not with her bulky skirts in the way and the narrowness of the passage. They both knew as much. His voice was soft, not at all out of breath. "Just a bit farther."

The ground rumbled, trembling on all sides, and dust rained down from between the cracks in the old stones.

"He's going to bring it down on our heads." The idea terrorized her.

They reached a landing. "No," Sin said. "This is his church more than it is our sanctuary."

Layla skidded to a halt. "What?"

With a tug he kept her going, past the stone sarcophagi of England's long-dead royalty, knights, and heroes. "Do not dally."

"Why," she hissed, "did you bring us here if he can follow?"

Sin stopped by a large black sarcophagus deep within the crypt. Intricately carved with *cross pattée* and *fleur-de-lys*, it was situated under an archway against the wall. He dropped her hand and began to slide the top down. The heavy lid moved easily under his strength.

"He is a guardian. Which means he cannot destroy the abbey. But he is also damnation, which means he cannot enter consecrated grounds." Sin got the top halfway off. "Now jump in."

Layla balked. "Why? No. Why?"

His smile was swift and tight. "Because he just might try it regardless of the laws. And, yes, you are. This is made of iron, painted with the blood of a Templar knight. Damnation cannot touch it and keep his strength. Does that answer all your questions?"

"Not hardly."

Another violent tremor rent through the abbey, and she nearly jumped out of her skin. Cursing under her breath, she gathered up her skirts and made to climb in. Only she paused as a new horror occurred. "Is there a body inside?"

His green eyes twinkled. "There shall be two. Yours and mine." When she glared, he shook his head. "No bodies inside, Layla. Now get in."

She did as told, hating every moment. The space was cold

and dank and narrow. More so when Sin climbed in after her. Trying to give him room, she pressed herself against the wall of the coffin, and cold seeped through her clothes.

"How long must we remain?" she gritted out as he settled down next to her, his body so close their knees bumped and his shoulder moved under the curve of her neck.

"'Til dawn." Sin reached up and started to draw the lid over them, blocking out the weak light. "Which is close. Be still now."

"We'll be without air." Trepidation had her voice rising.

"There are a few holes," he said calmly. "I've had to lie here before."

"When?" She didn't really care, but simply needed to hear the sound of his voice as darkness stole over her.

"Training. We have safe places to hide but must learn to use them." His voice was soft. "Not all of them are this accommodating."

"I do not want to know," she vowed tightly.

"Likely not," he agreed before closing the lid completely.

And then there was nothing but a blackness so dense even her superior eyesight could not cut through it. The air grew thin and close, pulled out of her lungs. Layla tried to tell herself to calm but the walls of the tomb seemed to push in at all sides.

A tomb. She was in a tomb. Sin's body next to hers only served to highlight how tight the space was, how little air they had to share.

A sharp sound left her, and it sounded much like a whimper.

"I'm frightened, Sin. I'm sorry... You must let me out." Stars sparkled in the blackness as her breath grew short. "I cannot. I don't like the dark. Sin..." Panicked, she bucked, bashing her head on the lid.

"Shhh..." Sin's arm drew her closer, and his warm palm smoothed over her cheek. An anchor in the darkness. Gentle yet firm. He touched his lips to her forehead. "Easy, Layla. Easy. I am here. I won't let you go."

Shaking, Layla leaned into him. Her throat was raw, her corset too tight. "I cannot breathe. Saint..." A sob left her.

"Focus on me, little bird." As he spoke, he reached behind her and grabbed hold of her bodice. The delicate fabric ripped like paper. Another firm tug and her corset strings snapped.

Air rushed into her lungs. Sin murmured soothing nothing sounds as he pulled the corset from around her waist. It fell behind her, and then his wide palm was firm against her back, rubbing slow, gentle circles over her thin chemise. "It's all right now. It's all right."

A shuddering breath left her, and she sagged into his hold. They were face to face, her legs tangled with his, her palm spread wide on his chest where she could feel the steady beat of his heart.

For long moments, she simply rested her forehead against his and just breathed, listening to his quiet sounds of reassurance, feeling his hand explore her back. Warmth stole over her; exhaustion flooded her limbs. Despite the utter dark, her eyes fluttered closed.

"I'm sorry," she whispered after a time.

Sin paused. "Why?" His voice was just as soft.

"I should not have panicked."

His sigh brushed over her parted lips. "Don't ever apologize for your fear. Feeling keeps you human."

Layla snuggled closer to his warmth, moving carefully for fear he'd realize and put a distance between him. But he remained as he was, gently holding her. Carefully, she pressed her palm just a bit more steadily against his hard chest. "Have you ever been afraid?"

The muscles beneath her hand went tight. Silence descended and, with it, the horrible pressure of the dark. Perhaps he felt her impending panic, for he let out a slow breath and his thumb brushed her jaw. "Oh, little bird," he said in a small voice, "I've been afraid for years."

It punched her heart, and she found herself stroking his chest, slowly, gently. "Saint, what happened to you?"

He tensed again, his hard swallow audible. "She broke me."

Gods, she wished she could see his face. "Who? The woman that fae reminded you of?"

Sin's fingertips dug into the small of her back before he seemed to force his hand to relax. "Do not make me speak of her in the dark."

Because one could not hide from nightmares in the dark. Layla knew this well. Jealousy wasn't quite the emotion she felt. It was a dark cousin of it, hateful and violent, for she knew Sin had been hurt by this loathsome mystery woman.

"No, Saint," she reassured. "We shall not speak of her now." Wanting to comfort, she leaned in and kissed him, her lips landing softly on his cheek, close to the corner of his mouth.

They both went utterly still in that pitch black space. Despite being fast friends when they were young, they'd never done more than hold hands as children. Layla had been fifteen when they'd parted, desperately in love with him, but a girl just the same.

This kiss was nothing more than a press of lips to skin. And yet the action felt irrevocable, as if she'd stepped over a line in the sand. Beside her, Sin's breath grew light, almost stopping completely. She could feel his shock, as if he'd been taken utterly off guard and didn't know what to do. His lean body was close to hers, enough for her to want to press closer and absorb all that lovely warm strength.

Neither of them moved or said a word. Layla's lips felt

full and sensitive. She needed to do that again. But before she could try, the trembling tips of his fingers ghosted over her jaw. When he reached the lower curve of her lip, he paused. Layla's belly clenched in anticipation.

The soft gust of his exhaling was her only warning. And then his lips touched hers. Hesitant, as if he too were afraid to break the spell, and yet he moved away slowly, lingering.

Heat bloomed over her skin and washed through her limbs. A small sound of want escaped her. And he heard it. Again his lips returned, his upper lip brushing against her upper lip, parting her mouth just a bit. Again his mouth drifted away.

Layla dared not move. Oh, but she wanted. For so long she'd dreamed of kissing Sin. Of him kissing her. Now it was time, and she wanted to relish every second. Her body felt heavy, languid. Only her mouth was mobile, throbbing and needy. She lay in the dark, listening to the sounds of their disjointed breathing and the frantic beat of her own heart.

More. More. More. Please give me more.

And he did. Light, exploring touches, as if he too wanted to take his time. She nuzzled in, and took her own kiss. His full lips were soft but firm. A puff of breath left them when she pressed another kiss there.

Trembling, she leaned fully into him until there was no more space between them. With a nearly soundless groan, he slid his hand up her back to rest between her damp shoulder blades. When he kissed her again, it was deeper and longer, parting her mouth with his.

The touch sent heat swooping down her belly and had her head spinning. There in the tense, heated silence, they kissed. Simply kissed, almost chastely. Exploring the shape of each other's mouths. Until they both began to shake, their breathing turning to pants.

Sin made a sound, needy and almost resigned. His hand found her jaw and cupped it. Angling his head, he came at her again. When his tongue delved into her mouth she gasped, and he went deeper, lapping her up as if she were sweet cream. And she'd never felt anything so decadently delicious.

Layla wanted a taste of her own. Copying him, she touched her tongue to his lower lip. Instantly Sin nipped it, drawing her in. "Yes," he whispered, licking into her. "Like that. Like that."

His quiet instruction made her needy for more. More of his taste, the feel of his mouth, of sharing the same breath. She surged into him, opening her mouth wider. And he groaned, holding her steady as he feasted on her mouth.

She grew dizzy with it. They kissed until her lips grew swollen and her jaw ached. And still he did not stop. Not until she whimpered and, acting on instinct, ground her hips against the hard length of him prodding her belly.

Sin stilled, his lips just touching hers. Their breath mingled as he pressed his forehead against her brow. And then he sucked in a deep breath. When he let it out, all the fine tension seemed to leave his body.

Layla clutched his lapels, wanting to kiss again. But he was withdrawing. She could feel it. A whimper of protest left her. Sin talked over the sound. "We should go."

"No."

His fingertips, still cupped on her cheek, twitched. "Not in this place, little bird."

And then she remembered where they were. A tomb. No, she supposed this was not the best place for them to be any longer. But she knew that the moment he let them out, he'd be withdrawn and emotionless Sin once more. She did not know if her heart could take it.

Chapter Seventeen

When the pale fingers of dawn crept over the sky, Sin and Layla left the cathedral. His suit was in bloody tatters, her gown ripped open along the back. Sin slipped his coat onto her shoulders but it did little to warm her. He was able, at least, to conceal them from humans as they trudged down the street. Layla's skin was wan, her eyes red and bleary. Sin tucked her against his side, dropped the glamour that hid them, and hailed a cab.

Even tattered, their clothes were too fine for a cabbie to ignore. Sin paid the driver an extra bob and then sat back in the ill-sprung seat, gathering Layla close once more. He could not seem to let her go.

She'd kissed him. He could think of little else as they rode along in silence. For years, he'd dreamed about kissing Layla. The reality made his dreams a pale ghost in comparison. Indeed he was haunted now, the memory of her sweet lips upon his so strong that he could feel them still. Her taste was in his mouth, luscious ripe pears. He'd had no idea kissing would be so addictive.

He'd been groomed to please a woman; knew how to make one quicken within moments, knew exactly what to do with his cock, his body. But he'd never had a kiss. Mab had not been interested in such sentimentalities. And he was glad for that. Glad he could save that one thing for Layla.

He wanted more. Now. Forevermore. And yet, when he thought of sinking his still-hard cock into Layla, he felt soiled. He wanted Layla but he could not rub off the taint of Mab.

The cab rolled to a stop and the driver turned. "Looks like there's some sort of trouble ahead, sir. Can't go any further."

Traffic had come to a standstill. Distracted with his thoughts, Sin hadn't paid attention. Now he smelled the smoke in the air, saw it billowing in black clouds just over the tree line.

"We'll get out here." Tossing the cabbie another coin, he moved to wake Layla, who had fallen asleep on his shoulder. "Little bird." He brushed a kiss across her cheek because he had to touch her. "Layla, love."

Her lashes fluttered, and then those glossy brown eyes focused on him. As with every time she looked at him, he felt it in his heart, in his cods. He wanted to kiss her soft, sleepy mouth once more. Instead, he touched her cheek. "Come along, now."

She bolted upright. "Sorry; I don't know what happened."

"You slept. We'll get you home, and you can sleep some more." But as they alighted the cab, Sin glanced up the road where people were gathering, and a sinking feeling settled in his stomach. Taking her hand, he moved forward, weaving past people idling on the pavement.

"Oh, Sin," Layla said at his side, her hand gripping his hard.

Her home stood black against the pale sky, a smoldering ruin of burnt timber and toppled-down stone.

"Hope no one was inside," a man said to no one in particular.

Sin wrenched around, tugging Layla with him. She trotted along, her cheeks shining with silvery trails of tears. "Did he do this?"

"That would be my guess," Sin grumbled, his stride brisk. They needed cover. A place to hide.

"Is he out here?" She glanced around.

"He might be." Sin kept them moving. "However, his power is low now that it's dawn, whereas mine is growing." Even so, he did not want another match until he'd seen Layla safe.

But where to take her? His friend Eliza had left him a manor house in Knightsbridge but it had been Mab's first. He'd refused to set foot in the place, no matter that Eliza had redecorated. It had not eradicated the memories.

He headed for Evernight House. He was still close with his cousin Holly, whom he'd grown up with. But Holly was off with her husband Will in America. It would have to do, and it was close by.

Two streets later, they were in front of the imposing townhome.

"I do not want to protest your choices," Layla said at his side, "but this place rather looks like one of those houses you read about in Gothic novels. The sort where the intrepid heroine goes to work as a governess and never comes out again."

He smiled. "Good thing you're not a governess. When this house was built, iron rods, blessed by Augustus, were set into the walls. It was done to keep fey out." Sin still remembered Mab's ire over this fact. Of course she'd made Sin spy for her, but it still gave him a sense of satisfaction that she couldn't enter. He glanced down at Layla. "However, it also makes this house one of the few places strong enough to deter St. Claire. It isn't foolproof. But it will do."

He took a step, then paused. "I should warn you, there are

traps set to keep unwanted people out. So do as I say until we are inside."

She made a shocked sort of laugh. "Traps? What is this place?"

"Evernight House. Holly's home."

Layla's eyes lit up. "I remember Holly. She never wanted to play with us. Always had her head in a manual."

"Yes. Well, she's an inventor now and is currently on holiday in America. Visiting Mr. Edison to talk about some sort of camera intended to photograph moving pictures."

"How extraordinary."

"Mmm. Let's see if I can get in now. Wait here."

It took some doing and the discovery of five new traps designed to maim, if not decapitate, an immortal, but Sin got through and then led Layla inside. Holly's codes had not changed, and he punched them into the control panel at the front door. Once inside, he shut them in and re-set the traps.

"No safer place in London," he said in the quiet gloom. The staff was off, and dusters covered the furniture, making them appear as ghostly white lumps. But he found a lantern and some matches in the butler's pantry. Lamp lit, he guided Layla up to the second floor.

"This is my room," he said, opening the door. She hovered in the doorway as he pulled dust covers from the chairs and bed. But when he went to the wardrobe and pulled a fresh set of linens out, she moved to help him make the bed.

They worked together, and it felt oddly domestic. Sin had funds enough, and Layla was an heiress. They need never make their own beds. But the idea of sharing a home with Layla felt rather like standing on a cold street and gazing into a window aglow with light. He wanted in.

"St. Claire had Augustus's wing," Layla said, breaking the silence.

Sin glanced up at her. Her features were set and pinched as she tucked in a sheet. "Yes," he said, the yawning pit of heartbreak opening up once more.

She blinked several times. "His wings are not like yours, are they?"

"How do you mean?"

"You said yours were a power, not part of your body." Sad brown eyes gazed up at him. "His are. Else there would not have been blood and bone."

Sin swallowed hard. "Yes, they're part of him." Which meant that Augustus had been weakened enough to allow St. Claire to rip the wing from his body.

"Do you suppose he's..." Layla licked her lips and savagely shook out the quilt. Dust flew in little motes.

Sin caught the edge and smoothed it down over the mattress. "I don't know. Augustus is strong. He should be able to heal just as quickly as I can."

"He's dying," she whispered.

Sin shot up straight, his hand clenching a pillow. "What do you mean?"

"Augustus told me that he was dying, or fading, rather. That he only had a small time left here." The pink curve of her lower lip plumped. "I do not think he'd let that...monster take his wing unless he..."

Sin tossed the pillow down and rounded the bed. She went willingly into this arms and he held her against him, pressing his lips to the crown of her head. She smelled of dust and soot and home. "It's all right, little bird."

She clung to him, her arms around his waist. "How can you say that?"

"What else is there to say?" He kissed the top of her head. Once. Then once more because he could. "Get into bed now. I'm going to turn on the heat."

"Turning it on?" She blinked up at him.

"The house runs on a radiator system through the flooring." He gave her a brief smile. "Don't ask. It's complicated."

"I'm sure," she murmured. Then a sad sigh left her. "Is St. Claire my father, do you think?"

Sin stilled. He thought back on the way St. Claire had been looking at her; it certainly hadn't been a fatherly expression. "I cannot say for certain, Layla. But I do not believe so. You look nothing like him, nor do you have his coloring."

She shuddered. "He's been courting me. I let him touch me." She rubbed her arms. "I feel vile now."

Sin squeezed her tight. "Do not think of it. I will not let him touch you again. I swear this."

"I believe you, Saint."

Her trust was a glorious thing. Reluctantly he let her go. "I'll see about finding you some new clothes."

She nodded, already toeing off her slippers. He should go. She'd want to remove her ruined dress. His feet stayed rooted to the floor. Layla looked up at him, her expression almost blank with exhaustion. "Sin?"

He shook himself out of his stupor. "Right. I'll leave you to it."

Layla nodded but, when he moved to go, she caught his arm. "Saint... Will you come back?"

"I'm not leaving the house, Layla." He was playing the ignorant but he did not have it in him to remain in this room at the moment. She was too tempting.

Unfortunately, Layla was never one to let him slide from the truth. "Will you come back to the room? Lie with me for a while?" She closed her eyes and a flash of pain and fear twisted her features. "I don't want to be alone."

God, he ached for her. Letting out a slow breath, he leaned

in and kissed the crest of her dirty cheek. "You will never be alone again, little bird. Rest now; I'll come back to you."

He always would. She was in his heart, and he was incapable of living without her. Whether he could give her what she needed was another thing entirely.

When he knew she was settled down, he got to work. First writing letters. Then he sought out one of the young lads who always seemed to haunt the stables behind the big houses that ran along either side of the Evernight estate. He gave him a bob to seek information about Layla's burnt-out house. Had the servants survived? If so, the boy was to find Mr. Pole.

"Only Pole, understand?" he told the little urchin.

The boy's speckled face wrinkled in a scowl. "What you take me for? Daft? I'll find him, quick as a duck."

"Give him direction to Evernight House."

His wide, blue eyes went round. "That horrible house? I heard tell it's haunted."

Sin wanted to laugh. "By me. I don't take kindly to unwanted visitors. But if you do as asked, I'll see you get a hot supper and remain unmolested by any wee ghosties."

Pale-faced, the boy nodded.

Sin handed him a bundle of letters. "You say you can read?"

The boy scoffed. "This here one at the top says, 'Lady Archer.' Gor, a true lady?"

"Indeed." Sin tapped the boy's shoulder. "Now off with you. I'll add a shilling for every note safely delivered."

"On my honor, sir." With a tip of his ratty cap, the boy took off running.

Archer

The days were growing short and cold. Archer had moved his chair as close to the hearth as he dared and still it was not enough. He ought to cover himself with a thick rug and be done with it. But the idea of doing so put to mind the image of an ailing old man, and he could not bring himself to do it. The irony was not lost on him; he was an ailing old man. The oldest human he knew of. He used to have nightmares of waking up to find that his physical appearance suddenly matched his true age, and Miranda would find him a withered old man.

He smiled at that fear now.

"What is that grin all about?" Miranda asked as she walked into the room.

As always, the sight of her took his breath and warmed his blood. She was simply the most beautiful woman he had ever seen. But it was her spirit, her bravery, and her unwavering love for him that made her irresistible to him.

"I was wondering how you would react if my appearance were to suddenly reflect my true age."

She sat on the arm of his chair and leaned against his shoulder, her fingers going to his hair to play. "That would be a shock," she teased. She toyed with a lock of his hair, and a shiver of pleasure went down his spine. "And what brought this on, may I ask?"

Archer rested his head on the curve of her breast. "Maudlin thoughts, Miri. Nothing more."

She leaned down and kissed the top of his head. "You always were a terrible liar, Ben." Her lips stayed pressed against him, and her warm breath ghosted over his skin. She trembled, and her voice came out rough. "Tell me, Archer. We are past hiding the truth from one another."

He closed his eyes, and his throat clogged. "Saying it aloud will make it all the more real."

Her arms closed around him, and she slid onto his lap. He held her close, taking in her vitality. And she warmed him, using her power of fire to send out luxuriant waves of heat. For his benefit, as if she knew perfectly well how very cold he was.

"It is cancer, Miranda."

She stilled. And then a shudder wracked her frame. "No." Heat swirled around them, the fire crackling and snapping in the grate. "No, Ben."

He kissed her cheek. "I'm so very sorry, Miri."

She started to cry, not the pretty, quiet weeping of a gentlewoman, but great heaving sobs. It ripped his guts out to hear it, and he gathered her as close as he could.

"Ben, I can't... I cannot live this life without you."

His heart stilled, and he cupped her damp cheek to tilt her face up. Her green eyes were luminous with tears. Gently he kissed the corner of each eye, his thumb wiping each drop. But they would not abate. "Miranda," he whispered. "My love. My heart. You are so very strong. So young—"

"Do not dare imply that I will get over you," she cut in fiercely. "Or so help me, Archer, I will... I will..." Her expression crumpled, and she sobbed once more, pressing her cheek against his as her arms wrapped tightly around his neck. "If I was the one ailing, the one who..." She swallowed hard, as if she could not say the words. "What would you do?"

He kissed her lips fierce and quick. "I would want to die with you." He hated those words. Hated death. "But, Miri, you will live on." Archer gave her shoulders a small shake. "You will. It is the only thing keeping me sane, the thought that your life remains."

She kissed him back just as fiercely, just as quickly. When she drew away, her gaze was brilliant green and irate. "I do not want to argue with you. But this isn't over."

He had to smile. He'd fallen in love with her sharp wit and cunning mind. His kiss was softer now, lingering. "We can do other things." Sadly, he was too weak for much, and she knew this well. It had been weeks since he'd taken her. Or she him.

Miranda, however, nuzzled close. "Come to bed, I shall take very good care of you."

His blood heated. "Of that I have no doubt. However, we've received a note from your brother." Her soft body tightened. Archer spoke over the protests he knew were coming. "St. John asked for your presence. He would not do so if he wasn't in need. I will not turn my back on him, and neither will you. Not anymore."

Miranda met his gaze. "Well, your penchant for tossing about orders hasn't diminished in the least."

"We were the ones to find him in Ireland. We were closest to him. I am ashamed of our unwillingness to give him another chance."

She looked away, her chin lifting. Archer took hold of it and turned her back to face him. "Miri, he is your family. I want that for you. At the very least, let us go to him and hear what he has to say."

She relented with a sigh. "I miss him, Archer. I do. But I find it hard to trust my family after all the lies they've told over the years."

He leaned his forehead against hers. "I know, love. But Sin is a good lad at heart. It will hurt you more if you do not go to him."

Miranda let out an unsteady breath. "Then let us go." She moved to rise but stopped and cupped his cheek. "Archer, I..." Her teeth came down hard on her lower lip.

He pressed his hand against hers. "I know, love. I know." After all, what was there to say? Death paused for no man.

Chapter Eighteen

Sin had shut himself off again. That much was clear. After bringing her to Evernight House in the early hours of the morning, Sin did not kiss her again. No, he hustled her off to bed, for which she was grateful. After all, she was dead on her feet and needed the rest. But he'd withdrawn. True, he'd returned to her as promised.

Layla had fallen asleep almost the instant her head had hit the pillow. But she'd awakened when he returned. Sin hadn't said a word as he crawled onto the bed, staying over the covers and spooning himself behind her. It was clear he thought her asleep, and she wasn't inclined to dissuade him of the notion, not when he seemed so on edge.

What she had wanted to do was turn and demand more kisses. But she rather feared he'd bolt if she did. So she'd let herself lean into his solid warmth and slept once more.

A few hours later, when she'd reawakened, he brought her some gowns. "Holly hasn't left much, and I'll admit this only to you. She is an atrocious dresser."

"Sin, you cannot say that about a lady. It's rude."

"She's not a lady. She's my cousin, and I'm certain she'd agree. But you're in the right." He flashed a grin. "I would not dare tell her."

She lifted a plain brown house dress up for inspection. All right, the gowns weren't inspired, but they were of good quality.

"I'm afraid her…er…underthings might not fit you." He'd gone pink at the tips of his ears. And she wanted to kiss him for it.

But he was correct in that as well. Holly Evernight's corset did not fit Layla's shorter torso. So she did without, which felt wonderfully freeing and slightly erotic. With the lack of a corset to hold her breasts in place, they gently swayed with each step she took, brushing her nipples against the soft lawn of her chemise. It was altogether too decadent. And yet she reveled in it, wanting to feel this way. Wanting to experience more touching with Sin.

After dressing, Layla ventured into the massive house, calling Sin's name. She found him in the kitchens, stirring a pot of oats. She had to grin. Sin had hated oats as a boy and so had she.

"You don't expect me to eat that lumpy mess, do you?" she said to him.

Sin gave her a stern look. "You'll eat your oats, young lady. How else shall you grow strong and tall?"

"On apple tarts and sweet buns?"

His dark brow quirked. "I'll add in honey and dried fruit but no more."

It was the only way she'd ever eat the otherwise bland porridge and he knew it. Layla got the bowls and spoons. They ate in silence. And when she did not engage him in conversation, Sin grew quiet, his expression drawn inward.

"What shall we do?" she asked him.

He stirred, seemingly pulling himself out of whatever place he'd gone. "I cannot find Augustus." He glanced at her, clearly seeing Layla's confusion. "Augustus and I are connected by thought. If I relax and seek him out, I can hear him. I haven't been able to do that since he left. Whether this is due to his will or some other reason, I cannot say."

"And St. Claire?"

Sin's green gaze flickered silver. "I can fight him, Layla, but I cannot guarantee that I will win." He pushed his bowl away. "In the days of old, there were many of us. Judgment and Damnation both. From what Augustus told me, there were great battles between, cities leveled in the process, the people's stories lost to time. They were equally matched, you see. One by one Judgment and Damnation fell, until there were only Augustus and the fallen who'd created Damnation. He went by many names, but Augustus called him Cain."

"As in the Cain of biblical lore?"

"The very one. Though Augustus swears he's older." Sin worried his bottom lip with his teeth. "Augustus created me—"

"How?"

He winced. "I've sworn an oath not to say, Layla. All you really need know is that it can be done. Damnation, however, are either born of Cain's sons breeding with humans or created straight from Cain. The difference being their wings. Did you see St. Claire's?"

"They were like yours, only black."

"Aye. Only one straight from Cain would have wings shaped as such. Others' are like that of a bat's." He sighed, his broad shoulders sagging. "Those originals were supposed to be gone, killed off in the wars. They are powerful, Layla. More than I am as a fledgling Judgment."

A chill worked over her skin, and she rubbed her arms. "Then we go into hiding."

His smile was tilted. "He will find us. In truth, I believe he's been tracking both of us all along."

"How?"

"I do not know. But he is the lord those demons were referring to in the alleyway, I'm sure of it. Damnation has the ability to put thoughts into another's mind. He's been talking to me. And laughing at you."

The cold within her grew, enough to make her shiver. "What has he been saying to you?"

Sin's gaze slid away. "Speaking of my secret desires. Of blood and death. Of destroying those who hurt me, and those whom I've never met."

As if he was disgusted with himself, he shoved away from the table and turned his back on her. Head ducked, hands low on his hips, he breathed deep and slow.

Layla stood as well, the porridge now leaden in her belly. "Saint, you think of those things?" She didn't mean it as an accusation, but he stiffened at her question.

His voice was low and rough when he spoke. "Yes, Layla. I think of that and worse. When I close my eyes at night, I dream of violence, of doing…unspeakable things. He plucked the thoughts from my mind and thrust them back in my face. He knows."

Slowly, she walked to him and laid a tentative hand on his shoulder. Sin flinched, his shoulders so tense she thought he might tear away from her. But he held still, and she let the weight of her hand sink more firmly onto his flesh, giving him that connection. "I think of those things too."

Her small voice seemed to fill the hollow silence. Sin turned. His expression was blank, all that perfect male beauty held in complete control. "Who hurt you, Layla?"

She had an idea that Sin would lay her enemies to waste. But she shook her head. "No one. Ever." Her grip on his shoulder tightened. "And yet the thoughts are there all the same. On the ship over, I stood at the rail next to a couple. We were staring out at the rolling sea, and the urge hit me like a wave that I should throw them both overboard. It was so strong that I had to grip the railing to keep myself still."

She took a ragged breath, her darkest confession leaving a hole of emptiness in her chest. "Does that make me evil?"

His hands cupped her cheeks. "I see your soul, Layla, and it is luminous. It glows with goodness."

Layla placed a shaking hand to his. "And do you see the darkness there too, Sin? Truth?"

His black brows furrowed, but he stared into her eyes. A tremor went through him. "Aye," he croaked. "I see glints of it. Smoke over diamonds."

That he told her the truth had her taking a relieved breath. "I think…" She bit her lip then forged on. "I think we hold both within us. Light and dark. Augustus once said the world was about balance and how we chose to live would determine our course."

"Yes." He sighed and leaned his forehead against hers. "The choice."

"You've chosen to live in the light, St. John. And those dark thoughts? What can they do to you? Nothing. Because your will is stronger. It always has been."

His sharp breath sounded tortured. "Layla, why do you always see the good in me when others only see the bad?"

"Augustus didn't. He chose you to be his champion." She tried to smile but her heart was too battered now. Her fingertips grazed his temple. "And I will always see the good in you, Sin, because I cannot do anything less. You have always been the happiness in my life."

A groan left him, and he closed his eyes tight. "And you are mine."

"Then kiss me," she whispered.

It was as if she struck him. Sin jerked his head back, his hands falling from her as if she were flames. He backed away a step, his eyes pained. "What happened last night... You were frightened."

She blinked at him, a hard, hot pressure building behind her ribs. "Are you saying you kissed me out of pity?"

"No." He scowled. "Never pity. But we were in that small space. And..." He ran a hand through his hair, sending the glossy crimson-tipped locks every which way. "I do not know how to make you understand—"

"Oh, I believe I am beginning to." Mortification washed over her, shrinking her skin over her hot cheeks. "You do not think of me as a man does a woman, is that it?" She choked out a bitter laugh and pressed her knuckles to her cheeks. "You think of me as a sister. You didn't want to kiss me at all. And there I was, a fool kissing you. Begging for more."

"Not think of you as a woman?" he repeated, his mouth falling open as if she'd slapped him. "Not want to kiss you? Sod it, Layla. The only woman I have *ever* wanted to kiss is you. The only woman I have ever kissed is you."

It was her turn for her mouth to fall open. He stepped closer, his eyes flashing. "From the moment you climbed up my tree and started giving me endless grief, you have been the only one I have ever wanted. First as my playmate, then as the woman I ached to have in my bed."

"Then..." She struggled to breathe. "Then why? Why push me away?"

"Because," he slashed the air in a helpless gesture, "sometimes what you want is not what you receive. I wanted you, always. What I got…" His hands gripped the back of his neck as he paced away.

It seemed he would stalk out of the room. But he stopped, his back stiff as starch. All at once his hands fell to his sides and his head dipped. When he spoke again, his voice was a jagged sound. "She broke me."

Dread was a dark thing creeping down her throat, headed towards her heart. "You said that before." Layla moved as slowly as she could, but she needed to be near him. "Tell me what was done to you, St. John. You hurt so badly. I cannot bear it."

He wouldn't turn. "A man should be allowed to keep some things for himself, Layla. This is my business alone."

"It is my business too," she said, coming up behind him.

He snorted, a loud and angry sound as he whipped around to glare. "How the bloody hell do you figure that?"

"Because you, St. John Evernight, are mine. Whether you will it or not. Your heart and soul have been mine to keep since I climbed up in that bloody tree to drive you mad. Mine to protect. And if you are bloody broken, then I bloody well will be here to help you put the pieces back together."

She stood before him, her breasts heaving against her bodice, her breath agitated.

He gaped at her as if she'd lost her mind. Annoyed, Layla did not break his stare, but lifted her chin. She was not leaving him. Never again.

Perhaps the stubborn arse finally saw that, for he swallowed hard and his expression crumpled. With a strangled sound he ducked his head and pinched the bridge of his nose. A harsh, choking sound left him as his shoulders vibrated with tension—a man trying his best not to break apart any further.

"Oh, Saint." Layla laid her hand upon his chest.

He let go then, his knees giving out on him. Sinking to the floor, he pressed against her, his face burrowing in the valley of her breasts. As he shook, she wrapped her arms around his shoulders and held on tight, curving over him so that she might give him shelter for once.

Sin gripped her hips so tightly she felt her bones creak. But she did not mind. Especially when he held on as though he feared she might disappear.

"Layla," he said in a ragged whisper, "I don't want you to know what I've become. I don't want you to hear those things."

She combed her hand through his cool hair, the strands like silk against her skin. "Answer this one question truthfully." When he stilled, she asked him, "If the tables were turned and all that you hold in your mind, all these deeds you're afraid to show me, were on me. If I had done them instead, would you walk away?"

Silence ticked through the room. Sin's deep breaths gusted warmth through her bodice. Making a small sound of defeat, he pressed his head more firmly into her. "I want to say yes to win this argument, but you asked for honesty. I would never turn away from you."

Layla leaned down and kissed the crown of his head. "Then I suspect you already know that I could never do the same."

When he sighed, she tugged him upward. Sin followed, not looking her in the eye. No, not yet. But he would. He had to, for she would not give up on him.

"Tell me something," she said, guiding him out of the kitchen and into the library where Sin had started a fire in the grate for more warmth. "It is clear you do not like to be touched. You tolerate it fairly well with me." He shot her a wry glance, but said nothing. Layla continued. "But mainly it is you touching me. Should I try the same without warning, you flinch."

He flinched then at her words but did not deny them. Together, they sat perched upon the edge of the velvet couch that faced the fireplace.

Back straight as an arrow, Sin frowned down at his bent knees, then cleared his throat. His voice was like rust. "You are correct. The touch of another is unpleasant for me." He glanced at her, his eyes rimmed in red, but quickly slid his gaze away. "It isn't with you, but I still have to tell myself that it is you, not..."

His teeth sank into his bottom lip, and then he truly looked at her, locking his green gaze to hers. "You promised not to turn away. But if I tell you all, will you promise not to take my sins onto yourself?"

Layla blinked, her mouth opening to agree, but she realized that he'd trapped her. He knew Layla would find a way to blame herself. For not being there, for not coming back to him soon enough, or—silly as it would seem—for him experiencing pain at all. A wry smile tugged at her lips. "Well-played, sir."

He did not smile but simply waited.

"This is emotional blackmail, you realize," Layla hedged.

His green gaze bore into her.

She sighed. "Very well. I promise."

Sin gave a slight nod. "I do not believe you," he said. "But I will remind you of that promise, regardless."

She gave him a quelling look, but he wasn't entirely incorrect. They sat in silence for a moment, then Sin began to speak, his voice low and slow as if he had to drag the words from within. "Do you remember when you left Ireland?"

"Of course I do. It was the worst night of my life." She had been fifteen and Sin sixteen. Layla had had great plans for them. They would marry as soon as she came of age and then live in a lovely manor house. She'd known then that she ought to think of babies and looking after their home, but mainly Layla had thought of them dancing and laughing for however long and loud they wanted. Of them traveling the world together and having adventures.

And then Augustus had ruined it all. "Augustus came to me late in the night and said to pack my things. We were to go. Immediately."

Sin frowned. "I did not know that."

She shook her head at the memory. "I refused. I did not want to leave you. Oddly, that upset Augustus even more. He put his foot down. We were going. End of discussion."

It had been the first time she'd had a true row with her guardian. "Oh, how I cried," Layla said to Sin. "I screamed at him, calling him a heartless rogue, a destroyer of all happiness. All sorts of childish insults. It was useless. Augustus remained firm. He wouldn't even let me say good-bye to you."

Sin's hand moved to hers, and their fingers twined. Layla held on tight. "In the end, he allowed me to leave you a note." She gave him a watery smile. "Such a pathetically short and uninformative note, considering the level of my heartbreak and despair."

The tip of his thumb moved over the back of her hand. "I felt much the same about that note. I grew so angry..." He let out a humorless laugh. "I froze the pond."

"And how did the locals take a frozen pond in the middle of summer?" she asked with a small laugh.

"I don't know," he said, frowning down at their linked hands. "I was not in any state of mind to care."

"Sin, you must understand how very sorry—"

"Layla," he cut in gently. "You promised not to blame yourself."

"Damn it," she muttered.

He gave her hand a squeeze. "I was angry and stupid in the way only a sixteen-year-old boy can be. I wanted answers. I wanted to know where you'd gone." With his free hand, he rubbed the back of his neck. "Had you left because of me? Had your guardian figured out that I was different? Dangerous?"

"Saint—"

"No interruptions, Layla." His tone was mild, almost distant. "And I wanted to learn about myself. What the hell was I? I knew I wasn't the only one in the house who was odd. Holly could manipulate metal. And our housekeeper, Nan, was certainly not normal."

Sin's fingers grew cold in her hand, his voice lowering. "It was Nan who started it all, really. She'd always told us tales of the fae folk, of how they were powerful and full of strange magic. The fae held the knowledge of the ages, could grant wishes..." Sin snorted. "Oh, she warned Holly and I, never seek them out. To strike a bargain with one was to court disaster, for they had ways of taking more than they offered.

"I did not listen, of course. In some ways it was a bit of a lark. Find a fairy mound, make a request to the winds for a fae to grant my wish. I didn't truly expect one to find me."

Layla swallowed down her trepidation. "But one did."

His jaw bunched, his fingers twitching. "Yes. One did."

Sin would rather be anywhere but where he was at the moment. Which was an oddity, considering Layla was the one true bright spot in his life. He could face an army of immortals, intent upon tearing his head off, but telling this woman his deepest shame was terrifying, as was the threat of seeing her pretty light dimming upon hearing his ugliness.

Layla sat by his side, her hand in his. She remained quiet,

though he knew it was taking all her patience to do so. He wanted to smile, but his body refused to do even that small action.

But he had to speak so he forced his body to obey. "I found her at the fae mound just outside the estate. Do you remember the place?"

They used to roll down the unnatural grass-covered hill, gaining speed until they came to a stop among the clover field at the bottom.

Layla nodded. "That place always gave me the chills, truth be told. When we'd grow silent, it seemed the hill was waiting for us to continue our chatter, as if it was listening."

He cut a glance at her, surprised at the fear in her voice. "Why didn't you tell me?"

Layla shrugged. "Thought I was being superstitious." She gave him a wan look. "So you went there?"

He nodded. "She was waiting for me. Mab, the queen of the fae. Later, I realized I'd played right into her hands. Nan was under her control. It was an easy thing to tempt a boy like me, one desperate for answers." He stared down at the floor, unable to look at Layla anymore.

"She had an affection for beautiful young males. Loved to collect them, keep them as her pets." He took a deep breath and ground out the rest through his teeth. "Keep them as her playthings."

Beside him, Layla tensed. Sin ignored it and continued before he lost the nerve.

"At the time, however, I simply saw the surface: a beautiful, magical creature who offered me everything I desired."

He did not want to remember, but it was there all the same. Mab appearing in her silken green dress, her long, dark red locks glowing like rubies in the sun, her purple eyes filled with tender sympathy. Her voice had been sweet, melodious. *"Tell me, dear boy, what is it that you wish?"*

"I asked to know who I really was, where I'd come from, and where you'd gone."

Layla sucked in a sharp breath, and his hand found hers. She was cold, her hand tense. Sin squeezed it in warning. He would not hear her regrets. He could not if he were to finish.

"She said she would grant my requests, but that I must make a sacrifice as well. A blood bond, and I would become her servant until I came of age." He snorted. "I had this fanciful image of faithfully serving a queen, like some modern-day knight."

Layla's hand pressed against his arm. "Saint..."

"It's all right, little bird. The past cannot truly harm us."

She made a sound of dissent. "No, but it can haunt us well enough."

He glanced at her then. "So let me tell mine and set it free."

Her soft brown eyes filled before she blinked. "Tell me."

"I gave her my blood bond, and she gave me my answers."

Her smile had been coy then, victorious. "Your girl is in Paris with her guardian. As for your origins, your sister shall arrive in the morning to tell you all."

"She did not lie," Sin told Layla. "Miranda did arrive in the morning. I was her brother. I had two other sisters as well, Poppy and Daisy. They thought I'd died at childbirth. Our mother was the head of a secret society who protected humans from supernaturals. And our father..." He tried to smile but couldn't. "Was a demented demi god of chaos who had killed our mother when she refused to tell him where she'd hidden me. My sister Poppy had defeated him. But the truth remained, I was the spawn of evil."

He could hear Layla swallow. "We did go to Paris at first," she said.

Sin sighed. "I know. I was set to track you down, and then Mab came for me. And I realized that she owned me completely. I was ordered never to write you or try to find you. And that was my first lesson, truth and promises could be manipulated into something as solid as air."

He did not want to say the rest. The ugly truth sat like a hot stone in his throat.

Set it free.

"She had me do her dirty work. To spy on my family. Betray them." Sin pressed his cold fingertips to his hot eyes. "To amuse her when required."

Layla's hand was a warm weight on his arm, but she did not speak. Thank god for small mercies.

"I came to her a virgin. And though I suspect it would be much worse for a girl—"

"Why?" Layla cut in fiercely. "Because a boy's feeling and experience has less worth?" Her glossy locks trembled as she gave a sharp shake of her head. "Do not make light of it."

"I am not," he said quietly. Well, perhaps he was. "Every experience I've had was something foul and against my will, Layla. But…Sod it. I felt pleasure," he rasped. "Do you understand? I did not want it, but some sick, twisted part of me responded to her. And I…" He closed his eyes. "I loathe myself for it."

She went still, and he could not look at her.

"That is what I mean when I say she broke me. She turned me against myself."

"I want to tear her apart with my bare hands," Layla muttered.

He could not help but lean against her shoulder. "I already took care of that. My first act as Judgment."

Big, brown eyes peered up at him. "You are certain she's gone?"

"Annihilated in both body and soul." He still felt the supreme satisfaction of remembering his lightning flowing through her body, vaporizing it, and the surge of his power sending her soul to hell.

The couch creaked as Layla turned towards him. "She is gone. But you and I? We're here."

Sin took in the familiar shape of her face. She was utterly lovely to him, fresh and pure, with her heart in her eyes. He wanted to hold her close and protect her from anything ugly or unkind. And he wanted to hold her close and demand that she never let him go.

But his skin felt too tight for his flesh, and his insides churned.

As if she read his thoughts, she put her hands in her lap, as if to assure she would not touch him. "I'm tired. We've only slept a few hours. Would you lie with me?"

That hot lump in his throat seemed to grow. He tried to swallow it down. "I will do anything for you."

Chapter Nineteen

Sin's heart thudded against his chest as they walked to the room they'd shared. At his side, Layla said not a word, but her cheeks were a soft shade of pink, her lips parted as if in anticipation.

Anticipation. He'd never felt that when faced with carnal acts. He'd felt dread, disgust, even fear at some points. He did not feel it now. No, his emotion was something altogether different.

He feared he would muck this up, that she would touch him or he would touch her and the memories would return. He felt hate that Mab still influenced his life. And he felt the overwhelming need to hold and stroke and kiss Layla once more. To worship her with all that he had.

He could please her. He knew very well how to do such things. But could he please himself? To truly make love meant both sides felt pleasure; he was sure of that much.

When they reached the room, he placed his hand on the small of her back and led her towards the bed. A cold sweat broke out over his skin, and he tried to breathe slowly, to focus on the feel of her firm back against his fingertips.

Layla stopped and turned to face him.

"Saint, I don't want to ask you to speak of details, but I need to know how..." Her cheeks pinked as she struggled to find her words.

He knew what she wanted. Guidance. To know what triggered his bad memories. Her care for his feelings struck him in the heart and made that shriveled organ swell.

She was so much smaller than he, the top of her head just reaching his chin. So delicate of form. But so much stronger of heart. With a careful hand, he traced the fragile ridge of her collar bone. His fingers stopped at the top edge of her bodice, then slowly followed the line down over the sweet swell of her bosom.

Layla's breasts lifted on a breath, but she did not move, only stood watching him. His thumb brushed over the little bow in the middle. Only then did he meet her eyes.

A pulse of power and want hit his gut. "Turn around," he whispered.

Without hesitation, she presented him with her back. In his world, the action was a level of trust most would never grant. That she bent her head forward a little, exposing her fragile nape, was even more so.

The gown she wore was plain, brown wool that buttoned up the back. He knew she did not have a corset beneath, only a chemise. It had been the best he could do without leaving the house. But the knowledge that there was so little between him and her bare skin has his cods drawing tight, his cock growing heavy with anticipation.

And yet the simple act of gently drawing the thick fall of her shining hair away from her neck gave him more pure pleasure than any sensual deed he'd ever done. Layla's long tresses flowed like silk over the back of his hand as he settled them over her shoulder.

Her skin was cream and honey, having a golden sheen that gleamed in the weak light. Unable to help himself, he ran his knuckles down her spine, from nape to the middle of her shoulder blades, where the bodice began.

A fine shiver worked over Layla as he did. He wanted to do it again, just to see her react. But he paused there, his fingertips rubbing the little nub of the topmost button.

"Before you left," he said, slipping one button through its hole, "I used to imagine us married."

She sucked in an audible breath, her shoulders rising. But she said not a word. So he continued, his fingers slowly undoing her buttons, making the edges of her bodice sag. "Truth be told, I imagined our wedding night more than anything."

He could see the crest of her smooth cheek and it plumped on a smile. "Of course you would," she murmured. "And what did you imagine, Saint?"

His lips twitched. "Keep in mind, I was a lad at the time. My imagination is much improved now."

"Hedging, are we?"

He ran his thumb over one of the bumps on her spine, the thin chemise moving with him. "I imagined undressing you. Just as I am now." Her bodice parted, revealing more of her thin underclothes. "Opening you like the very best Christmas package."

She drew in a breath. "And then what would you do?"

Sin gave in to temptation and rested his forehead on her shoulder. Her scent and warmth surrounded him. Summer cherries, wood smoke, honey on buttered toast. She did not truly smell of those things, but it was as close as he could come to describing her.

He tilted his head and skimmed his lips over her silken skin, loving the way goose bumps broke in his wake and how she delicately shivered. The line of her hair was damp, and he nuzzled her there. "Definitely this," he whispered, giving that fragrant spot a soft kiss, all the while lightly running his knuckles along her back.

She swallowed. "What else?" Her voice was smoke.

Slowly he kissed his way back down her neck to the curve where it met her shoulder. His tongue flicked out to catch a taste. Salt and sweet. Layla's breath stuttered. Sin paused there, his body exquisitely tight and hot, his own breath unsteady. There was only one chance for a first time, and he wanted to enjoy his with Layla.

With painful slowness, he spread his palms wide on the narrow expanse of her back. Layla's body tensed, her ribs expanding and contracting with every quick breath she took. But she did not pull away. No, she leaned into his touch, letting her head fall back against his shoulder. Giving herself to him.

Sin closed his eyes, his lips still resting on her skin, the very spot where her pulse pounded. "Now this," he murmured against her skin, "held top place in my fantasies."

He slid his palms around her ribs, moving under her gaping bodice. When he reached the rounded swells of the sides of her breasts, she sucked in a tiny gasp. Sin went achingly hard, but did not stop, not until he cupped her sweet, warm breasts in his hands.

They both trembled. Sin waited, soaking in the feel of her filling his palms, and then he squeezed, kneading her tender flesh. Layla moaned, her head lulling on his shoulder, her eyes closed tight. "I think I shall faint," she said weakly.

"No, you won't," Sin promised, a smile pulling at his lips. "You don't want to miss the best part." He ran his fingertips around the stiff points of her nipples, rubbing the linen back and forth over her skin. She whimpered sweetly. Then Sin gave those sensitive tips a hard pinch.

Layla cried out, her back arching, pushing her breasts further into his touch, even as her body sagged into his. Her capitulation unhinged him. Need surged through him so hard he bucked his hips forward, grinding his hard cock against her plump bum.

With a groan, he clamped down on her shoulder, his teeth sinking into her flesh, holding her there as he squeezed her breasts. And Layla gave another hard cry, her body shaking.

Hurting her. Stop.

Cursing, he let her go, stepping back. His breath came in uneven pants, his fists clutched tight to his sides. She turned, her gaze dazed, and wrapped her arms around him as if he hadn't just flung himself away from her.

"Saint." She kissed his neck. "Why did you stop?"

"God, Layla." He shivered, trying to control himself. "I don't know how to do this."

Her soft lips caressed his jaw, his cheek, the edge of his lips. "Do what?"

Her touch, the lazy way she explored him, her warm body molding to his as if she wanted to meld them together—all of it went to his head, made him dizzy, had his eyes closing so he could just feel her. Sin took a breath and tried to focus. "I only know how to fuck. Not make love."

He opened his eyes then. She smiled up at him as though he was something precious, not a man incapable of giving her what she needed. "I have not taken a lover, so I cannot profess to know the difference. But I know this. I waited for you, Saint. You are the only man I've ever wanted. Whatever we do, however we do it, will be right." She touched his cheek. "Because it will be you and me together."

Sin swallowed convulsively. He wanted to kneel at her feet, hold her tight, and never let go. "I was too rough with you just then."

"Truly?" She frowned. "And here I thought you were wonderfully wicked."

"Hell." He rested his forehead against hers. He'd done so many terrible deeds, let so many people down. And yet here she was, the woman he'd given his heart to so many years ago, wanting him just as he was. "I adore you, Layla."

He could feel her smile. "Adore me some more, Saint. Preferably until I lose my senses."

"Now that," he said with a growing grin, "I can do."

Layla had stood on stage before hundreds, sang for kings and queens, poets, and artists. She'd held people captive with a perfect pitch. None of that prepared her for the breathless rush of anticipation and pulsing pleasure of being with Sin. When he touched her, she burned incandescent with desire. When he worked his fingers and lips over her body, she both sighed in relief and ached for more, more, forevermore. Would it ever ease, this wanting of him? Layla thought not.

He stood before her now, his eyes hot with lust, his mouth slightly swollen from their kisses. "Layla." His voice was thick and rough. "I need to know that you understand what will happen here. That I intend to take you, make you mine."

She caressed his jaw. "Yes. And you will be mine as well."

"Always." He cleared his throat. "I would have honesty between us. Before he left, Augustus told me it would be safest if you were to get with child." He frowned, stepping closer. "I do not want you to think that is why—"

Layla kissed him softly before stepping away. "I know

you, Sin. I know us. This is greater than circumstance. This is fate."

His eyes closed, and he leaned his forehead against hers. "Yes, it is."

Her belly fluttered. "Would you regret a child?"

He pulled back to look at her, his expression fierce. "It would be my honor. A joy, Layla."

Warmth swelled within her. "Well, then. There is nothing more to worry over."

The blunt tips of his fingers ran up and down the curve of her neck, and he watched the action as if he were deciding how best to take her apart, one decadent taste at a time. "Grant me permission to control this." His green glaze flicked to hers. "Trust me to take care of you, and I promise, love, I'll give you pleasure."

Tension rode over his lean frame, and she knew he was holding himself in check for her. Tenderness swamped her breast. Sin had never been given the choice in his wants and desires. That he trusted *her* enough to ask now made her want to protect his love with all that she had.

"Do what you will," she said, "for I am yours."

His gaze grew more intense, as if he was searing the sight of her into his memory. "We are each other's."

His hand, warm and strong, slid to her nape, holding her there. Layla leaned into the touch. "Then, I should like to undress you."

Sin's lids lowered. "Would you now?"

She grasped his hand to give him a soft kiss in the center of his palm. And his breath hitched. So Layla did it again. "It is about your pleasure as well. Between us, St. John, it will always be about equal pleasure, both given and received."

"Take off my shirt, Layla." His voice was a deep command that stirred something within her belly.

Layla stepped forward so that they were toe to toe, his warmth and power surrounding her. He stood perfectly still, his eyes on hers, his breath slow and even. Her hands shook only a little as she pushed the button at the top of his collar through its slit. Each button released with a little pop of sound that somehow made that empty space between her legs clench every time.

Still he did not move. She stared into his eyes as her hands slid down his taut chest, along his narrow waist. His nostrils flared as she grasped the loose sides of his shirt and slowly gathered the fabric in her hands, pulling it from his trousers.

"Lift your arms." Her voice did not sound like her own. It was rougher and yet weaker.

He obeyed, raising those strong arms that could carry her with ease. Layla drew the shirt over his head, coming up onto her toes, for he was so much taller than she. And her breasts brushed his bare chest, only the thin fabric of her chemise separating them.

They both trembled at that small contact. She tossed the shirt aside, and he slowly lowered his arms, the sinewy muscles along his shoulders bunching and moving beautifully beneath his smooth skin.

But no matter how badly she wanted to drink in the sight of a half-undressed Sin, she did not glance down at his torso. She kept her focus on his eyes. There would be time enough to explore. For now, it was about him knowing he was loved.

Sin ran his knuckles along her bare arm. "Now you."

His hands found her waist and gently pushed the loosened gown over her hips. The heavy fabric slithered to the floor with a hiss, leaving her in the knee-length chemise.

Layla's breaths grew unsteady as she reached for the closure of his trousers. The hard length of his arousal butted up against the fabric, stretching it tight. She could not help it;

she pressed the heel of her hand over the rounded tip, and he grunted, swaying into her touch.

"Layla." His voice was a near growl of sound. "Keep on with that, and we won't be going slowly for much longer."

Smiling, she ducked her head, her forehead touching the smooth, hot cap of his shoulder. She made short work of his buttons, for she didn't want to go very slowly after all. But before he could be revealed, she looked back up to meet his gaze again.

Layla heard his trousers fall. He peered at her, his expression almost sleepy, as he skimmed his palms over her shoulders. Her chemise dropped to the floor. Cool air kissed her skin.

For one silent moment, they stared at each other. Then, as if by mutual agreement, they looked down. A ragged breath caught in Layla's throat. He was so perfectly formed, his body chiseled and strong, a study of lean muscle and graceful lines. His chest was bare of hair, his flat nipples sugar brown and tight.

Sin stepped forward and the hot, smooth tip of his cock touched her belly. It took all her attention. He was very thick down there, pulsing with need, the crown so swollen it looked pained. A pearl of moisture adorned the little slit at the tip.

His chest rose and fell in agitated movements, and she became aware of her own nakedness. Of the rounded swells of her breasts, the way her stiff pink nipples stood at attention, nearly touching his chest. She felt beautiful just then, sensual, powerful in her own right. Because she affected him as much as he did her.

Sin's hands ghosted over her arms, running up and down, sending shivers of pleasure along her skin. "Never in all my days have I seen anything as lovely as you, little bird." He cupped her cheeks, tilting her head up. His eyes creased at the corners as he looked at her. "You are the sun around which my world revolves."

"Sin." She couldn't say anything more. Her heart was in her throat.

His head dipped, and his lips came close enough that she felt their heat. "If I forget to say so when we are joined, I love you, Layla." He kissed her then, soft, sweet. "Always."

Afraid that she might topple, Layla wrapped her hands around his wrists and kissed him back. "And I love you, Sin. Madly. Completely. Eternally." With each word, she kissed his lips, and he sighed.

And then he bent and swung her into his arms. The bed was cool and soft, his body warm and hard as he settled next to her, pulling her close. He cradled her jaw as he kissed her, a melting glide of lips and tongue.

"Layla." His voice was soft but urgent. "It feels like my whole life I've been dreaming of you. Wanting you just like this, soft and yielding in my bed."

His long lashes rested along the crests of his cheeks as he closed his eyes and kissed her again.

And her heart ached even as her body ignited. Tenderness, bittersweet and heavy, swelled through her. This man, capable of leveling London, needed her.

He kissed her for long, languid moments, until her lips swelled against his, until she grew restless and clutched his shoulders, her body at once flushing hot then shivering as though cold.

Sweat dampened his temples, his color high. And all the while, the hard length of his sex pressed against her belly, a reminder that he would soon push that blunt instrument deep inside her. She wanted that. Suspected he'd fill all her empty places so well she'd never want him to leave her.

"I love kissing you," he said against her mouth. "I didn't think..." He licked into her mouth again and made a noise of contentment.

"Didn't think what?" she asked in a haze as she nipped his upper lip, then the bottom.

"That I would like kissing." He said it so simply, distracted as he was. He tilted his head and surged in deeper.

Layla's heart stilled. He'd never kissed another. Only her. Her fingers twined into his hair and she petted him, moving down to his strong neck, along the shifting muscles of his back.

As if her touch spurred his, his warm, rough palms caressed her sides, and he slowly worked his way down her body, lips mapping the line of her neck, down to her breasts. When he kissed her nipple, she gasped, a jolt of heat going down her middle. When he sucked it into his warm, wet mouth, she nearly came off the bed.

He chuckled darkly, his teeth catching the stiff bud and tugging. Layla saw stars. "Sensitive," he said. "And delicious." His tongue flicked her.

"Do it again," she whispered. "Please."

"That and more, love," he said, licking the lower curve of her breast. "Just keep talking to me. Let me hear your beautiful voice."

"I love the way you smell," she told him as he moved over her, surrounding her with his warmth, his mouth and hands learning her body. "Like warm spices and cool rain. Your voice is a rumble that goes straight to my heart and makes it beat faster."

He hummed in approval and moved lower.

"I love your mouth," she said. "The way it moves when you talk, the way it curves when you smile. I love to feel it on my skin. Kiss me, Sin. Kiss me and don't ever stop."

Kiss her he did. Over every inch he could find. Slowly, lingering in the oddest places—the crook of her arm, the dip of her waist, the inside of her knee. Spots she would have never considered sensitive until now. Until his thorough care and gentle caresses made her so attuned to his touch that, with each kiss, her body fairly vibrated with need.

Her lids lowered, her breath came in frantic pants. Sweat glistened over her skin, her nipples so tight they throbbed. And that swollen, slick spot between her legs, the one he'd ignored, ached.

Her fingers opened and closed as if wanting to grab onto the pleasure and haul it close. "Sin," she begged. "Sin."

There were no other words. He'd become the entirety of her vocabulary.

From between her spread and trembling thighs, he glanced up, his eyes molten silver and jade. Thick locks of inky hair tumbled over his damp brow. He was a dark angel, intent on driving her mad with lust.

A slow, wicked smile curved his lips. "Yes, love?"

She undulated, trying to push her sex closer to those lips. But his hand upon her hip kept her where he wanted. "Kiss me," she said.

He placed a lazy kiss on the curve of her inner thigh, and her body twitched. "I am kissing you, sweets."

Cheeky rat. She wiggled again, lifting her breasts as if the very air could relieve their ache. She was so very wet between her legs. Wet and hot. And he knew it. Layla moaned. "It hurts, Sin. I need you."

His expression abruptly turned fierce. With a groan, he surged forward and kissed that needy spot the way he kissed her mouth, open and wanting, desperate, as if she were his only sustenance.

She broke apart, heat flaring so hot and sure that she

could not breathe. Sensation rolled over her, red and strong. Like blood. *Life*, she thought, *this is life*.

Sin was rising, his hips sliding between her thighs, his chest pressing against her breasts. He stared down at her with flushed cheeks. And the rounded crown of his sex notched against her opening. "Layla," he whispered, "I'm going to take you now."

She could only nod, weak and shaking but needing more. The emptiness inside her contracted in anticipation.

He pushed forward. Gods he was big, so very thick, so very present. Her flesh stretched around his, working to accommodate that unyielding hardness. A whimper escaped her, her hips wiggling as if to make room for him.

He paused, and she felt him pulsing. "All right?" he ground out.

"More."

He eased back a bit and then sunk deeper. By the time he was fully seated, they were both shaking. A rivulet of sweat ran down his cheek as he hovered above her. He stayed still, letting her grow accustomed to him. "Breathe," he told her.

So she did, and the stiffness in her limbs eased. "You are enormous," she informed him tartly.

He laughed then, a husky chuckle, his expression so light and happy it was almost boyish. "To be sure." He circled his hips, grinding against her in a way that was utterly wicked. "How does the saying go?" he asked thickly, green eyes going dark with heat. "The better to tup you with."

She fought a laugh. "St. John, that is not how the story goes."

He dipped down, his lips brushing hers. "That's how our story goes." He kissed her deep and sure as he pulled back and thrust hard.

Oh, my.

She thought no more. He loved her with steady, smooth strokes, putting his whole body into the motion. "Yes," he bit out when she wrapped her legs around his waist to hold on tight and lifted her hips to meet his. "Like that."

His thrusts came faster, finesse giving way to greedy grunts. The hot tension was building within her once more, that sharp edge that bordered pain. Perhaps he too felt it, for his brows furrowed, his lips parting as he drew in air. "Layla, I don't think I can last."

Last? She did not want to linger. Perhaps later, when she'd quenched her thirst for him. Now she chased that feeling, the hard coil in her lower belly that twisted. "Sin, I think I . . . It's here again. That ache."

He rotated his hips, and it lit her up, all those aching spots of hers flaring hot. "Come for me, Layla. Let go, love. I have you."

His words set her free. She arched into him, her fingers digging into his sweat-slicked shoulders. She came on a wordless cry. Groaning, he bucked against her, his body shaking.

They fell together. And when they came down, their bodies limp and slack, she could only cling to him, pressing her cheek against the crook of his neck. Her voice, when she could find it, was rough as sand. "That was . . . I have no words."

He stirred, turning to his side to face her. "Everything," he rasped. "It was everything."

She could not agree more.

Chapter Twenty

Lena

With Augustus missing a wing and Lena draining her powers to keep the hole in his chest sealed, they made slow progress from Vienna to London. She managed to secure railway tickets for them but the endlessly rocking carriages clearly taxed Augustus's strength, and he'd soon grow whey white, his brow dotted with sweat. As Lena could not stomach the sight of her proud and once strong man waning with each passing day, she found reasons to take breaks, settling them into hotel rooms for the night.

Once tucked up in a bed, she'd feed him a good, hot dinner, force him to drink down some hearty ale, and then watch him sleep.

Asleep, Augustus was no less commanding in appearance. He was Michelangelo's David—big, bold nose, hard brow, stern eyes, pouty mouth. Yet he was no youth. Augustus was sheer masculinity, painted in olive tones and ink black hair.

Her fingers itched to trace the line of his furrowed brow, down along his firm cheek, to the puckered curve of his upper lip.

He breathed softly, evenly, the thick clumps of his lashes fluttering against his cheek.

In all the years of knowing him, Lena had never before seen Augustus at rest. Sleep simply was not something an ancient immortal did in the presence of another, unless there was absolute trust. And while Augustus had always claimed to want her, she knew he did not trust her. With good reason.

A pang of guilt speared her heart. She'd tricked him into laying with her.

"What," came his rasping voice, "are you scowling about?"

Lena blinked and met his gaze. Eyes the color of coffee stared back at her. Lena wanted to move back from the pillow on which she lay with her head so close to his. But she stayed put. "When we were together, you under Apep's spell, I felt..." She drew in a sharp breath through her nose. "I felt so very dirty, Augustus."

He frowned. "How heartening to know I made you feel like filth."

A humorless laugh left her. "Dirty because I was tricking you, old friend. You were there, present in the moment, and yet not. There was a distance in your eyes, a glassiness. I was using your body, not engaging your soul."

He was silent, his dark gaze moving over her face. "Did I enjoy it, at the very least?"

This time she laughed outright. "What a question." Heat suffused her cheeks. "You were quite enthusiastic."

His color heightened as well. "Gods, you make me sound as though I were a randy youth."

"Is that such a bad thing?"

His mouth quirked. "I'd like to think I displayed some skill, not gone at you like a bull in heat."

Lena could not help but lightly flick a lock of his dark curls back from his brow. "Stop fishing for compliments. Your skills were…"

"Exceptional?" He flashed a shockingly boyish smile.

"Exemplary."

For a long moment, they smiled at each other; then his faded. "Why, Lena? All you had to do was ask. I feel cheated. Out of having you and of knowing about Layla."

It was difficult to breathe. "I know," she rasped. "My regret is more than I can express. But, Augustus, I am not a good soul. I do these selfish things. I take what I want."

"And yet you risked your life and the regard of your peers to keep St. John's identity a secret from Apep."

"That was nothing—"

"It was you and I who created the SOS. You could have been Mother, but you let the Ellis women lead. Always in the shadows, operating where no one could see you but where it was most needed."

A lump of hot discomfort lodged under her breastbone. "What will happen to the SOS if you are gone?"

His gaze slid away, a new tension clenching his jaw. "It will change. Enoch is going to split open the gateways, and there will be no way of closing them."

Lena lifted off the pillow. "He cannot. That would be…"

"Chaos," Augustus finished for her. "And yet, no matter how I try to see another way, it all leads back to the same road. To Layla helping him break down those walls and being consumed by Damnation. To St. John becoming…" He went silent, his eyes closing.

His color was fading, and Lena spied the silver blood seeping from the wound in his chest that would not properly close. She pressed her hand to it and he shivered.

"What does he become?" she whispered.

"Me," Augustus said. "He becomes final Judgment. Alone."

Such bleakness in his words. And Lena knew he felt that chasm of loneliness within himself. How very hollow and cold it felt. She knew this because she'd experienced the same throughout her long life. Only with him did she feel wholly herself.

Slowly, she eased to his side, resting her head close to his. His scent was so familiar to her she could no longer define it, only feel the utter comfort of drawing it in and knowing he was near. He stirred as if he'd just noticed her proximity to him. Lena spread her fingers wide over his solid chest, pushing her power into his wound, willing it to heal.

"Augustus," she whispered, "I've loved only two beings in my long life. The child I bore and the male who gave her to me."

He sucked in a sharp breath, and then his head turned in her direction. Coffee-colored eyes now glassy and rimmed in red stared as if seeing her for the first time. "Lena..."

She blinked rapidly. "You truly thought I did not? How could you? I would not have resisted so hard, sunk so low in my need to have you, if not for love."

His palm was too cold, his touch too weak, for her liking; Augustus was never cold when in good health. But she welcomed it anyway as he cupped her cheek. "Lena, we've been walking this earth alone for too long. I'll give you an eternity of love if you'll simply let me." His thumb traced her trembling lower lip. "Entrust your heart to my keeping. I will never take it for granted."

Lena allowed herself to nuzzle into his touch. "Layla first."

He blinked slowly. "Yes, Layla. I must see her once more. Help her."

Lena allowed herself one kiss, softly, tenderly upon his

parted lips. A bolt of pleasure and happiness went through her at the touch. And he sighed as if he too felt the same. So she kissed him once more. "Stay strong for our child, my love. And then I am yours."

For the first time in his life, Sin indulged in pleasure. He let it wash over him, permeate his skin, fog his mind.

He spent his time with Layla, discovering every hidden spot that made her shiver and moan, soaking in the sounds she made and the way she moved. But for every discovery he made, she made one herself.

In the dark corners of his mind, he'd been afraid to let her touch him. He'd been toyed with, forced to respond, so many times his body had felt as if it were covered in dirt. And yet, when Layla laid her hands on his body, there was only relief, a shivering pleasure, a need for more.

Layla washed him clean with her touch, her laughter. He hadn't expected to laugh in bed. Never thought to do it. Yet they spent long hours tangled up, laughing over nonsensical things, touching as though they'd just discovered the concept.

"It is joy," she told him at one point, her glossy hair spreading over her back like a dark wave.

"It's you," he countered.

"It's us." She pulled him close to kiss him. He went willingly and fell all over again.

Finally they slept, Layla's head upon his shoulder, her arms wrapped tight around his waist as though she feared to let him go. Perhaps he had the same fear, for he woke early to find his hands in her hair, fisting the heavy locks, his leg flung over her hips, pinning her down to the bed.

For all that, Layla slept on, a look of peace and bliss smoothing out her pretty face. His heart ached with love for her, but his mind was not at ease. There were things to do and the world to face.

Sin slipped out of their bed and dressed quietly.

Pole had arrived, looking a bit worse for wear but stoic as always. He brought with him two footmen and three housemaids. The cook and housekeeper had apparently fled. But Pole took control and had one of the housemaids head to the market with a footman while the rest began opening up rooms.

"Was the strangest thing, Sir," he told Sin as they sat at the kitchen table. "I had this undeniable compulsion to leave the house. Almost dreamlike, if you don't mind me saying so. I ended up on the street in my nightshirt only to find the other servants there too." The older man's hand shook as he took a sip of the Irish whiskey Sin had insisted upon. "Next thing we know, the whole house blows like a bonfire on Guy Fawkes Night."

Pole shook his head. "Can't understand what happened. Or why we were somehow called out."

Sin could understand the hows but the whys were a mystery to him as well. Damnation was hardly one to spare lives. Especially not when one was in the midst of blowing up a house to make a point of scaring his prey.

Sin could only offer a forced smile and click glasses with Pole. "Here is to your health. I am happy to see you alive and well, Mr. Pole."

"You're a good lad. And Miss Starling?" Pole took another sip of whiskey. "She's well?"

"Hale as ever. She's sleeping. It was a long night for us all."

The boy returned shortly thereafter, bringing word that he'd delivered his notes. "You think this house is frightful," he told Sin as he tucked into a bowl of porridge. "You should see the Archer place." He shuddered. "Thought they'd lock me up and use me bones for their soup."

Sin chuckled. "We toffs like our houses to be dramatic. You did well, lad. Mr. Pole will set you up if you're wanting work."

Sin left the boy to his meal and went to find Layla. She was reading in the newly uncovered library, a cheery fire crackling in the hearth. "I'm so glad everyone got out. Pole brought me some tea and told me the story." She gestured to the tea service. "Would you like a cup?"

"No." Sin paced to the hearth, picked up a strange-looking clock device and then set it back down, aware that anything in Holly's house could be deadly. He'd have to remind the servants to keep dusting to a minimum. And to stay out of Holly's rooms. He walked back to the sofa, sat next to Layla, then stood again.

"You're making me dizzy, Saint. Do sit." A soft flush covered her cheeks when she looked at him now.

Sin knew the reason for it, and for a moment all worries vanished. There was only the memory of Layla in his arms, her slim body warm and smooth, her lips mapping paths over his chest. He took a ragged breath as he stared down at her.

The flush on her cheeks deepened. She knew very well where his thoughts lay, and she gazed at him through lowered lashes. "That look in your eyes. It's as if you'd like to devour me."

He found himself lowering to her side. "I would. Over and over."

Her smile was cheeky as he cupped her nape and drew her close. God, kissing her filled him with utter peace and yet shook him to the core. It was the one thing they'd shared with no one else, only each other.

He reveled in the heady sensation, just kissing her softly, not too deeply, taking languid tastes as he stroked her cheeks. How long he held and tasted her, he could not say. Long enough that his cock grew heavy and his body went lax against the pillows.

She sighed into a kiss, her fingers threading through his hair. Shivers of pleasure went down his spine. She nipped at his lower lip. "Why were you pacing?"

Sin breathed in her scent, sweet and warm like cherry tarts. He kissed her again. "I invited my sisters here," he murmured against her lips. "Not certain if they'll show, however."

Layla stroked his hair. "When are they to arrive?"

Sin only wanted to kiss her now, and his lips found the fragrant little spot just below her ear. "Quarter past the hour, if they decide to come." He nuzzled his way down her neck, his hand testing the weight of her soft breast.

Regrettably, Layla jumped up with a gasp. "Look at me. I cannot greet your sisters in this housecoat."

"You're beautiful." He tried to pull her down. "Come, kiss me some more, little bird." It felt good to make demands, to know that she wanted Sin for who he was, not his looks or what he could do for her.

Even if she was unfortunately distracted at the moment. She gave him a quick kiss on the cheek. "There. That will have to do—"

He caught her mouth with his and gave her one slow, searching kiss. Her gaze was fairly dazed when he pulled away, and he chuckled, brushing his lips over the tip of her nose. "Go on then, pretty yourself up. Though you'd look perfect in a sack."

Layla's lips pursed but her eyes shone with happiness. "You only say that because a sack is easily removed. No..."

She evaded another kiss. "I'm off before you seduce me again."

He was grinning long after she quit the room. But silence soon descended and he had the mad desire to follow and stay within the orbit of her warmth and happy laughter.

Running a finger along the back of the couch, he wondered if his family would ignore his call for help. A hollow well spread out from the center of his chest. If they would not come, he'd find another way. He had Layla now. But if he were brutally honest with himself, he wanted his family back as well.

A chime rang through the house and a moment later, Layla bustled into the room, her eyes gleaming like burnished mahogany. "Well, someone answered the call."

He wanted to smile at her excitement but his insides were too twisted.

Pole walked Daisy and Ian Ranulf in, and Sin's muscles clenched. His sister Daisy had always been the happy one. Plump and blonde with blue eyes and a cheeky tongue, she was also the most physically affectionate one. She eyed him now with caution, and his heart thudded against his ribs.

"I know we are supposed to be cross with you," she said. "But I cannot look at you and not offer a kiss, brother."

She came to him, her blue velvet skirts swaying, and bussed a quick kiss over his cheek. "You look well, St. John." She peered at him. "Better, in fact." Her glance cut to Layla. "I wonder why."

Ian grasped Sin on the shoulder in greeting but his gaze strayed to Layla, and his nostrils flared. He glanced back at Sin, but before he could say a word Archer and Miranda entered, followed by Poppy and her husband Winston.

They'd all arrived. They'd come even though they thought him a traitor.

Archer gave him a quiet look, a bare nod, and Sin realized that perhaps it was the husbands who had influenced this reunion. Sin didn't know whether to be amused or insulted. He settled on apathy at the moment. Archer had certainly had a stake in getting Miranda to make peace with Sin.

Miranda gave him a short nod, her gaze cold as ever. "St. John."

Not a one of them calling him Sin anymore. He took a breath then gestured to the numerous seats set up around the fireplace. "Please be seated." He ought to formally introduce them to Layla, but the tension was thick enough as it was and he wasn't about to subject Layla to any possible snubs.

When they'd all settled, he took a chair next to Layla, close enough to touch her if he felt the compulsion.

"Miss Layla Starling," he said, gesturing towards her with his chin. "My family. Daisy and Ian Ranulf, Poppy and Winston Lane." He did not mention their early meeting with Poppy, for he knew his sister would not approve. "Lady Miranda and Lord Benjamin Archer."

He glanced around the room. "Miss Starling is my good friend from childhood and currently under my protection." *Mine, mine, mine.*

A few brows lifted in surprise but not a soul made comment on why Layla should need protection. Instead there were polite but bland murmurs of greeting.

Layla's happy demeanor from earlier had faded into a faint moue of disapproval. And it pained him that she should witness his family looking upon him as though he were a criminal.

This was foolish, asking for their help. He ought to have solved the problem on his own. Sin's fists tightened, and he nearly stood to tell them all to leave, that it had been a mistake calling them here.

Then Layla's soft hand settled on top of his. That small but reassuring weight bolstered him, wrapped around him just as sure and strong as any armor.

Sin's gaze went hard. "It is clear that you are reluctant to be here. I have been reluctant to make contact. But none of that matters anymore. There are greater things at play than our personal wants, and I intend to set a few things clear."

Chapter Twenty-One

To say Sin's family was intimidating was an understatement. They were a handsome lot to be sure. Layla wondered if the blood of immortals and Others was somehow predestined to physical beauty, for everyone in the room—yes, even the badly scarred man they called Winston—was beautiful in their own way.

Regardless of their physical appearance, they all radiated power of various levels. Winston and Archer were clearly human, though Archer's body seemed to give off a faint silver glow, one that shocked Layla, for she had not previously been inclined to notice such things. But it was there—a bit like what she saw in Sin when he turned Judgment. Had Archer the blood of Judgment in him from some distant ancestor? The man was clearly ailing, so he could not be of full blood or he'd have healed himself.

The man called Ian stared at her with an intensity that was unnerving, though she wondered if he was aware of doing it. There was nothing untoward about the look. He was currently stroking his wife's hip where she sat perched upon the arm of his chair. Rather, his nostrils flared slightly as if he were taking in Layla's scent and trying to define it. She supposed that made sense. Sin had told her Ian was a lycan, a being capable of turning into a werewolf. He was the king of the lycans, in fact. Layla entertained herself by picturing him wearing a great golden crown with a snarling wolf carved in the front.

Her small smile made the beautiful one, Miranda, raise a brow. Gods, but she looked so very much like Sin. She had his sculpted features: the high-cut cheekbones, the thin straight nose, the lush but shapely lips. It almost hurt to look upon her. Sin was a beautiful male but Miranda was stunning.

And she was not happy to see them. Nor were any of his family, apparently. Poppy, the leader of the SOS, seemed indifferent. Daisy, Ian's wife and a strange being who clearly had a mechanical heart—Layla could hear it ticking away—was a pretty woman with a sweet smile, as if she would always be smiling, regardless of uncomfortable situations.

This definitely counted as uncomfortable. The silence was deafening.

Sin cleared his throat. "For the past year and a half, I've been in communication with Augustus."

Silence took on a heavy, hard feel.

Sin stared back at his family and the square line of his jaw hardened. "He has been mentoring me, if you will."

"Why would Augustus do that?" Miranda asked, her tone cutting.

Sin didn't flinch. "Well, I suppose he felt he had things to teach me." He glanced at Poppy, who seemed to know some of the truth, and then back at the rest of them. "This family has always been entwined with him in some way or other. I believe Augustus sees us as his to protect in his own way."

Sin left the rest unsaid but Layla heard it loud and clear, and believed his family did as well. Sin was part of this family whether they objected or not.

Daisy had the grace to duck her head, while Ian and Archer seemed to give the barest nod at the same moment. Looking at them, Layla suspected they were close friends.

"And you, Miss Starling," Miranda said, looking at her with those eyes the same exact shade as Sin's. "Augustus has been seen with you quite a bit."

"He is my guardian," Layla said with pride. "He raised me."

"Bloody hell," Poppy said in a low tone. "You all think me capable of secrets? Augustus wrote the manual."

"I was unaware that his guardianship of me was a secret," Layla said.

"Forgive me, Miss Starling," Ian said, his tone laced with a hint of Scottish brogue, "but you aren't quite human yourself, are you?"

"No. My mother was called Lena."

An instant and menacing growl rumbled in Ian's throat, drawing Layla up short, the tiny hairs along her neck and arms rising. Sin tensed, leaning forward in his seat. "Tone it down, Ranulf. She is mine."

A flush went through her at his claim. But Ian was glaring, his pupils turning to slits, rather like a wolf's. Daisy cupped the back of his neck and gave it a squeeze. "Calm yourself, my dear pest. You know very well a person's nature is not beholden to that of her parents." She made a soft snort. "Or we'd all be raving, evil lunatics in here."

Ian winced. "Apologies, Miss Starling. I've had bad dealings with Lena." He waved a hand that appeared to be tipped by claws. "'Tis no excuse, merely to point out that my reaction was not intended for you."

"It's all right. I suspect we are all on edge."

Sin glanced at her and then set his arm on her chair, seeking her hand. She laced her fingers with his cold ones and realized how tense he really was.

"There is a guardian-level Damnation demon in London," Sin said.

Poppy sat up straight, her fine nostrils flaring on a sharp breath. Only Ian seemed as affected. The rest merely looked confused.

"At the risk of acquiring stomach upset," Winston drawled, "what, pray tell, is a Damnation demon?"

Layla rather liked him just then.

Poppy's pale hand drifted to his shoulder. "It is quite like Apep. Only worse."

At that, Winston winced, and Archer muttered, "Christ."

"Who is Apep?" Layla could not help but ask.

"Our father," Poppy said shortly. "A lovely fellow who wanted to steal my husband and my son's souls."

Right. That one. He sounded delightful.

"Apep," Sin cut in, "was a sort of Damnation, actually. Augustus told me he was one of the first trials. He fancied himself a demi god after he broke from Damnation."

"Always with the secrets in this family," Miranda muttered.

"So this Damnation fellow," Winston cut in, "what can you tell us about him?"

Sin rubbed the back of his neck. "This one goes by the name St. Claire, though I doubt it's his real name. He's a direct get of Cain, the original Damnation. We ran afoul of him last night and barely escaped. He destroyed Augustus's home, which is why we are here. What you must understand is that this being is unlike anything our civilization has seen in a millennium. He can level the city if so inclined. He can send utter terror into most minds, leaving the victim helpless to defend himself."

"Well, isn't that charming," Daisy said with a little frown. "So we shall not be having him to tea."

Ian spread his palm out on her curvy thigh. "Surely he is not a match against all of us."

Sin's voice was cool and deadly. "The last time Damnation ran amuck, it leveled Pompeii." He gave a tight smile. "Oh, aye, it was no volcano that caused the destruction. It was a war between Damnation and Judgment."

Archer cleared his throat, his voice coming out husky and tinged with pain. "Judgment. You speak of the soul eaters."

Sin met his gaze. "Yes. Augustus, as you know, is Judgment. He is the father of them all. Probably why he calls himself Father in the SOS. He defeated that Damnation, and had believed them all destroyed." His jaw tightened. "St. Claire had Augustus's wing."

Poppy went pale. "What? How?"

"He'd clearly ripped it off." Sin's expression pinched. "We do not know if Augustus lives."

Poppy ducked her head, and Winston pulled her onto his knee, his arm going around her thin shoulders. "When you met with this St. Claire last night, what did he want?"

"He wanted Layla," Sin said. "I was disinclined to let him have her."

"And how did you get away, if he is as powerful as you claim?" Miranda added with a disbelieving look.

Layla bristled.

Sin merely looked at her. "I am not without power, Miranda. As you well know."

"Oh, I know. As I know of your penchant for falsehoods."

Archer murmured a reprimand under his breath, but Miranda ignored it.

Daisy wrinkled her nose. "You must admit, St. John, you have yet to be forthcoming with us in all your dealings."

Poppy gave Sin a hard stare. "You are keeping things from us again. Do not deny it."

Sin's expression was perfectly blank. A sign that Layla now knew meant he was hurting but did not want it to show. "I made a vow to Augustus to hold my own council on many things."

Miranda snorted. "Quite convenient, that. Tell me, did he ask you to interact with Mab? To become her lover?"

Sin's grip on Layla's hand went tight before slipping away. "Augustus had nothing to do with her."

"So I thought," Miranda said with a scoff. "And here you are again, in the thick of things, full of secrets, and not divulging them when they are needed."

Poppy peered at Sin as though he were an insect. "She speaks true, St. John. Mab's plans might have destroyed all the GIM. Which includes your sister."

Daisy flushed pink at this. And Layla remembered that GIM were those with clockwork hearts. She did not know the particulars of Mab's threat to them but it had to be horrid if the expression of agony on Ian's face was anything to go by. He said not a word but he would no longer look at Sin.

Sin who sat rigid and silent as they all took turns sniping at him.

"You warmed that evil woman's bed knowing she was making those you love suffer," Poppy said in a low voice. "Why? You never said."

Sin's jaw bunched, his eyes narrowing and turning a silver-green. But he would not speak. It seemed he'd lost the ability in the face of their ire.

"And now you expect us to believe that Augustus has willingly made you privy to all his secrets—"

Layla snapped. "Oh, enough! All of you."

Three sets of feminine eyes glared at her with varying levels of annoyance. She did not care a whit. Layla leaned forward, her fist bunching. “How dare you give Sin a hard time, toss his love back in his face?”

Miranda raised a red brow. “Miss Starling, you do not know—”

“Oh, I know enough. I know that he is your brother. And you turned your backs on him when he needed you most.”

“He was in league with—”

“Are you quite serious?” Layla all but hissed. “How can you not even entertain the possibility that he was acting under duress?”

“Layla,” Sin began, but she held out a hand.

“No, Saint. No more.” Her glare went round the table, taking in the shocked expressions. “A blood slave, forced to do whatever that foul bitch… Bother, I am new to this world, and I’ve heard of blood vows. It shocks and disgusts me that you, who have lived with these laws for years, did not think of it.”

A ringing silence met her. And Layla grabbed Sin’s cold hand. “He is the best man I know. Loyal to a fault—”

“Layla…”

“Protective of those he loves. How could you not see he was doing his best in the only way he could?” She rose to her feet, her body quivering. “How could you not have done *your* best to save him?” Her teeth met with a click. “I cannot… No. I cannot stand to look at any of you. You don’t deserve him.”

She’d have pulled Sin with her but she gathered he’d not go lightly. So Layla quit the room by herself, her eyes burning but dry, before she did these ladies and gentlemen harm.

Layla exited in a flutter of irate skirts, her head held as high and proud as a queen’s. Ringing silence followed. Sin found her rather magnificent. He fought a smile and looked back at his family. "So then, that was Layla."

"She's wonderful," Ian said with a wolfish grin.

"Yes," Sin said. But as soon as the dust settled and the silence returned, he thought of Layla's words. She'd told them of his deepest shame. Suddenly he felt ill, his skin crawling with humiliation. It was a sad truth that a large part of him would rather have their anger than their pity.

The feeling grew worse when he spied their horror-stricken faces.

A strangled noise left Miranda. "You…A blood slave to Mab?"

Now that Layla had swooped in like a defending angel and said the words, Sin felt his own hurt and resentment bubble up within. They *had* turned their backs on him. Without a second thought. "Is it so shocking?"

Daisy made her own little noise of distress, and then he was smothered in velvet and bosom as she hugged his head so tightly he could barely breathe. "Oh, dear boy. My little brother. How could we?"

"Daisy," Ian drawled. "He's in danger of inhaling your breasts."

She drew back. "Right, sorry. But they're inescapable, really."

Sin let out a weak laugh, and she replied by kissing his cheeks and forehead before sitting down next to her husband once more. And he sat there a little dazed. He'd missed casual affection, but his heart hurt worse. He'd missed their love.

Poppy cocked her head and peered at him. "Brother, Layla was right to chastise us. There is no excuse for our behavior. We have wronged you. It was badly done of us."

"Badly done?" Winston said with a scoff. "It was shoddy

behavior, at the very least." He pulled his pipe free of his twisted mouth. "My deepest apologies, St. John."

"Christ," Ian said with a slap of his hand to his thigh, "we're making it worse. A man does not need a room full of people falling prostrate on the floor, begging forgiveness. He needs only one emissary. Take Miranda." Ian cocked his head towards Sin's silent and frowning sister. "She's the one who cocked it up in the first place."

"Ian!" Daisy clouted him on the head, or tried to.

Ian was quite good at ducking. "I only speak the truth."

An awkward silence fell over the room. Sin would not look at Miranda. He couldn't. But he saw her rise and then she was kneeling before him. Tears glistened in her eyes, the same jade green as his. "Ian speaks true," she said in a husky voice. "Sin... I've been so distrustful of my family, save my sisters."

Hurt punched through his chest. Yes, they'd had each other, always. Sin had been the one taken away and hidden.

Miranda's hands clasped his. "No one was what they claimed to be. And then to find out I had a brother. I'd always wanted one. It hurt all of us to believe all these years that you'd died. When I found out you were still alive..." She shook her head, tears breaking free to run down her cheeks. "I was so angry with Mother. I was angry that we did not get to care for you, see you grow."

"Miranda," he croaked, not wanting to hear any more.

But she squeezed his hands tight, sending flares of warmth up his arms, the power of heat and fire that only they shared. "I think... I think I was looking for something to keep you away. Because it hurt too much to know how we'd failed you. I was afraid to love you because you might be taken away once more."

Sin pulled her close then, and she hugged him tight, her

slim body shaking. "Forgive me, St. John. I love you so. If it takes the rest of my life to do it, I will make this up to you."

A soft cry from Daisy, and then they were both smothered again. Little flowers popped up on Miranda's hair, and Sin laughed—Daisy usually chose to use her powers for beauty rather than for defense. A cool hand landed on his shoulder as Poppy came close and kissed the top of his head.

From beyond the wall of sisters hugging him, he heard Ian groan. "Make them stop, Lane," Ian said to Winston.

"You only say that because you're in danger of weeping," Winston said dryly.

"Don't think I missed you wiping your eye, Lane," Ian retorted.

And Sin laughed again, pressing his own damp cheek to a soft arm, Daisy's he supposed. They were all too close for him to properly tell. When they pulled away, he realized he had to trust them if they were to trust him. Some secrets were harmful if kept for too long, and what he'd become was one of those.

"Augustus made me Judgment," he said.

And the air seemed to leave the room.

"You took the elixir," Archer said in a slightly awed voice.

"Yes." It wasn't really an elixir. But Sin would keep that much of Augustus's secrets. "Unlike you, however, I had someone to teach me." Sin let himself change, going crystal clear and unfurling his wings.

"Jesus," Winston said. "You look just as Augustus did when I saw him in that alley." The alley where Winston had been mauled by a mad werewolf. Augustus had swooped down and saved him, though Winston bore the slashing scars on his face.

They all looked awed, but Archer and Miranda appeared haunted. Sin knew Archer had been slowly changing to

Judgment. Not realizing that was what he'd been becoming, he hadn't the skills to change at will.

"Wings too?" Miranda reached out then halted.

"You may touch them," Sin said.

And she did, shock and awe still on her face.

Archer stared. "Have you done it? Taken a soul?"

"Yes, when warranted. I've been in Rome, acting there." Sin vanished his wings and changed back into his human form. "Out of all of us, I am the one most likely to vanquish St. Claire. Some of you might succeed in wounding him, but he will destroy you and those you hold dear."

He looked around the room. "Poppy and Win, you have a child. Archer and Miranda are mortal. Daisy is GIM but he is quite capable of persuading you to rip out your own heart."

Ian growled, but Sin merely gave him a long look. "You know a little of Damnation; that much is clear. Tell me I am wrong."

"You are not," Ian grumbled. "Nor am I willing to risk my Daisy. However, myself? My fellow lycans? We will stand with you."

Daisy's face pinched but she bit down on her lip as if to stifle her protest.

"Thank you," Sin said. "But lycans cannot effectively fight Damnation. It is said that Damnation's first servants were the wolves and the serpents. He could turn your will at a thought."

Ian bristled. "Are you saying you believe me to be that weak of mind?"

"You? No. But your wolf? Those of your men? We cannot risk it."

"Canny wee angel boy," Ian said under his breath as he glared down at his claws.

Sin sighed and ran a hand through his hair. "London is

in danger of falling. We need to prepare. Ian, you are able to mentally reach out to other lycan, yes?"

"That I can," Ian said.

"Then have them search for Augustus." Sin glanced at Daisy. "The GIM too, if you please. As for the rest of us, there is a good chance that Others with evil in their hearts will strike when Damnation does. As it is, there is a contingent of raptor demons who serve him."

"We need Jack," Winston said. "He is Nephilim."

Yes, out of all of them, only Jack had the strength to help Sin fight St. Claire. "I'd like to ask Jack to guard Layla. I cannot worry about her and fight Damnation as well."

"Consider it done." Jack Talent walked into the room, towering over everyone with his great height. At his side was his small and delicate-looking wife. "Apologies for the delay. Mary and I were at the theater and did not receive word until it let out."

Sin stood and grasped Jack's massive hand. "Appreciated, Jack." He turned to the room. "Now if you'll excuse me, I'll go see to Layla."

Ian grinned, flashing long canines. "Aye, attend to your lady love, and perhaps afterward, ask her to give us simple folk another chance? I'd quite like to keep my head, ye' ken?"

Sin laughed. "I'll see what I can do."

She was a coward, shouting at Sin's family and then running away. She ought to have stayed. She'd left his side, left him to face their ire without her. Layla pressed her knees closer to her chest and hugged herself tight, huddling in the corner of the large velvet sofa in her room. She needed better control.

Half the hour had dwindled away since she'd gone at their

heads. Layla was still riled but she fancied that, if Sin had been rejected by his family, he'd have sought her out by now. Or perhaps he was angry with her for spilling his secrets. She winced. She had not meant to do that. Or had she? Layla's thoughts were a muddle.

A soft kiss at her cheek made her yelp and jump. Sin's grinning face hovered over her shoulder, and she scowled. "You scared the life out of me."

He kissed her again, close to the sensitive corner of her mouth. "Not *all* the life, I hope. I'm rather attached to you."

His voice was soft and tender. And she watched him as he rounded the sofa to crouch before her.

"Sin," she said, "I'm sorry—"

His lips on hers rendered her silent. He kissed her softly, deeply, as if her lips were warm wax and he was shaping them to his. His breath flowed into hers, his familiar scent surrounding her. He pulled away, his green eyes searching her face. Silvery tracks of dried tears trailed his cheeks.

"You've been crying." She touched his cheek, tracing a line.

Sin pressed his hand to hers, trapping her palm against his skin. "Have I? I suppose I was overwhelmed. Don't hold it against me, eh?"

Ridiculous man. "Did they shout at you?"

"No." He leaned in and kissed her again. "I think you might have shamed them into the next century. They love me. And I love you."

Warmth went through her and she smiled. "I love you too."

His answering smile was so tender and carefree, she now was in danger of crying. Sin cradled her face in his hands and kissed her cheeks, her brow, the tip of her nose. He finished with a soft kiss on her lips. "Your love, Layla, is the greatest gift of all. What you did for me back there..."

"I know," she said mournfully. "I went off like a raving lunatic. Your family surely hates me now."

He shook his head, his thumbs stroking her cheeks. "No one has ever stood up for me in that manner. It made me feel…I don't even know how to describe it, but Layla, I will spend my entire life making certain you feel the same, that you know how loved you are by me."

"Saint, you're an immortal," she felt compelled to point out.

He was busy kissing his way down her neck. "Precisely. Which means an eternity of practice. Mmm…You smell delicious. Your ire has the scent of roasting chestnuts."

A scandalized laugh bubbled up within. "Don't tell me such things. I'm horrified."

She could feel him smiling against her skin. "Why? It's wonderful." His warm hands coasted down her neck, along her sides, brushing the swells of her breasts and lingering there. Sin's voice grew deeper. "And your arousal. Gods, Layla. When you're aroused…warm butter and sugar."

The tips of his thumbs flicked over her nipples, and Layla arched into the touch, her lashes fluttering closed. "I never thought your sense of smell was so developed."

"Only for you, it seems." His tongue traced the line of her neck, and still he played with her nipples, rubbing them, pinching them so lightly it made her breath come quick. "Like that, do you?"

She shivered with delicious heat. "More," she whispered.

He groaned, tugging at her aching nipples. "Are you all sweet and slippery for me, Layla?"

She loved that he was like this with her—free, relaxed, and slightly devious. Her fingers trailed over his hot neck, sliding beneath his collar. "Yes, Sin."

He hummed in appreciation. "Lift your skirts and let me see."

Heat rippled over her skin, and her limbs grew both tight and heavy. Her fingers struggled to gain purchase on her skirts, gathering them up, slowly exposing her stockinged legs.

Sin sat back on his haunches, watching her progress. His gaze blazed when the skirt reached the tops of her thighs. "Layla, love, you aren't wearing knickers."

"Apparently not," she said with a little smile. The air was a cool kiss on her wet sex. And she shivered in anticipation.

His voice grew thick and rough. "Part your thighs more, little bird, so I can see all of you."

The demand had her thighs clenching. Layla wiggled a bit, arching her back, letting the tender tips of her breasts push against her bodice. She caught Sin's gaze and her smile felt languid, coy. "No," she said.

Sin raised a dark brow, but his lips curled too. "No?"

His reproachful glare sent little flutters through her belly. They grew stronger when he placed his hands upon her knees and firmly wrenched her legs open. Layla bit her lip as he slowly looked her over, his thumbs rubbing her sensitive skin. "Naughty, Layla," he whispered, "hiding this pretty, pink quim from me."

At his words, her sex contracted, and his nostrils flared on a sharp breath. His voice grew lower still, rougher. "Touch it. Tell me how it feels."

Her breath left in a gust, and she stared at him wide-eyed, her heart pounding against her breasts. He looked at her from under thick, black lashes. "Go on, love, play with that little button for me."

Perhaps she ought to be shy or scandalized by his demands, but the way he looked at her, as if she was the only thing in his world, as if she were utterly beautiful, made her want to please him. The mere thought had her flushed and aching. And so, with a shaking hand, she reached down between her legs.

A moan left her as her finger slipped over that swollen bit of slick flesh, and pleasure skittered down her thighs and up her torso.

"That's it," Sin murmured darkly. "Show me how you like it."

Slowly she moved her finger in a light, teasing circle, all the while watching him watch her. His broad chest lifted and fell with each unsteady breath he took. A flush ran over his cheeks, his lips parting as though he were thinking of kissing her where she played.

"Dip those fingers in, Layla. Are you ready for me?"

With a shiver, she obeyed his command, plunging her finger into her tight heat. She'd never done that before, never explored so far, and to have him watching her every move made it both illicit and wonderful. Only with Sin would she feel free to touch herself. To play. For they were playing, weren't they?

As if she'd asked the question aloud, Sin caught her gaze, and a slow, heated smile pulled at his mouth, one that promised she'd be well-pleased. "Oh, yes, little bird, you love it, do you not? Spreading those legs wide, letting me watch?"

Her lids fluttered, wanting to close. But she wanted to see him more. He leaned in a little, his grip on her thighs firm. "Give me a taste."

Her sex tightened around her fingers, all of it so slick and hot and swollen. Layla drew out. Her glistening fingers shook as she reached out and painted his lower lip with her arousal.

He groaned, his lids lowering as his licked, tasted her, then caught her forefinger, drawing it in deep. His mouth was warm and wet, his tongue flickering over her fingertip. She felt it between her legs, over her stiff nipples.

"Sin." Her breath hitched. "Now. Come to me now."

She hadn't meant it as a command, knowing he did not like those, but Sin didn't appear unsettled. No, his expression grew fierce, his hand going to the buttons of his trousers, where his erection pushed against the fabric.

He took his cock in hand, and again she marveled at its thick length. Was it normal to adore that part of the male anatomy? She did not care. She wanted it in her and arched her back, spreading her legs wider.

Sin's eyes flashed silver green as he stroked himself. "Greedy girl. You need me?"

"Desperately."

His voice grew husky. "You love me?"

"Eternally."

His free hand slid up her thigh and grabbed her hip. He pulled her forward, just this side of rough, and rubbed the crown of his cock over her sensitized opening. That was all the warning she had before he thrust inside, filling her up with one push.

It tore a garbled cry from her lips, her body tensing before going liquid with pleasure.

Sin ducked his head, his lean body hunched over hers as if to shelter it. "So very good," he said. "Always ecstasy with you, Layla."

He moved in and out, a lovely invasion and retreat that stuffed her full and left her achingly empty over and over. And she could not help but move with him, lifting her hips to greet his return, drawing them back to prolong his retreat.

Sin's gaze stayed locked with hers, his parted lips brushing her lips so that they shared the same breath. Every few thrusts in, he would kiss her, a light taste of her mouth before drawing away.

Layla shuddered. There was something decidedly wicked

about doing this fully clothed, with only where they were joined exposed. It drew all her attention there, to how wet she was, the air cool on her burning thighs, to how very thick and hard he was, working her body as if each pump of his hips was an exquisite agony.

Pleasure licked over her skin, making her flesh quiver. But her heart was this soft and aching thing within her chest, swelling with tenderness for Sin, for he looked at her, his gaze wide and just a bit battered, as if he did not know what to do with his feelings. He'd told her he did not know how to make love. How very wrong he was, when she felt his regard with the whole of her body.

A lump rose in her throat, and she cupped the sides of his sweaty neck, feeling the heat of his body. "Sin," she said, drawing him closer. His chest pressed against her, his mouth found the crook of her neck as she held him in her arms.

A tremor went down his back, and he puffed out a breath. "Layla. Layla." He thrust hard and fast then, uncoordinated and desperate. And she held him throughout as he let himself go.

"Just this, Sin," she whispered in his ear. "Just you loving me. Me loving you. Always."

He thrust harder, hitting some spot within that made her shudder, had her sex swelling with near-painful pleasure. "Always, Layla."

He reached down, and his thumb found the sensitive place that she'd played with before. He pushed down, and she flew apart, a cry ringing out. On it went, hard and startling. She couldn't think, could barely hold onto his collar. He worked her there, prolonging her pleasure, until, with a shout of his own, he thrust one final time, pushing hard against her sex.

Panting, he sagged against her. Layla gave him a weak kiss on his damp temple. Her body was so warm and satisfied, little tremors of pleasure still running through her, that she could fall asleep just like this, with him deep inside her, his lips on her neck.

But he suddenly chuckled, deep and disjointed. “Ah, Layla love, you slay me in the most perfect way.”

She had to smile. “You did all the work, sweet Sin.”

He lifted his head and gave her a look so tender it took her breath. His thumb brushed over her lower lip. “No, Layla, it’s all you. You love me. That makes all the difference in the world.”

Chapter Twenty-Two

Lena

They had just pulled into Victoria Station when the world caught up to them. Lena felt the presence of power before the train had stopped. From beyond the window, billows of white steam and black coal smoke mixed to gray, and the shrill whistle of the train announced their arrival. But somewhere out there on the platform filled with bustling travelers, an immortal waited.

Augustus stirred, his heavy lids opening as though by force of will. "London?"

"Yes." She leaned back from the window, where she was exposed. "Something is out there. Can you stand on your own?"

A weak smile. "I can make a good show of it."

Lena wasn't certain about that, but pride was a valuable commodity, and she was not about to stomp on Augustus's. "It feels like a primus but off somehow."

"Fallen," Augustus said, closing his eyes and inhaling. "No, the son of a fallen. Nephilim. I do believe it is Jack Talent."

"Wonderful." The one being who had most cause to hate her. He had every right. He represented her greatest dishonor.

Augustus looked at her then with solemn eyes. "Behave."

"Are you trying to cause a row? Because you are off to a good start."

The corner of his pale lips lifted. "Merely attempting to stop one, love."

Lena had extreme doubts as to the possibility of that. This meeting would not be pleasant. But she held her tongue as she helped him out of their car and onto the platform. Not wanting to take chances, she instantly cloaked them to all humans.

Others, however, could see them well enough, and they had not gone two steps before Jack Talent, that hulking behemoth of a man, emerged out of the mists. At his side was a pretty little GIM whom Lena recognized to be Mary Chase. Though she'd heard they'd married, so Lena supposed she was Mary Talent now.

Anger radiated off them in palpable waves. And though Augustus stood at Lena's side, they only had eyes for her.

Talent took a hard step in her direction, his big fists clenched. Looking at him now, with his great height and massive build, she ought to have known he was never a mere shifter, but had the blood of angels in him.

"You," he said.

"She is my mate," Augustus cut in with a surprisingly hard voice. "Hurt her and you destroy me."

Talent hesitated and scowled. "Shit and piss, Augustus. You'd put me in this bind?"

Mary, who was still at his side, glared as well, her gaze cutting between Lena and Augustus. "You are Father of the SOS. Your knowledge saved Jack and me once. Which holds us in your debt, but what she did to Jack..." Mary's frame vibrated with rage. "I cannot..."

Lena let go of Augustus and stepped forward. It hurt her stubborn pride to do it but she knelt before Jack Talent. "Your blood and suffering are on my hands. I meant to use your blood to borrow your likeness only. I thought to protect St. John from discovery. But my servants abused you. That is inexcusable." One slash of her nail over her wrists and her blood flowed free. "Thus I offer you my blood."

Crimson drops fell to the pavement between Talent's booted feet. She held her hands up higher. "It is all I have to give. But Augustus must be helped. He is innocent in all this."

Above her, she heard Talent sigh. "Get up with you. I don't want your blood."

Lena rose and faced him. Shadows danced in the dark green eyes that glared down at her, so haunted, and yet there was peace to be found within those depths as well. "Whatever your actions, whatever pain inflicted upon me, those roads led to me being with Mary. I'll not take that back for all the bloodshed in the world."

"Let me hit her then," Mary grumbled.

Talent nearly smiled but then frowned as Augustus fell to his knees. Crying out, Mary rushed to his side but Lena was quicker. Wrapping an arm around his shoulders, she lifted him to standing.

"What ails you?" Talent asked him.

"He has been wounded by a Damnation demon," Lena answered. "I haven't the power to fully heal him, nor can Augustus restore himself."

Grimly, Talent bent forward and rested a hand upon Augustus's shoulder. "May I have a look?"

Augustus's eyes opened, revealing reddened rims and irises that were clear as glass. "By all means, Master Talent."

Gently, Talent parted his shirt. “Hell.” The fist-sized wound that Enoch had punched through Augustus’s chest remained, oozing silver blood. “I spoke too soon about the bloodshed. Mary, a knife, if you please.”

Mary Talent reached down, pulled an elegant stiletto from her boot, and handed it to Talent. Without pause, he took the knife and sliced it across his palm. Blood bloomed, the scent rich and delicious, like spiced pudding. Lena bit her lip to keep still. She understood why her servants had lost their heads when faced with Talent’s blood; it was ambrosia to demons, even Damnation.

He paid her no mind, however, and pressed his bleeding palm to Augustus’s wound. A faint sizzle filled the air. Augustus inhaled sharply, his head jerking up. Color returned to his cheeks, though not as robust as it ought to be.

When Talent pulled back, Augustus’s chest was smooth, and Talent’s palm was healed. “Better,” Talent murmured, satisfied. “St. John sent us to look for you two. A Damnation demon has destroyed your house and attempted to take Layla.”

Augustus sucked in a sharp breath, and a bit of his old fire flashed in his dark eyes. “Where are they now?”

“At Evernight House. Safest place they could figure. However, I doubt that will keep the bastard out for long.”

“It won’t keep him out at all,” Lena said. “He is biding his time for whatever he has planned.”

“As I feared.” Talent braced Augustus’s shoulder once more. “It would be best if I carry you, Master Augustus. But only if you will it.”

“Pride means nothing if one is dead,” Augustus said. “Idling in the open invites temptation. Take me to Layla and St. John, Master Talent.”

With the utmost care, Jack Talent lifted Augustus in his arms, and Lena felt a fresh surge of guilt for wronging the man who would treat her love with such respect. So many regrets. She vowed she would not have any more before her time here was done. She followed them out of Victoria Station and prepared to face her daughter.

Before dawn, Layla left Sin sleeping and crept downstairs to find something to eat. She found herself hungry more often, as if something inside her was clawing at her stomach, demanding more and more food. It had been this way since she'd begun to change.

She had just turned the corner towards the stairs when she ran into Ian Ranulf. Sin had told her that his family planned to stay at Evernight House for the moment, where they would be strong in number and ready to protect each other if needed.

But she'd forgotten that fact until she came abreast of Ian. He really was disarmingly handsome—nothing close to Sin's male beauty, but charismatic, with brilliant blue eyes that seemed to glow like the moon in the dim light.

"Lass," he said with a nod, "I hope St. John conveyed our apologies for our behavior earlier."

Sin hadn't. He'd been busy. Layla was determined not to flush but the damn wolf-man noticed anyway, and he grinned. "No, I suppose he had other things on his mind."

"You are very forward, Mr. Ranulf."

His grin grew. "It's just Ranulf. Or Ian, if you prefer. And I've been told as much on occasion." He inclined his head, his expression warming. "I meant no disrespect. Truthfully, it eases my mind to know young Sin has found such a loyal and protective mate to walk through life with."

Her blush must be crimson at this point. "Yes, well, thank you."

But when she moved to go, he touched her arm. "At the

risk of causing further offense, I wanted to say that I've been catching your scent."

"My scent?" Mortification surged through her. Good gravy, she did not want to think about her scent now.

Ian grimaced. "I seem determined to stick my foot in it tonight. No, lass. I meant, when you've shifted, I've scented you. At first, I thought you were a lycan."

"Truly?" Despite her embarrassment, she was intrigued.

"Aye, there's something a wee bit lupine in your scent. But it isn't lycan, no. And I had the devil of a time placing it until we were in the same room together." He moved closer, lowering his voice as if he were imparting bad news. "It's jackal, ye ken?"

Layla frowned, but her heartbeat kicked up. "No, I'm afraid I don't understand."

"There's nothing as keen as a lycan's nose, aye? It's a strange thing, but we have what you might call collective scent memories. What my ancestors scented long ago is stored up in here." He pointed to his head. "I know what the paint drying on the temples of Luxor smelled like because one of my kin was there."

"And this jackal?"

"St. John mentioned the Damnation demon, and it hit me. They smell of jackal and brimstone. You, Miss Starling," he gestured towards her, "smell of jackal, sugar-spice, and fresh rain. Just as Judgment in full fighting form smells of fresh rain."

Layla's mouth fell open. "Sin never scented that on me."

"Aye, I suspect St. John has bonded with you to the point of which he scents your emotions and not your similarities to him."

Her head began to pound, her eyes hot. "What are you saying?"

His blue gaze bore into hers, serious and solemn. "I think you know."

That she was both Damnation and Judgment? Layla bit her lip and glanced around, trying to make sense of it. "But how?"

Ian frowned too. "I was thinking on Lena. She was a clever devil, always hiding her true self and thoughts from others."

"You knew her well." It wasn't a question. Ian's tone and expression told its own story.

He made a face, not of disgust this time but of discomfort. "Aye, well, I suppose I should tell the truth. We were lovers at one point in time, before I met my Daisy."

"Oh." And what more could she say? The man before her appeared no older than thirty, and yet he'd been lovers with her mother.

He grimaced. "And you thought the conversation was awkward before, eh?"

She had to laugh. "I do admit, I view you in an entirely new light, Ranulf."

"You really ought to call me Ian at this point," he said with a quick smile. His expression grew serious. "Truth is, when Sin said you were Lena's, part of me wondered if you were mine. The timing was right, ye ken?"

"But I'm not?" Her stomach fluttered at the possibility of facing her father.

He shook his head, appearing surprisingly mournful. "As proud as I would be to call a lass such as yourself my kin, I'd know by scent alone. I've no jackal in me, lass. It isn't my scent I'm catching on you, but hers.

"Once, when Lena shifted into a swarm of spiders"—at that he shivered—"there was a hint of something in the air. Jackal and brimstone."

"How could she hide that scent?"

"Some beings can hide many things if they've a mind to do it." Ian touched her arm again. "I know not who your sire was, but think on it, lass. My sense of smell does not lie. You have both Damnation and Judgment in your flesh and blood."

Dread filled her, even as Ian finished, his words heavy as her heart. "Given that this Damnation demon is hunting you, I'd say there's a good chance he thinks you're one of his own."

"But that doesn't make any sense," she said. "For if Damnation is the scent of my mother, then the Judgment you sense in me would be that of my father."

Ian frowned. He made to speak but Layla was already turning, heading back to her rooms. She needed Sin.

Chapter Twenty-Three

Layla had gathered up her skirts to climb back up the stairs when the front door opened. The wind whistled into the house, bringing with it the scent of Augustus, of rain and another scent: that of brimstone.

She halted and caught Ian's eye. He appeared shocked as well, and they both gaped at each other for a tense moment, then Ian's mouth filled with fangs. With a growl, he spun round and sprinted down the stairs. Layla followed, her heart in her mouth.

The front hall was a long, cavernous space laid out with black marble. Ian was charging across it, headed for a delicate-looking woman with midnight hair and eyes. The woman did not flinch in the face of a snarling, spitting mad lycan, whose jaw had begun to lengthen into a snout.

At her side was a pretty, well-dressed woman with brown hair, who held an arm around a pale and slumped Augustus.

A tall man with enormously broad shoulders stepped in front of Ian, putting his massive hand upon the lycan king's chest to stop him. "Hold, Ian. I've made my peace with her."

Ian pushed up against the man's chest, but his wild glare went past him to the woman's. "I've a few words of my own, *mo mhac.*"

Layla had spent enough time in Ireland to know a bit of Gaelic. Ian had called him his son, though the big man with light brown hair and blunt features had little physical resemblance to Ian.

And then she remembered: Ian had been hunting Lena because she'd done a great wrong to his adopted son, Jack Talent. Layla's gaze flew to the woman with black eyes and found her staring back, her expression at once rapt and fearful.

Lena. This was her mother. A hum went through her body as if she were a tuning fork just struck. At the same moment, Ian lunged around Jack, ready to pounce upon Lena's small frame.

But as if he'd been lifted by an invisible hand, Ian flew back and was pinned to the wall. The man all but howled his fury, his body growing more lupine as he struggled, unable to free himself.

The commotion brought everyone in the house to the hall. Sin was suddenly by Layla's side, his hand a welcome warmth at the small of her back. But then he strode forward. "Augustus." He glanced at Ian. "Calm yourself. Jack brought her here. Can you not see?"

Daisy ran into the fray, fearlessly touching Ian's lengthened cheek. "Ian, my lovely pest, take a breath."

The man obeyed, and he seemed to sag, his shape returning to that of his human self. "All right. I'm calm." It was a growl of annoyance. "Now kindly release me." He glared at Augustus, who cleared his throat.

"I'm not holding you. I haven't the ability to do so."

Ian's glare slashed to Lena. "Afraid I'll still do you harm, witch?"

Lena had yet to look away from Layla, but she did so now as if with reluctance. “Hardly.” Her voice was black ice over stone.

At Layla’s side, Miranda and Archer and Poppy and Winston gathered.

“I do love reunions,” Archer murmured, as he leaned heavily on his silver-topped cane. “Most especially when Ian is in a snit.”

Winston appeared pale, making the red slashing scars that covered half his face stand out more. “Nothing quite like a lycan in a temper.” But he frowned. “If Augustus is not holding him, who is?”

Poppy left them and strode towards Augustus. “Father, you are unwell.”

“A bit of an understatement, my dear.” He accepted her arm with his free hand, clenching it tight. “St. John, release the man.”

Sin shook his head. “It isn’t me.”

Slowly, Augustus’s red-rimmed gaze traveled to Layla. She felt it like a soft thud against her heart. He’d never looked at her in such a manner, as if she were something utterly new, precious, and wondrous. “Layla,” he said, “let him go.”

She sucked in a breath, aware of all eyes upon her. Aware that the small woman who emanated enormous blasts of power was staring at her in much the same manner as Augustus.

Had she been holding Ian back? She thought of how she’d wanted to stop him. It had been an instinctual desire. Another breath and she thought about him falling free of the wall.

Ian tumbled forward, catching himself in an instant. “Bleeding hell,” he said with a faint laugh in her direction. “I had no idea you were that powerful, lass.”

"Neither did I." But she did not address him. She addressed her parent. For she knew then, without doubt, that when Ian had scented rain upon her, he'd been scenting her father, Augustus. "Did you know?" she asked him now.

Augustus swallowed convulsively. "No. Not until now." He bit off whatever else he wanted to say, and she glanced at her mother. Gods, this was her mother.

"You kept the knowledge from him."

The woman blinked. She was utterly beautiful in a cold and still sort of way. Did she feel anything? Any remorse? Any love for the daughter she'd discarded?

When Lena spoke, it was a near whisper. "I've done many wrongs, as you can see."

Sin stepped towards Layla, his eyes creased with worry. "Let us go to the library. We can talk."

Daisy took Ian's arm and then gave a cheery smile. "Right, then, the rest of you lot, breakfast in the dining room. Chip chop."

Poppy gave her a sidelong look. "I do love how you believe we'll follow your orders, sister." Yet she moved towards the dining room without hesitation.

And Layla was left alone in the hall with Sin and her parents.

I'd rather be eating breakfast. Layla stuffed that thought down and sat across from her parents. Augustus slumped against the bolsters of the blue velvet couch, his posture so unlike him, he almost appeared a stranger to her. In a way he was—the man she'd always believed to be her guardian, now her father.

Her fingers were cold, and as she tucked her hands beneath her thighs, her gaze moved with great reluctance to Lena. Emotions rocked through her, all of them strong and disparate: love, hate, happiness, sorrow, anger, yearning. She didn't know what to think or to feel.

Sin leaned a hip against the side of her chair, and his hand settled on her nape. Grounding her. He too knew what it meant to be without family, to have them suddenly appear back in his life. How had he handled meeting Miranda and Archer when they'd arrived in Ireland to tell him he was not who he thought?

He gave her neck a squeeze, and she realized he'd read her conflicting emotions quite well.

"Well, then," she got out. "This is quite awkward."

The fingers at her nape began to massage her locked muscles.

Augustus gave her a wan smile. "Quite. May I present you to Lena, your—"

"Mother," Layla finished for him, getting a dark pinch of satisfaction in seeing the woman twitch when she said it.

Lena might have been carved from pure marble but she blinked, a slow sweep of lashes. "I went to see you sing. In Vienna."

Layla did not know whether this pleased or angered her. A little bit of both, really. Or a lot. "I've lost my voice."

She did not know why she said it; this woman wouldn't be her sounding stone. But Lena's expression softened a bit—the difference between marble and sandstone.

"It will come back."

Layla flinched as if struck. "How can you say?"

"Because it happened to me."

Augustus straightened. "You sing?"

Her thoughts exactly.

Lena shrugged one thin shoulder. "Not as beautifully as Layla but I am proficient." A strange smile curled her rose-bud lips. "Strange gift for Damnation but all of us have it, with varying degrees of talent." Her dark gaze pinned Layla's. "Do you know what your name means?"

"I hadn't thought on it that deeply," Layla admitted.

"Layla is Arabic for night. I knew when you were born that you had the gift of song. I saw it in your soul. Thus you were Layla Starling, my little night songbird."

"Yes," breathed Sin, his expression fond.

Layla realized he'd known that all along, and that, in hearing Lena's explanation, he'd softened towards the woman.

Lena nodded, then told them of how she'd made a bargain with Apep, Sin's sire, and tricked Augustus into laying with her. Layla was appalled but said not a word, her gaze flicking between Augustus and Lena. Her father appeared grim but not particularly angry.

He glanced at her. *How could I be?* Layla jumped at the sound of Augustus's voice in her head. Sin had warned her of this talent, but it was the first time Augustus had utilized it with her. *When it gave me you? My pride and joy, my daughter.*

Layla blinked rapidly, her eyes watering. *I have always thought of you as a father. Always loved you as one.*

Emotion flared bright in his eyes. She felt his love for her like a warm hug around her heart.

"There is something neither of you know," Lena said, cutting the moment short.

"Lena," Augustus murmured, exasperation and a wry fondness tinging his tone.

He loved this woman, Layla realized.

Yes. Since the beginning.

She bit back a smile.

Lena looked at them as if she knew perfectly well they were silently conversing. "When I made my bargain with Apep, it was under the agreement that I would not get anything out of it other than..." Her pale cheeks flushed, a sight that seemed somehow wrong on her stoic face. "Other than being with Augustus."

"Oh, hell," Augustus said then.

"Yes," Lena said as if he'd made perfect sense. "I did not expect to get with child. But when I did, I was forced to give you up. I was not allowed to keep you, and if I had tried, Apep would have claimed you."

Layla sucked in a painful breath. "So you gave me to my father."

"Yes." Lena blinked again. "I could not risk telling him the truth. I knew he'd try to go after Apep. It would not work, however. The contract was binding. I was only set free when Winston and Poppy Lane, with the help of Jack Talent, destroyed him."

At her side Sin stirred, his voice coming out rough. "So then, had you not told Apep of my existence, Layla would not have been born."

"That is one way to look at it, St. John." Lena's lips pursed. "You've the look of your aunt, a great sorceress who was gone long before you were born. As does your sister. But you've Apep's hair, those crimson-tipped locks."

"Jolly good," Sin muttered, then his grip on Layla's neck turned soft. "Thank you, Lena, for setting into motion the acts that would bring my soul's mate into existence."

Lena reared back as if she did not know what to do with his praise, but Layla reached up and squeezed his hand.

"My boy," Lena said, "you are born of Apep, one of the original Damnation, and made into Judgment by Augustus, *the* original Judgment. Not only are you viewed as an abomination as well, but a traitor to your kind."

Augustus spoke up. "Enoch, which is the true name of the demon who took my wing, is the natural-born son of Cain, the first and strongest Damnation. In his eyes, Layla might be converted to her rightful place by his side, but St. John must be destroyed."

"What makes me the lucky girl who gets to be converted?" Layla's heart pounded as she spoke. A certain dark rage was swarming in her belly. No one would hurt Sin. Not as long as she drew breath.

"Enoch is the last living male Damnation. As part Judgment, you are still extremely powerful, and thus considered a good candidate for breeding."

Sin shot up from the chair, his skin clear, wings snapping outward. "I will end him. Today."

"He is stronger than you, young one," Lena said without emotion. "He nearly bested both Augustus and me. And while your mentor might be weakened, to take us both on is no small feat."

Sin did not flinch. "I know all this. It doesn't matter. If I die trying, I will have, at the very least, tried."

Layla had a good lot to say about Sin dying for her honor but she was not able to voice it, for a cry in the hall had them all turning.

"That was Miranda," Sin said.

They found her crouched next to Archer, who lay sprawled upon the black marble, his skin white and shining with sweat.

"I am all right," he told them.

"No," said Lena, "you are at death's door."

Chapter Twenty-Four

Augustus

He could feel the pull, that insistent tug on his soul that demanded he leave this plane of existence and return to the world where he had been born. He did not fear fading. His heart hurt, however, for those he would leave behind. Layla, his child. He'd loved her from the moment he'd laid eyes upon her. And though he'd only now known she was his flesh and blood, he'd always been a father to her, as much as he was able.

He would miss Poppy, whom he had both mentored and worked with as an equal. He would not get to see her child grow to manhood, or hear her no-nonsense tones, telling him he was wrong about one thing or another.

It hurt to think about those he'd leave behind. But he could not linger forever. His time was rapidly dwindling, and there was one thing he would do before it ended.

"Lena," he called, knowing she was in the other room,

sitting with Layla. They both entered. And though their coloring was different, when they stood side by side, he could see the similarities in them. The same doe-shaped eyes, the same fine but short nose and oval face.

Layla had his lips, he realized with a jolt. Womanly on her, but the same curve to the upper lip and pout on the bottom. Her coloring was lighter than his as well, but he remembered that, as a younger lad, his hair had been mahogany, not black. Just like hers.

He smiled at them. "Such a pretty picture, my lovely ladies."

Lena pursed her lips. "Sentimentality makes me ill, and you well know it."

"Perhaps that's why I indulge in it," he teased. "To see you riled up."

Layla inclined her head towards Lena. "He once told me that his ability to aggravate others was part of his charm."

Lena did not take her eyes from him. "Daughter, when a man has to tell you what makes him charming, he is selling himself on the cheap." She flashed a quick fang at him when he laughed. "However, in this case, I shall have to agree."

"I regret nothing." A wave of lethargy hit him, and he leaned against the pillows. "I need you to bring Archer and Miranda to me."

Lena's expression grew sharp. "Have you the strength?"

It was not a question of what he had, but what needed to be done. If he did not act, a man would die, a heart would be broken, and he found he could no longer bear to witness those things. In truth, this was the only thing he had the strength left to give. He could not even help his child fight Enoch.

Layla glanced between them. "What's this about?"

"I've enough," he said to Lena. "However, it will be gone when it's done. Are you ready?"

He did not want to ask it, but she needed to know it was her last chance.

Lena did not hesitate. "I will not leave your side."

Layla huffed. "Anyone care to enlighten me?"

"I am going to perform my last act as Judgment," he said to her. "Find Sin and bring him here as well." Augustus closed his eyes to rest for a moment. "And be quick about it, the both of you."

They did as bided. Sin arrived first.

"Help me into that chair," he told the lad.

Grimly, Sin took his arm and guided him into the chair. "What's all this about?"

"Do not ask me questions you know the answer to." Augustus settled into the chair with a sigh. So very tired. He glanced at Sin, who now crouched next to him. "When I go, you will be final Judgment."

Sin blinked in shock.

"There is no one else. And your heart and soul are pure, St. John. More than you believe them to be. I've told you this before."

Sin cleared his throat, his eyes going glassy. "So you have. But I fear I will fail you."

"Will you try your best?"

"Of course."

"Then you will not fail."

They were interrupted by the arrival of Archer, stubbornly limping along, though he let Miranda and Layla hold on to his arms and provide some support. Lena trailed behind.

Archer's gaze was sharp on Augustus, his weakened body jerking as Miranda helped him into the unoccupied armchair by the fire.

"It bothers you to see me thusly," Augustus said. He was

too far gone to hold his human appearance any longer and was fully transformed to Judgment, his wing laying limp at his side. When he faded and went to There, his lost wing would be restored, as would his strength. One thing to look forward to.

"I do not mean to be rude," Archer said through labored breaths. "But it is true. I see you and remember my curse, the years of isolation and fear that I lived in it."

"And yet it was never a curse."

"It was for me."

"Because you were ignorant of what you were and did not have one to teach you how to use it."

Archer shrugged. "True."

At his side, Miranda held him up. "Do not forget that the witch who gave him the elixir made it harder to accept Archer's state as anything other than evil."

"Yes; Victoria. She was a rare error in my Judgment. I did not realize the depth of her insanity until you'd already dispatched her." Augustus gestured to the seats drawn near him. "Take a seat."

When they had, he looked them over with a keen eye. They both possessed an honest core and a fierce will. Ones that shouted they wanted to live. They had a curiosity about life. And Archer was a healer. More than enough reason for Augustus.

"Do you remember," he asked Archer, "what it felt like when you were altered?"

Archer's tight expression smoothed over. "Yes. I remember the strength, the heightened senses."

"You miss it," Augustus said.

Archer blinked, his mouth curling down at one corner. "Yes." A grudging admission. But honest.

"It is nothing to feel shame over, lad."

A wry smile flitted over Archer's mouth. "And yet I do."

"So then, if I offered to restore your strength, to make you wholly and fully Judgment," Augustus countered, "would you say no?"

Miranda uttered a small gasp as Archer went stock still, his face leaching of color.

"You are dying," Augustus said baldly. "Every Other can see that plainly. If I had to guess, I would say you will be gone any day now."

"Hold your tongue," snapped Miranda, her face flushing in pain and rage. "How dare you speak so blithely?"

"I state the truth, however painful it might be." His gaze went back to Archer, who had yet to move, let alone speak. "Well?"

No one stirred, all eyes riveted to Archer. The man cleared his throat. "You speak true. But no, I would not."

"Even if it meant you would never die?"

"Especially then."

"Ben!" Miranda lurched forward, her fingers digging into her husband's coat sleeve. "You cannot refuse. This is your chance—"

"To what?" he snapped with surprising vigor. "Watch you grow old and die? While I remain the same?"

"You'd rather I watch you die now?" she said hotly.

Archer's jaw clenched.

Augustus spoke before they could argue again. "You answer under the assumption that what I offer you I would not offer to your wife." At that, they both looked at him with twin expressions of shock. Augustus allowed a small smile. "I am not one to break apart soul mates. And the fact remains that this world is now more open to Others. Judgment angels will be needed now more than ever. Yet only St. John and Layla remain. They need help."

"You..." Miranda swallowed hard. "You would turn us both?"

"You are both worthy, strong, brave. The real question is, are you willing to fight for what is true and right? It is not an easy life."

Miranda let out a hard breath. "It is not in my or Ben's nature to run from a fight."

At her side, Archer was still quiet and pale. "You ask me to willingly become the very thing I fought to escape for a century. I lived behind a mask because the world could not look upon my face. I find it hard to accept going back there."

"St. John will teach you how to hide your true form and pass as human."

"It is quite easy when you are full turned," Sin added.

Archer glanced at Miranda, and he leaned into her embrace. "Miri, the decision is yours."

"Why mine?" she asked, searching his face.

"For wherever you go, I shall follow."

Her lashes fluttered closed, and she leaned her forehead against Archer's. "When you thought yourself cursed, I found you beautiful. To know that we shall be together all time? To know that we can help Sin protect those we love? How can we say no?"

Archer's kiss was brief but clearly tender, then his gray gaze met Augustus's. "We accept. With gratitude."

"Very good." He turned to Lena. "If you drain them, it will go faster."

She nodded. "If they allow it."

"When Judgment is properly turned," Augustus explained to Archer, "the person is first drained of nearly all their blood. This helps the transformation, for there is less resistance in the body. Usually by lance. But if you agree, Lena can...well, there's no better way to put it, drink your blood with much better efficiency and less pain. She is also better able to monitor how much blood loss is enough."

A moue of distaste twisted Miranda's features. "I do not relish the idea of becoming a meal. However, I will defer to your wisdom."

Archer laughed shortly. "As my wife agrees, so shall I."

"Sin?" Augustus held his arm out. "Would you?"

St. John stood and collected the implements he had put aside. A lance connected to a rubber tube and two vials. While St. John readied the equipment, Augustus addressed his rapt audience. "The procedure is simple, really. Once you have been drained of your human blood, you shall drink down a vial of mine."

Archer leaned in, his expression curious. "The elixir was your blood?"

"Yes."

"And we only need a small vial? I cannot see how that is possible when we will have lost so much."

"Yes, but mine is stronger. Once it hits your system, the change will occur. Do you remember it?"

Archer's laugh was dry. "Oh, quite well. And it was not pleasant."

Sin laughed as well. "An understatement, if ever I've heard one."

Yes, Augustus thought as he watched them, he would miss his brood. But that they were all together once more filled him with satisfaction. He would leave this place knowing he'd done the best he could.

Chapter Twenty-Five

Lena

Lena pulled her fangs from the man called Archer's neck. His blood had the foul taint of deadly sickness, unlike the sweet richness of his wife. It left Lena's stomach full and faintly rocking. She ignored it and wiped a drop of his weak blood from her lip.

Archer lay white as a sheet, his wife senseless at his side. Miranda had already been given a vial of Augustus's silver blood. She twitched and whimpered as her dry veins grew dark, mapping her flawless face like gray rivers just beneath the skin.

Archer's breath, however, slowed dangerously.

"Give him the vial," Lena said to her wide-eyed daughter.

Layla quickly tilted the glass to Archer's pasty lips, and as a newborn babe to his mother's teat, he sucked the silver blood down. They needn't worry about putting it in his vein; the blood would seep into his system as soon as it entered his mouth.

As expected, Archer grunted, his big body going taut on the bed.

"What happens now?" Layla asked, staring at the couple in fascination. They had been strapped down with thick leather bindings—one of the marvels of Evernight House being the endless supply of chains and straps in Holly Evernight's dungeon lab. Lena supposed the girl used them to hoist engines and the like, but one could never be too sure of another's hidden proclivities. After all, Evernight was mated to a sanguis demon with a reputation for randiness.

Smiling slightly at the thought, Lena stood. "Watch them for a while." She leaned down and pealed back Archer's eyelid. His eye was unfocused, but the once-human gray pupil was already turning clear. A look at Miranda's showed the same: lines of clear seeping into the jade green. "They will make it through."

Her tender-hearted daughter's shoulders sagged. "Good."

"You care for these people you've just met?" Lena glanced down at the handsome couple. Beauty was always appreciated but she had little use for it anymore.

"Of course," Layla said, watching them as well. "They are Sin's family. It would hurt him if they did not pull through. And they are good people. I can see it in their eyes."

Lena nodded. "That is your father's talent. I am glad you have it."

Layla shook her head, her short laugh bemused. "I still cannot believe he is my father." Firelight caressed her skin, turning the color to warm ivory. "Well, that is not precisely correct. He always felt more of a father to me than a simple guardian."

"He loved you from the start." Lena fisted her skirts behind her back where Layla could not see her shameful need to touch, to hug. "I would not have left you with him if he didn't."

Layla's brown eyes met hers. "Did you miss me?" Her gaze slid away. "Never mind, do not answer."

"With every breath." Lena reached out to touch her but hesitated. "I built a wall of coldness around my heart to keep Augustus out. By the time you came along it was so thick, I found it better to retreat behind it than feel the agony of leaving you behind."

Layla closed her eyes, and Lena could not resist the temptation any longer. Her daughter's skin was smooth as satin, warm and flush with health. She stroked her cheek. "So many things I did wrong, so many regrets. But having you was never one of them. You are the best and brightest part of me. And of him."

A small sob broke from Layla, and Lena's resolve crumpled. She pulled Layla close, holding her daughter as tightly as she dared. Her own heart was breaking, those walls crumpling like dust. "I should have liked to have known you better."

Layla shuddered. "You're fading with him." It was not a question.

"He is my heart. And I have withheld mine from him for too long."

Layla pulled back, her cheeks wet but her eyes fierce. "Good. If you..." Her breath hitched. "If you both are to leave, that you go together and you bring him peace is a comfort to me."

Lena wanted to hold her daughter again, perhaps do some sort of motherly thing—brush out her hair and plait it while they spoke of fashions or some other frivolous topic. But she felt Augustus waning, their connection already strong enough for her to know the time had come.

She could not say good-bye. She was still too much of a coward. Sorrow made her insides quake. She held herself together with force of will. It made her movements clumsy as she grabbed hold of Layla, cupping her cheeks and pressing a hard kiss to her forehead.

Lena drew in Layla's scent, stored it in her memory. "Know this. You are loved. So very much."

She could not stand another moment. Kissing her daughter one last time, she turned and strode from the room without looking back.

Augustus

Lena strode into his room, her ink black hair flowing free down her back like a banner, her lithe body clothed in a simple silk gown of crimson. She was the most stunning creature he'd ever beheld. And she was crying, silent tears tinged with red that rolled down her white cheeks.

She did not halt until she was on the bed, in his arms. "Hold me."

He could barely move, the pull of the other side so strong. But he managed to bring his arms around her narrow waist. She felt like home.

"It is done," she said, her words encompassing the whole of their remaining tasks.

Quite suddenly, he wanted to weep. He would not see his daughter again. But Lena was warm in his arms, where he'd wanted her to be for all these long, cold years.

"Lena..." He tried to say more, but his mouth wouldn't work. Fear took hold.

As if she felt him slip further, she lifted her head. Her dark eyes were clear and focused. "Look at me," she said. "I choose you, Ramiel." His true name, the one he'd been given at birth.

With the last of his strength, he spoke. "And I you, Melaina." For he knew her birth name as well.

Wings the color of the darkest night unfurled from her back and curled around him until they were cocooned. Her fangs extended, and she slashed her wrists. Fragrant blood bloomed. She pressed it to his dry lips, and it flowed honey-sweet over his tongue. His body began to glow with both heat and light as she said the words he'd been waiting to hear. "From flesh to bone to blood of heart, shall our souls be entwined, never to part."

When she lowered her wrist, her offering flowing through his veins and going straight to his tired heart, he had the strength to give the words back to her.

As soon as they were uttered, the bed and London fell away from them. The world came into focus again, and they were lying in a field of white flowers, her black wings a sharp contrast. Lena blinked up at him, and then her gaze focused just above his head. Her dark eyes gleamed. "Your wings are restored."

He felt them, substantial, a welcome weight. Augustus stretched them wide simply to enjoy the sensation. "So they are." He touched her cheek. "Regrets?"

She glanced around. "I regret we appeared in a bed of flowers and not a nice silken nest of pillows." Her smile was sly, almost shy. "However I am certain we can make do."

A chuckle bubbled up within his chest, and he ran the back of his hand along her cheek before undoing the button at the top of her collar. And the next one. "We have an eternity to get it right."

She scoffed as he slowly parted her gown. "We shall get it right from the first." She arched her back, slipping free from the crimson silk. "Come here and let me set you straight."

He went willingly, an apt pupil, more than ready to take on whatever lessons she sought to give.

Chapter Twenty-Six

A sob tore out of Layla as soon as the door to the room closed, leaving her alone. She knew without doubt that Lena had said good-bye. Just as when Lena had left to take care of Archer and Miranda, Augustus had pulled Layla close and hugged her tight. He'd kissed her brow and said he loved her. That he would always love her. And she'd known he too was letting her go.

She could feel them fading. Her parents. One she'd never truly known, the other she'd never truly let play the role. Everything in her wanted to run from the room and track them down. To fling herself on them and beg for them to remain.

But Augustus could not, and Lena would follow him. If she stayed, Augustus's curse to remain alone and weak would be for eternity. Layla was not so selfish to deny her parents their chance at love. But her heart broke all the same. She felt abandoned, like a child once again.

Biting her lip to keep it all in, she glanced at the couple lying in bed. She sent for Daisy or Poppy to watch over them. Miranda and Archer were unclothed, covered with eider-down quilts, but vulnerable. It seemed right that one of Miranda's sisters should be here.

And Layla needed Sin. More than she ever had before. Sin would make things bearable. She moved to go to him when a great tremor rent through the house. Everything shook; vases toppled and paintings fell from their hooks.

The room rocked and swayed. And it seemed the very earth roared, the sound so loud her ears rang. *Sin*, she thought frantically; *something has happened to Sin.*

Sin felt the exact moment Augustus faded. It hit him like a bolt of lightning straight to his heart. His body bucked, and he was flung back from his spot by the window. Power such as he'd never experienced surged through him.

He fell flat on his back, unable to move. Pain. Pressure. He was going to break apart. Voices in his head endlessly babbled, a cacophony of sound that rose to a single ringing pitch.

Images flashed before his eyes, scenes of death, violence, love, birth, the mundane, the profane. His lids fluttered, those strange scenes flickering so swiftly that they blinded him.

He understood now what Augustus had endured. Too much. Too much of everything. He hadn't warned Sin.

Anger roared within, but the pain was taking him.

And then he realized he was not alone. Someone else was there. Dread pulled at his heart.

Dimly, his focus settled on a face: Enoch. Laughing, leaning over him.

You failed, and now she is mine.

Layla burst into the room she shared with Sin, her body trembling with the need to be held by him, to see his face and know he was all right. She stopped short so quickly that her heels skidded on the rug.

All the blood rushed from her face, shock and terror tingled on her skin. She could not breathe, could not speak. This had to be a lie, an illusion. But she blinked and nothing changed.

The room was singed black, as if a fire had flared bright then blown itself out. Blood dripped from the walls, splashed over the singed curtains.

Drip, drip, drip.

A steady shake rose up her back and down her legs. Layla's focus narrowed and a strangled sound bubbled up. A headless body on the floor. Blood, so much blood—silver, streaked with scarlet. The body long, lean. Scuffed boots, black trousers.

No, no, no.

"Yes, yes, yes."

Her gaze snapped up, and there he stood, the bastard St. Claire. Enoch, she supposed. She did not care. He smiled at her—a lazy, evil smile with a hint of fang. His skin was earthen red, his wings a dull black.

"You are not dreaming, Layla dearest."

He moved, and she saw what he held.

Her entire world froze solid. She would not look. She could not.

He raised his hand. Sin.

The shaking within her started to break free, a pitiful wail of utter loss rising.

Sin's head in Enoch's hand. That beautiful face slack with death. Those glorious eyes dull and unstaring. And silver-streaked blood dripping down onto the carpet.

She screamed then, so hard the window blew out, shattering and falling like crystal rain. A surge went through her and her back jerked. Wings, glossy black and batlike, spread behind her. She felt them twitch, but still she screamed, her rage blasting towards Enoch, whose smile only grew.

He tossed the head at her feet. "Catch me if you can, girl." And then he flew out the window.

With a snarl, she took off running. She had never flown, did not know how. But she did not slow. Layla leapt from the second-story window, hurtling herself after Enoch. Her body hovered for an instant, weightless and buoyant, and then began to plummet.

No. Fly. Fly.

The command tore through her, and the muscles along her back tightened. A jerk and a flap and she lifted, awkward and too slow. But she flew.

Enoch was a blot against the light of the moon. She willed her wings to beat faster, to move her where she needed to go. They were slow to respond, but she followed.

He was toying with her—stopping mid-air, flying in a loop around the backdrop of the moon. Bastard. Bloody fucking bastard.

Suddenly she was shooting through the air. She collided with him as he hit the bottom of one of his showy loops. Layla saw a flash of surprise in his eyes, then a grin of satisfaction before they both fell.

As they tumbled, she clawed at him, gouging his tough skin, black blood splashing hot over her face. He simply laughed and laughed as if she pleased him immensely. It lit her rage. Even as he spun so that he would take the impact of their fall.

People screamed as Layla and the demon smashed into the pavers so hard that broken slate and dust flew upward. She did not care who saw. She punched and punched with all her might, her limbs shaking, power and loss throbbing in her breast.

Enoch took the hits for a moment, then thrust her away. Easy as flicking off a bug, and she tumbled back, rolling along the upturned ground. Her back crashed into something hard and sharp. Where were they?

Trafalgar. They were in the square. Hundreds of humans scurried around, wild-eyed and shocked.

Enoch stood, his wings stretched wide, his body lengthening to inhuman heights. Nine, ten, eleven feet. "Shall we dance, little girl?"

Layla rose to her feet and found herself clutching foot-long scythes of obsidian. She had no notion how they'd got there but she suddenly felt as though her mother was at her side, guiding her. *Never falter. Kill without hesitation.*

That she would do. She had nothing left to live for but revenge.

Chapter Twenty-Seven

Sin. Sin." Something slapped at his face. "St. John!" Another slap, this one hard enough to rattle his brain. Sin lashed out, catching hold of a neck as thick as an ox's.

He grasped it hard and squeezed.

"*Oof.* Piss and shit."

A blow to his arm made him lose his grip. Sin lurched upward, his body sluggish and tender. The world was hazy and too bright. Blinking, he tried to focus.

Jack Talent knelt before him, rubbing his neck with an irritable expression on his face. "Next time I take you unaware, give me a good punch instead of going for the neck. Bloody hell that's murder on the throat."

Sin rubbed his eyes. "So noted." Gods, his throat was shredded. He peered at Jack. "Did you try to strangle me as well?"

Jack fell back onto his rump. "Hardly. We found you laid out and senseless. We've been trying to wake you for half an hour."

Sin realized then that his sister Daisy was at his side,

her soft arm around his shoulders. When had she embraced him? His mind was a muddle, his senses surging and fading like the tides.

Mary was there as well. Sin accepted the glass of brandy she handed him. "Jack thought it best to take a direct approach and knock you awake." She shot her husband a look that spoke volumes as to what she thought of that plan.

"Worked, didn't it?" Jack groused, taking a glass as well. He drank it down in one gulp.

Sin did the same, welcoming the burn along his tender throat. "What happened?"

He was not in his room but in bed in a guest room that he knew to be down the hall from his. Jack and Mary exchanged a look as Daisy's grip upon his shoulders tightened.

Sin was ready to start shouting when Daisy spoke. "We found you in your room. It had been destroyed by fire, the windows blown out."

He sat straight, his heart racing. "Layla?"

"She is gone." Daisy skittered back when Sin shot out of bed. "We heard her scream. In rage, Sin. In rage."

Sin was already bolting from the room and seeking out his. Destroyed. He stood amongst the wreckage, fear and foreboding pressing in on his heart. The scent of brimstone was so strong it burned his nostrils.

Jack trotted in behind him. "She wasn't taken," he said. "Ian came into the room in time to see her shoot out of it. She was flying, Sin. On wings like mine."

"Then she has fully matured." He took a breath. He needed to calm. His newly acquired powers slipped and skittered around in his flesh, out of control and barely contained. "Where is Ian?"

"Something has happened," Mary said, coming into the room. "It felt like an earthquake but demons are popping up all over London. Not in disguise but as they are. The city is in chaos."

Sin glanced out the window as if seeing London for the first time. Black smoke billowed from numerous points on the horizon. He could hear the screaming now. The confusion and fear of humans slammed into his senses like a cold fist.

Sin tried to shake it off.

"Ian, Poppy, and Win went to help," Daisy said, suddenly there. "Miranda and Archer still sleep like the dead. Mary and Jack stayed to watch over them."

Sin knew without asking that Jack was itching to get out there and kill demons. But he would not risk the safety of his family to do so.

"I've got to find Layla." He studied the horizon again. At the center rolled the biggest column of smoke.

"Trafalgar," Jack said at his side.

And that was where he would go.

Archer

In Archer's experience, newlywed couples often thought of "in sickness and in health" in vague terms of dabbing a sweaty brow when one had a fever, perhaps administering pain powders for a headache. It was not until they were into the meat of the relationship when they realized what sickness could mean. That perhaps death was waiting on the other side of that fevered brow.

Archer and Miranda's start, however, had been forged by fire, haunted by death and murder. He'd been willing to give up his soul to save her, and she'd risked her life to save his. Therefore, one long, torturous night of holding each other as Augustus's blood tore through them was of little consequence.

Being deathly ill to begin with, Archer had the worst of it. He'd known what to expect, and yet it still shocked him, how his body felt as though tiny beasties were eating him up from inside to out. It hurt worse seeing Miranda pant and grit her teeth, determined not to scream.

Eventually, they fell into an exhausted sleep, too weak to do anything more than hold each other's hands.

Awareness eventually crept over him like little cat feet dancing up his spine. He took a breath and felt the clean movement of air traveling through his lungs. No pain. Oh, but the surge of power. Strong, pure, heady. His cock grew hard with it.

On that odd realization, his eyes snapped open.

At the very same moment, Miranda's eyes snapped open. She let out a startled yelp, catching sight of him.

And Archer could only gape at his wife. "God's teeth," he said on a breath. "Just look at you." She was the most exquisite crystal sculpture come to life.

"Look at you," she retorted. "My beautiful man." With a shaking hand, she reached out and touched the corner of his mouth. "This was the face I saw for the first time." Her smile was tilted. "Well, half of it at any rate."

Her smile faded as she spied her hand, and she lifted it high, wriggling her fingers experimentally. "Gads, that's a strange sight."

Quite suddenly, all he could do was laugh. His chest rumbled with it, and it felt delicious. "What a pair we make now. Perfect fiends."

Her gaze met his, and though she had not a spot of color in her, he could well see the heat flare in her eyes. Like a spark to tinder. In a blink, she wrenched off the covers, her eyes traveling over his nudity. He laughed again. "Not much to see, is there?"

Though now that she'd uncovered them, his gaze riveted to her perfect, pert breasts, like the palest liquid silver. His cock throbbed with impatience.

Miranda's gaze narrowed on it. "Oh, I see well enough. And I want to feel this," she wrapped her hand around his length, her grip assured and wonderfully tight, "inside of me."

Archer groaned, but he was already moving, rolling her over and pinning her to the bed. He thrust into her without warning, knowing she was ready. He could smell her arousal. He could hear the tiny creaks of the bed as he pumped. He could feel everything.

Archer grinned down at his wife, her lips parted and panting. "Oh, my darling Miri, what fun we shall have."

Her smile was wide as she wrapped her arms around his shoulders. "All that I am, all that I become, is for you."

He'd said those words to her long ago, when she'd first unmasked him. Aching in his heart, he leaned down and kissed her. "Only you, Miri. Only you."

Chapter Twenty-Eight

Sin had been correct: When she needed it, Layla's fighting instincts would kick in. The thought of Sin hurt so badly that she forced it away as she ducked a blow. She was fighting for him now. Later she would mourn. Later she would let her heart break.

Now, however…She grabbed hold of Enoch's wings, using them for leverage, and fell back, flipping the bastard over her head. The second he landed, she turned and slammed her elbow into his nose. It crunched flat, blood spraying.

Still the bastard did not stop laughing at her. It drove her to madness. Again and again, she smashed down into his face, turning it to pulp.

Around them, the square was in ruins. Nelson's great column had toppled, and water shot up in an unchecked blast from the broken fountainheads. Small fires burned, but a massive ring of never-wavering fire cut the square off from the rest of the world.

Enoch had done that, heedless of who saw and who was hurt. Humans had burned, deaths so horrible that she'd screamed and launched herself at him again. She hadn't his strength or his powers. Only this new body of hers, skin a shimmery pale ruby, as if she were made of rose gold, her wings awkward but powerful, capable of knocking statues over with one blow.

Layla swung her elbow down once more, but Enoch caught it. She'd known he'd been toying with her but she hadn't realized how much. His grip crushed her bones, and she wailed despite herself, agony racing through her arm. He leapt easily to his feet, his face already healing, taking shape, the blood drying and flaking away like dead leaves.

Chuckling, he wrenched her useless arm behind her back and hauled her against him.

"Mmm, I do love to dance with you, Layla." He ground his erection into her backside. "You are a worthy partner."

Sickened, she thrust her head back and saw stars when her skull met with his face. His grip slipped, and she turned round to punch his throat. He countered with a slap, hard enough that she staggered back. Blood pooled in her mouth.

Enoch grabbed her by a wing and twisted. Pain ripped down her spine. "Now, now, I should hate to tear these off," he said lightly. "They will take some time to regrow and it hurts like the devil." He grinned wide. "I've met him, you know. Bit of a bore. However, I do suspect he'd like you."

"Perhaps I shall offer him a dance as well." Layla kneed Enoch in the stones.

Like all males, he hunched over with an "*oof!*"

With a thought, she called forth her blades once more. She'd lost them somewhere along the way, but a voice in her head whispered that they would always return to her. Cool obsidian pressed against her palms. Layla swung, but not soon enough.

Enoch lashed out and an invisible blade sliced through

her middle. Her vision dimmed, her knees gave out. She crumpled to the ground just as she heard a shout.

That voice. She knew it.

"Layla!"

Through the black edges of her sight, she saw him walking through the fire, his body gleaming, his eyes brilliant green in all that crystalline beauty. Wings flared out behind him; lightning crackled over his frame.

"Sin." He was here. He was here.

Enoch grinned down at her. "How weak of mind you are to believe my illusions."

A sob ripped from her. She'd played right into his hands. Leaving Sin and destroying London with her rage. Enoch's massive hand wrapped around her neck, squeezing so tightly she could barely draw a breath. He held her close as Sin strode across the square. "Unless you'd like me to tear her head off," Enoch said, "I suggest you stop."

Sin halted, his chest heaving with each deep breath he took. His body trembled and Layla knew he felt the same rage she had, that he was struggling to keep control.

Tremors went through the earth. In the distance came the sound of church bells clanging as though the shaking ground had rung them.

"You will not hurt her," Sin ground out. "It is me you want to destroy."

Enoch's thumb ran down the side of her neck. "True. I'd much rather fuck this one."

Blasts of icy cold mixed with flares of heat. Overhead clouds gathered, black and filled with flashes of light. Sin's eyes flickered clear and then green again. He was shaking so hard his wings fluttered.

And Enoch laughed. "I see you have Augustus's powers. Hard to control, aren't they, boy?"

Sin did not answer, but Layla looked at him anew. Good God, it was true. Power rolled over him in violent waves. He was as volatile as liquid nitrogen. That would be a comfort but Layla understood as clearly as Enoch did: Sin out of control meant he was less able to direct his powers.

"Are you going to fight me?" Sin said. "Or hide behind Layla?"

"Oh, we shall fight," Enoch said. With that, he dragged Layla back until her wings met the cool granite of the plinth that had once held Nelson's column. She'd barely blinked when he conjured two great spears of obsidian and slammed them through her wings, pinning her to the plinth.

She screamed and Sin shouted, rage and horror tinging his voice. He launched himself at Enoch, trying to get past him to free her. But the Damnation caught Sin in his arms, and they both went tumbling.

Pain shot through Layla as she watched them roll in a fury of fists. Lightning arched and crackled around them, singeing the air. All the while the earth trembled, great chunks of it rising, bringing forth the scent of soil.

Enoch flew through the air as Sin struck him full force in the chest. He landed with a thud, his body sliding a few feet. Sin stretched out a hand, and the toppled column lifted from the ground. He swung his hand forward, and as if heeding his command, the column flew across the square and crashed into Enoch.

The demon's legs twitched then stilled. Instantly, Sin sent a blast over the column and Enoch's legs disappeared under a wall of crystal clear ice.

Sin turned and his gaze clashed with hers. "Layla," he whispered, the desperate sound carrying over the space between them.

He took one step in her direction, and then ice exploded,

sending a blast of frost over everything. Enoch stood tall and unharmed. He took a deep breath and seemed to expand. "Do you not realize, boy? You cannot win. We are evenly matched. Final Judgment and Absolute Damnation. We could fight forever, grind this town to dust, and it would not end. Your family will be hunted, humans destroyed. And all that will remain will be you and me and this pitiful half-breed girl."

"And yet I will not stop protecting Layla," Sin said. "Not while I have breath in my body."

Layla felt the truth of his words. Sin would fight for her without end.

"Good," Enoch bit out. "For with every blow we exchange, with every earthquake you cause, more and more of my brethren come into this world. Augustus foresaw this, as did my maker. You and the girl. Abomination and betrayer. Two beings that should not be." He spat a glob of black blood on the ground. "You upset the balance. And now the worlds have collided."

Layla's heart pounded, pain throbbing in her wings. No; she was the one who'd upset the balance. She was both Judgment and Damnation. And she had to choose a side or the imbalance would remain.

"If I vow to remain with you," she called out to Enoch, "will you vow to leave Sin be?"

"No," Sin shouted, the sound so loud her ears hurt. He whipped around, his expression shattered. "No, Layla. Never."

Enoch was the cat eating the canary. "Done."

Layla held Sin's gaze. "You cannot control this. It is my vow to give. My decision."

In an instant Sin was in front of her, his eyes wild. He wrenched the spikes free. With a cry, she sagged against him. He held her close, his body so alive and strong. She soaked up his heat, reveled in the fact that he was here. "I thought you dead," she said, clinging to him. "His illusions. I saw your body."

Sin's fingers threaded through her hair to the point of pain. But she welcomed it. His heart beat a furious rhythm against his chest as he pressed his lips to her temple. "I cannot live without you, Layla. Stop this madness."

"Enough with this stalling," Enoch called out. "I tire of waiting."

Sin snarled, his body turning as if to attack, but Layla held him back. His eyes were wide and green, pain in his gaze. "Layla."

She touched his cheek. "Saint, love without trust means nothing. I choose this."

He sucked in a sharp breath. "You tear my heart out."

She said nothing more but moved away. His arms fell at his sides, his body trembling once more. She knew he was fighting the instinct to haul her back with all he had.

Hear my words, she said silently, hoping he would. Remember what I said. *Trust, Saint. Trust.*

Sin watched the woman he loved more than anything walk away from him. Nothing compared to that pain. He couldn't look at the bastard she went to. He would break if he did. She was sacrificing herself for him. He was not worth that.

A growl tore from him, and he took a step forward, ready to pull her back into his arms, her plea be damned, when her voice, clear as crystal, rang in his head.

Hear my words. Trust, Saint. Trust.

He halted, brought short by it. Trust? His body tingled, the powers he'd acquired still running amok just beneath his skin. She wanted him to trust her. She had a plan.

His gaze snapped to her retreating form, her slim back ramrod straight.

Enoch opened his arms to her but it was Sin's eyes he met. Smug, sodding bastard. He was so sure of his victory. Sin ground his teeth, let him see his hatred and frustration, let it pour out of him in punches of power so strong the entire square frosted over. The ring of fire that Enoch had created died on a hiss, and all that was left was silence and cold.

The world around them was deserted.

Layla stopped before Enoch, her body so much smaller, her skin a shade of rose gold that glittered in the gray, frozen square. "You vow not to touch St. John Evernight, by thought, power, or physical reach?"

Enoch sliced his wrist open with a claw. His blood was the color of garnets, nearly black in the fading light. He held his wound aloft. "Your vow, Layla Starling, daughter of Melaina, that your soul will be mine."

An obsidian blade appeared in her hand. She sliced her wrist and blood the color of her rose gold skin welled up. "I vow that our souls will remain together."

"Good enough."

Sin's heart pounded so hard he thought it might just fly free of his chest. His body clenched tight. He had to trust her. Trust. He'd never given that to anyone but her. Not fully. God. He could not lose her.

But his woman did not look back at him. She raised her wrist and pressed it to Enoch's. Their blood combined with a smoking sizzle of sound, and Sin's body swayed as if hit.

He choked on his rage when Enoch hauled Layla to him and kissed her, his dirty hands grabbing her bottom and squeezing as if he owned her.

And she went willingly, rising up on her toes, her mouth opening to his.

Sin's vision went red even as his heart ripped in two. A sound tore through the square, one of shock and pain. Was it him? He took a breath, blinked.

Layla held onto Enoch with a grip that bowed her body. Sin took a step closer as Enoch's larger body started to twitch. The demon writhed in Layla's grip, black lines of his veins suddenly visible against his red flesh.

The devil?

And then it hit him; she was sucking out Enoch's soul.

Sin rushed forward just as Enoch's eyes opened wide, glowing yellow one moment then leaching of color the next.

"Take it all," he shouted, as Layla bent over Enoch's sagging frame.

A shudder went through her and then, with a gasp, she let go, her lips leaving the demon's with a loud pop. Sin grabbed her arm, yanked her back and, with a whip of lightning, sliced Enoch's head from his body.

Absolute Damnation shattered like glass before disappearing in a puff of white smoke.

Sin stared at the spot for a long moment before wheeling around.

Layla swayed on her feet, taking long, deep breaths. Her flesh rippled, her eyes flickered black, yellow, brown, silver, gold, as if her body could not pick a color. Sin longed to hold her but she was too unstable.

"Let it ride out," he whispered, trying to soothe, for he suspected she was experiencing much the same power surge as he had. "It will settle, love. Do not fight it."

With a cry, her body went rod-straight, a strange dark light shooting from her eyes, and she crumpled. Sin scooped her up before she could hit the ground. He cradled her body in his arms, drawing his wings around them.

In the cocoon of darkness he held her, murmuring nonsense

words of comfort, telling her how very brave he thought her, how much he loved her. He did not know how much time passed; all that mattered was that she was in his arms. They were together, and they would always be. That he knew to the marrow of his bones.

A soft sigh left her and she stirred. Her thick lashes lifted, and Sin found himself staring at eyes the color of old gold. "Sin?"

"Here, love." He cupped her cheek with a clumsy hand. "Right here, little bird."

She struggled to sit and he helped her, still keeping her within the circle of his arms. Lowering his wings so she could see the square, Sin peered down at her. "All right, then, love?"

She shuddered and leaned closer. "Yes. All right. Strange but I do not hurt."

He kissed her, a soft touch of lips to lips. "I suspect you shall feel that way for a bit."

Layla really looked at him then, her gaze moving over his face and body. "You are final Judgment now."

"And you?" He kissed her again because he could. "Are Absolute Damnation, are you not?"

Slowly she smiled, and it was brilliant. "It worked."

"How did you know?" If he thought about what happened too hard, he'd start to shake once more. It was nothing he ever wanted to experience again.

"Augustus said that Damnation had the ability to eat a soul and, in doing so, would take on the other's power."

Gently he stroked a lock of her tangled hair back from her face. "But how did you know you could overpower Enoch?"

Layla leaned into his palm. "I am the daughter of Final Judgment and Lena, the most cunning Damnation to have lived. How could I fail?"

A chuckle rumbled in his chest and he gathered her close. "So you are."

Her lips found his neck and she pressed little kisses along his skin. "I am sorry I gave you a fright. But I could hardly explain myself then."

"I heard you," he said, closing his eyes and resting his cheek to the top of her head. "You asked for trust."

She pulled back and her eyes glowed a soft gold. "And you gave it to me."

"I give you that and more, Layla. I give you my heart, my soul."

Layla cupped his jaw, her touch so tender it made him ache. "And I promise to keep you well. I love you, St. John."

Happiness bloomed over him, warming the air between them. Something tickled his ankle, and they both looked down to find themselves sitting on a bed of grass dotted with bluebells. That was new. Layla laughed, delighted, and he joined her, pulling her down upon it. "I love you too, little bird. Forevermore."

Epilogue

In the small hours of the night, when the sky hovered between ink black and dove gray, Sin stood upon the narrow terrace of St. Paul's golden gallery.

Archer came up alongside Sin. In silence, they stared down at the city spread out before them—at the twinkling lights of the gas lamps, dotted here and there by brighter electric lights that had popped up more and more in recent years, at the black smoke drifting from the countless chimneys, and at the always-moving waters of the Thames.

All was quiet now. But it would not remain. Humans had seen the truth of their world, and nothing would ever be the same. Sin saw the future stretch out in a vast maw of unrest and adjustment. Wars would be fought, civilization rearranged. It was not pretty. But he also saw peace, and he saw the love his family would have in their lives.

"I cannot get past the strangeness of seeing myself this way," Archer said quietly. He held out his hand, now crystal clear, reflecting the moonlight. "It brings back old memories." Behind his back enormous wings spread wide. Sin knew it would take some time for Archer to control his appearance.

"When I was first turned," Sin said, "I stared in the mirror for two weeks straight."

Archer snorted. "I stared in the mirror for a hundred years, wondering what the bloody hell I was becoming."

"Yes, but now you know better."

Archer glanced at him. Truthfully it was odd to see another of his kind. They were a sight, appearing as living crystal. It was hard to focus on Archer's clear eyes.

"And you?" Archer asked. "How do you feel? Is holding Augustus's old power any different from what you were before?"

Sin knew Archer asked because the scientist in him would always question, always want to know the hows and whys of things.

"Be grateful you are simply Judgment."

Archer's crystalline face frowned. "That bad, eh?"

Sin chuckled. "You must remember those early days when you struggled not to tear the knobs off doors or to keep from tearing your trousers when you tried to step into them. Imagine that to the tenth power."

Archer made a sound of amusement. "Remember them? My dear boy, I'm living them over again. This morning, Miranda and I... Well, never mind that."

"We all heard the bed break," Sin muttered. "And thank you for that lovely moment. Truly."

Archer laughed then, a great roll of sound that echoed over London. At the booming sound, Archer immediately reined it in, grimacing as though chagrined. "Pardon."

Sin smiled. "I'll teach you how to control it."

"I suspect you will. I am sorry, however, that Augustus is not here to teach you this new state of being."

Sin shrugged. "That is the nature of the beast. If he were here, I would not be final Judgment."

Sin heard a soft rustle, and a moment later Layla landed beside him. He wrapped an arm around her waist and pulled her near. "Hello, little bird."

Layla kissed his shoulder, which was as high as she could reach without tugging him down, and then said hello to Archer. "What are you two doing up here?"

"Flight practice," Sin said with a kiss to her head.

The night before, Layla had begun to sing Puccini's "O'Mio Babbino Caro" in notes so clear, so powerful, she'd made dour Poppy weep and drawn a crowd to the gates of Evernight House.

"What changed?" Sin had asked Layla afterward.

"I suppose I did," had been her reply. "I'm fully turned now. Mother said my singing would come back, and she was right."

"Did you feel this change? Is that why you sang?"

She had smiled at him then, her face incandescent and so beautiful it had taken his breath away. "No, Saint. I simply felt joy. Singing was the only way to properly express it."

Joy. It was an addictive emotion. And one Sin was still growing accustomed to feeling. At the moment, it filled him as he held Layla close. "Where is my dear sister?" he asked while nuzzling the soft skin on her neck.

"Here." Miranda's face peeked out from over the curve of the dome.

"Bloody hell, woman," Archer groused. "Must you crawl along the very edge of the place?"

"It isn't as though I'll fall," she said with a cheeky grin. The wind picked up, lifting the long strands of her crystal clear hair. It was an odd effect but beautiful. "Are we flying or not?"

"Flying," Sin said. "Remember, use the air currents to your advantage."

And as they took to the night, Sin had to grin. A strange new world indeed.

Did you miss Archer and Miranda's love story?

Discover how the Darkest London series began.

Please see the next page for an excerpt from

Firelight.

Chapter Two

Getting married was a happy dream that had filled Miranda's girlhood thoughts and promptly left as she grew older. She well knew the face that looked back from the mirror each morning. She was not foolish enough to pretend that she was without beauty. Vanity may be a sin but so was lying. She was fair of face and form, though she knew many a girl who looked better.

However, as a woman without fortune or title, she received few offers of marriage. The most consistent offers came in the form of teasing shouts from market vendors when she walked to Covent Garden each Saturday morning. How then, she thought as Daisy pinned white roses in her hair the following morning, had it come to this?

Perhaps it was a dream. The woman in the mirror didn't look at all like her. She was too pale. Her pink gown, one of many provided by Lord Archer's money, ruffled and frothed around her like a confectionary. Miranda turned away with disdain. It was the image of an innocent and a maiden. She was neither. And yet *he* had come for her. Why?

She did not believe Father's nonsense about him wanting her for her beauty. There were plenty of pretty daughters of utterly bankrupt, thus desperate, nobles for a wealthy man to choose from. What, then, did he want? *What has the world come to when men such as he are permitted to roam the streets…* Perspiration bloomed along her upper lip. And yet Lord Archer did not know precisely what he was acquiring when he took Miranda as his bride, did he?

To create fire by mere thought. It was the stuff of myth. She had discovered the talent quite by accident. And had burned through her share of disasters. Father and Mother had forbidden anyone to ever speak of it and, more to the point, for Miranda to ever use her talent again. Poppy had simply disappeared in the library to search for an explanation; she never found one. Only Daisy had been impressed, though quite put out that she did not possess a similar unearthly talent. As for herself, the question always remained: Was she a monster? Both beauty and beast rolled into one unstable force? Despite her desire to know, there was the greater fear of putting the question to anyone and seeing them turn away as Martin had. So she kept it inside. She would not tell her husband to be, no. But she took comfort in the notion that she was not without defenses.

Poppy and Daisy's mutual disregard for Father kept them at a distance as Father hovered by her elbow, guarding all possible attempts to escape. Their chatter was no more than a din, Father's hand upon her arm a ghost, as they made their way to the small family chapel by the river.

Reverend Spradling met them at the door. The brackets around his fleshy mouth cut deep as his eyes slid from Miranda to Father. "Lord Archer is…" He tilted his head and pulled at the cassock hugging his bulging neck. "He is waiting in the vestry."

"Grand," said Father with an inane smile.

"He wants to talk to Miss Ellis in private," the reverend interrupted as Father tried to walk through the doorway. "I told him it was inappropriate but he was most insistent."

The two men turned to Miranda. So now her opinion mattered, did it? She might have laughed, only she feared it would come out as a sob.

"Very well." She gathered her skirts. Her fingers had turned to ice long before, and the ruffles slid from her grasp. She took a firmer hold. "I won't be but a moment."

Slowly, she walked toward the vestry door looming before her. She would finally face the man who would be her husband, the man who sent brutes to hospital and caused women to swoon with terror.

He stood erect as a soldier at the far end of the little stone room. Women, she thought, letting her gaze sweep over him, could be utterly ridiculous.

She closed the door and waited for him to speak.

"You came." He could not fully stamp out the surprise in his deep voice.

"Yes."

He was tall and very large, though there wasn't a spare ounce of fat discernible over his entire form. The largeness of appearance came from the breadth of his shoulders, the muscles that his charcoal gray morning suit—no matter how finely tailored—could not completely hide and the long length of his strong legs encased in gray woolen trousers. It was not the elegant, thin frame of a refined man, but the brute and efficient form of a dockworker. In short, Lord Archer possessed the sort of virile body that would catch many a lady's eye and hold it—were it not for one unavoidable fact.

She lifted her eyes to his face, or where it ought to be.

Carved with a Mona Lisa smile upon its lips, a black hard mask like one might wear at Carnival stared back. Beneath the mask, his entire head was covered in tight black silk, offering not a bit of skin to view. The perversity of his costume unnerved, but she was hardly willing to swoon.

"I thought it best," he said after letting her study him, "that you enter into this union with full understanding." Black-gloved fingers ran over the silver handle of the walking stick he held. "As you are to be my wife, it would be foolish of me to try to keep my appearance from you."

He spoke with such equanimity that she could only gaze in amazement. A memory flickered before her eyes like a flame caught in a draft, a vision of a different man, in a different place. A man who also hid in shadows, whose gloriously strong body had haunted her dreams for months afterward, made her want things she hadn't the name for back then, things that made her skin heat on many a cold night. It had shamed her, the way she had coveted the dark stranger. But it could not have been Lord Archer. The stranger had a voice like shadows, rasping and weak, not like Lord Archer's strong, deep rumble.

"Look sharp, Miss Ellis!" The walking stick slammed on the stone floor with a crack, and she jumped. "Do you still intend to proceed?" he asked with more calm.

She stepped forward, and the man went rigid. "Who are you? An actor of some sort?" Her temper swelled like fire to air. "Is this some joke Father has concocted to bedevil me, because let me tell you—"

"I am Lord Benjamin Archer," he said with such acidity that she halted. His eyes flashed from behind the mask. "And it is no joke I play." The hand on the walking stick tightened. "Though there are days I wish it to be just that."

"Why do you wear that mask?"

"Asks the woman whose beauty might as well be a mask."

"*Pardon me?*"

The immobile black mask simply stared back, floating like a terrible effigy over broad shoulders.

"What is beauty or ugliness but a false front that prompts man to make assumptions rather than delving deeper. Look at you." His hand gestured toward her face. "Not a flaw or distortion of line to mar that perfect beauty. I have seen your face before, miss. Michelangelo sculpted it from cold marble three hundred years ago, his divine hand creating what men would adore." He took a step closer. "Tell me, Miss Ellis, do you not use that beauty as a shield, keeping the world at bay so that no one will know your true nature?"

"Bastard," she spat when she could find her voice. She had been beaten once or twice, forced to steal and lie, but no one had left her so utterly raw.

"I am that as well. Better you know it now."

She gathered up her train, but the heavy masses of slippery fabric evaded her grip. "I came of my own free will but will not abide by cruel remarks made at my expense," she said, finally collecting herself. "Good-bye, Lord Archer."

He moved, but stopped himself as though he feared coming too close. A small gurgle died in his throat. "What will it take?"

The tightly controlled urgency in his voice made her turn back.

"If you find my character and appearance so very distasteful," she said through her teeth, "then why ask for my hand?"

His dark head jerked a fraction. "I am the last of my family line," he said with less confidence. "Though I have love for Queen and Country, I do not desire to see my ancestral lands swallowed up by the crown. I need a wife."

The idea that she would procreate with the man hadn't entered her mind. It seemed unimaginable.

"Why not court one of your nobles?" she asked through dry lips.

He lifted his chin a fraction. "There are not many fathers who would give their marketable daughters up to a man such as me."

It irked her that his words made her chest tighten in regret.

Lord Archer tilted his head and assessed her with all the warmth of a man eyeing horseflesh for purchase. "Your appearance may matter little to me but when the time comes for my heir to enter into society, your stunning looks will help a great deal to facilitate him."

She could not fault the sensibility of his plan. Even so...

"Why do you wear that mask?" she asked again.

The mask stared back.

"Are you ill? Have you some sort of sensitivity to light upon your skin?" she prompted.

"Sensitivity to light," he uttered and then gave a short laugh of derision. He lifted his head. "I am deformed." That the confession hurt his pride did not escape her. "It was an accident. Long ago."

She nodded stupidly.

"I realize my appearance is far from ideal to an attractive young lady in search of a husband. On the other hand, I can provide a lifestyle of wealth and comfort..." He trailed off as though pained by his own speech and then shifted his weight. "Well, Miss Ellis? What say you? This is between us now. Whatever your decision, your father may keep what little funds he hasn't managed to squander without fear of retribution from me."

"And if I say no? What will you do? Is there another girl

you might ask?" She shouldn't care really, but her basic curiosity could not be quelled.

He flinched, a tiny movement, but on him it seemed as obvious as if he'd been struck by a blow.

"No. It has to be you." He sucked in a sharp breath and straightened like a soldier. "To speak plainly, there is no other option left to me. As to what will I do should you say no, I will continue to live alone. In short, I need you. Your help, that is. Should you grant it, Miss Ellis, you shall want for nothing."

The man in the black mask seemed to stand alone, apart from everything. Miranda knew loneliness when she saw it. Her mind drifted over another memory, one hard repressed. One of herself standing in the very same corner of the vestry, watching as Martin cut their engagement and walked away. And it had hurt. God, it had hurt. So much so that the idea of doing it to another made her queasy.

Lord Archer had shown his weakness, given her a chance to cut their agreement. He'd given her power over him. The man was clearly intelligent enough to have done so with purpose. A chance at equality was unexpected.

Still, none of that might have mattered. Foolish was the woman who gave away her freedom out of sympathy. No, it was not sympathy or the hope of power that prompted a decision; she felt something when in the presence of this strange man, a tingling thrill that played over her belly, the sense of rapid forward motion though her body stood still. It was a feeling long dormant, one gleaned from taking a sword in hand, swaggering through dark alleys when all proper girls were in their beds. It was adventure. Lord Archer, with his black countenance and rich voice, offered a sense of adventure, a dare. She could do nothing short of picking up that gauntlet, or regret it for the rest of her days. Perhaps, then, she could help them both. The idea of helping rather than destroying filled her with a certain lightness of heart.

Miranda collected the blasted train that threatened to trip her and straightened. "We have kept my father and sisters waiting long enough, Lord Archer." She paused at the door to wait for him. "Shall we go?"

Fall in Love with Forever Romance

NACHO FIGUERAS PRESENTS: WILD ONE

Ralph Lauren model and world-renowned polo player Ignacio "Nacho" Figueras dives into scandal and seduction in the glamorous, treacherous, jet-setting world of high-stakes polo competition. Sebastian Del Campo is a tabloid regular as polo's biggest bad boy, but with an injury sidelining him, he's forced to figure out what really matters...including how to win the heart of the first woman who's ever truly understood him.

Fall in Love with Forever Romance

HAPPY EVER AFTER IN CHRISTMAS
By Debbie Mason

USA Today bestselling author Debbie Mason brings us back to Christmas, Colorado, where no one in town suspects that playboy Sawyer Anderson has been yearning to settle down and have a family. But when his best friend finds out the bride Sawyer has in mind is his off-limits baby sister, it might be a hot summer in Christmas in more ways than one…

Fall in Love with Forever Romance

THE BILLIONAIRE BACHELOR
By Jessica Lemmon

Bad boy billionaire Reese Crane needs a wife to convince the board of Crane Hotel that he's settled enough to handle being CEO. And beautiful Merina Van Heusen needs money to save the boutique hotel she runs. But what will they do when love intrudes into their sham marriage? Fans of Jessica Clare and Samantha Young will love this new series from Jessica Lemmon.

A SUMMER TO REMEMBER
By Marilyn Pappano

In the tradition of RaeAnne Thayne and Emily March comes the sixth book in Marilyn Pappano's Tallgrass series. Can Elliot Ross teach the widow Fia Thomas to love again? Or will the secret she's hiding destroy her second chance at forever?

Fall in Love with Forever Romance

FOREVERMORE
By Kristen Callihan

Sin Evernight is one of the most powerful supernatural creatures in heaven and on earth, and when his long-lost friend Layla Starling needs him, he vows to become her protector. Desperate to avoid losing her a second time, Sin will face a test of all his powers to defeat an unstoppable foe—and to win an eternity with the woman he loves. Don't miss the stunning conclusion to *USA Today* bestselling author Kristen Callihan's Darkest London series!